The Connellys of County Down

Also by Tracey Lange

We Are the Brennans

The Connellys
of County Down

Tracey Lange

CELADON
BOOKS

NEW YORK

THE CONNELLYS OF COUNTY DOWN. Copyright © 2023 by Tracey Lange. All rights reserved. Printed in the United States of America. For information, address Celadon Books, a division of Macmillan Publishers, 120 Broadway, New York, NY 10271.

www.celadonbooks.com

Designed by Donna Sinisgalli Noetzel

Library of Congress Cataloging-in-Publication Data

Names: Lange, Tracey, author.
Title: The Connellys of County Down / Tracey Lange.
Description: First edition. | New York, NY : Celadon Books, 2023.
Identifiers: LCCN 2022028594 | ISBN 9781250865373 (hardcover) | ISBN 9781250865397 (ebook)
Subjects: LCGFT: Novels.
Classification: LCC PS3612.A566 C66 2023 | DDC 813/.6—dc23/eng/20220616
LC record available at https://lccn.loc.gov/2022028594

Our books may be purchased in bulk for promotional, educational, or business use. Please contact your local bookseller or the Macmillan Corporate and Premium Sales Department at 1-800-221-7945, extension 5442, or by email at MacmillanSpecialMarkets@macmillan.com.

First Edition: 2023

10 9 8 7 6 5 4 3 2 1

To all the O'Hares of County Down

Especially Louis O'Hare

R.I.P. Dad

*Fairy tales do not give the child his first idea
of bogey. What fairy tales give the child is his
first clear idea of the possible defeat of bogey.
The baby has known the dragon intimately ever
since he had an imagination. What the fairy tale
provides for him is a St. George to kill the dragon.*

—G. K. Chesterton

The Connellys of County Down

Chapter One

When the unit intercom buzzed and the cell door rattled open on its old metal track that morning, Tara breathed a heavy sigh of relief and swore it was the last time she'd ever hear that racket in her life. For 525 consecutive mornings that noise had signaled the start to a day that looked just like the one before, another day when she was told exactly what to do and exactly when to do it.

She'd been restless most of the night, wired with anxiety. Until she walked out the door of that place, something could still go wrong. That wasn't likely. She had yet to see one woman's release date changed this late in the game. But that's how it was when she let herself want something so damn much. The closer she got to getting it, the more she doubted it.

Jeannie had snored like a trucker as usual, but Tara hadn't bothered nudging the upper bunk with her foot to get her cellmate to turn over and quiet down. It wouldn't have helped. When the alarm went off at 6:30 a.m., Tara was sitting on her bunk, back against the cinder block wall, knees pulled up to her chest. While she waited she listened, peeled apart the sounds that fused together to create the early-morning white noise of prison life: the ring of a telephone and the guards' distant conversation, echoes of a cough here and a clearing of a throat there, bodies turning over in their bunks—seeking, for the last few moments of rest, a comfortable position on a metal frame covered by a two-inch mat.

Less than an hour to go. They'd told her to be ready to leave her cell by seven thirty, before morning roll call. The discharge process would be fairly quick, then her sister, Geraldine, would be waiting outside in the parking lot. Tara had hoped her brother would pick her up; Geraldine had a way of shredding Tara's nerves in short order. On their last phone call three days ago Tara subtly asked about it—*I know how busy you are, Ger. Maybe Eddie could make the trip.* But Geraldine shot that down, saying Eddie shouldn't lose a day's wages and rock the boat at work by asking for time off, never mind so he could pick his sister up *from prison*, she had added, whispering the last two words, no doubt in case anyone around her overheard.

Jeannie started moving around above her, but Tara didn't get up right away. There was nothing for her to do at the moment. The running around had been done yesterday: returning library books, tendering all prison-issued clothing and linens except for what she was wearing, stopping by medical to get cleared. She wasn't prescribed any pills to take with her. Unlike the majority of the women at the Taconic Correctional Facility she'd managed to sidestep any dependence on drugs—prescribed meds or contraband narcotics. Though she'd started smoking cigarettes again, a habit she'd quit almost ten years ago.

Her packing was done, and she'd said most of her goodbyes the night before. It was more emotional than she thought it would be, saying goodbye to some of the girls. Prison made for unexpected friendships. There were women from all walks of life serving time at Taconic. Medium security was a catchall for everything between white collar and the most serious felonies. If someone committed fraud or laundered money, they generally went to minimum security, aka prison camp. If the crime was serious, the sentence long, and the person had priors, they usually did their time in maximum. Tara had hoped for minimum; transporting stolen opioids was not a violent crime. But because it was across state lines and she had a previous assault charge on her record, the Bureau of Prisons points system dictated she do her time in medium.

It worked out okay. She'd always known how to take care of herself. It came from growing up in a home with little parental supervision, in one of the poorer neighborhoods of Port Chester, one of the poorer towns in Westchester County. But Eddie always had her back when they were kids, when her tendency to buck the rules would land her in the hot seat. He would either help her get out of trouble or suffer alongside her. In Taconic, she was utterly alone.

Her show-no-fear strategy had gotten her into a little trouble initially.

When she didn't follow all the guards' rules she was restricted to her cell until she figured it out. When she didn't follow all the inmates' rules she paid a physical toll, though that was just the one time. For the most part she stayed on the fringe and observed until she learned how it all worked. In the end, prison was a lot like high school. There was a hierarchy, with the most significant offenders at the top. They had committed major crimes and would be there the longest, though most of those women weren't very scary. A lot of domestic abuse victims who'd finally struck back or addicts who had committed enough drug crimes to earn a long mandatory sentence. Everyone else resided within a tentative clique of some kind, sometimes determined by race or language or religion, sometimes by education or employment background. Repeat offenders tended to hang together, as did the lowest and most hated on the totem pole: the child abusers.

Like in her years at Port Chester High School, Tara was able to avoid making any real enemies at Taconic. She kept friendships pretty loose, other than Jeannie, but got along with most of the women there. Most of the guards too, except for a few menacing assholes—including a couple of female guards—and she made damn sure never to get caught alone with them. That was one thing she wouldn't miss. Being so vigilant all the time was exhausting.

Jeannie's bare lower legs appeared over the side of the top bunk as she finally sat up. "When you leave," she said around a yawn, "I'm taking that bunk. Tired of climbing up and down."

Tara stood and stretched, headed over to the sink to brush her teeth. She glanced at the sheet of polished metal that was supposed to pass for a mirror. All she saw was a distorted pale face framed by blurry copper waves. "You should switch the mattresses," she told Jeannie. "Mine's thin as paper."

Jeannie nodded, her black corkscrew curls bouncing on both sides of her round face. She half slid, half hopped down from her bunk, kissed her fingertips, and pressed them to the eight-by-ten school portrait of her eight-year-old daughter, Chloe, which hung on the wall opposite their bunks. Then she started changing into the forest-green top and pants every inmate at Taconic wore. She had four months to go on a ten-month stint for repeatedly writing bad checks. Her dickhead boyfriend put her up to it and walked away scot-free when she got busted. Funny how many of them had a similar story, doing time for some man.

While Jeannie dressed, Tara turned to the small desk they'd shared since becoming cellmates six months ago. She opened the midsize cardboard box that held the belongings she was taking: her many sketch pads and pencils, some drawings and family photos that had been taped above her bunk, a large stack of homemade cards from her ten-year-old nephew, Conor. The letter from her father was in there, though she wasn't sure why. She'd read it once and never responded.

She pulled out the handful of cigarettes she had slid in the box the night before and studied them. She should just leave them behind, quit cold turkey as she exited this place. Jeannie didn't smoke, but she could trade them for something. Someone was always hunting for cigarettes. Tara folded her hand around the Marlboros that had been smuggled in by a guard or somebody's family member or friend during a visit. She never knew who or where the cigs originated from, just traded for them when she got the chance, usually food, sometimes one of her sketches. If Geraldine saw them, Tara would never hear the end of it. But just the thought of her sister made her want to light one up, so she slid them back in the box.

Next Tara pulled out a folder, laid it on the desk, and touched her fingertips to it. "This is for Chloe," she said, glancing at the school portrait. "It's the last four installments. You can give them all to her next weekend or dole them out over the next month." Jeannie's mother was taking care of Chloe while Jeannie served her time, and every weekend, without fail, they made the four-hour round-trip from Albany to visit her.

Tara hadn't had a visitor in over four months. Her family lived thirty miles away.

Jeannie shook her head and pressed a fist to a hip. "I can't believe you did all this, T."

"I wanted to finish the story." It was more like a comic book. Chloe had cerebral palsy and walked with two canes. Not long after Jeannie moved into her cell, Tara caught her crying one night because she had nothing to send her daughter for her birthday. A couple days later Tara offered her a comic strip that depicted Chloe using her special power—canes that became ultramagnets at her command—to save a dog from an evil dogcatcher. Chloe loved it so much Tara expanded it to a series over the past few months, giving the heroine a nemesis, Dr. Doom, who was trying to take over Chloe's hometown.

"Does she finally get rid of that Dr. Doom?" Jeannie asked.

"She turns her canes up to their highest magnetic strength and uses them to crush him." Tara smacked her palms together. "She lets him live, but he's harmless after that."

Jeannie laughed. "She's gonna love that." Her head tilted. "You know, these comics have meant so much to her."

Tara shrugged a shoulder. "I'm just glad she liked them."

"I bet Conor loved his too."

"He said in his letters he hung them all up in his room."

Jeannie's brows pinched together in concern. "You sure you gonna be okay, going back to live with that brother and sister of yours?" She was twenty-six, four years younger than Tara, but Jeannie had a natural mother hen thing going on. And she made no bones about how little she thought of Eddie and Geraldine. *What kind of brother and sister don't visit more when they live right down the road? That ain't right.*

Tara had given up making excuses for them. "I'll be fine," she said.

"Connelly." The raspy voice belonged to Linda Morelli, a short, compact guard with a gray flattop. "You ready to check out of this place?" she asked, crossing her arms.

"Yes, ma'am."

"Well, let's go." Morelli tossed her head down the cellblock. "I have the privilege of escorting you through processing."

"I guess this is it," Jeannie said. "Damn. Who's gonna listen to all my stories about Chloe and nag me to exercise? God knows who I'm gonna get up in here next."

Tara folded down the flaps on her box. "Hope it's someone who can sleep through your snoring."

But Jeannie didn't smile. "I mean it, T. I don't know how I would have survived without you in the beginning."

"You would have been fine."

Jeannie, quite a bit taller and wider than Tara, enveloped her in a hug. "You stay in touch, and be good now. No more running drugs for that asshole."

"You too," Tara said. "No more writing bad checks for that other asshole."

Morelli cleared her throat. "If this is gonna take a while, I can come back later."

Tara stepped away from Jeannie and smiled at her. "We'll talk soon," she said. Then she picked up her box and followed Morelli.

Relief rushed through her whole body as she stepped out of that cell for the last time.

But then a wave of panic sideswiped her so suddenly she stopped walking for a moment to catch her breath, pretending to get a better grip on the box in her hands.

It was impossible to put into words how much she wanted to leave Taconic behind. The crushing claustrophobia she had to beat down every time they locked the cell doors, the mind-numbing sameness of every day, the tragic stories of the women around her—many of whom missed their kids so much they cried through the night, or were so hungry for intimacy they turned to each other, or were in so much emotional pain their only release was to make it physical by cutting themselves with dull blades pried from cheap commissary razors.

But when she looked ahead, down that cellblock toward the exit, the overwhelming openness of it all hit her and she still felt a sense of power-lessness that came with having little control over her own life. She had no money and would be living off her sister and brother. Employment would be tough to find with a record. There was no way she'd be allowed to teach art to kids anymore, which never paid well but she'd loved the work. She would be on parole for two years, at the continued mercy of the corrections system. And she had no idea what Roland Shea might be expecting at this point. It better be nothing. He'd already cost her the last year and a half of her life.

Morelli turned back. "You all right, Connelly?"

Tara drew a deep breath and pushed her shoulders down. "I'm fine," she said, picking up her pace.

Yeah, there were some serious obstacles coming her way. But she would figure it out, with or without anyone's help. She was used to do-ing that.

Morelli led her out of the block and across the scrubby courtyard, to the far building that housed Receiving and Departures. It had been her first stop upon arriving at Taconic, when eighteen months had felt like a life sentence. They made their way through a series of locked doors and gates before stopping at a small inventory room. Morelli handed her a bag of clothes and pointed her in the direction of the bathroom, where she changed. She had asked her sister to pick out a few items from her closet, but for some reason Geraldine sent clothes she'd bought from a second-hand store: an amorphous T-shirt and jeans that were so big Tara had to fold over the waistband so they stayed up.

She leaned forward, arms braced against the sink beneath her, and took a close look in the mirror. God, she was so washed-out. The plain white shirt didn't help, but it was more the pasty skin combined with light eyes. The freckles glared more than ever. Her reddish-blondish hair was long now, past her shoulders, and frayed on the ends because she hadn't had a cut in months. Other inmates did the haircutting, and some of them were pretty good. But it was customary to offer a solid tip—food or postage stamps—and Tara had been frugal. She was lucky enough to get money deposited into her inmate account every month like clockwork. Her brother and sister had done that for her, and though it was probably guilt money for not visiting more, she was grateful. Having the ability to buy the things she needed from the commissary helped her make it through.

She gathered the prison uniform into the plastic bag and headed back out to the inventory counter. Morelli took the bag from her and gave her another one, which contained the clothes she'd arrived in. She would have worn them home, but it was against the rules. A fresh set of clothes was required for release because the prison didn't wash the old ones, and there was no telling what shape they'd be in after sitting on a dusty shelf for years, or whether they would still fit. They were the only personal effects Tara had brought with her. She'd known the day she was starting her sentence. It was all prearranged thanks to a plea deal. Eddie had driven her to Taconic on a frigid gray November morning over two

Thanksgivings ago. They didn't talk on the ride, not a word. There was too much to say. But when they got there, Eddie gave her a long, fierce hug, whispering into her ear—*Stay strong, Tare.* And he cried as he drove away, his big shoulders shaking behind the wheel of his old pickup.

"You don't have a jacket?" Morelli asked. "It's chilly out there today."

"I have a hoodie from when I got here." She pointed to the plastic bag of clothes.

Morelli sighed. "Okay."

Tara pulled out her soft black zip hoodie and slipped it on over the T-shirt. It felt good to wear something of her own again, a connection to who she was before this place.

"Next," Morelli said, "you sign this." She slid a piece of paper and a pen across the counter.

Tara scanned the document, a contract whereby she vowed not to commit any crimes, not to consort with criminals, to abide by the terms of her parole . . . A deterrent, as if she needed one. She signed the contract.

"This is a copy of all your release paperwork," Morelli said, handing over a manila folder. "Your parole officer's info is in there. Don't forget to make contact within twenty-four hours or you'll be in violation. Grab your box and come this way." She turned and headed farther down the hall.

They made a left around a corner, and Tara could see it. The exit door at the far end of the corridor. There was a large window in the upper half of the door, and sunlight poured through the crisscross wiring embedded in the thick glass. She was just about there, and Geraldine would be waiting on the other side. *In the same old white minivan,* she'd told Tara. Her sister had no good reason for driving a minivan, no husband or kids or cargo to lug around. She just had a pathological need to prove to everyone how practical she was. But in that moment Tara didn't care. She was getting the hell out of here.

They arrived at a Plexiglas window and Morelli moved behind it, used one of her many keys to open a lockbox and remove an envelope. "Wow," she said, "you have over a hundred dollars saved up in your inmate account." She slid the envelope and a clipboard across the counter to Tara. "Your driver's license and a prepaid Visa card are in there. Just sign that receipt."

Tara signed again, removed her license and the Visa card from the envelope, slipped them into the front pocket of her jeans. She had plans for that money and wanted to make sure she didn't lose it.

Morelli pointed down the corridor to the bulky desk sitting maybe ten feet from the exit. "Now we head over there and you officially sign out. Then, you blow this joint." She angled her head and squinted at Tara. "You know, Connelly, I've been here almost twenty years, walked I-don't-know-how-many women through this building on their release date. And I *always* know if I'm gonna see them again."

Tara stared at her and held her breath, wanting to hear her next words but dreading them just as much. As if Linda Morelli had her own special power, and Tara was doomed to whatever verdict she predicted: she would make it or she wouldn't, yes or no.

"But I can't figure you out," Morelli said. "You're a smart girl, smart enough to keep your head down and get along in here. Yet you were dumb enough to get mixed up with a drug dealer and his business." She shook her head. "I just don't know."

So, a sentence of maybe.

Tara met the older woman's gaze head-on. "Sorry to break your record, Morelli, but you can bet your ass you'll never see me again."

Morelli flashed her a wide grin and said, "Hope not." Then she turned, waving for Tara to follow. They moved to the desk by the exterior door, where Tara was supposed to sign one last form. Morelli was in the middle of explaining it—a liability release stating she was no longer an occupant of a New York State correctional facility—when the desk phone rang.

Morelli held up a finger and answered, listened, said, "Yeah," and, "Understood," a few times.

Tara waited and looked out the exit door again. For the first time in 525 days she was about to step out into the unblemished fresh air, where the breeze would touch her skin without trailing through chain-link fence and barbed wire first. She'd leave the window open in Geraldine's van on the drive, let the wind rush through her fingers and her hair. Eddie and Conor would be home later, and her chest lifted at the thought of wrapping her arms around both of them. Goodwill surged through her, and she didn't care that they hadn't visited more. She just wanted to go home.

Morelli hung up the phone. "Appears we have a little holdup."

Tara pulled her eyes from the door. "Sorry?"

"That was a call from the warden's office," Morelli said, nodding toward the phone. "Someone wants to talk to you before you leave."

"Who?"

Morelli shrugged. "Above my pay grade. Should only take a few minutes, but I got an intake arriving soon, so I'm going to have you wait in there." She pointed to a door behind her, a door with no window in it.

Tara felt a sharp constriction in her chest. "What are you talking about? Let me sign that last form and I'm done, I'm outta here."

Morelli gave her a pointed look. "We have to do things right, Connelly." She started waving Tara toward her. "Let's go. It's policy, I can't have more than one inmate in this area at a time."

Tara froze. Was Morelli kidding? In five steps Tara could be out the door and there'd be no concern about too many inmates in this area. Was she technically even an inmate anymore? Who wanted to talk to her and why did she need to wait in some room? Something was wrong. Maybe another inmate had lied about her, implicated her in some infraction in exchange for favors or a reduced sentence. It happened all the time. She backed up a step toward the exit.

"Stop," Morelli said, raising her voice. "Don't be stupid, Connelly. I'm sure it won't take long—"

"*What* won't take long?"

"I don't know, they just told me to hold you for a minute. All I'm asking is that you wait in there."

No, she was asking Tara to move away from the exit and farther back into the building, to step into another locked room while someone else decided her fate. Fuck that, she'd done her time. She turned around and headed for the exterior door. Four steps to go. Three . . . two . . .

But Morelli was too fast. Her hands wrapped around Tara's forearms and yanked them behind her.

Tara was stopped cold, her five and a half feet and 120 pounds no match. Besides, fighting was pointless—what the hell was she thinking . . . Her head started to spin with the infractions she was racking up: insubordination, resisting, erratic behavior.

"Please wait," she said, hating the pleading wobble in her voice. "Wait. It's okay, I'll go."

But it was too late. She recognized the feel of cold metal and the sound of clicking gears as the cuffs encircled her wrists and squeezed tight.

Chapter Two

Brian had carefully planned his visit to the Taconic Correctional Facility that Monday morning. He was there to see Tara Connelly. She wasn't expecting him, and timing would be key. Better to talk to her after she changed into civilian clothes, avoid the power imbalance that came with a police detective sitting across from someone wearing a prison jumpsuit. But he wanted to catch her before she left the building so he could say what he needed to say without her family around. The optimal moment would be at the tail end of her discharge process. She would be excited about leaving, looking forward to going home. Hopefully she'd be open to hearing his apology. Maybe she'd even be willing to accept it.

But he couldn't control that part, her reaction. He just needed to see her, make sure she was okay, and say sorry, for his own sake. Then he could move on, become unstuck from this guilt quicksand that had been pulling at him for eighteen months.

He'd checked in with the warden's office earlier, and they promised to call him when Tara was nearing the final sign-out. In the meantime he waited in his car in the parking lot, checking emails on his phone. Most of them were messages about new cases waiting for his attention, but there was also an update about Roland Shea. Apparently he'd been at his home as of thirty minutes ago. Brian had asked an officer working the early shift to verify Roland's whereabouts, even though it was doubtful he'd pick Tara up that morning. He hadn't visited her once the last eighteen months; Brian had checked. But he felt better knowing exactly where that dirtbag was, confirming he would not be part of her homecoming. That was the last thing she needed.

While he was scrolling, a new text appeared. It was from Hank: *Still at the dentist?*

Brian checked his watch before responding: *Yeah. Be in by 9.*

He'd worked with Hank the last six years, and known him much longer, since Hank was also his uncle. They were tight, but there was no need for him to know what Brian was up to that morning. His uncle would never understand this whole thing. In his eyes it would be inappropriate and unprofessional, and Brian couldn't really argue with that.

A couple minutes later he got the call. Tara was almost finished and he needed to get in there if he wanted the chance to talk to her.

He hopped out of the car, bent down to check his reflection in the window, and ran fingers through his dark hair. He'd grown out the crew cut a couple years ago to a medium wavy length. Susan, his ex-wife, asked him to do that the whole last year they were married, but he refused. Probably because he knew by then it wouldn't have helped. When she was offered her dream Realtor job at Sotheby's in Manhattan and he said he wouldn't move, she used it as justification for cheating on him with—and eventually leaving him for—Slick Rick the Finance Prick: *You're just so stuck, Brian . . . the only thing you're passionate about is your job . . . nothing ever changes.* And his personal favorite, *It's like being married to an old man.* Apparently he'd missed the line in the wedding vows about promising to "grow and change as a human being" until death did them part.

Continuing to use the window as a mirror, he stood up to his full six feet and straightened his tie. At least he didn't look like an old man. No sign of gray at his temples yet, and he'd only had to loosen his belt one notch since he graduated from the academy. In his opinion he looked right about his age of thirty-three. He had a sport coat in the trunk he could throw on, but that felt too formal. Maybe he should lose the tie and just go with the blue button-down, open the collar . . .

Maybe he should stop worrying about shit that didn't matter. This wasn't a date. He was a cop and she was a criminal. He just wanted the chance to get something off his chest. After that, Tara Connelly would become a distant memory.

～

He hurried across the parking lot, rehearsing the brief lines he'd decided on. He would offer them up right before she walked out the door. The whole thing would take less than thirty seconds.

When he entered the building Tara wasn't in the discharge area. A female guard with short gray hair sat behind the desk, talking on the phone. Her name tag said L. MORELLI. She nodded at him and held up a finger while she finished her call.

After she hung up he flashed his badge. "Detective Nolan," he said. "I'm looking for Tara Connelly."

"She's in there." Morelli flicked a thumb over her shoulder toward a closed door, which likely led to some sort of holding room. "I was told someone wanted to talk to her. Is that you?"

Brian nodded.

"I hope it's not more bad news for her." She stood and gestured toward the phone on the desk. "That was the main office. Her sister can't pick her up this morning. She's gonna have to figure out a ride."

While she unclipped her key ring from a belt loop and sorted through keys, Brian tried to prepare himself. It had been a long time, and she might look quite different now. There was no denying it. A year and a half ago Tara Connelly had been very attractive, with her strawberry blond hair, pale blue eyes, the smattering of light freckles across her face. And, at least in Brian's experience, she'd been strong-willed and stubborn, tough in the way people were when at a young age they had learned to be disappointed by life. She stuck to her guns once she made a decision, even a bad one. *A woman who knows her own mind*, his mother would have said with an approving smile.

But Brian saw it often, the changes people underwent while serving time. Sometimes they gained substantial weight from being sedentary. Which was preferable to those who came out skin and bones because they developed a serious drug habit on the inside. Some people aged disproportionately fast because of the lack of sun and sleep or an overabundance of anxiety. Other inmates changed their personalities, exiting much angrier than when they entered or more fearful. Sometimes they just went quiet and flat, like some inner light had been extinguished. He hoped she still had her spunk after being in this place.

Morelli found the right key and swung open the door. She led him inside a small room with a metal table and two chairs, one of which was occupied. Tara raised her face.

Damn. She looked the same.

Her gaze zeroed in on him. "What the hell are *you* doing here?"

When she shot out of her chair he realized her hands were behind her back. She appeared ready to lunge across the table at him. It seemed he needn't have worried about her lively spirit being crushed.

"Jesus Christ," she said. "Did you screw with my release, Nolan?"

"What? No." He held his hands up in innocence and turned to Morelli. "Why is she cuffed?"

"She started resisting, and I needed her to calm down while we waited for you."

"I didn't mean for you to . . ." He dropped his head and rested his hands on his hips. "Take them off."

"All right, but you're responsible." Morelli pushed off the wall, walked behind Tara, and removed the cuffs.

This was not a good start. Right before Tara was about to walk outside, Morelli had apparently locked her in this room with no explanation. And it was Brian's fault. "Look," he said to her, "there's been some confusion. You are free to go."

Tara rubbed her wrists while her eyes flicked between Morelli and him, like she didn't trust it.

"Although I guess your sister can't pick you up," he said. He looked to Morelli for confirmation and she nodded.

Tara's shoulders slumped, and she exhaled in resignation. "Figures."

Brian didn't know what to do. She'd just suffered a bad scare and learned she didn't have a ride home. It seemed self-serving to insert a quick apology at this moment so he could check it off the list and be on his way.

She crossed her arms and narrowed her eyes at him. "Did you come all the way here to tell me that?"

"No, I just found out myself." But that led to the question of exactly what he was doing there, and he wasn't getting into it in front of a guard. An idea sprang to mind, and he acted on it, even though he suspected it was a bad one. "I was actually here on another matter," he said. "But I thought I'd offer you a ride home."

Her eyes widened in disbelief. Or maybe dread. She looked at Morelli. "What are my other options?"

"We can get you a bus ticket, but it'll take a while," Morelli said. "Or we could call you a taxi. But that'll cost you most of that commissary money you saved up."

Tara's arms dropped to her sides in defeat.

Brian cleared his throat. "I'm headed back to Port Chester anyway, so it's no problem . . ."

She shook her head but eventually said, "Fine," through clenched teeth. Then she grabbed her box from the table and walked past him, out into the hall.

"Damn." Morelli cocked a brow. "What did you do to her?"

He pressed his lips together for a moment. "I helped put her in here."

⤙

It didn't take Brian long to doubt the wisdom of offering the ride. Tara made a lot of angry noise while moving through the final stage of her release: slamming her box on the desk, tossing the pen down when she was done signing the last form, rushing out the exterior door. Now she was stalking across the parking lot at a rapid clip. If his legs weren't longer than hers, he would have had to jog to keep pace. It was shaping up to be a fun drive.

"It's the black SUV parked near the end," he said, pointing to an unmarked Ford Explorer in the first row. He didn't mention that she'd been in that car before, but the way her steps slowed while she stared at it said she remembered.

As they got closer he asked if she wanted him to put her box in the trunk.

"No." She held it tight against her chest and stopped by the passenger door. "I assume I can sit in front this time, where I'm not trapped inside."

He gave her a serene smile and unlocked the car. "Of course."

After climbing in she forced the box down into the space by her feet.

Brian started to reach for his Ray-Bans in the center console but figured he'd look even more cop than he already did, so he left them off and settled for flipping down the visor. They belted up and he pulled out, moving across the long parking lot toward the exit. They had to wait in line behind several cars to check out with the guard, and as Brian made slow progress toward the gate with one hand on the wheel, he noticed Tara's eyes trained on the section of tall chain-link fence that rolled back and forth, letting one vehicle at a time pass through. She shifted in her seat often, legs twitching, full of anxious energy. He turned to her. "We're almost there."

A moment later they pulled up to the gatehouse, presented their IDs to the guard, and the gate rolled open. Brian gunned the gas as soon as he could, and after he turned onto the main road she stilled. But her gaze was glued to the side mirror, watching Taconic slowly fade away behind them. She stared until he turned south on the Saw Mill River Parkway half a mile later. Only then did she seem to take a breath and lift her head to look out the window, at the trees and road signs and world rushing by.

He'd never picked someone up from prison before, but he imagined the relief she must be feeling in that moment, some level of emotion about the idea that she was free, so he just let her take it in for a while. Besides, there was no rush to reach for awkward conversation. He had thirty minutes left to recite his practiced apology—*Miss Connelly, I want to acknowledge that our investigation back then did not go as planned. Although you refused to cooperate, the end result was regrettable.* He checked on her occasionally though, and caught her sniffing and swiping fingers across her cheeks a couple times.

Where the hell was her family this morning? He knew from her file that her mom died when she was young, and her father vanished a few years later. But she had an older brother and sister who should have been there.

The quiet started to weigh on him after about ten minutes. So did the delicate floral scent that had to be coming from her hair, which seemed surprising considering she'd just been released from prison. She hadn't so much as turned her face toward him yet.

"Well," he said, "you look good."

Her head finally swiveled his way, but her forehead was wrinkled in question or doubt.

"I mean, you know," he said, glancing over at her. "You look healthy."

"Really?" she asked in a flat voice. "Must be all the prison food and cigarettes."

There was no good response to that, so he just stared ahead while she lifted partway out of her seat to dig a Visa card from her jeans pocket.

"You can drop me at the toy store in town," she said. "I'll walk from there."

The toy store. That's what the leftover commissary money was about. She lived with her nephew and probably had saved up to buy him something. "That's fine," he said. "I'll wait and take you all the way. I assume we're going to your old house . . ."

"You remember where it is, right?" She thrust the Visa card in her hoodie pocket and zipped it up. "The place you arrested me one morning in front of my brother and my nephew while we were eating breakfast."

He kept his voice level. "I remember." Perhaps this was his penance, this drive with her. Having to sit next to someone who was so angry with him it pulsed off her in waves. But he wasn't going to be cowed into silence. "So you'll be living with your brother and sister again?"

She let out a complicated sigh that ended in "Yes."

Maybe a sore subject. Brian never understood people complaining about their siblings. While growing up he often wished for a brother or sister, particularly after his parents died when he was fifteen. All these years later he still longed for someone who'd known them the way he had, someone who shared those memories and could help keep his parents alive in his mind. Hank was the closest thing Brian had to that, but they generally avoided the subject of Brian's parents. The discussion would inevitably work its way around to the night they were killed in an apparent robbery gone wrong, and that was just too painful for both of them.

Another ten minutes went by and he was still reaching for something to say, maybe news to report about Port Chester. But not much had changed while she was gone. As they approached the south end of town they were greeted by the abandoned hospital campus, which had sat lifeless since 2005 and served as a testament to a town stuck midtransformation. Port Chester was a gateway to New England and had served as a transportation hub going all the way back to the 1600s, when it was considered a major seaport, given its location on the Byram River and Long Island Sound. It had the oldest school district in Westchester County, and its economy had been through several evolutions, from boatbuilding and farming to foundries and manufacturing.

But it had been hurting since factories started closing doors in the 1980s. Some revitalization in the early 2000s had attracted a younger crowd, happy to ride the Metro-North two hours round-trip to get to their jobs in the city every day if it meant getting more bang for their buck. Though it hadn't done much for the longtime residents. Brian saw it on the job every day—increasing auto thefts, robberies, domestic violence calls—largely the result of a shortage of jobs and affordable housing. Something like 75 percent of the kids in the school district qualified for the free lunch program. And in recent years, like many hurting towns, it had become fertile ground for a thriving drug trade. But Tara already knew all about that.

So they stayed quiet while he pulled off the highway and headed north on Boston Post Road. Port Chester was more working class and diverse than any neighboring towns, which was evident in the bustling half-mile strip of ethnic restaurants, markets, and specialty stores that lined the main drag. It ran parallel to the Byram River two blocks to the east, which served as the state line between New York and Connecticut for a couple of miles.

The toy store was located just off Main Street, and the OPEN sign in the window was lit up in bright colors.

"You really don't have to wait," she said. "I can walk."

"No, it's fine. I want to grab a coffee anyway." He nodded toward the Dunkin' across the street.

She chewed her bottom lip while she debated, but then she climbed out, leaving her box on the floor of the car. It was all bent out of shape crammed down there, and the flaps were halfway open. When he glanced inside it, he spotted notebooks and a few loose cigarettes tucked against the side. Maybe, like a lot of inmates, she'd traded most of her commissary money for cigarettes the whole time she was in there.

Brian shot Hank another text—*Running late. Closer to 9:30*—and figured he better get some coffee. It wasn't until he was placing his order that he realized he should have asked if she wanted something. A memory flashed across his mind then: sitting across from her in an interview room at the station with Hank at his side, the first time they questioned her. They kept her there for two hours that night, and she went through four cups of coffee. During a lull in the questioning, when he and Hank were keeping it friendly, playing good cop–good cop for the time being, Brian made some remark about how much coffee she drank. Her response still made him smile—*I'd prefer tequila, but I'm guessing that's not an option.*

Black with two sugars. That's how she'd taken those coffees. As well as the others he'd watched her drink during follow-up interviews, which got less friendly each time. She hadn't had a decent cup of coffee in eighteen months. He bought her a large and added extra sugar.

On his way back to the car he spotted her through the toy store window, studying the LEGO sets like her life depended on picking the right one. He'd met her nephew once, the unfortunate morning she mentioned earlier. The kid had to be maybe ten or eleven now . . .

He went inside and walked down the aisle toward her. "A guy I work with has a kid about your nephew's age. I went to his birthday barbecue last weekend and this one"—he carefully pointed with an index finger so as not to spill the coffee in that hand—"was a huge hit."

Her eyes flicked to the complicated spaceship set, but she made no move to pick it up. Maybe eighty-five bucks was more than she had.

He held up one of the coffees. "I picked this up for you." When she didn't reach for it, he placed it on the shelf next to the LEGOs. "Just thought you might want one. I'll be outside." He turned and left the aisle, but stopped around the corner. When he peeked a few moments later, she was sipping the coffee and examining the spaceship LEGOs up close.

⤝

Once she got back in the car with her shopping bag he knew he only had a few minutes. He headed north on Main, under the elevated train tracks, where downtown gave way to a residential area. Tara and her family lived in an older part of town, where a lot of the Colonial-style houses had been converted to multifamily dwellings. Most were in need of significant maintenance or updating, and grass grew between gaping cracks in the pavement, much of which had buckled over time from bulging tree roots. Gentrification would eventually move in this direction, but for now there were lots of holdouts. People in this neighborhood could get a good price for their house, but not enough to afford another place in Port Chester. Or anywhere else in Westchester for that matter.

They only had half a mile to go. Brian took a breath and was about to start his little speech—*Miss Connelly, I want to acknowledge . . .* —but she bent down to her box, started moving things around to make room for her purchase. He waited so he wasn't apologizing to the back of her head. Then he was making the left onto Gillette Street, and two blocks later they came to the end of the cul-de-sac, where the Connellys lived.

She sat back up but he still didn't say anything because she was staring up at the house, scrutinizing it, and it felt like he'd be interrupting something.

The house looked about as he remembered it: a run-down two-story with a partial daylight basement. The whole thing rambled up the steep hillside behind it. It was a faded yellow with chipped white trim and a lot of worn latticework under the porch, which ran the width of the house. A wilting white shed sat in the side yard, under the thick branches of a maple tree.

There was no car in the driveway and no movement inside. No one was home to greet her.

When she reached down for her box Brian realized he was out of time. It was now or never. *Miss Connelly . . .* Shit. That was too stiff.

Her hand wrapped around the door handle and pulled.

"Tara."

She turned to him with slightly raised brows, probably surprised to hear him say her first name, and in such a soft tone. Her icy blue eyes searched his and his rehearsed lines went out the window.

He swallowed. "I never wanted you in there. I'm sorry it all went down the way it did."

She blinked and pulled her head back a bit. He didn't drop his eyes while she studied him because she was clearly trying to read his intentions. Though it felt a little dangerous, staring straight back at her. Especially when her gaze softened just a touch for the first time that morning. Maybe she was thinking about the last time they saw each other, the day of her third interview at the police station.

But when she spoke the edge was back. "Have a nice life, Nolan." She climbed out of the car with her box and hip-checked the passenger door shut. Then she walked up the path and the porch steps, never looking back.

"You too," Brian said to the empty car.

He waited while she searched under the cushion of a worn wicker chair and came up with a key, let herself into the house. Then he drove off, headed back toward town, toward the station and the full day ahead of him. Hank would be waiting, chomping at the bit. They had a meeting that afternoon with the Westchester County prosecutor's office to talk about their ongoing investigation into a drug trafficking ring that was operating out of Port Chester. A ring that was headed up by one Roland Shea.

Brian glanced at the yellow house in his rearview once more. A weight had lifted from his chest when he offered that apology, a more heartfelt one than he'd originally intended. He'd been thinking about her for so long, she'd taken up residence in his brain. But he'd done all he could for her now, and it would be a relief to let her go.

It was unlikely he'd see Tara Connelly in the future. He lived twenty minutes away, over in White Plains, and really only worked in Port Chester. Like a lot of cops, he preferred to keep his professional life and his personal life—what little he had—as separate as possible. His path would probably cross Tara's only if she returned to criminal behaviors.

So with a little regret—maybe more than a little—he hoped to never see her again.

Chapter Three

_____

Geraldine checked the clock on the wall above her desk to see it was already twelve thirty. Crap on a stick. She really should head home. Tara likely arrived—to an empty house—three hours ago. But Geraldine still hadn't dug into the quarterly tax payments, which was the whole reason she didn't drive up to Taconic that morning in the first place. The due date was coming up fast, and she hadn't even started the process. Normally they were completed and ready to go this time of the month, which is why Mr. Bertucci entrusted the task to her and her alone. _Who needs a fancy computer program, Geraldine,_ he'd say, tapping an arthritis-bent finger to his temple, _when I have you, the human calculator?_ He liked to tell her she was the reason he was still in business, a last bastion mom-and-pop payroll service fighting to stay alive among the cheaper online options. When he was forced to retire a few months ago because of Mrs. Bertucci's worsening Alzheimer's, he had put Geraldine in charge and hired her a part-time assistant named Rita.

For the most part Geraldine loved the job she'd had for the last fifteen years, same one since she was twenty-two years old. She found a soothing rhythm in putting numbers in boxes, printing checks, conducting direct deposit transactions. Seeing in black and white the fruits of her labor as the hours rolled by, knowing people were getting their much-needed paychecks thanks to her.

But since she became manager her duties had changed. Now she had to deal with clients directly, take meetings, field phone calls—which made her so nervous she found herself hiding armpit sweat stains, talking over people, and laughing too loudly. And it meant she had to hand off several payrolls to Rita. Geraldine was supposed to be the boss, but Rita was always questioning her methods, making suggestions for becoming more efficient. No matter how many times Geraldine explained that she and Mr. Bertucci had always used the same tried-and-true system for processing payrolls, Rita insisted on doing things her way. And she was so darn fast.

Geraldine refused to assign any more payrolls to her though, for fear of losing control of the office. So lately there just weren't enough hours in the day to get everything done. That very morning she'd come in specifically to start on the quarterlies but then decided to double-check the payrolls that were going out that afternoon. Time-consuming, but worth it. Especially after last week, the mishap with Dunbar Construction's payroll.

Dunbar was one of their biggest clients. They employed a lot of people, including her brother, Eddie, and due to a data entry error on a spreadsheet the paychecks for all twenty employees were incorrect. There'd been angry phone calls, a conference with Mr. Dunbar to explain and apologize, and the whole process had to be reversed and refigured. Geraldine apologized profusely to Mr. Bertucci, who had held up a hand—*Everyone makes mistakes, Geraldine. But if Rita screws up like this again, she goes.*

Geraldine considered telling Mr. Bertucci it was actually her mistake, not Rita's. But it would have shaken his faith in her, caused him to lose sleep worrying about his business. So, really for his sake, she decided not to mention it. Besides, there would be no such mistakes in the future—Geraldine was double-checking everything now.

She looked down at the jam-packed accordion folder labeled QUARTERLIES, the one she'd been trying to get to all morning. For the previous three months she'd been slipping the pertinent paperwork in that folder so it was all in one place, but she'd been too busy to separate it by company like she usually did, so it was also in chaos. The first step was to simply organize it.

But she was feeling rushed, pressured to get home and see her sister. And she had to stop at the grocery store on the way, get something for dinner . . . Hell's bells. Geraldine had planned on picking up pork chops, but was Tara still a vegetarian? Did they allow that in *prison*? After eating Geraldine's perfectly good meat-and-potatoes dinners since she was a little kid, Tara up and decided to go veggie five years ago. So now, after a year and a half, Geraldine was supposed to start worrying about a special diet again. But then Tara had always made Geraldine's life more difficult than it had to be.

It was pointless to try to work on the taxes now. There wasn't enough time to do everything she needed to do, and if she stopped in the middle she might lose track and make a mistake. So she locked the folder in her bottom desk drawer, set the alarm, and left the office.

As she drove to Stop & Shop and pictured her sister wandering around the house alone, a combination of guilt and worry pulled at her. When she called Taconic that morning to say she couldn't get there, she'd assumed their tax dollars paid for a shuttle or taxi to get released inmates home, but now she wasn't so certain. She should have just gone to pick her up. Eddie wouldn't be happy. He had wanted to take the day off, even pull Conor out of school for pity's sake, just so they could be home when Tara arrived. But that was a bad idea, disrupting their routine that way. So Geraldine insisted they go on with their normal day, said it would give her and Tara time to catch up.

But "catch up" was really a euphemism for Geraldine laying down some ground rules with her younger sister. For that's the other thing that had Geraldine so preoccupied lately, the idea of Tara coming home. Geraldine loved her sister, and she was excited to have her back. But they couldn't be more opposite, and Tara would have to understand things operated differently now. She might not like it, but while she was gone Geraldine had brought order to the house, new routines. Tara would have to get used to it.

Once inside the grocery store, Geraldine couldn't remember any good vegetarian recipes, so in the end she bought the pork chops, along with extra bread and a bag salad, and she picked up the cake she'd ordered. Vanilla layers with chocolate buttercream frosting. Tara's favorite.

It was when she was loading the groceries in the van that she noticed a large sign in the window of Harriet's Secondhand Store: 20% OFF EVERYTHING. Harriet's was already cheap, it would almost be like getting stuff for free.

She checked her phone: 1:40. Tara had been home for hours now. And Geraldine didn't need any more clothes or anything for the house. Eddie was complaining lately about a lot more clutter around the place already.

But maybe there'd be something cute for Tara, a welcome-home present.

Geraldine locked the van and headed into Harriet's. She would be even later for her sister, but maybe it would help if she was bearing a gift.

~~

When she finally pulled up to the house at almost three o'clock, she gathered the groceries but left the Harriet's shopping bags in the van. She'd grab those later. Geraldine hadn't found anything for Tara, but she'd gotten a great deal on some used clothing and house decor. And her loyalty points earned her an extra 10 percent off her purchase.

The bubble of anxiety in her chest inflated as she climbed the porch steps. She hadn't seen Tara in four months, since she visited Taconic last December. She only went a handful of times—holidays, Tara's birthday, last summer on the anniversary of their mother's death. Father Pat encouraged her to go more often, and she didn't like to disappoint him. But it was just so depressing, sitting across from her sister at a cafeteria-style table in that cold dreary hall. So much noise echoing off the walls: gates and buzzers, people coming and going, kids running around. Guards walking close by, watching them and listening to their conversation, which was stilted and painful. Particularly when Tara seemed to keep glancing over Geraldine's shoulder, as if wishing someone else would appear. Besides, Tara had made her own bed, getting involved with a *drug dealer*. She'd brought shame to the whole family.

Geraldine took a deep breath, swung open the front door, and there was her sister. Lying on the couch in the living room, sound asleep.

Geraldine didn't move right away, just stood in the doorway, grocery bags in hand, taking stock. Tara didn't appear any worse for the wear. Actually, she looked quite young, curled up on her side like that, hands tucked under her cheek. She used to fall asleep that same way when she was little, snuggled between Geraldine and Eddie while their mom told them one of her fairy tales. How strange to think that same little girl was now an *ex-convict*.

People usually saw a resemblance, though everything about Geraldine was just a bit . . . more. She had seven years, four inches, and fifty pounds on Tara. Her hair leaned more orange-red compared to Tara's rosy-blond, and where Geraldine's freckles were dark scattershot across her face, Tara's were a light dusting along her upper cheeks. To Geraldine, even her own voice always seemed louder and squeakier by comparison. Tara was blessed with their mother's finer features and subtle grace, while Eddie and Geraldine both inherited their father's broad body parts and rougher edges. Though, Tara was the only one who became a criminal like their father. No wonder. She'd idolized him when she was a kid.

Had Tara been sleeping since she got home? Geez Louise, Geraldine could have stayed at work after all. She kicked the door to slam it shut behind her, maybe harder than she needed to, which caused Tara to bolt upright.

"Sorry," Geraldine said, bustling across the living room to drop the grocery bags on the kitchen counter. "Didn't mean to wake you." She turned to face her sister, who was looking around the room and blinking, like she was trying to get her bearings. "Welcome home, Tare!"

Tara stood, raking hair back from her face. "Thanks."

Geraldine hugged her, and Tara hugged her back with surprising warmth. "Wow. First day home and you're napping?" Geraldine asked.

"I didn't get much sleep last night."

"You were probably too excited, right?" Geraldine pushed her fists against her hips. "I'm sorry about not getting up there this morning. Work has been CRA-zy." She waved a hand. "But I figured Taconic probably has buses that run people home."

"No, actually. It doesn't." Tara gestured toward the staircase off the living room. "I was going to get settled up in my room but there's a padlock on it. I saw one on your door too. Since when do we have padlocks on our doors?"

Geraldine winced. "Since I started my eBay business." Well, she was going to start an eBay business, just as soon as she had time.

"You have an eBay business?"

"Just trying to bring in a little extra cash. But no one's home all day and I need to keep my inventory safe."

"Inventory? Is that what all these knickknacks are about?" Tara threw her chin around the room, toward the Hummel figurines crowding an end table, the collection of vintage milk bottles lining the tops of the kitchen cabinets, the variety of small carved wooden cats set up along the mantel.

Dang it. They weren't *knickknacks*. "Yeah, I just have those out 'cause I was dusting them earlier. But I have to keep it all close by because I work with it at odd hours. You know, like at night? And your room was right across the hall from mine."

Tara nodded slowly. "Soooo, am I sleeping on the couch now?"

"Oh, no." Geraldine laughed, putting a hand to her stomach. "Of course not. We got you all set up. Follow me."

Tara lifted a beat-up cardboard box that was sitting on the floor by the sofa, and Geraldine led her away from the main staircase, back through the kitchen. When she started up the steep narrow stairs by the back door, Tara stopped.

"Wait a minute. You put me in the attic?"

"It's not an attic, Tara. There's a window, and it has its own exterior door so you have some privacy." Geraldine smiled wide. "We figured you'd appreciate that after, you know, where you've been." That wasn't quite truthful. Eddie thought Tara might like her old room back, but Geraldine insisted she'd prefer a separate space. "And we cleaned it out, moved your furniture in." She climbed the rest of the stairs and opened the door, led Tara inside, and gestured around the room. "I had Eddie paint the walls and add those shelves, and I put up that clothing rack. The baseboard heater works real well, and before summer we'll get you an air conditioner."

Tara's eyes roamed around the room.

Geraldine took a closer look. The queen bed was made up with Tara's old paisley quilt, her rustic oak dresser and matching desk were along one wall, across from the shelves Eddie had made. But the place did look pretty bare. Nothing hung on the white walls—she'd wanted to have Eddie paint them a color but didn't know what Tara would like. Nothing sat on the shelves or covered the rough wood floor. "I brought all your pictures up from your room," she said, pointing to a pile of framed photos and artwork in the corner. "But I didn't know where you'd want them . . ." Shoot. She could have set some of them around the room. That would have helped.

"Where are all my clothes?" Tara asked, setting her box down on the dresser.

"Right here." Geraldine yanked a suitcase out from under the bed and dropped it on top.

"There's no way that's everything."

"Well, no. But it's everything you should need for a while. I left the winter stuff and some of your shoes in the closet—"

"I want the rest of my clothes, Geraldine. And all my books."

"Sure, sure. No problem." She held up her hands. "Just give me a few days to get things sorted out in your old room. I got so busy lately and"— she pulled her fingertips to her chest—"I'm embarrassed to say it's a bit of a mess. Just let me go through it, and I'll get all your stuff to you real soon."

Tara glared at her, and Geraldine's panic spiked. She wouldn't put it past her sister to demand to be taken to that room right then. Like she was entitled to do that after being gone the last eighteen months.

Geraldine tossed her hands up. "I thought you would like the peace and quiet, you know, your own place. I figured it would be a nice 'welcome home' surprise."

"*Welcome home?*" Tara said. "You didn't show up this morning, Geraldine. No one was here when I got home, I find a padlock on my bedroom door . . . Some welcome home."

It did look bad. Geraldine could see that now. But she couldn't offer Tara her room or her stuff back right then. "If you hate it up here," she said, injecting a mild quiver into her voice, "you can move back to your room soon. I'm just trying to bring in some money. We lost your income, Eddie was out of work again for a while earlier this year, and we were paying off your lawyer. Things have been really tight."

Tara's shoulders drooped, her eyes slid to the side, and Geraldine knew she'd won.

"No, it's fine," Tara said. "But I want the rest of my things by the end of the week." She turned and reached into her cardboard box, pulled out a stack of Conor's letters and drawings. Geraldine had sent dozens to her the last eighteen months.

Geraldine hesitated by the bed, reached for the gold cross around her neck. It wasn't like Tara to make things this easy. "You're okay with the changes I made?"

"Seems like you have everything under control," Tara said without looking up.

That was true. It had to be if her sister was already noticing it. And that's what was so worrisome about Tara coming home. Geraldine had never, despite all her best efforts, been able to control her younger sister.

After displaying Conor's cards on the shelves, Tara moved to her suitcase on the bed and unzipped it.

Geraldine watched, feeling useless but uncertain what to do. She wanted to tell Tara how nice it was to have her home, that she'd missed her, that she'd worried about what Tara might be going through in that awful place. And Geraldine wanted to apologize for not showing up that morning. She had treated her sister's homecoming like any other day because she was afraid of screwing it up. But that's exactly what she'd done.

Tara started pulling clothes out of the suitcase, searching for things. Probably eager to change out of the used Harriet's clothes Geraldine had sent her, which, to be fair, were clearly too big. Tara kept yanking up the jeans, and they certainly weren't her style. But Geraldine hadn't had time to go through her sister's things and guess what she'd want to wear home.

So in the end all she said was, "I'll start on dinner and let you get unpacked." Then she headed down to the kitchen to put the groceries away, breathing a sigh of uneasy relief.

Relief at the thought that her sister was home and willing to adapt to the changes Geraldine made without causing much fuss.

Uneasy because that idea seemed way too good to be true.

Chapter Four

The attic above the garage. Yeah, it had its own exterior door, which was off-kilter and drafty as hell. And it was as far away as it could be from the bathroom. Tara almost demanded her sister unlock her old room and give it back. But it was true Tara had created even more financial hardship for her family over the last year and a half. Besides, Geraldine had seemed on the edge of tears. Maybe she really believed she was doing the nice thing, giving Tara some space. The problem with Geraldine wasn't that she didn't try, she just never seemed to try the right thing.

After she left, Tara slowly spun about, assessing the room that had always been used for storage. When they were little she and Eddie used to play among the boxes and old furniture in the dusty, shadowed room, bringing to life one of their mom's fairy tales, The Connellys of County Down. In the story, Geraldine, Eddie, and Tara had to pass through the dangerous Fairy Forest on their quest to reclaim Connelly Castle, a grand stone masterpiece surrounded by beautiful gardens, majestic woodland, and boundless wildlife. Tara and Eddie would pretend the attic floor was the spongy bog they had to cross without getting sucked under. The delicate cobwebs were booby traps, and disturbing one would incur the fairies' ire and bring misfortune upon the offender. They spent hours up there, getting lost in the fantasy of it.

Eddie and Geraldine had put some work into the room, spruced it up quite a bit. Tara had wandered around the empty house earlier that day and not much else had changed, though there was a lot more of Geraldine's tchotchke crap lying around. The padlocks on the bedroom doors were a bit of a shock, but Geraldine had always been paranoid about being robbed, like the Connellys had much worth stealing. At the other end of the upstairs hallway Eddie's room was tidy as always, if a little sparse, his bed made, clothes put away, and surfaces free of clutter. Next door was Conor's small room, in the same state of mild mess she remembered. The comic strips she sent him from Taconic were indeed hanging above his desk. And the mural she'd painted for him years ago was still on the wall, a large depiction of Finn McCool, a heroic warrior in medieval Ireland whose adventures had become the stuff of myths over time. Tara had painted him standing tall, blond hair flowing, mighty sword at his side. He looked down on Conor's bed, as if watching over him while he slept.

When she couldn't get into her old room, Tara had eventually surrendered to the heaviness that pulled at her limbs. It wasn't until she flopped down on their old plaid couch that she realized she was exhausted. Not just because she'd slept little the night before, but also because she hadn't truly relaxed—not all the way, where even her tiniest muscles and nerves went slack—since the last time she was in this house. She was overtaken by the silence and a warm drowsiness that came with being somewhere safe after so long. Her sleep was so deep it had taken a minute to orient herself when Geraldine got home.

She took her time organizing her new space. It had been a while since her time had truly been hers. No guards or buzzers telling her where to be next. This room belonged to her, and none of the furniture was metal or bolted down. She could set it up however she liked.

First she shoved the bed farther from the window so the early-morning sun wouldn't blast through directly onto her face. She stacked her sketch pads and pencils on her old desk, laid clothes in dresser drawers. It was a relief to change into an old wrappy tunic over a pair of comfy jeans, her own soft clothes, which fit just right. Geraldine had provided enough clothing for her to get by for a while, but there were specific items she'd been looking forward to that weren't there: some favorite T-shirts and vintage blouses, her black moto boots. Also a silky dress that was too floral and old-fashioned for Tara to wear, but was one of the few keepsakes she had of her mother.

A random nail in one wall was about the right height for her favorite print, a black-and-white drawing of the Manhattan skyline she bought at the Met years ago after taking a free art history class there. Last thing she did was swoop one of her old tapestries across the steepled ceiling with thumbtacks. It was an abstract pattern in various shades of blue, and it helped warm up the whole space.

The exterior door led to a rickety staircase that descended the side of the house. She stepped out onto the small landing and had a seat on the top step, around the corner from Geraldine's eyeline, and lit up one of her remaining cigarettes. Maybe this room had its benefits after all.

It was a cool afternoon but the sun was strong and still fairly high in the sky. Their street had always been quiet. There were only three houses spread around the cul-de-sac, with the Connelly house in the middle. Mrs. Savalas's little split-level next door was lifeless, empty rooms through the dingy windows and a yard overtaken with weeds. Mrs. Savalas had been good to the Connelly kids while they were growing up and often fending for themselves. She would find excuses to stop by and check on them, drop off hot food, hand-me-down clothing, and sports equipment. She'd brought Tara to Urgent Care when she fell out of the big maple tree in the yard and broke her arm in fifth grade because, as usual, their father was not around. And after he left for good Mrs. Savalas vouched for them when nosy social workers came by to see how they were doing. Tara had missed her funeral a few months ago, after the emphysema finally won the battle. She'd had to settle for sending a card.

She inhaled the smoke, held it in her mouth for a moment before drawing it into her lungs and then slowly blowing it out in a long trail. She waited a bit, repeated. The whole ritual relaxed her, but sitting still also allowed the questions to start poking her: How would she get around? She'd sold her car, along with her laptop and cell phone, to help pay for that attorney and her fines. Where the hell was she going to get a job? An associate's degree in early childhood art education from Westchester Community College didn't qualify her for much. She'd worked part-time at a fancy private school down in Rye teaching art to elementary kids for five years, but no school could hire her now. The only other thing she was qualified to do was wait tables. She'd always meant to go back to school, get her bachelor's degree, but she never had the time. Before going away, her life largely centered around work, Eddie, and Conor. That's what happened when your single-dad brother suffered long-term effects from a traumatic brain injury and needed help paying bills and raising his son.

Eddie. How it was possible to so look forward to seeing him, while simultaneously being so disappointed in him, was beyond her.

Six times. Tara had seen her brother exactly six times since he drove her to Taconic that cold November morning. She didn't expect Geraldine to come often. She was freaked-out just saying the word *prison*, let alone being in one. But Tara expected more from Eddie. They spoke regularly, and he always took her calls, any time of the day or night. He kept her up-to-date on Conor and encouraged her through the darkest days, especially early on, when she felt so low she was scaring herself—*You got this, Tare. You're the strongest person I know.* But she hadn't actually seen him in close to a year.

She'd made a lot of excuses for him: he was busy with work and Conor, his memory sucked and he was terrible with logistics, his migraines or moods were probably acting up. But she would never forget the painful disappointment she endured weekend after weekend, every time hers wasn't the name called over the intercom to the visitors center.

Whatever shitty excuse her brother and sister had for not visiting more, they'd made sure to put $100 in her inmate account every month. They'd sent that money without fail—$2,700 total, including extra for holidays. She had no idea how they'd come up with that kind of cash, but it got her through.

Eddie's truck turned the corner onto Gillette Street up ahead. A two-tone Ford F-150, shiny red with a wide white band around the middle. The thing was like twenty-five years old and had to be pushing 250,000 miles by now, but Eddie kept it in immaculate condition. Tara always figured it was because caring for that truck was one thing Eddie knew he couldn't screw up too badly. If he made a mistake, was late with an oil change or put the wrong kind in, he could fix it, and the truck wouldn't be hurt or disappointed in him.

She used her sneaker to snuff out the cigarette, flicked the stub into one of the trash bins under the stairs. Before heading down to the kitchen she grabbed Conor's gift. She'd gone with Nolan's spaceship suggestion in the end, though she'd kept it hidden so he wouldn't know. For the first time since he dropped her off she recalled his apology and wondered about the agenda behind it. He helped send her to prison because she wouldn't rat out Roland, and now he was apologizing for it? Admittedly it was hard to forget what happened during that third interview, the last time she saw Nolan before she went away. And apparently he remembered how she took her coffee. But she knew from personal experience that his job was more important to him than anything else.

On second thought she grabbed one of her sketch pads as well. What better way to show Eddie and Geraldine how she spent their money, make them understand that, although it hurt when they stayed away, she hadn't felt abandoned by them? And for that she would always be grateful.

~

Downstairs Geraldine was setting four places at the small round dining table off the kitchen. She wore a ruffled apron that had pictures of fried eggs all over it and said BE CAREFUL WHAT YOU WHISK FOR! Tara was about to offer to help when she heard rapid-fire feet running up the porch steps.

Conor's face appeared in the front door window. Behind his glasses his eyes went saucer-wide when he saw Tara, and an impossibly huge smile broke across his face, revealing two big front teeth with a gap in the middle. He flung the door open. "Tara!"

Before she had time to say anything he threw himself at her, his thin arms squeezing her around the middle. He'd grown at least a few inches since she left.

She wrapped her arms around him, breathed in the little-boy shampoo-and-sweat smell of his floppy brown hair. "Hey, Con-man." It felt so damn good to hold him again, except it made her heart heavy to wonder what else she had missed in addition to those few inches.

"I can't believe you're home." He let go and ran to the door. "Dad! She's here!"

"Gracious, Conor," Geraldine said from her place by the table. "The whole neighborhood knows now."

He gave her an autopilot "Sorry, Aunt Geraldine."

Tara took a deep breath and swallowed the threatening lump while she listened to Eddie's heavy tread climb the porch stairs. His blue baseball cap with the Dunbar logo came into view first, followed by his round ruddy face, mostly covered in a full ginger beard. He wore a flannel over a white T-shirt, jeans, and work boots. Eddie had always been thick, "farm strong," as an old baseball coach used to call him. But it looked like he'd packed on a few extra pounds while she was gone.

He stopped in the doorway, filling the space, and stared at her. After a moment he let out a long breath and his broad shoulders relaxed.

Conor waved toward Tara. "She's home, Dad."

Eddie nodded, and spoke in his gravelly voice: "Yep. She's home." Then he took three steps forward and enfolded Tara in a tight hug, the kind that said he meant it. She stayed stiff at first, determined not to let him off the hook that easily. But the longer it went on the closer she came to tears.

With a gruff sniff he pulled back, keeping his hands on her shoulders. His expression was solemn as he looked her up and down, studied her face. "You okay?" he asked.

The response that sprang to mind was snide: *If you were so worried about that you might have visited more.* But when she looked at his furrowed brow and watery eyes, she couldn't say it. "I'm okay," she said.

He pulled her back in for another hug. This time she hugged him back.

Over his shoulder Tara could see Geraldine and Conor watching, a little wonder in their expressions. Eddie didn't often get emotional. He seemed so relieved to have her home. And maybe he was feeling some guilt. Whatever it was, it felt like he was trying to make up for all the lost time with this one hug.

It was Conor who finally broke the silence. "God, Dad. Let her breathe."

Eddie stepped back, and they all laughed together.

~

The look of awe on Conor's face when she presented the spaceship LEGOs was well worth all the weeks she'd given up her commissary. He wanted to get started on it right away, but Geraldine called them to dinner.

When they sat down to eat, Tara kept the conversation focused on them. She wasn't ready to get into her time at Taconic. Being home still felt not quite real, as if she might jinx it by talking about it and wake up back in her cell bunk. And if questions about her future came up, she had no answers. So she asked them to bring her up to date on everything she'd missed.

With great pride Geraldine talked about her promotion at work and Father Pat's request that she organize the collection volunteers at Sunday morning Mass. "The whole thing was a mess," she said, shaking her head. "Some rows were never seeing the basket and others were being hit twice."

Eddie had been working with Dunbar Construction as a carpenter and equipment operator since he graduated from high school. But apparently last year he'd stepped down to general laborer.

"Why?" Tara asked. "That's more brutal work and a worse schedule. Not to mention less money." But she could guess the answer. Eddie was a top-notch worker, but his frustration level soared when the tremors started in his hands or his response time suffered because he was having one of his rough days.

He shrugged. "I got tired of screwing things up. It became too risky."

She hated to hear that. It wasn't like Eddie to give up. He'd pushed through so much adversity in his life—losing their parents, surviving a car accident that left him with a traumatic brain injury, being a single dad—with a quiet but firm determination. Usually while cheering the rest of them on.

She pointed to his beard. "What's happening there? You going for a ZZ Top thing?"

He shot her a look. "It's not that long."

"You still working out?" she asked.

He shot her a more exasperated look. "When I can."

Conor sat beside her, bouncing a bit in his seat while he ate, glancing often in her direction, like he was afraid she might disappear again. He answered all her questions: his fifth grade teacher was okay, he had all As, and no, he didn't have a girlfriend—he rolled his big brown eyes at that. His favorite video game was *Fortnite*, he was still playing Little League baseball, and his favorite position was shortstop.

"Coach says he's the fastest on the team," Eddie said with a beaming smile.

"Yeah, but I don't know if I'll make the traveling team this year,"

Conor said, using a knuckle to push his glasses up his nose. "My hitting's not good enough." He looked at Eddie across the table. "Can you take me to the batting cages tomorrow, Dad?"

"I don't know, Con. I have work on the other side of town tomorrow."

"I can take you to the batting cages," Tara said.

"Would you really?" Conor asked. His glasses had slid halfway down his nose again. The frames looked too heavy, cumbersome.

"Sure. We'll go after school."

His eyes and smile lit up.

"Whoops," Geraldine said with a wince. "Tomorrow is CCD."

"CCD?" Tara turned to Eddie. "You put him in catechism classes?"

He shrugged a shoulder. "Ger thought it would be a good idea."

Tara stared at him, waited for further explanation. Eddie hated those classes as much as she did when they were kids. The unsmiling nuns, a lot of fire-and-brimstone Bible stories, so many rules. She'd convinced Eddie to stop going to church and CCD a couple years after their mother died because their father just didn't care. Geraldine begged them to start going again because she feared for their immortal souls, but they refused.

"Conor's been doing very well," Geraldine said, flashing him a proud smile. "He's making up for lost time, you know. Father Pat says he can probably start receiving Communion next year."

Tara checked on Conor, who moved his food around with his fork, his mouth puckered to the side. He didn't look too stoked about the idea of receiving the Body of Christ.

Geraldine really had taken the helm, and Eddie had apparently just rolled over.

"Okay," Tara said. "Then I'll pick you up from CCD and we'll go after."

Conor perked up. "Great."

"How will you get there?" Geraldine asked.

"I'll borrow one of your vehicles."

"Well, I'll be at work."

"You can drop me off tomorrow and take my truck," Eddie said.

"But will she be covered by your insurance?" Geraldine asked him. "We didn't look into that."

"She's just driving around town."

"Most accidents happen within a mile from home."

Eddie took a breath. "It'll be fine."

"And what about dinner?" Geraldine asked. "We eat at six thirty—"

"Jesus, Geraldine," Tara said, letting a hand drop-slam to the table. "I guess we'll eat a little later tomorrow night."

Everyone froze.

Geraldine's gaze dropped and she started playing with the napkin in her lap. Eddie and Conor became spellbound by their food, and, just like that, familiar patterns had settled back in.

This is what was so damn difficult about Geraldine. Tara could only take so much of her sister's incessant worrying, her need to follow any rule she could get her hands on, even arbitrary ones. Who gave a shit if they ate dinner an hour later? But no matter how far Geraldine pushed Tara past the limit of normal human patience, when Tara finally reacted she felt like a bitch. Because Geraldine wasn't trying to drive her crazy. She just got so stuck on her schedules.

This was not how Tara wanted her first night home to go. "Maybe you and Eddie can eat at the regular time," she said, "and just save us some."

"Yes," Geraldine said. "That could work." But she didn't look at anyone, just grabbed plates and started taking them to the sink. "It's shower time, Conor."

He stood and brought her his plate and glass, then came back to stand near Tara's chair. "Will you come up after and do the LEGOs with me?"

"Sure."

He smiled and pushed his glasses up again before heading to the stairs. Geraldine probably bought him those glasses at some discount place. Tara started a mental Conor To-do List: get him out of CCD, buy him a new pair of glasses.

Eddie piled more food on his plate. "Hey, Ger," he said. "You have any trouble getting up to Taconic today?"

Geraldine turned from the sink, wiping her hands on a towel. "I didn't actually go."

"What do you mean?"

"I got so busy at work. I went in really early, thought I would get it done fast, and it just took longer." Her hands were twisting that towel now like they were trying to wring water out of it. "And I thought they'd have a shuttle . . ."

Eddie turned to Tara. "How did you get home?"

She paused for an instant. This was not going to go over well. "Believe it or not, I caught a ride with Brian Nolan."

His jaw dropped.

"Who?" Geraldine asked. Her hands stopped moving.

"*Brian Nolan?*" Eddie yanked his hat off his head. "The asshole who put you in there?"

"*Eddie,*" Geraldine said. "No potty mouth while Conor's home."

Tara nodded at him.

"What the hell were you thinking, Tara?" he asked.

It was a fair question, one she was still asking herself. She shrugged a shoulder. "I just wanted to get home."

"Je-sus Christ." Eddie jammed his hat back on his head. "How could you get in a car with that fuckin' guy?"

"Language, Eddie!" Geraldine said.

He looked at her like she was out of her mind. "And why didn't you call me if you couldn't get up there?"

"'Cause I kept thinking I would leave, and something else would come up"—her hands worked the towel but it wouldn't twist any tighter—"and then all of a sudden it was too late."

Tara nudged her brother's arm. "It's okay. It was a little awkward, but fine."

Eddie was huffing and shaking his head like he wasn't ready to let it go.

"Listen," Tara said, "I wanted to talk to you both about something. Come sit for a minute, Ger." She hopped up to grab her sketch pad and sat back down, laying it across her lap.

Geraldine took her seat across the table.

"I wanted to thank you both," Tara said. "The money you put in my account was a lifesaver, and I know twenty-seven hundred is a lot of money." She stood the pad on end on her lap. "I wanted to show you what I spent most of it on."

But when she raised her eyes they were giving each other quizzical brows.

"Twenty-seven hundred?" Geraldine asked.

"Wow," Eddie said, looking at Geraldine. "Did we put that much in?"

"Of course not. We couldn't."

Tara looked from one to the other. "How much did you put in?"

Geraldine shrugged. "I'd have to look at the account, but I tried to send a couple hundred dollars now and then, and on special occasions . . ."

"Wait." Tara laid the sketch pad back down. "You didn't put money in there every month?"

"You know we couldn't do that." Geraldine flipped her palms up on the table. "My goodness, on top of the mortgage and taxes and Eddie's medical bills, we were still paying off your lawyer and your credit card for the first year. And you told us not to worry about sending you money, remember? You said—"

Tara held up a hand. "I know what I said." She did the math, added up the sporadic deposits she got around the holidays. They'd sent around $900 over the course of the eighteen months. Who the hell had sent the rest? She lowered her hand and her head, not sure which weighed heavier: the disappointment that they hadn't sent it or the need to know who had. "I just . . . I assumed it was you."

Eddie cleared his throat. "I'm sorry, Tare."

"It's okay. I'm sure you sent what you could."

"No," he said. "I mean I'm sorry to say this, but I think I know who put the rest of that money in there." When he tilted his head and gave her a pointed look, she knew who he meant. "Who else could it be?" he asked.

Tara closed her eyes and felt her whole body sag. Eddie was right. There was only one person it could be.

But the last person on Earth she wanted to owe anything to was Roland Fucking Shea.

Chapter Five

———————

Brian stretched his back, shoulders, and arms as much as possible within the confines of the driver's seat. He'd been sitting in the same position for hours and was starting to feel it. Hank had been in the passenger seat just as long, but he intermittently laid it all the way back for a while and extended his legs. Brian didn't have that option. He had to keep his eyes trained on Roland Shea's front door several blocks away.

Roland lived just south of Port Chester, where the homes were a little bigger, more spaced out, separated by old-growth trees and leafy shrubs. The Tudor he lived in was nice, but not too nice, and it was in his mother's name even though she resided full-time in Florida. He was good at flying under the radar.

It wasn't a bad setup for surveillance. The neighborhood was quiet enough that they could be parked a ways down the street and still have a clear view, but not so quiet they would be noticed in the middle of the day. A camera outfitted with a telephoto lens sat on Brian's lap so he could zoom in to make out faces or license plates or take pictures.

The sound of the seat lever whirred as Hank eased back again.

"Maybe it's your turn to watch the door," Brian said.

"Talk to me when you're my age." His uncle closed his eyes and crossed his arms, having ended the discussion by pulling the seniority card. He liked to use it sometimes to stick Brian with the grunt work or heavy lifting. He also used it years ago to get Brian transferred to Port Chester, and then again when he requested that he and Brian partner up. It would have been nice to work more often with some of the other detectives in the department. But Brian didn't have the heart to talk to his uncle about it because he knew Hank believed it was his job to keep Brian safe. It had been that way since the day Brian's parents died.

Hank was twenty years older than Brian but still in decent shape. His tall frame carried his beer gut fairly well, and his thick hair was only partially streaked with gray. *Don't have a wife anymore to fatten me up or nag me bald,* he liked to say. Which always triggered Brian's Uncle Hank guilt. After Brian lost his parents he moved in with Hank and Rosemary, who had no kids of their own despite ten years of trying. Maybe their marriage would have lasted if they hadn't had to take in their teenage nephew. Things had been strained enough between them before Brian came to live with them, his aunt moving through life in a sad haze after not being able to conceive, his uncle avoiding it all by focusing on problems he could solve at work instead of the ones he couldn't solve at home.

Like uncle, like nephew. That's what Susan used to say, maybe even put it right in the divorce papers—Brian didn't know because he never read them. *The most important thing to you is your work, catching bad guys.* Which was probably inevitable when both his parents had been murdered. Based on precious little evidence left at the scene of the crime, the prevailing theory was that his parents had come home and surprised an armed intruder who likely panicked. But Brian would never know for sure what happened because the trail went cold almost immediately, and the Nolan double-homicide case remained unsolved to this day, along with eight other Westchester County homicides in 2001. Whoever did it had gotten away with it, which meant there was no one Brian could tie his anger to or pin the blame on.

Except himself. A curfew of ten o'clock just hadn't seemed reasonable to fifteen-year-old Brian, especially after a big win for his baseball team that evening. So, for the first time ever, he'd blown off his curfew. And he knew in his heart the only reason his parents had gone out that night, leaving the house empty and inviting, was because they were looking for him.

Susan knew all that. They'd talked about it. The problem was she wanted him to do more than talk about it. When her Realtor career started to take off, she wanted him to move in a different direction, think about a job in the private sector, some kind of sales or high-end security.

She claimed it would be healthier for him and their marriage. Brian had never understood why she married a cop if she didn't want to be married to a cop.

A UPS truck pulled up in front of Roland's house. The driver approached the front door, dropped off a large Amazon box, and rang the doorbell before he took off again.

Normally Brian and Hank would not be stuck with this task; they'd find some shift cops to pawn it off on. But they had to keep a close eye on Roland now. During their meeting last week the prosecutor's office reported they were finally close to bringing an indictment against Roland, they just needed a little more time to dot the *i*'s and make sure the charges would stick. Everyone in that meeting was part of a task force created to investigate the dramatic spike in opioid overdoses in and around Westchester. They'd been working on Roland for two years, quietly building a case against him based on witness testimony and undercover surveillance, but they were afraid of jumping the gun. No one wanted him to get away. Not again.

They had been this close with him once before, thought they had him dead to rights. They'd been surveilling him for almost six months when a patrol officer watched a vehicle pull up to Roland's house one evening, then drive off in a hurry a few minutes later. On a hunch the officer decided to follow. He let the driver cross the state line into Connecticut with a busted taillight before he pulled her over. She refused his request to search her vehicle, but when he ran her license and saw a previous assault charge on her record, he conducted the search based on probable cause. Which was when he found a baggie filled with bottles of oxycodone sitting under the passenger seat.

It should have been a cakewalk. Bring the driver in and make an offer: turn in the boss and walk away or go to prison. Brian and Hank assured the rest of the team it would work, especially when they learned the driver was a young art teacher who still lived with her family. Poor thing probably just needed money and got sucked in by Roland. She'd be scared to death and roll over on him in the first five minutes. The whole task force had prepared for his imminent indictment and arrest.

They had not, however, prepared for Tara Connelly.

Roland's front door opened, and Brian zoomed in with the camera.

He felt his whole body tense up when the man himself stepped outside. Roland was taller than Brian by a couple inches, but lanky. His jeans slouched low on his hips, and a loose Donald Duck T-shirt hung from his shoulders. Barefoot and carrying a plastic bag, he headed for the large recycle bin at the corner of his house. Roland Shea was personally responsible for countless lost and ruined lives. But apparently he still gave a shit about the environment.

Brian zoomed in a little closer, studying him. What the hell had Tara seen in this guy? Maybe it was the surfer look he had going, wild blond hair he often wore in a man bun, his face shaded in perma-scruff, the black bracelets. Or maybe she found the cartoon T-shirts charming. Whatever it was, it prevented her from turning on him.

Roland dumped a load of liquor bottles in the bin, grabbed his Amazon package, went back inside without looking up and down the street. He didn't seem to have any extra bodyguard-types watching over him or the house, just the one goon he kept around all the time. And he'd had people over every night lately. All indications he was feeling pretty comfortable at the moment, which was right where they wanted him.

"Shea on the move?" Hank asked without opening his eyes.

"Just taking out the recycling."

"What a noble fuckin' citizen."

Many people wanted Roland put away, but Brian believed it was quite possible no one wanted it more than Hank, for a few reasons. Number One: he considered it a personal failure that he and Brian had not been able to deliver Roland a year and a half ago. Which was only compounded by Number Two: the son of one of Hank's oldest buddies on the force OD'd on Roland's heroin just last year. They knew it was Roland's because of the Yankees logo on the little glassine envelope found in the kid's bedroom. And Number Three: Hank had made a vow to the boy's father that Roland would go down for it.

When Tara wouldn't flip on Roland and ended up going away for him, he didn't thank his lucky stars and find another occupation; he continued his operation. But he was smart about it. He streamlined his business and focused solely on heroin coming straight from Mexico. He started stamping the Yankees logo on his product, because even drug dealers understand the power of branding. Customers appreciated the relative safety and certainty of a known entity when it came to their heroin. Roland worked with only a trusted skeleton crew now, and they were experts at covering their tracks. They sold in small quantities, and they never made deals via phone calls or social media. It was all word-of-mouth or encrypted messaging.

Hank raised his seat, reached for his coffee cup, realized it was empty, and dropped it back in the cupholder.

Brian figured this was as good a time as any to bring something up with him. "I saw Rosemary last night."

His uncle's head spun his way. "Where?"

"She came out to the cemetery with me." Brian visited his parents' gravestones regularly. It was where he conversed with them in his mind, kept them up to date on his life. As if the setting made it all more official and upped the chances they were listening.

Hank grunted in response, looked out his window. He probably knew what was coming.

"She said you've been drunk dialing her again lately," Brian said. "Since she told you she was getting married."

"What does she expect?" His uncle coughed a bitter laugh. "She asks to meet me for dinner, we talk old times and have some laughs. Then, when we're about done with a pleasant meal, she lays it on me. Tells me she's suddenly marrying some guy."

Brian sighed. Hank knew very well his name was Marty, and he was a high school teacher Rosemary had met at church. "She wanted you to hear it from her," Brian said.

"She wanted to gloat."

"You know that's not true."

Hank turned to his window again.

Brian didn't push it because Hank knew damn well Rosemary would never gloat. He was just still hung up on her, even after all these years. "Stop calling her, okay? It really upsets her."

"Then why does she take the calls?"

When Brian asked Rosemary the same thing, she didn't respond other than to give him a pointed look. Because Brian already knew the answer. She still took Hank's calls for the same reason Brian still indulged long nights at the bar with him. "Because she worries about you."

His uncle's eyes drifted to his lap, and he let out a sigh so full of regret it could have brought Brian to tears. Then he shifted around in his seat. "I gotta take a leak."

Brian checked his watch. "Replacements should be here in a few." He reached into the backseat for the clipboard they would hand off to the next crew, noting Roland's quick trip to the recycle bin.

"You still going out with that girl in your neighborhood?" Hank asked. "What's her name again?"

"Ashley."

"What does she do?"

"She's in marketing, or maybe public relations." That's as specific as Brian could be. "And we're not really 'going out.'"

Hank grunted. "Friends with benefits?"

Brian shrugged.

"You know, that's not going to get me any grandkids."

"Exactly."

Hank shook his head. "If you're not careful you're going to end up a sad bachelor, like your uncle . . . Hold up. Looks like Roland's got visitors." He grabbed a small pair of binoculars from the center console.

Brian looked up to see an older model red-and-white pickup pulling into Roland's driveway. He zoomed in with the camera. A big guy stepped out of the driver's side, but a denim cap and a full red beard covered most of his face.

"That guy look familiar to you too?" Hank asked.

"Maybe." Brian searched his memory, tried to place him, catch hold of a name that felt just out of reach.

Until someone hopped out of the passenger seat of the pickup.

Shit.

"I'll be *goddamned*," Hank said. "Did you know she was out?" Undoubtedly he was referring to the strawberry blonde who walked around the truck to stand by the guy. She was wearing an off-the-shoulder blouse with billowy sleeves under denim overalls, hair pulled up in a loose bun. Brian remembered pegging her style as girl next door with flair.

A fleeting spark of excitement at seeing her again went cold as Tara and the guy—Brian recognized him now as her brother—walked toward Roland's house.

"Guess she didn't learn her lesson." The satisfaction in Hank's voice was unmistakable. In his mind she was the reason they didn't get Roland off the street a long time ago. "I should call her PO," he said. "Get her sent back for violating parole."

It looked bad, her being there, less than a week after she got out. But maybe she deserved the benefit of the doubt. Brian regretted not giving her that once before. And Hank might learn all kinds of things if he started digging into this, including who drove her home the morning she was released. "You can't do that, Hank."

"Why the hell not?"

"Because then Roland will know we're watching him."

His uncle stared at him for a moment, like he was getting ready to argue.

"Besides," Brian said, "we might be able to use this at some point."

Hank trained his binoculars on Roland's house again. "Maybe . . ."

Hoping that was the end of it, Brian looked through the camera just in time to see Roland open the door to his guests. His eyebrows lifted in surprise, but a welcoming smile spread across his face as he shook hands with Eddie and slapped him on the back. Then he turned to Tara and opened his arms wide.

It was impossible to deny the disappointment that came with watching her step right into them.

Chapter Six

————————

Eddie hadn't expected such a warm welcome when they knocked on Roland's door. He was sure the raging headache he'd had going on all day was about this meeting. That tended to happen when his stress level kicked up. The last time he and Tara saw Roland was before she went away, and that conversation had not gone well, to say the least.

It was hard to make himself shake Roland's hand, withstand the backslap and phony hello: "Eddie, dude. Good to see you."

But when Roland raised his arms looking for a hug from Tara, it took everything in Eddie not to step between them. He didn't though. Tara had said to just follow her lead.

After a long moment—too long—Roland let her go, looked her up and down. "Well, my Irish lass, doesn't look like the big house did you much harm."

Grade A Asshole.

Tara offered a small smile. "Hi, Roland. We just need a minute."

"Yeah, yeah. Of course." He waved them inside, through a small foyer, into a living room that had seen some action lately. Dirty glasses were planted on most surfaces, empty pizza boxes and leftover crusts littered the floor. The leather couch was hidden under random clothing, half-eaten bags of chips, video game controllers. Even if Roland invited them to have a seat, which he didn't, there was nowhere to sit. So they stood in an awkward circle around his coffee table.

Eddie recognized the jacked guy in a tight black T-shirt sitting at the kitchen island with a coffee mug in his hand. One of Roland's security people.

Roland turned toward him. "Scott, you remember our old friends, the Connellys."

Scott's only acknowledgment of Eddie and Tara was a dark side-glance before he went back to reading his phone.

Eddie took a wide stance and crossed his arms. He was pretty much there to be the muscle too, back up his sister. Might as well try to look the part. He was about the same size as Scott, though definitely softer around the middle.

Roland pulled his shoulder-length hair back and bound it with a band. "Pardon the mess, had people over last night."

"No problem," Tara said. "Sorry we couldn't call first. I didn't have your number anymore. I just wanted to talk to you—"

A sudden burst of loud angry music cut her off. Roland held up a hand and slid his cell from a back pocket. "Sorry, sweetheart. Must take this." He headed for the kitchen. "Only be a minute."

She nodded at him before he disappeared around a corner, then she rolled impatient eyes at Eddie.

He'd tried to talk her out of this whole thing. She didn't need to be anywhere near Roland Shea ever again. But Tara said this was too important. When Eddie offered to go see him alone, she said she needed to say it for herself. That was probably code for: *I better handle this, Eddie. You'll just screw it up.* Which was fair. It was Eddie's fault Tara had ever gotten mixed up with Roland in the first place.

Roland walked back in the room, sliding his phone in his back pocket. "Sorry about that. Please . . ." He nodded at Tara to continue.

"Roland, I just wanted to thank you. For the money." She used her hands and talked fast. "I didn't expect it at all, and it wasn't necessary—I never would have rolled over on you. But it was a huge help to me in there, and I will pay back all of it as soon as I can—"

"Whoa-whoa-whoa," Roland said, his brows lifting high. "What money are we talking about?"

"The commissary money."

Roland just stared at her and shrugged.

Eddie felt as confused as Tara looked. It had to be Roland. He had the means and the . . . What was the word? It was hard to think around the pounding in his head. The motivation. No one else they knew had the means and motivation to do it. That's why Tara was so determined to risk coming here—to thank him, vow to pay him back, and make sure there was no expectation on Roland's part.

Tara cocked her head. "You didn't put money in my inmate account at Taconic?"

"No, babe. Wasn't me." He brought a hand to his chest. "I'd've been happy to, but I figured your family was looking after you." His accusing eyes slid Eddie's way. "I mean, I couldn't have used my name, of course, but I would have figured something out . . ."

Tara was already holding her hands up. "No, no. That's okay. I just assumed . . ." She gave her head a quick shake, then looked at Roland head-on. "It doesn't matter. I just came here today to make sure we're all square at this point. That all our business is finished."

A mix of pride and wonder washed over Eddie as he watched his sister. The way she held Roland's eye without blinking, her chin raised. How she said just the right thing, exactly what she meant. Tara had always been good at showing no fear, even when it was right there under the surface. Whether it was when they got caught cutting school or skipping church, or when their mom died and left them with their useless father, or when the cops tried to get her to turn on Roland. Even the morning Eddie dropped her at Taconic, he'd been the one to shed tears, not her.

Roland put a hand to his heart, his wrist wrapped in a half dozen braided bracelets. "Tara, sweetheart . . ."

If he called her sweetheart again Eddie was pretty sure he'd crack Roland across his scruffy face, Scott or no Scott.

". . . yes. If that's what you want, our dealings are finished."

She nodded once.

"And," Roland said, extending the hand out toward her, "if you need some money now, a little cash to get set up, I'd like to help." His other hand pulled a thick wad of rolled-up bills halfway out of his front jeans pocket. "No strings. In my opinion, you've earned it."

Eddie saw his sister's eyes drop to the cash. It had to be tempting. Tara had no money of her own. Just yesterday she had to ask him for some so she could buy a few things from the grocery store and get a haircut. Eddie hadn't even blinked, just handed over more than she asked for. He'd been in that position before himself, living off other people, and it was an awful feeling.

But Tara just said, "No thanks," and turned for the door.

Roland watched her go, a mild look of regret on his face. "Let me know if you change your mind," he said.

Tara never looked back, just headed outside to the truck.

Eddie followed but stopped at the door. "Stay away from her, Roland. I mean it. She's done enough for you."

Roland snorted. "It's not my fault she went to prison, dude."

Eddie felt the burn rise in his cheeks. For a split second he saw himself lunging forward, wiping that smirk off Roland's face, and forcing him to accept the blame for what happened back then. He even felt a twitch in his right arm, like it was itching to take the swing.

Over in the kitchen, Scott stood from his stool.

Roland just waited, a snide smile on his face.

As always Eddie could not come up with a worthy response. He badly wanted to hit Roland with a line that would put him in his place, maybe scare him a little, but words failed him. Especially with the hammering inside his skull, which had intensified. So he had to settle for slamming the front door on his way out.

~⪡~

Eddie had taken a sleeping pill, but it wasn't doing the trick. It was the migraine he'd had all day. Although it eased to low-grade after they left Roland's, his head still ached, and it would be tender tomorrow. A second pill would knock him out, but then he'd sleep half his Sunday away, and he promised Conor they would go to the batting cages. A choice between getting shitty sleep or being a shitty dad. Tara had taken Conor to hit balls a few times since she got back, and she thought, with pointers from Eddie, Conor could improve quickly. *He needs some batting tips. And it wouldn't hurt you to get out and get some exercise,* she'd added. A dig at the weight he'd gained while she was gone. Tara was the one to drag him on runs, nag him about working out. She had cooked meatless meals and fought with Geraldine to keep sugar in the house to a minimum. All that had changed when Tara left.

He'd been taking the pills over a year now—something else his younger sister would not approve of. Sleep had never come easily, at least not since the night he was fourteen years old and his father wrapped the Ford Mustang they were riding in around a tree at high speed. Eddie woke up in the ICU four days later to learn from his sisters that their father had walked away from the car crash and then run away from home. They didn't need to tell him why, that their dad didn't want to deal with the aftermath. Specifically, cops who would quickly realize the Mustang was stolen and discover Bobby Connelly's long and illustrious career in auto theft. Eddie was no help to the police. He had no memory of the accident, and neither he nor his sisters offered up the fact that stolen vehicles often spent a few hours at their house before delivery. Eddie hadn't seen or heard from their father since. Though every month for many years after he left he sent envelopes with a few hundred in cash.

While Eddie had always battled insomnia, it was worse after Tara went to prison. Even more anxiety haunted him during those dark, solitary hours when he couldn't get his mind to rest. And his doc said the insomnia had contributed to—if not caused—the seizure. He'd been seizure-free for years, then one night at the dinner table five months after Tara left: wham. He was sitting with Geraldine and Conor, working on his meat loaf, when a wave of nausea hit, his ears started to ring, and he experienced an otherworldly bout of déjà vu. Next thing he knew he was on the floor, looking up at two frightened faces. His doctor prescribed antiepileptic drugs along with the sleeping pills, both of which made him tired all the time. He missed some work, stopped running and working out with the weights in the basement. He also lost his driver's license for ten months, until he was medically cleared to drive again.

He never told Tara about that seizure, and he made Geraldine and Conor promise to keep quiet about it too. She had enough to worry about at the time.

Someone shuffled past his bedroom door. He checked the clock: 10:35. It had to be Conor. His small bedroom, an old deck Eddie had enclosed and insulated, was at the very front of the house, next to Eddie's. The other bedrooms were on the far side of the staircase: Geraldine's room—formerly their parents' room—and Tara's old room, which she used to share with Geraldine when they were growing up. How they ever shared a room Eddie didn't know. His sisters were from two different planets.

He listened to his son descend the stairs, then got out of bed to see what was up. Not that he didn't trust Conor. He was a good boy. He did well in school, was already way smarter than his father. He tried hard in baseball, made do with secondhand everything—or made do without—and did all that was asked of him without complaint. Even going to those CCD classes, because it meant so much to Geraldine. Eddie said no at first, but she had this way of nagging, wearing him down with her emotional pleas, like it was the most important thing in the world to her. Conor made it easy. *It's okay, Dad. I'll just go,* he'd said. *Let's not argue about it anymore.* And Conor had been doing that nervous thing he tended to do, swinging his arms against his hips like a ringing bell. The more anxious he was, the faster the swinging.

Not wanting to wake anyone else, Eddie climbed down the steps quietly, assuming Conor was getting a snack in the kitchen. But it was dark downstairs. The only light came from the soft overheads on the porch. Conor was standing out there, on the other side of the screen door, wearing a T-shirt and flannel pajama bottoms. No glasses, which was rare, since he was practically blind without them. Eddie was about to call out to him when he heard Tara's voice.

"Hey, Con-man. What are you doing up?" She was on the other side of the living room window, folded up in one of the wicker chairs on the porch. She had a cigarette between her fingers and reached over to place it on the edge of a nearby flowerpot she appeared to be using for an ashtray. Geraldine would hit the ceiling.

Conor took the seat beside hers. "Couldn't sleep. And I smelled *that* through my window." He threw his chin toward Tara's cigarette.

She looked above her to the second story, right where Conor's room was. "Sorry about that."

He shrugged.

Maybe Eddie was intruding, skulking in the shadows and eavesdropping. But it stirred something in him to see them sitting there, side by side in the quiet night. They were so easy together. Conor wasn't like that with most people. Neither was Tara.

"You know," Conor said, "Mrs. Jenkins, the health teacher, said smoking is terrible for you. It could even kill you."

Tara nodded. "Mrs. Jenkins is right. I'm afraid I developed a bad habit while I was gone."

While she was gone. That's how they'd always referred to it. *While Tara's away we can use her room for storage. Tara will be gone for Christmas again this year.* Like she was on a trip. Naming it directly would have meant thinking about where she was.

Then Eddie heard his son ask Tara a question he hadn't had the balls to ask her himself.

"Was it scary there? In prison?"

She took a moment, maybe deciding how much he could handle. "Yeah, it was sometimes. Especially at first, not knowing anybody or how it all worked. But I figured it out, even made a few friends. My last cellmate, Jeannie, has a daughter a little younger than you. I drew some comics for her too."

"Did she have a special power?" Conor asked.

"Yeah, but hers was different from yours. Everybody has their own special power."

Eddie smiled to himself. Conor loved those comics she'd sent him, about a boy whose eyeglasses activated his superhuman intelligence. They covered half a wall in his room.

"You know," Tara said, "drawing those comics helped me get through that place. But it was stressful, being there, and boring most of the time, which is why I started smoking. I'm working on it though. I have a plan to stop soon."

Conor didn't respond.

Tara's shoulders slumped. "This really bothers you, doesn't it."

He nodded.

"Well . . ." She reached for the cigarette, studied it for a moment. Then she brought it to her lips and took a long drag, the tip glowing bright. After she blew a trail of smoke in the opposite direction from Conor, she pressed the cigarette into the dirt of the plant to put it out. "I just quit," she said.

"Really?"

"Yep. I was looking for a good reason to quit, and I can't think of a better one than you."

A small ache lodged in Eddie's throat. He wished he could talk to Conor like that, be so open with his feelings. But he was always afraid of saying or doing the wrong thing, looking stupid or weak in front of his son.

"It's not going to be easy, you know," Tara said. "They say smoking is the hardest habit to break." She leaned forward, elbows on her knees. "I'm going to need your help."

Conor leaned forward on his knees too, so their heads were close together. "What can I do?"

"Let's see." She thought for a moment. "When I get a really bad craving, I'm going to come find you, and you'll need to tell me a joke."

"A joke?"

"Yeah. A knock-knock joke, or why'd-the-chicken-cross-the-road joke, whatever. Just something to distract me. Do you know some jokes?"

He scratched his head. "Only a couple. But I could get more, from kids at school."

"I think you should do that. You'll need to have a few lined up, a craving could hit anytime. I might come wake you up in the middle of the night. Or show up at school in the middle of the day," she said.

Conor laughed.

"What? I'm serious." Tara held out her fist. "Deal?"

He bumped it. "Deal. But only if you come up and tell me a story."

For about two seconds Eddie worried whether it was normal for Conor to still want to hear fairy tales at ten years old. But then he remembered he'd listened to his mom's stories until he was eleven, and he would have kept on listening if she hadn't died.

"I don't know," Tara said. "It's pretty late."

"Just a quick one?"

She made him wait a bit, then she grinned. "Okay."

Eddie headed up the stairs and got back in bed before he heard them go past in the hall. Then he lay in the dark, head angled toward the wall he shared with Conor, and listened to Tara tell the story of the mighty Finn McCool. Eddie didn't catch every word of the soft, melodic voice Tara used to paint pictures of a misty landscape and ancient ruins, like their mother used to do. But it didn't matter. He already knew the story backward and forward.

When a Scottish giant threatened Ireland, Finn used his exceptional strength to hurl chunks of the Irish coastline into the ocean to build the Giant's Causeway, a bridge across the Irish Sea to Scotland, so he could challenge the giant to a proper duel. But when Finn realized just how large the giant was, he had to rely on his wits instead of his muscles. He lured the giant to Ireland, wrapped himself in a blanket, and lay in a crib. When the giant arrived at Finn's house and saw the enormous baby, he assumed its father must be massive, and he ran back home, breaking up much of the causeway as he went so no one would follow him. What was left became one of the natural wonders of the world. Tara always finished the story by telling Conor he reminded her of Finn McCool because he was both strong and smart.

Conor knew his mother, talked to her every couple weeks on the phone. But he saw Andrea only a few times a year, when she made the trip up from the city in her skintight clothes and loads of makeup. She was a hostess at some club down in the West Village and still very much a party girl, even after a couple stints in rehab. Not really equipped for visits from her young son. She and Eddie met at a bar one night eleven years ago while she was staying with her parents in Port Chester. They tried living together for almost two years after Conor was born, but between her drug use and his bouts of depression and foggy days, it was a disaster. When Eddie finally offered her an ultimatum—stop using or leave—she chose to go. Tara had been more of a mother to Conor than Andrea ever was.

Geraldine tried with Conor, in her own way. She loved him, and she was good with the details: due dates for school stuff, his practice schedule, making sure he brushed his teeth twice a day and got to bed on time. But it was hard for Conor to see past the nervous Nellie and have much fun with Geraldine. And all her rules stressed him out.

It was a gift, hearing Conor and Tara together on the porch that night. When Eddie thought about it, he'd seen a few changes in Conor just in the short time Tara had been home. Smiling more, talking about his day at the dinner table, excited about baseball rather than defeated. Tara did that for him. Eddie wished he could do more for her now—find her a job, get her a car . . . something. God knows he owed her.

And if he spent the rest of his life making it up to her, it still wouldn't be enough.

Chapter Seven

The headquarters for Rudy's Value Maids was a gloomy affair buried in the back of a low-end strip mall, and the acrid aroma of mildew and disinfectant burned Tara's nostrils. She sat across from the owner, Rudy Russo, a thin middle-aged guy with dark spiky hair, a wishbone mustache, and a Hawaiian shirt. They'd barely started the interview when he had to answer his phone. Now his pale arm darted about as he barked at someone on the other end.

"I already explained this to you, Carla," he said. "Tell him no credit cards or checks, cash only. That's how it works . . ."

While Tara waited for Rudy, who was probably committing some kind of tax fraud, she let her eyes wander around the dreary office. Beat-up vacuum cleaners and grubby-looking mops lined one wall; shelves along the opposite wall were filled with various cleaning solutions and supplies. On top of a file cabinet in the corner was a stack of gray aprons that said VALUE MAIDS across the chest in a no-frills font that seemed indicative of the whole operation.

"Sorry about this," Rudy said, pointing to his phone. "Now she doesn't know how to work the lockbox." He smirked and rolled his eyes.

Tara held up a hand. "No worries."

He got back on the line, started talking through the lockbox process in a slow, singsongy voice. Like he was speaking to a child.

Eddie had driven her to the interview, and he hesitated to let her go in alone—*This place looks sketchy, Tare*—but he settled for waiting outside. She would have driven herself, but after this interview they were both meeting with her parole officer. Tara had spoken to her PO only briefly on the phone last week, to report when she arrived home and schedule their first appointment, which had to include a family member. She wasn't sure what to expect, but there'd been lots of talk in Taconic about the godlike powers parole officers wielded over their parolees. Landing this job today would help Tara start off on the right foot.

She was also getting desperate. She hadn't been able to land an admin or retail position anywhere, not even a waitressing gig. A couple of other, more reputable housecleaning services had turned her down too. They never said outright it was because of her record; employers in New York weren't supposed to discriminate on that basis. But it was fairly obvious when they shifted from enthusiastic to *We'll let you know* after the subject of a criminal background check came up. And there was no use lying to them; that would only make her look worse.

So, yes, she was hoping to impress her PO. But she also needed a goddamn job.

Rudy finally hung up. "Sheesh. It's just not that hard, know what I mean?" He shrugged. "Okay, where were we . . . Right. It sounds like you have a lot of availability?"

"Yes. I can work as many hours as you can give me."

"And you have reliable transportation? I can't tell you how many of my girls swear they do, then they can't get to a job and I gotta scramble to figure it out."

The thought of being one of Rudy's girls made Tara's stomach turn. But she reminded herself it would be temporary. "Transportation won't be an issue." She, Eddie, and Geraldine would just have to make it work with two cars for a while.

"That's what I like to hear," he said, looking down at her résumé. "Used to be a teacher, huh? You don't have cleaning experience, but you worked in the service industry before. That helps." He kept reading. "What about the last year and a half? You weren't working?"

This was always the tricky part. He hadn't mentioned a background check. She didn't want to lie, but she also didn't want to bring up her record if she didn't have to. "No, I had stuff going on, took some time off. But I'm ready to get back at it."

Rudy stared at her for a moment with narrowed eyes. Then he gave her a snide smile. "So if we run your criminal history, it's gonna come up clean?"

"I didn't realize that was a requirement."

"As you can imagine, Tara, I gotta be careful. My girls go into people's homes, unsupervised." His fingertips went to his chest. "Puts me in a very liable position."

Tara sighed and started to rise from her chair. "Okay, well thanks for your time—"

"Hold up," Rudy said, raising a hand to wave her back down. "I didn't say you couldn't have the job. I just like to know who's working for me, know what I mean? Now, you got good experience, flexibility, you seem eager . . . I'd really like to help you out."

She offered a small smile. "I'd be grateful if you gave me a chance."

He returned the smile. "That's nice to hear. You wanna just tell me what's on your record? Maybe we bypass the whole background check."

It was probably a fair question; he had to make sure he wasn't hiring a violent offender. So she answered. "It was a drug trafficking charge."

"So you did time." It was more a statement than a question. Obviously she wasn't the first ex-con to apply for this job.

She nodded.

Rudy sucked in air through gritted teeth. "Ouch. That makes it hard to get work. Explains what you're doing here. I bet Value Maids was bottom of the list for you, am I right?"

Tara shifted in her seat. "Not really . . ."

He held up a hand. "I get it. You on parole now?" When she hesitated to answer he leaned toward her and lowered his voice. "I've helped out other girls in your position. In my humble opinion, everyone deserves a second chance, know what I mean?"

"I'm on parole."

His head bobbed up and down in understanding. "Well, I think we could make this happen, Tara. I know how it works, I can help with your PO, sign all those forms so they know you're behaving, staying employed, that kind of thing. I can bring you on at fifteen dollars an hour too—lot higher than minimum. And I'm dialed in with all the property management companies in town, so I could get you as much work as you want."

Tara didn't believe for one second this was about benevolence. It was probably quid pro quo: he sweetened his offer because it assured "his girls" would work hard and stay quiet about his scam, especially the ones on parole. This was no dream job, but that money would give her a little breathing room.

"You do good, and I'll send you to the nicer places," Rudy said. "You know, the ones that are a little less disgusting." He raised his eyebrows. "How does all that sound?"

"That sounds great," Tara said. "And I'm a hard worker, I won't let you down."

Without taking his eyes off her he pushed back against his chair and propped an elbow on an armrest, ran his thumb and forefinger down his long patchy 'stache. "No, I don't imagine you would."

She waited to see what was next, if he would ask further questions or get going on the paperwork. But he didn't.

"So, when can I start?" she asked.

"As soon as we come to"—his shrug was breezy—"an arrangement."

That's when she knew the catch was coming. All through the good news he offered she'd been waiting for the bad. "An arrangement?" she asked, keeping her voice steady.

"Yeah, you know. I do this for you, get you all set up, make your PO happy. And maybe we spend some time together, get to know each other a bit. Like, after hours. We could hang out, have some fun." He winked at her. "Bet you could use some fun if you just got out, know what I mean?"

Tara clasped her hands together in her lap. There was no mistaking his meaning, and the way he was looking her up and down now, with no shame, made her skin crawl.

"I'm thinking we could take care of each other," he said. "You're not gonna get a better offer. I know damn well you went to the other cleaning services before you came here, and they turned you down. Let's face it, you're only here because no one else will hire you."

Her instinct was to jump out of that chair and run out to Eddie, drive away from this place and never look back. But then Rudy would just get away with this. She could report him, maybe to her PO. But her word wouldn't count for much against a local business owner and employer. And, apparently, Rudy was already getting away with it—*I've helped out other girls in your position.*

She reached down into her bag and pulled out a form, tossed it on the desk. "Just sign that so my PO knows I showed up for the interview," she said without looking at him.

"Sorry." He shook his head. "I only sign paperwork for my employees."

Tara didn't actually need his signature, she'd met her interview quota already. But she wanted to make him pay in some small way, do *something* to wipe that smug smile off his face. She leaned forward, put her forearms on his desk. "You see the big dude waiting outside in the red pickup?"

Rudy maintained a pointedly disinterested expression while his gaze flicked to the parking lot behind her. But she saw it, the instant his eyes must have landed on Eddie. His cheek twitched.

"That's my brother," she said. "If you don't sign that form I'm going to go out there and tell him what you tried to do to me. And he will come in here and mop this dirty fucking floor with your scrawny little ass until it sparkles. Know what I mean?"

He looked at her a long time, and Tara made sure to sit very still and hold his gaze. The truth was Eddie couldn't afford to get into fights. It would bring on a migraine and make him nauseous for days, exacerbate his TBI. Tara would never put him in that position. But she'd always been good at bluffing.

Rudy glanced down at the form. He sucked his teeth and did his best to look bored. But eventually he picked up a pen and signed it. Then he waved her away.

It was hard to enjoy the tiny victory because her whole body started trembling, in revulsion and anger. But after she grabbed the form from Rudy's desk she forced herself to walk out of there, not run, even though she could feel his eyes on her the whole time. With relief she yanked open the exterior door and stepped through.

But right before it closed behind her Rudy shouted out one last thing. "You'll be back, princess. You can't escape your past."

When she got to the pickup and climbed in next to Eddie her muscles went weak with relief.

"How'd it go?" he asked, starting the truck. "Did you get the job?"

She shook her head and fiddled with her bag for something to do. Because if she looked directly at her brother she would cry.

"Hey," Eddie said. "You okay?"

No, she wasn't okay. But if she didn't pull it together he would figure it out and go after that asshole, and she didn't want that.

So she swallowed it all down and turned to him. "I'm fine. But let's get going. Don't want to be late for my PO."

〜

The meeting with her parole officer was in New Rochelle, about fifteen minutes away. The drive gave her time to calm down, though she still felt shaky when they arrived at Westchester County Parole Services, a squat stucco building with dark windows located right off the interstate. The episode with Rudy had more of a hold on her than she cared to admit. She could tell herself all day he was the sleaze in this equation, but his proposition had made her feel cheap and humiliated. And like she'd narrowly escaped something. Maybe because there was a very fine line between her and the women who'd been too desperate to turn him down.

Eddie followed her into the lobby, pulling at the neck of his collar. Tara had told him he didn't need to dress up for the meeting, but he insisted on wearing a button-down. "Listen," he said. "I'm just going to keep my mouth shut, let you do all the talking. I don't want to screw anything up."

"You don't have to say much, she just wants to meet a family member, make sure I have some support."

They located Community Supervision Services on the second floor, and the receptionist directed them down a long unadorned corridor bathed in harsh fluorescent light. Tara had been in a lot of government buildings in her life, and they all seemed to offer the same drab hopeless ambience. When they found the right door and knocked, a voice called for them to come in.

The woman who stood behind the desk as they entered looked to be midthirties. Her black hair was pulled up in a tidy bun, except for a straight curtain of bangs that ended just above her eyes, and she wore a white blouse and dark pants, business casual attire that flattered her short curvy shape.

Tara introduced herself and Eddie.

"Nice to meet you both. I'm Doreen DaCosta with Parole Services for the state of New York. We talked on the phone last week." There was no missing the Bronx accent, the mix of bristly attitude and musical lilt, the nasal twang in *New Yawk* and *tawked*.

Once they were all seated Tara pulled a stack of paperwork from her bag. "I filled out all the forms you asked for, Ms. DaCosta. And I have a list of places where I've applied for a job, but no luck yet."

DaCosta offered no response, made no move to take the papers, just clasped her hands together on the desk. Her long and pointy press-on nails were purple with fine swirls of glitter. "Thanks for bringing all that, Miss Connelly, but I'm afraid there's something else we gotta talk about first." When she spoke everything seemed to move to the rhythm of her speech: her head, her shoulders, her large gold hoop earrings.

Tara glanced at Eddie and lowered the paperwork to her lap. "Okay."

"I received a report that you already violated your parole."

"*What?*" Tara asked.

Eddie leaned forward in his chair. "How?"

"Did you visit Roland Shea, a known drug dealer, at his home last Friday afternoon?" DaCosta asked.

Tara drew in a sharp breath. Wait, that wasn't a parole violation, was it?

"Do you recall signing a contract when you were released from Taconic whereby you vowed not to consort with known criminals, particularly ones related to your own past criminal activity?"

In the periphery Tara saw Eddie drop his head.

"Yes, but—"

DaCosta held up a hand and splayed her fingers. "Miss Connelly, I'm only interested in helping people who truly want to reenter society successfully. I don't tolerate violations, it's that simple."

"I understand," Tara said. "But I didn't realize it was a violation, and I had to talk to him."

"Well, I hope it was worth it, because this is grounds for revoking your parole."

"Wait." Tara slid forward to the edge of her seat. "You can't do that."

DaCosta pulled her chin into her neck. "I most certainly can."

"No, I mean . . ." This couldn't possibly be happening. "If you could let me explain—"

"You've been out only a week and a day. If you can't abide by the terms of your parole for that long there's no hope for the next two years." She closed the file in front of her, the one with Tara's name on it, and pushed it aside. "I have a call in to my supervisor about remanding you back into custody to finish out the rest of your sentence."

Remanding you back into custody . . . All the air was sucked from Tara's lungs and everything became blurry as her eyes filled. For the second time in the space of an hour she felt utterly powerless. She was aware of Eddie's eyes on her, imploring her to speak up, convince this woman she was making a mistake. But it was hard to find the words through the fog of panic. She had never hyperventilated before, but it felt like that's what was happening, like she was getting too much air. Or maybe she wasn't getting enough.

Eddie spoke in his low rumbly voice. "Ms. DaCosta . . ." He pulled his hat off his head and held it between his hands. "All Tara's done since she came home is try to find a job and take care of her family. I don't know how many interviews she's been on looking for work. She cleaned our house, even the yard. She's been cooking healthy meals and spending time with her nephew." His voice caught on that last part and he cleared his throat. "Now, I was with her when she went to Roland's house, and she had a damn good reason for being there. If you could just hear her out . . ."

DaCosta studied Eddie's big earnest face for a moment, then she looked at Tara. "I'll hear you out, but don't lie to me or you'll make this worse." She raised her eyebrows to emphasize her warning.

Tara took a breath, swiped at a couple of tears, and thought about the best way to explain this because she would get only one shot. "Someone put money in my account while I was at Taconic. I thought it was my family, but it wasn't. I mean, they put some in"—she gestured toward Eddie—"but someone else put a lot of money in there. I assumed it was Roland because we don't know anyone else with that kind of extra money." She held up a hand, as if swearing that what she was about to say was the truth, the whole truth, and nothing but the truth. "The only reason I went to his house was because I wanted to tell him that I would pay back every single penny. I was afraid he expected something from me in return."

It might have been wishful thinking, but Tara could swear a glimmer of understanding flickered in the other woman's eyes.

"That's the God's honest truth," Eddie said. "That's exactly what Tara said to Roland."

"It turned out it wasn't even him," Tara said. "I've had no contact with him since, and I never will again."

DaCosta sat there, lips pursed and arms folded on her desk while she considered it all.

"Ms. DaCosta," Eddie said, "I'm sorry we broke a rule. We didn't mean to, and it won't happen again. But, ma'am, we need Tara at home. *My son* needs her at home."

She drummed those nails against her desk for a moment. "You've been looking for work?"

"Yes." Tara shuffled through the papers she brought. "This is a list of all the places where I applied so far, with signatures." She pulled it out and laid it on the desk.

DaCosta glanced at it. "You're living with family as planned?" she asked, nodding toward Eddie.

"Yes. My brother and his son and my older sister."

"When I send you across the hall for a piss test after this meeting," she said, pointing a finger that way, "is it gonna come up clean?"

"Yes. I don't use."

DaCosta held her hand out for the rest of Tara's paperwork. She took her time scanning through it—leaving Tara to continue to wonder if she'd be sleeping at home or in a jail cell that night—then she leaned back in her chair and linked her hands in front of her. "You find out who gave you that money?"

"Not yet," Tara said. "I called the Department of Corrections, but they said the deposits were anonymous."

"You got any theories?"

"There's a chance it was our father," Tara said, glancing at Eddie. They'd talked this possibility through. "We haven't seen him in seventeen years, but he used to send us money, and he wrote me a letter when I was at Taconic." She shook her head. "But I never responded, and I just can't see him setting up payments. He was a cash man, preferred to leave no trace."

"So you're afraid somebody might come calling."

"Yeah. I mean, who gives someone almost two thousand dollars without wanting something in return?"

DaCosta nodded, as if to say that was a fair question. "Tell you what, Miss Connelly. I'll make you a deal. I *will* be checking out your story, but for today I'll accept your explanation as to why you were at Roland Shea's house and let this infraction go—as long as you understand that will only happen once."

"I understand."

"But in return, I want you to let this money thing go for now."

"Let it go?"

"Mm-hmm. I get why you want to know who gave it to you, but whoever it is, they don't want you to know. It happens." She shrugged. "And you'll only break more rules by trying to investigate it on your own. What you need to be focusing on right now is rebuilding your life. Finding a job, being back with your family, nailing down goals for the future. So I'll send you home today, if you agree to drop it. We got a deal?"

Tara didn't respond right away. Was she really supposed to just forget about that money?

"Of course we have a deal," Eddie said, elbowing Tara.

"Yes," Tara said.

DaCosta angled her head. "Don't test me, Miss Connelly. For the time being I want you to consider looking into this matter a parole violation. You got it?"

"I got it."

"Good. Then let's review your parole plan." She pulled Tara's folder back in front of her and opened it up.

They spent the next thirty minutes going over a plan for "successful reentry." Initially Tara would be checking in with DaCosta in person monthly, and by phone weekly, and she had to undergo regular drug screening tests for a while, which was standard with a drug charge. She was not permitted to leave Westchester County for any reason without prior approval, and she would continue to document her attempts to get a job. Much of the focus was on the home environment; DaCosta asked lots of specifics about who resided in the house, their ages and occupations, their daily routine. Eddie had to jump in when Tara couldn't recall certain information, such as Geraldine's work address, details about the household budget and schedule. DaCosta even commented on it—*I can see why you brought him in as a support.*

But it was hard to focus on paperwork and particulars when she'd been so close to returning to prison that very afternoon. There was no doubt Eddie's impassioned plea had saved her. Her freedom felt so fragile, and, right now, she owed it to her brother.

So while she listened—but not really—as DaCosta rattled off community resources available to assist parolees, Tara reminded herself to thank Eddie for not keeping his mouth shut that day. Maybe the line separating her from Rudy's victims wasn't quite so fine after all.

Chapter Eight

The *Q* on the accordion folder stared up at Geraldine like an accusing eye every time she opened the drawer. She still hadn't started on the payroll quarterly taxes, and they were officially late. Never before had she fallen behind like this. She always gave herself an early deadline of one week, just like she always set her watch five minutes early. But that deadline was long gone, and the real deadline, the one set by the IRS, was today. Not good, but manageable. She was still within the grace period and could avoid significant late fees.

But she had to find a long, uninterrupted period of time to attack them or she would make errors, and she couldn't start on them right then. Mr. Bertucci was on his way in to meet with her about the recent payroll error. Not Dunbar Construction. There'd been another one since then—smaller, only three paychecks affected over at the Round the Corner Bookshop. But another error nonetheless. Geraldine was rushing to finish their payroll on time, and she had failed to factor in overtime and PTO. Rita had shaken her head—*There are automated programs that would prevent that kind of mistake.*

Geraldine had sent Rita on errands so she wouldn't be here when Mr. Bertucci came in.

She closed and locked the drawer with the *Q* folder in it, deciding she'd work on the quarterlies at home that night. That paperwork shouldn't really leave the office, but she'd have some peace and quiet at home, and no prying eyes. Though, she'd also promised Tara she would get the rest of her clothes and books to her soon. What the rush was Geraldine didn't know; it's not like Tara had a job to go to yet.

It was nice having Tara back at times. She'd given the house a thorough cleaning and tidied up the yard. Dinners were livelier. She asked Conor all about his day and his friends; somehow she remembered all their names. She played video games with him and they joked around a lot. Geraldine was never good at making Conor laugh. And Tara liked to tease Eddie, ask him when he was going to lose the neckbeard and find a girlfriend. Though it wasn't kind when she poked at him about his weight—*Sure you need that third helping, Eddie?* Still, it felt like she had lightened the whole house up a bit.

But she'd been home less than two weeks, and she was disrupting everything. Keeping Conor up past his bedtime with the fairy tales, nagging Geraldine to relegate her "clutter" to her own rooms, wanting to cook organic vegetarian dinners, which were far too expensive. Eddie had to take a morning off work to go to a meeting with her parole officer, for pity's sake. She wasn't interested in atoning for her crime; she made that clear when Geraldine suggested she go to confession—*I'd rather stick needles in my eyes.* Rules had never mattered much to Tara. She let everyone else worry about the rules while she did what she wanted. Like when Geraldine used to try to implement chore charts, curfews, and consequences, and Tara flat out ignored her. Or when Geraldine would have to take time off work to meet with school officials because Tara got caught smoking or skipping class again. She'd always been good at creating chaos.

When Geraldine looked outside to see Mr. Bertucci's old Cadillac pulling in, she straightened up her work space. A cluttered desk would not instill confidence. She opened her top drawer and swept most of the papers in there. Not all of them, she didn't want to appear idle.

When Mr. Bertucci walked in, she had to force the smile to stay on her face. He looked older than when she'd seen him last, which was only a few weeks ago. He wore his usual dress pants and a sport coat over a crisp white shirt—he took pride in supporting a fellow countryman by buying his clothes from the local Italian tailor—but they seemed to hang off him. Maybe he'd lost weight, or he was stooping more. And the long wrinkles in his face seemed to have deepened.

Geraldine stood behind her desk. "Hello, Mr. Bertucci. It's so good to see you."

"Ah, Geraldine." He walked over to take her hands in his. "It's been too long, eh?"

"Can I get you anything?"

"No, please, don't go to any trouble. Sit, sit." He sat across from her. "Tell me, how are you?"

Geraldine loved how old-school Mr. Bertucci was, from his clothes to his approach. He always made time to ask questions about how she was doing. "I'm great, thanks."

"Good, that's what I like to hear. Your family is well too? Eddie and young Conor?"

"Very well."

"Is Tara settling back home all right?"

Geraldine nodded. "And just so you know"—she lowered her voice—"Tara doesn't have keys to the office or anything." The last thing Mr. Bertucci needed to worry about was a criminal having access to his records.

He waved a hand. "I know Tara's a good girl at heart. And you're a good sister, taking care of your family like you do." He looked around the office and raised his bushy brows. "No Rita today?"

"I asked her to go to Staples and the post office after lunch. I wanted a little time to check over the last few payrolls she processed."

He gave her a pointed look. "Any more errors?"

"No." She folded her hands on the desk. "Mr. Bertucci, I can't tell you how sorry I am about the bookstore checks. I know it was a small error, but *no* error is acceptable."

"Geraldine, my good friend. Please stop." He leaned forward, his kind but tired eyes on hers. "I know how hard you work. I could not have asked for a better right hand these fifteen years. Anna and I"—he pulled his hand to his chest—"are so grateful. Especially now, when she needs me with her more than ever." He sighed as his hand slid down to his lap.

"How is Mrs. Bertucci?" Geraldine asked.

His shoulders lifted. "One day she knows me and things are good. The next, not so much."

"I'm sorry. She's such a wonderful woman." Mrs. Bertucci had always been kind to Geraldine.

"She has a fondness for you too." He patted his knees. "Come, I'm not here to burden you with my problems." He sat up a little straighter. "Mistakes happen, Geraldine. But when I see two errors in two weeks it tells me something might not be quite right, eh?"

Geraldine pulled her hands under the desk, where she squeezed them so tight her nails dug into her palms. She didn't know how else to control herself while possibilities raced through her mind: Mr. Bertucci asking to see all current payroll reports or the quarterly tax receipts.

"So, I ask myself," he said, "what could be the problem? And I think maybe you need more help, that you have too much on your plate."

"Oh, no, Mr. Bertucci."

"I know you are always trying to save us money where you can. But maybe we need Rita to put in more hours, so you can focus on overseeing things."

Gracious, that was the last thing Geraldine needed. It was hard enough inventing busywork to occupy Rita lately so she didn't realize how overwhelmed Geraldine was. What Geraldine needed was time to catch up. "That's so kind. But, really, it isn't necessary."

He nodded. "Then I wonder if it's worth thinking about some new"—he made circular motions with his hand, searching for a word—"program for the computer. I know, I know. You're like me, you appreciate the old ways. But maybe something that would make your job easier."

"Well, I could look into that, if you want me to." She scrunched her face. "But, honestly, I think the reason our clients stay with us is because we do things the old-fashioned way, you know? When they call the office, they get a live person, not voice mail. If they have a rush job or a special request, we can accommodate them. They like knowing who's handling their payroll, that it's not some machine."

"You're right, Geraldine. It's our customer service that keeps us in business. I just want to make sure you have what you need." He held up a finger. "Including a different assistant, if that's necessary."

The idea of a different assistant was appealing, but she couldn't make that change now. She didn't have time to train someone new. Besides, Rita was a mouthy thing. If Geraldine fired her she would probably go to Mr. Bertucci and open a can of worms.

"I had a heart-to-heart with Rita yesterday," she said. "I'd really like to give her another chance."

Mr. Bertucci studied her for a moment, then he chuckled and shook his head. "I don't know why I was worried. As always, you have everything under control." He shrugged. "It's probably just the stress. I worry about my Anna. Never get old, Geraldine." He gave her a sad smile before he stood, patted his pockets, looking for his keys. "Can I at least make the bank deposit for you? I drive past there on my way home."

He meant the client payments that usually flowed in early in the month. He would know they hadn't been deposited yet. Geraldine ran the office, but he still checked the account balance. The problem was Geraldine had been late sending out the invoices for last month.

"That's okay," she said. "I'm giving it a few more days before I process and deposit payments. Easter was last weekend and the mail always moves a little slower around the holidays."

He waved a hand. "Right, right. Well, you take care. Just let me know if you need anything, eh?"

"Will do."

He was almost out the door when he turned back. "Oh, the quarterly taxes get off okay?" he asked.

Geraldine could feel the burning glare of the Q like a laser shooting right through the wood and metal of her desk.

She smiled. "Yep. Right on time."

He lifted his brows. "Stupid question." After waving once more he was finally out the door.

~

Geraldine sat rigid at her desk for a long time after that, afraid to move because her stomach was doing somersaults, and she might be sick if she stood up. She had been mildly dishonest with Mr. Bertucci a few times lately, letting him think those errors were Rita's. But never before had she outright lied to him like she did that day. And about something so important. Mr. Bertucci had always been good to her. He treated Geraldine more like a daughter than her own father ever had.

Which is why she couldn't tell him she was in over her head in this management position. She couldn't fail him that way. She just needed to focus, get caught up on everything.

She picked up her long to-do list, considered which task to tackle first. There were so many to choose from: payroll reports, new direct deposit accounts, workers' comp audits, clients waiting for return phone calls . . . It all felt so overwhelming the letters blurred on the page. If she was going to get anything done that afternoon she needed to clear her head.

Harriet sent a text blast earlier that morning letting her rewards members know she had received new stock in overnight: *Casual and athletic clothing! Like-new table linens! Collectible dolls!* That was just the ticket. She wouldn't buy anything, but spending a half hour browsing would quiet her mind. Then she would return to the office, focused and ready to get back to work.

Chapter Nine

————————

When Tara first saw the online ad for a graphic illustrator she almost kept scrolling. Those jobs were never local, usually in Manhattan. And she didn't have the education—or the wardrobe—for such a position. She had no formal training, just years of studying and working at it when she could.

But this job was right in town, and the only minimum qualification listed was "proficient in Adobe Creative Cloud," which she was. Sort of. The ad was vague—*multifaceted illustrator*—but it mentioned character art and toy concepts, and maybe they wouldn't require a background check for such a position. So, what the hell, she borrowed Eddie's cell phone, since she still didn't have one, and per the instructions in the ad, texted her interest in the job, along with sample pictures of her drawings, mostly the comic strips she'd worked on at Taconic. Someone named Gordi responded before she handed the phone back to Eddie. The next morning, after dropping her brother at work, she headed over to the west end of town for an interview.

Eddie let her borrow his cell for the day, and the GPS took her to a commercial area of town with ramshackle houses mixed among small businesses and old brick apartment buildings. When Tara found the address for the interview she almost didn't get out of the truck, let alone knock on the door. Not when she saw the house it was attached to: a drab beige two-story with brown shutters and a sagging stoop, fronted by a neglected lawn. A beat-up Prius sat out front, along with a couple of bicycles and an electric scooter. She double-checked the address, rang the doorbell, and was greeted by a couple of pale early-twenty-somethings who both wore *Fortnite* T-shirts and looked like they didn't get out much.

The pudgy one with glasses and a mass of brown curls smiled and stuck out his hand. "Ms. Connelly? Gordi Cohen." He nodded to the guy next to him, a slumped string bean with a straggly ponytail and droopy eyes. "This is my business partner, Lance Richman."

Business partner? They looked like they were barely out of high school.

She shook hands. "Just call me Tara."

Since she was pretty sure she could take them both if they tried anything, she accepted Gordi's invite to come inside and followed them into an open kitchen-dining-living area that had been transformed into what looked like a video game command center. Triple-screen stations were set up in two corners, backlit by a rainbow of colors. Shelves lining the walls were crammed with headphones, controllers, microphones, webcams. Bubbly graffiti art covered much of the wall space. Conor would have been in heaven.

Gordi went full tilt welcoming her. He walked her around, showed off high-tech PC equipment she'd never heard of, offered coffee and pastries. She accepted coffee and sat across from them at a rectangular folding table in the middle of the room. Gordi leaned back in his chair, crossed an ankle over the other knee, and kicked things off by asking if she was familiar with any video games or YouTube channels. Which is when Tara began to suspect this was a complete waste of time.

"Only through my ten-year-old nephew, Conor. He plays games. *Fortnite* is his favorite," she said, pointing to their T-shirts.

Lance opened a folder and slid one of her comic pictures into the middle of the table. It was a frame depicting the hero, Crushin' Conor, creating a diversion to distract bad guys while his friends escaped captivity. Lance pointed to the picture.

But Gordi spoke: "He's your nephew?"

"Yes."

"That's perfect!" he said, clapping his hands. "He's our target audience." He went on to explain that he and Lance had started a YouTube channel a couple of years ago, posting videos of themselves playing *Fortnite*. Apparently they'd been playing religiously since the game was released. "We're highly ranked," he said.

"We're not that highly ranked," Lance said.

"We're pretty good."

"We're okay."

"In any case," Gordi said, "our videos are geared toward the younger crowd. We keep them clean. Upbeat music, no swearing, no talking anybody down—which parents appreciate. And the kids love when we give each other a hard time, play off each other."

"I'm the straight man," Lance said. "In case you were wondering."

Tara smiled. She could see it, how these two would be entertaining, Lance's deadpan to Gordi's energy.

"Glad you cleared that up for her, Lance," Gordi said. "So, over the last couple years we gained a following, got a few thousand subscribers."

"Is that a lot?" Tara asked him.

"It's respectable."

"Not really," Lance said.

Gordi sighed and adjusted his glasses. "It was a good start. But a few weeks ago we had a couple videos go viral." He shrugged. "I can't really tell you why, they were like most of our videos. Us playing and critiquing each other."

"I was extra funny that day," Lance said.

"Yeah, that must have been it." Gordi shook his head at Tara. "Anyway, all of a sudden we're getting thousands of new subscribers every day. We're over fifty thousand and counting, and we want to keep growing, try to get some sponsors. Which is where you would come in."

Tara raised her eyebrows in question. This was interesting and all, but she had no idea what she could do here.

"We need help with our platform."

"It's lame," Lance said.

"It's a little basic," Gordi said. "If we want to keep gaining subscribers, we need to diversify. Games are exploding right now with the younger crowd"—he mimed the explosion with his hands—"so we're getting into different games. But we also need to have more fun with our images. We want to bring in more graphics, change up our thumbnails every day."

"Thumbnails?" Tara asked.

"They're like snapshots of the videos we're posting. They attract views while kids are browsing." He turned to Lance, who spread out more of her comic strips: Conor outsmarting an evil cyborg, Captain Chloe holding Dr. Doom up high between her magnetic canes, Mighty Mike—another inmate's seven-year-old son—breathing in a puff of superhuman strength from his inhaler. "Tell us about Chloe and Mike," Gordi said.

"They're kids of friends of mine. Chloe has cerebral palsy, that's why I pulled in the canes. And Mike has asthma."

The smile that broke across Gordi's face was warm and earnest. "We love your characters, and your style. It's exactly the kind of thing we're going for."

"Yeah," Lance said. "You're good."

She looked across at the two of them. Both were probably a decade younger than she was. They obviously spent most of their time in front of a screen and maybe still lived off their parents. But they liked her work. They were excited about it.

Gordi leaned forward, elbows on the table. "Do you mind if I ask where you got the idea for these comics?"

"From old stories my mom told my sister, brother, and me. She grew up in Northern Ireland and used to read old Irish fairy tales to deal with the tension." Then Tara remembered how young they were. "Do you guys know anything about the Troubles over there?"

They shook their heads.

"Well, there was a lot of violence between Catholic nationalists and Protestant unionists in that part of Ireland for a long time. Street fights and bombings and sniper attacks. Catholics were in the minority and could be pulled over or stopped on the street and searched for no reason, sent to jail without a trial. It was a really scary time, and my mom found comfort in the fairy tales. Then she told them to us when we were little. In a lot of the stories regular people take on special powers. That's where I got the idea for the comics."

"Wow," Gordi said. "That's awesome."

Lance nodded. "Cool."

They exchanged a look and a nod, then Gordi continued. "So, Tara, here's the deal. You would start by helping us improve our existing platform. And we need to design some merchandise."

"Yeah," Lance said. "We really need merch."

They were talking like she already had the job. And there'd been no mention of a background check.

"After that, you could create some new characters and video content. You could even branch out into graphic novels if you wanted to. We could all go pretty far together. But"—he winced—"we should talk wage."

She was so excited about the possibility of the job she hadn't thought about the wage. They couldn't be making real money on ads yet, if they were making anything at all. But there was potential, and she was pretty sure she'd love the work.

Gordi rubbed his chin with his hand. "We want to offer you this job—we knew that as soon as we saw your work, and meeting you sealed the deal. We'd like you to start as soon as possible. Like tomorrow, if you can."

A bubble of excitement filled her chest. This all might go south, be over before it really got started. But she liked these guys and their audience, and she already felt ideas brewing, just based on being in their work space. After so long something good was about to happen.

Lance grabbed an envelope that was sitting on the corner of the table and pushed it across to Tara.

Gordi pointed to it. "All we need is for you to fill out the usual paperwork and do a criminal history check. But first, we really need to discuss wage . . ."

And there it was. Criminal history check. Tara barely registered the hesitation in Gordi's voice as it trailed off after "wage." She was too busy listening to a door slam on this particular dream. Rudy Russo had been right. She couldn't escape her past.

"You see, money's pretty tight," Gordi said. "My grandparents moved to Florida, and they rent this place to us dirt cheap. We have part-time jobs and a little funding, but—"

"Let me save us all some time." She slid the envelope back across the table. What the hell had she been thinking? These guys essentially worked with kids, albeit virtually. They didn't want a felon on their payroll. "I just got out of prison."

It was almost comical, how wide their eyes grew.

"I thought maybe it wouldn't matter for this job, since I wouldn't be working with customers or around money. But I get it," she said, standing up. "Sorry I wasted your time. I think what you guys are doing is pretty cool." She flashed them a small smile and headed for the door. The disappointment was growing heavy, and she wanted to get outside before the tears came.

"Uh, Tara?"

She turned to see Gordi stand.

"Is that for real? You were in prison?"

She nodded.

Lance stayed in his seat. "That's kind of badass."

Gordi nudged his glasses. "The only reason we asked for the background check is because my mom said it was a good idea. She's a lawyer." He shrugged like that explained it.

"I understand," she said. "I was there for a year and a half on a drug charge."

They side-glanced each other.

"Are the drugs an issue now?" Lance asked.

"No. They never were. Honestly, I was desperate and made an incredibly stupid decision."

Some agreement must have passed between them in the look they exchanged because Gordi grinned at her. "We can live with that if you can live with minimum wage for a while." He slipped his hands into his jeans pockets and bounced on his toes. "What do you say?"

⌒

Tara was so elated she decided to pick up groceries on the way home and cook something special for everyone that night. She took her time deciding on a recipe and choosing fresh ingredients at Stop & Shop, which was a luxury after being at Taconic. By law the prison system had to accommodate a vegetarian diet, but it didn't mean they had to worry about how it tasted. She'd had enough beans and peanut butter to last her a lifetime.

She had to use Eddie's debit card to buy the groceries, and she went through the self-checkout because, as unlikely as it was a cashier would notice she clearly wasn't an Eddie, her mind quickly went to a security guard stopping her on the way out of the store and calling the police. While she loaded the groceries in the truck and headed home, she reminded herself she'd soon be able to use her own debit card. Though minimum wage was barely going to cover living expenses, and it wouldn't be long before Geraldine started dropping hints about Tara contributing to the household budget.

Eddie was great about it, told her to take her time, there was no rush. He was overeager to offer her his phone, his truck, his debit card. But there was still tension between them, the tension of unsaid things. They had yet to talk about Taconic, including the fact that he hadn't visited much. And she didn't want to have to ask him to explain.

It was later that afternoon while she was prepping dinner that Gordi's question came back to her: *Where did you get the idea for these comics?* Mom's stories. She'd told them those fairy tales at bedtime most nights, the four of them—five on the nights Dad was home—piled on the twin beds in Geraldine and Tara's room, the soft light of a lamp creating a warm bubble around them. Her mother in one of her flowy dresses, auburn waves loose around her shoulders, her lyrical Irish brogue making the story that much richer. While she spoke they would all stare up at a poster of the lush landscape of County Down, narrow glens and marshy hollows giving gentle rise to the granite Mourne Mountains close to the sea. When she finished telling the story, if their father was present, he would promise to take them all there someday. Mom never refused to tell them a tale, even when she was quite sick near the end. The story they requested the most was the one she made up about them, The Connellys of County Down.

Tara was so young at the time that she remembered only the basics: she, Eddie, and Geraldine had to make it through the wild and tricky Fairy Forest and get to Connelly Castle on the other side. They each had some kind of special power, which they used to save one another along the way. But Tara couldn't remember those details. Eddie couldn't either, especially since his accident. She used to question Geraldine: *What were our special powers? How did we save each other?* But she always said she didn't remember either, and Tara should get her head out of the clouds, worry more about staying out of trouble than some old fairy tales.

Tara was spreading whipped potatoes on top of mixed vegetables when the whole crew piled in through the door. Eddie was covered in drywall dust and immediately went up to shower.

Conor, wearing baseball pants and cleats from practice, ran into the kitchen and leaned over the dinner. "Veggie shepherd's pie?"

"Yep."

He pumped his fists. "Yes!"

"No cleats in the house, Conor," Geraldine said, rolling her eyes at the veggie dinner or the cleats or both.

"Sorry." He spun around to head back toward the door and bumped the end table covered with Geraldine's figurines. One of them—a girl holding a basket of flowers—fell off the edge and hit the floor, breaking into way too many pieces to be glued back together again.

"Dang it, Conor, you broke it." Geraldine stared down at the fallen figure, her face twisted into something close to horror. "How many times do I have to tell you to take your shoes off at the door and NO RUN-NING in the house? You have to be more careful!"

Conor's eyes went wide, and he started knocking his arms against his sides. "I'm sorry, Aunt Geraldine."

"Don't you understand? She was part of a collection. Thanks to your carelessness, now there'll be an odd number—"

"*Geraldine*." Tara laid her hands on Conor's shoulders. "Dial it back."

Geraldine's lips twitched like she was going to say something, but then her mouth closed and her chin started quivering.

"I'm really sorry," Conor said, sounding close to tears himself.

When Geraldine looked down at him her eyes softened, and she nod-ded. Then she headed upstairs.

Conor dropped to the floor and started picking up pieces.

"Let me do that, okay?" Tara said, kneeling beside him and taking the broken porcelain from his hands. "This is so not a big deal, Con-man. Geraldine just had a rough day at work or something."

He nodded but there was no confidence in it, and she wondered how often this had happened while she was gone, Geraldine causing Conor anxiety over her ridiculous rules.

Tara reached out and knocked over another figurine. A pink-cheeked cherub holding an apple shattered against the floor.

Conor's jaw dropped.

She winked at him. "Now there'll be an even number."

The corner of his mouth tugged up.

"You know what?" she said, pulling him up with her. "I could really use a joke."

He didn't even hesitate. "What do you call a fake noodle?"

"I don't know."

"An impasta."

She laughed. "Go wash up before dinner, and don't worry about this."

Conor smiled, his eyes full of gratitude under those long lashes. "Okay." He took his cleats off and placed them side by side near the front door before he went upstairs.

She was in the middle of sweeping the broken pieces into a dustpan when Eddie's cell started buzzing. Tara recognized the number—a contraband cell phone Jeannie had used to call her from Taconic a few times—and she was immediately conflicted about answering. Today was Thursday, the day Jeannie worked in the prison commissary. Earlier in the week, before making the deal with DaCosta, Tara had asked Jeannie to see if she could find out who gave her that money. She'd promised to call that afternoon to let Tara know if she had any luck.

Tara sat at the table and answered. "Hey."

"Hey, T," Jeannie said. "I'm on Lana's phone again so I only got a minute." Her voice was low. It was an hour before dinner at Taconic, downtime when inmates could visit other cells as long as they weren't on restriction. Jeannie was likely tucked back in Lana's cell, with Lana keeping watch for guards.

"How much did all this cost you?" Tara asked.

"Just some ramen and floss."

"Bullshit." That might get you a cell phone for a few minutes, but it would have taken a lot more than that for someone to risk their cushy position in the commissary by digging up confidential info.

"Don't even worry about it. After all the comics you drew for Chloe? Girl, please. How'd the interview go?"

"Good. I got the job."

"No shit? That's great." There was a muffled sound as the phone moved away from Jeannie's mouth. In the background Tara heard her say, "All right, Lana. Chill out." She lowered her voice when she came back on the line. "So listen, I got an answer for you."

"Is it reliable?"

"Definitely. Lana's worked in the commissary for years, she has access to it all. I saw the actual credit card receipts myself. Always the same person, a hundred dollars on the fifteenth of every month, the whole time you were here."

For a split second Tara wanted to hang up. She didn't want to know. *For the time being I want you to consider looking into this matter a parole violation,* DaCosta had said.

"Hang on," Jeannie said. "I wrote it down." There was some shuffling on the other end of the line.

Tara tightened her grip on the phone.

"Okay, here it is," Jeannie said. "Brian Nolan."

Until that instant Tara hadn't realized how much she'd expected to hear her father's name. "What did you say?" she asked.

"Brian Nolan. *N-o-l-a-n.* Who's that?"

It simply couldn't be.

"Tara? Who's . . . damn, I gotta go." Her last words were a rushed whisper: "I'll call again soon." The line went dead.

Tara lowered the cell phone to the table. Never in a million years would she have guessed *him.*

She sat there for a long time, telling herself it was a mistake, there'd been some confusion on Jeannie's part. But, underneath that, she was also considering the alternative, that it wasn't a mistake, and she wondered why the hell Brian Nolan would ever do something like that.

And what, exactly, he wanted in return.

Chapter Ten

———————

"What the hell," Hank said, slamming down his desk phone after apparently hitting another dead end. "*Someone* knows where he is."

Brian looked across their desks, which faced each other, and watched his uncle grab a pen and scratch lines through a name written on his blotter. He pressed so hard the tip of the pen went through several layers of paper.

Roland Shea was missing. They'd been watching him 24/7 for weeks, waiting for the prosecutor's office to be ready to make the move. Then, two days ago, under another team's watch, Roland pulled a bait and switch and disappeared. He drove to Costco, parked his car in the busy lot, and entered the store. But he never came back out. At least, not back to his car. And he hadn't returned home. No one had seen him around town. He was just gone, in the wind.

"You know," Brian said, "he's done this before, taken off for a few days. I don't know if it's business or pleasure, but he comes back, usually in a week or so. You keep calling around and asking questions, someone might tip him off."

"What's your point?" Hank asked, without looking up from his list of names.

Brian didn't bother responding. It was no use when Hank was like this. He'd been in a foul mood since Roland went missing. And Brian knew he was also on edge about Rosemary's upcoming wedding next month. She and Marty were planning a very small event, just a trip to the justice of the peace because the Church didn't allow marriage after divorce, not even for a devoted member like Rosemary. Hank didn't know it yet, but she'd asked Brian to be there—*You're like a son to me, Brian. It would mean the world if you would stand up with me during the ceremony.*

This wasn't the first time he'd been in this awkward position, having to choose between his aunt and his uncle. When Rosemary finally ended their marriage and moved out of their sad, lifeless house, she asked Brian to go with her. It had been tempting. Brian knew Rosemary would create a warm environment with home-cooked dinners and conversation, as opposed to fast food on trays in front of the TV with Hank. But Brian couldn't do it. Even at sixteen he knew that once Rosemary left, Hank would have no one in the world except him.

It turned out for the best. When Brian stopped caring about anything and started sleepwalking through life for a few years, it was Hank who saved his ass on numerous occasions. When Brian showed up high to school or baseball practice, Hank talked the principal and coach into giving him more chances. Senior year Brian got busted playing mailbox baseball with some buddies, and shortly after graduation he caused a minor accident while driving over the legal BAC limit. In both instances Hank showed up in time to talk fellow cops out of arresting him. He never gave up on Brian, and he rarely got angry. Instead of punishing him, he'd take him to Yankees games, or they'd go deep-sea fishing off Montauk Point for a weekend. And it was Hank who helped Brian find direction and purpose with the police force after he quit college and floundered in dead-end jobs for two years. He and his uncle had been looking out for each other for a long time.

Brian's cell buzzed. A text from Ashley: *Hey stranger, it's been a while. You around tonight?* She'd signed off with a large kiss emoji. He lowered the phone and checked around to make sure no one had seen it. That was all he needed.

He hadn't seen Ashley for a while, and he was beginning to think maybe this thing had run its course. Ashley was attractive. She made no demands, and she liked to laugh. Hanging out with her was easy. It was just harder to get excited about seeing her the last few weeks.

"You know what I think?" Hank asked, propping a hand on the arm of his chair.

"What's that?" Brian poised his thumbs over the keyboard on his phone, not yet sure how he was going to respond to Ashley.

"I think that Connelly woman has something to do with it."

Brian's head snapped up. "What?"

"She's a known associate, Roland's old girlfriend. She gets out of prison two weeks ago, shows up at his house a few days later, and now he's gone."

"But *she's* not," Brian said, tossing his phone on the desk. They had guys cruise past the Connelly house the last few days to make sure. "So what's your theory there?"

"I don't know. Maybe they're cooking something up to get her back in the game, working with him again. Or maybe he's off getting some love nest ready for the two of them and she's going to join him."

As curious as Brian was to know what Tara and her brother were doing at Roland's house that day, he thought Hank was dead wrong. Call it a gut feeling. Though, it was possible his gut feeling was compromised when it came to Tara Connelly.

He shook his head. "I don't know. Feels like you're reaching."

"Oh yeah?" His uncle stood and leaned forward, fists braced against his desk. "She went to prison for the guy, Bri. Maybe she loves him, maybe she's owed something. Either way, she might be one of the people he trusts most right now." He pushed off the desk. "I'm going to update the chief," he said, stalking off toward the stairs.

Perhaps Brian would meet Ashley that night, have a few drinks, and go back to her place. Take a break from the pressure of dealing with a missing Roland Shea and a frustrated Hank Doyle.

His desk phone rang and he grabbed the receiver. "Nolan."

"Yeah, Nolan." It was the desk sergeant. "You got a visitor. A Doreen DaCosta from Parole Services."

"Did she say what it's about?"

"Nah. She's waiting for you in Interview Three."

Brian hung up and made his way through the bullpen, wondering what someone from parole wanted with him. He usually worked with POs only when he needed information about a person on their roster or they needed backup tracking someone down. He couldn't recall working with a Doreen DaCosta before, and that would be a hard name to forget.

He arrived at Interview Room Three to find her standing by the metal table, wearing a light trench coat and an identification lanyard around her neck. She had to be a foot shorter than him, even with the thick bun on top of her head.

"Ms. DaCosta? I'm Brian Nolan."

"Hi, Detective Nolan. I'm with Parole Services for Westchester County. Nice to meet you." She was a fast talker who packed her words with Bronx punch.

Brian shook the hand she offered, which had extra-long glittery nails. "You too. What can I do for you?"

"I'm Tara Connelly's parole officer, and I have a few questions, if that's okay with you."

"Sure."

"Detective, did you put money in her inmate account while she was at Taconic?"

He was so startled by the question it was like she'd spoken a foreign language and he needed a moment to translate. "Sorry, what are you—"

"It's a yes or no question, Detective."

Clearly she'd done her research and already knew the answer. Her bald stare and arched eyebrows dared him to lie to her.

He rubbed the back of his neck with a hand. "I may have put a little in there."

"A hundred dollars a month for eighteen months."

He didn't say anything, which said it all.

DaCosta crossed her arms. "You got some kind of relationship with Tara Connelly?"

"No."

"Was that your own money you put in there, or someone else's?"

"It was mine."

"Did she ask you to do it?"

"No, she didn't—"

"Did someone else ask you to do it?"

Jesus. Brian was usually the one firing rapid questions, trying to keep suspects off-balance while he got at the truth. "No, no one asked me to do it."

She took a step closer to him and narrowed her eyes. "Just what were you hoping for in exchange for that money, Detective?"

Brian's hands flew up and he swiped them out to the sides, like he was an umpire declaring himself safe from her insinuation. "Absolutely nothing—she doesn't even know about it."

"Then explain to me why you did it."

He took a breath and chose his words carefully. "Look, I didn't feel quite right about what happened back then. We were after her boss, she got pulled into the middle of it and ended up going away for him."

"Are you saying she wasn't guilty of the crime?"

"No, she was guilty."

She shook her head, which sent her hoop earrings swaying. "Then you need to help me understand what you did, Detective. Because from where I'm sitting, I should report this to the ethics committee for further review."

Brian pulled a shaky hand through his hair. He needed to make her understand or this would escalate quickly. He had no doubt Doreen DaCosta would report him if she believed his intentions were nefarious; she was obviously protective of her parolees. Which, ironically, made him grateful Tara was one of them.

But how was he supposed to explain what he did when he didn't entirely know the answer himself? He rested his hands on his hips and did the best he could. "I knew her family was financially strapped, and I wanted to help her out in some small way. We put a lot of pressure on her, and it all happened fast . . . She seemed like a good person caught up in a bad situation."

"You're describing most of my roster, Detective."

He nodded. "I know. You and I work with a lot of the same people day in and day out. But haven't you ever stretched the rules to give someone a small break?"

Her eyebrows lifted. "Yeah, I have. In fact, just the other day, when I had Tara Connelly crying in my office because I told her I was gonna revoke her parole."

"What—Why?"

"Because your partner reported seeing her at the home of Roland Shea."

Hank had reported her after all. But he never mentioned it to Brian.

"When her brother almost started crying too, I gave her a chance to explain," DaCosta said. "You wanna know what she was doing there,

Detective? She assumed Shea gave her that money, and she went to his house to tell him she would pay it all back. She was afraid of what he might want in return."

Brian dropped his head into his hands. It was his fault Tara had been at Roland's house that day. What a fucking mess. He'd only meant well, but he should have thought it through more. One of his mom's sayings leaped to mind: *You know what they say about good intentions, sweetie.*

"You picking up what I'm laying down, Detective?" DaCosta asked. Her voice went higher when she was angry.

"Yes. Just tell me you didn't remand her."

"I didn't remand her."

"Does she know it was me?"

"No, and I told her not to pursue it. But she might find out. The intelligence network inmates got going in the prison system rivals the CIA."

Brian gave her a weary nod.

She rolled her eyes, spoke in a low voice, almost to herself. "What the hell am I supposed to do with this . . ."

"I apologize, Ms. DaCosta."

Her hand whipped up. "I asked around about you, and I heard good things. The deposits were anonymous, you seem sincere, and I'm inclined to believe what you're telling me. Now, you haven't talked to her since she got out, have you?"

Only the morning he drove her home from Taconic, when he spent close to an hour alone with her. It was too much. If DaCosta knew that she'd have no choice but to report him. "I haven't talked to her since she got home," he said. Which was technically true.

"That helps. But—and hear me loud and clear, Detective—the best thing you can do for her now is leave her alone. She should be focusing on getting her life together. And you should be worrying about your job, because she could end your career." She pointed a finger at him. "Stay away from Tara Connelly, for both your sakes. Understood?"

That had been his plan in the first place, so he wasn't sure why he was fleetingly reluctant to answer. "Understood."

"Good." She reached for her bag on the table, shaking her head, as if she couldn't believe she had to deal with such nonsense. "I'll see myself out." Then she yanked open the door and left.

Brian pulled a chair out from the table and dropped into it, needing a minute to process it all. He'd been busted, and his job might be at risk. But all that was background noise. What kept replaying in his head were DaCosta's words: *I had Tara Connelly crying in my office because I told her I was gonna revoke her parole.* She must have been truly scared. Brian had seen her in what had to be some of the worst moments of her life, and he'd never seen her cry. Not during any of the interviews, not even when they arrested her.

He looked around the sparse windowless room, his eyes roaming over the one-way mirror on the wall, the small black box bolted to the table that housed the controls for the recording equipment. All three of her interviews had taken place in this room, including the first time they brought her in, when she drank four coffees and joked about tequila.

He and Hank mostly tried friendly chitchat that night, thinking they could schmooze her into giving up her boss, but she kept claiming she didn't know how the pills got in her car. When it became clear she wasn't going to turn on Roland as quickly as they'd assumed, an exasperated Hank had stood from the table, ready to end the interview, and told her they'd give her a few days to think about whether she wanted to cooperate. When she didn't respond, Brian gave it one more shot.

"Miss Connelly, we can only assume you're protecting this guy. I don't know you, but, frankly, that doesn't ring true to me. Troubled woman taking the fall for her man? That's a little cliché, isn't it?"

Without skipping a beat she said, "Kind of like brooding Irish cops who are all about the job?"

He hadn't meant to smile—he shouldn't have—but he did a bit. And she side-smiled in kind. Their little moment had abruptly ended when Hank yanked open the door and called for a uniform to take her home.

Brian stood and headed back toward the bullpen.

It wasn't difficult to understand why she risked her parole by going to talk to Roland. Tara was a survivor. A quick read through her file told the story: grew up with no money, lost her mother to lung cancer at nine years old, criminal father gone by thirteen, older brother half living in the hospital for much of her teen years. She was arrested for assault at twenty-two, sentenced to prison at twenty-eight. No one came through all that without significant trust issues. The last thing she probably wanted was to feel like she owed anyone.

He and Hank had used that assault charge to lean on her, told her it would assure a longer sentence. She'd been arrested years before for assaulting another female, a known drug user. Naturally they assumed it was a fight over drugs or money. It came up during the second, far less easygoing interview, when they laid on the vinegar because the honey hadn't gotten them anywhere. They started by showing up at her house on a Saturday morning to arrest her, believing that would get her attention. When the little boy started crying at the breakfast table, Tara winked and smiled at him, told him it would be okay. All while Hank was cuffing her hands behind her back. That's when Brian had started to feel queasy.

It wasn't until she was already in prison that he decided to find out more about that assault charge. He tracked down the old report to get the details. Tara hadn't gotten physical over drugs or money. She had punched her nephew's mother in the face when she discovered the woman was high as a kite while taking care of the boy, who was two years old at the time.

The same day he looked into the assault charge he scheduled anonymous monthly payments to her inmate account. It wasn't like him, making an impulsive move that could call into question his motives. His ex used to say he didn't have a spontaneous bone in his body.

Hank glanced up from a file when Brian sat at his desk. "Where were you?"

"Just checking in with a contact. Thought they might have seen Roland."

Hank's brow lifted in question.

"No luck."

His uncle grunted and went back to reading.

The last thing Brian did before attacking his to-do list for the rest of the day was text Ashley back: *Sorry, can't tonight. Work crazy. Not sure when it'll let up. B*

Hopefully she'd take the hint.

Chapter Eleven

Eddie grabbed a large push broom and started on the subfloor they'd finished laying down that day. They were working on the renovation of a large strip mall, one of Dunbar Construction's biggest projects at the moment. The other guys had left, so it was a good time to sweep. He had to wait for Tara anyway.

He'd been sharing his truck with her for four days now, since she got that job. He still didn't fully understand what she was doing other than drawing. Though Conor did. She picked Conor's brain over dinner every night about games he and his friends played, their favorite characters and YouTube channels, trying to get the lay of middle-school-gamer land. Conor loved being the expert: *God, Tara*—exaggerated roll of the eyes—*It's* Call OF Duty, *not* Call TO Duty. Most important, Tara loved the job. Even though she was making no money and working for a couple of kids.

Eddie liked carpooling with her, having company at the beginning and end of the day. They picked up coffee from Dunkin' in the mornings and argued over who got to pick the music—Eddie's classic rock or Tara's emo indie stuff; in the afternoons they talked about their days. Last Friday she even came out for a couple of beers, met some of the guys from work and their girlfriends and wives. But he couldn't help feeling it was strained. No matter what Eddie did for her it never felt like enough. They still hadn't talked about her time in Taconic. It was like a live wire that sat between them, and they both just danced around it.

Though she'd given him an opening just that morning. When they loaded up in the truck she said she hadn't slept well because she had a dream she was back in Taconic. Eddie had offered a sympathetic grunt and said, "Shoot. That's gotta be brutal."

Without turning from her window she said, "No. What's really brutal is being in there and dreaming that you're home."

One thing they did talk about on their drives was Brian Nolan. Eddie had been royally pissed off when he found out Tara broke her word to DaCosta, and he made her promise not to do anything about what she learned. But it didn't stop him from worrying about Nolan's agenda. It wouldn't be the first time a cop with power thought he could take advantage of a woman in a weak position.

He was never sure when his day would be done so he let Tara take the truck, which meant he sometimes ended up sitting around for a while. It wasn't so much the waiting that bothered him, it was the waiting while covered in dirt and grime. He craved a hot shower, not just to get clean, but also to let the heat start working on the aches and pains. His body, much like his brain, felt too used up for thirty-two. That's what happened when you spent your days cleaning and prepping construction sites. Hours on end of loading and unloading lumber and equipment, building and taking down scaffolding, digging trenches and backfilling holes. But it was the only position where he could be confident he wouldn't screw up something important. He'd had enough of that—losing his balance because a blazing migraine came on without warning, destroying pallets of expensive materials because his hand jerked the forklift, not being able to hear anybody over the tinnitus that screamed in his ears some days. At least he avoided the humiliation of getting demoted. Instead Eddie had told Mr. Dunbar when it was time for him to take a step down the org chart.

"Eddie?"

He looked up to see Lorraine Grady coming through the glass front door. She was the lead office admin who'd been with Dunbar almost as long as Eddie had. She was Mr. Dunbar's right hand, and he often had her on-site at his biggest projects, working in one of the temporary trailers.

"Hey, Lorraine. Didn't know anyone else was still around." He bumped his cap up, stood the broom tall, and rested both hands on top.

She shrugged and laced her fingers together in front of her. "I was just finishing up some stuff." Lorraine tended to slouch a bit, as if apologizing for being so tall.

Eddie felt his face heat up when he thought about how many times

Tara had told him to just ask Lorraine out already—*What the hell are you waiting for, Eddie?*

"How's Conor doing?" she asked.

"He's good. How about Katie?" Lorraine's daughter was in the same fifth grade class as Conor.

"Fine." She laughed a little and shook her head. "A handful right now. She always is after she gets back from visiting Disneyland Dad."

Eddie smiled. They were friendly and had commiserated over their exes before. Lorraine's moved somewhere upstate a few years ago, right after she caught him cheating on her and they split. He sounded almost as useless as Conor's mom.

Lorraine spun a slow circle, checking out the space. Construction business casual best described the way she dressed: heavy-duty jeans and rubber-soled shoes, durable company-logo shirts, and little makeup. But whenever she visited the work site she wore a bright-pink hard hat. She wasn't wearing it this afternoon though. Her straight brown hair fell loose to her shoulders. "It's coming along, huh?" she said.

"Yep. Tomorrow they'll start on the underlay, get the flooring in next week."

When she faced him again, he ran a hand down his face and beard, hoping to brush some of the dust away.

"We're ahead of schedule." She pointed toward the office space next door. "I heard they even sprayed the insulation in the new addition today."

"That's true. Actually, you probably don't want to be in here very long," he said. "That stuff's not good for you to breathe in."

Her thin eyebrows arched. "It's not good for you either."

Eddie shrugged.

"That's kind of why I came to find you, Eddie." Her fingertips started playing with the hem of her shirt. "I found out there's a project leader position opening up soon. No one knows yet, it won't be posted for a few days."

"Oh yeah?"

She nodded. When he didn't offer anything else she took a step toward him.

Eddie straightened up. He was taller than Lorraine, but not by much.

"I think you should try for it," she said.

"The project leader job?"

"Yes." Her hands fluttered about while she talked. "Think about it, Eddie. You've been here fourteen years. You've worked every position there is on the crew. All the guys respect you. Mr. Dunbar knows the project leaders talk to you all the time, ask questions and get your take on things."

That was true. Eddie was kind of a go-to since he'd been around it all forever. But that was a long way from overseeing projects and men. "I don't know, Lorraine. That's a management position."

"Exactly. So it's more money, nicer hours, and less physically demanding work. Which would be better for your health." She meant his "condition." She knew about his TBI. Lorraine was the one he had to call when he couldn't make it in because he was sick or when he needed help with his insurance claim forms. She even drove him to Urgent Care once after he fell off a ladder and broke his arm, and she gave him a ride home many times when he lost his license after that seizure last year. So why was she suggesting he go for a management position?

"I appreciate the thought," Eddie said, walking over to stand the broom against the wall so he didn't have to look at her. "But there's a lot of complicated paperwork involved in that position."

She followed him. "Not that much. It really just comes down to a few forms, and I could help you learn those."

He took a breath before he turned to her, frustrated that she was pushing him this way. Filling out forms and meeting with the bosses? Lorraine knew his limitations, she knew what everyone thought of him—*Poor Eddie. Nice guy but he's only half there sometimes.* She needed to let this go.

But when he turned to her to say just that, she was looking at him with big hopeful eyes. He couldn't remember the last time someone looked at him that way.

She stepped close enough that he could have reached out and touched her narrow shoulders. "Look, Eddie, I wouldn't be talking to you about this if I didn't think you'd make a great project leader. And before the interview we could go through the forms together."

He swallowed. "You really think I could do that job?"

"In your sleep."

"What about when I have . . . bad days?" He didn't have to explain. She'd seen those days, when he was hurting and couldn't concentrate worth a shit.

She gave him a breezy shrug. "People here will be happy to help you those days." She smiled wide and it reached her hazel eyes. "Including me."

And then, because he really wanted to keep looking at that smile, he agreed to give it a shot.

~

When Tara pulled up a little later and he climbed in the truck, he knew right away something was off. She didn't say anything, just stared through the windshield, a wrinkle between her brows.

"What's wrong?" he asked.

"There's something I have to ask you, Eddie." Her voice sounded small and fragile, like it could easily break. "Why didn't you visit me more at Taconic?" She turned to face him, and his heart broke a little. She didn't look angry. Just sad and hurt.

Maybe it was the bad dream she had the night before that had finally brought this question to the surface, but he should have expected it at some point. He didn't answer right away because this was too important and he had to get it right. He had to make her understand that he'd planned to go to Taconic every Saturday morning for eighteen months. But then he had the seizure and couldn't drive. And even if Geraldine would have driven him—which would have been a fight because she was flat-out scared of going there and didn't think Conor should be exposed to that—the meds made him nauseous and sapped all his energy and caused tremors for months until they leveled out. And once all that passed, and he got his license back, how was he supposed to face her? *Sorry I didn't visit, Tare, but I was such a fucking disaster the last year that most of it was a blur. I'm on a bunch of pills now, and I'm beyond broke because I missed so much work. In the meantime Geraldine took over the house, including your room, and I let her do it.* Every Saturday he found an excuse not to go, vowing to go next time.

Tara was watching him, waiting, giving him time to get his thoughts together. But that wasn't going to help. He'd abandoned her in there, and there was no defense for that.

He cleared his throat and tried to sum it up. "It was just too hard, Tare. I'm sorry."

Her shoulders drooped with disappointment, and she faced front to start the engine.

He scrambled for something to offer her. "Listen, I'm going to try for a project leader position."

She turned to him in surprise. "Really?"

"Yeah. Lorraine thinks I have a chance."

"That's great, Eddie."

"If I get it, it'll be more money. I can help you get a new laptop or pay Nolan back."

Her smile was tinged with doubt. "The best thing you can do for me right now is help me get my stuff back from Geraldine."

As a rule he avoided getting between his sisters or taking sides, figured they should work out their own problems. But right then, more than anything, he wanted to do something for Tara.

"You got it," he said. "But drive fast. We need to beat her and Conor to the house."

Fifteen minutes later Eddie stood next to Tara in front of the door to her old bedroom. They'd taken a quick look through kitchen drawers and side tables for the key to the padlock Geraldine had put on there, but no luck. They didn't have bolt cutters at the house, and his electric drill was dead and buried in the old shed somewhere. So the fastest option was force.

He turned to Tara. "You sure you want to do this? There's gonna be hell to pay."

"I've waited long enough, Eddie. I want the rest of my things."

The whole situation reminded him of when they were kids, trying to talk each other into—or out of—doing something stupid, like jumping off the shed roof or racing their bikes down the hill behind their house.

But this was different. Tara had been beyond patient. It was Geraldine's own fault it had come to this.

He braced his arms against the doorframe, raised his boot, and leveled a hard kick just under the padlock. That's all it took for the hasp to come loose from the door. He had to pull on it once to fully remove the ends of the screws, then the door was free.

"Okay," he said. "Let's make this quick." He gave the door a push, but it only opened halfway before it hit something and stopped dead. The room was pitch-dark, which was strange because it meant no light was coming through the windows. Given the musty odor, no air was getting in either.

Tara reached in to flip on the wall switch for the light. Then they both stared for a long time.

For the first few seconds Eddie couldn't have actually named a single thing that was in that room. There was so much *stuff* his eyes didn't know where to land first.

"Oh my God," Tara said, pulling her hand to her mouth.

The space was crammed from wall to wall with haphazard piles of . . . everything. The mess went almost to the ceiling across the room, completely covering the windows, and then cascaded down toward the door, like an avalanche. There was no apparent order to it. Eddie's gaze roamed over mounds of clothing on top of overstuffed cardboard boxes. Dolls and blankets and fake flowers spilled out of big black trash bags. Clear plastic bins were filled with dishes, pots, and pans. Tall stacks of magazines and newspapers were mixed in, some of which were trying to fall over but had nowhere to go. He checked behind the door to see piles of books on top of a couple microwaves.

The sheer amount of shit was staggering. And it *was* shit. One thing was crystal clear about the mind-boggling mess: there was nothing of value there. Yet Geraldine was guarding it all like national treasure.

Tara bumped into Eddie as she backed away from it, like she was afraid of what she was seeing. So was he.

Their eyes met but neither of them spoke. She spun and headed across the hall to Geraldine's room, touched the padlock on it, then turned back to him. "Do it."

He took two quick steps and kicked her door open too.

It wasn't quite as bad in here. She'd left narrow paths to her bed and closet. But it was pretty damn close. Eddie didn't know how anyone could live this way, sleep and function in this airless space, where he couldn't find the floor and it felt like mountains of crap could close in on him at any moment. "Jesus Christ," he said. "What the hell is she doing?"

But Tara wasn't there. He stepped back into the hallway to find her standing before the linen closet at the end of the hall. The door was open, no padlock on that one. The closet shelves were stuffed with so many Harriet's green plastic bags some had spilled out onto the floor.

Eddie's head began to throb. Geraldine wasn't just saving things or trying to be thrifty. This was something bigger. Darker.

Tara stepped forward and began yanking bags out of the closet.

"What are you doing?" he asked.

"What does it look like?" She pulled bags off shelves as fast as she could. "We're getting rid of all this shit."

That was tempting, but Eddie didn't know if they could just rip the Band-Aid off this particular wound. This was more a sickness of some kind. "Wait . . ."

"We'll load it in your truck and take it to the dump."

"Stop, Tara." When she ignored him he caught her in a bear hug from behind and moved her away from the closet before he let go. "Just stop for a minute, will you?"

She turned on him. "*Why?*"

"Because I don't know if that's the right call." Eddie looked from her old room to Geraldine's room to the closet. "There's something very wrong here, and I don't know if throwing it all away will fix it."

"What the hell are you talking about?"

"I think Geraldine needs help. Like, professional help. This is beyond . . ." Eventually he just shrugged. "It's beyond us." He pulled his cap off, rubbed his pounding temples.

"Are you all right?" Tara asked. Her eyes filled with worry, same way they always did when his brain started acting up. It had been that way since she was twelve years old.

"I'm fine." But he slumped back against the wall behind him, already feeling the migraine coming on.

She looked toward the closet, like she wanted to keep pulling bags. But then she sighed and put a hand on his shoulder. "Okay, Eddie. I'll do some research and we'll talk to her tonight, after Conor goes to bed."

He gave her a weary nod.

"But I'm going to need your support," she said. "Geraldine will fight us on this. It won't work unless we stay united."

She was right. Geraldine would deny anything was wrong, try to talk her way out of it. Eddie was going to have to back Tara up.

As he stood in the hall, surrounded on three sides by such suffocating clutter, one thought wriggled through the pain clouding his mind and took hold: it was like his sister was trying to bury herself alive.

"Okay," he said. "I'm with you."

Chapter Twelve

———————

Five days later Tara sat across from Eddie and Geraldine in the waiting room of Judy Horowitz, a mental health counselor. She was in private practice and worked out of a small brick building off Boston Post Road. There was no receptionist, just an elegant sign on the door inviting clients to take a seat in the waiting area. The space was cozy, with padded chairs and soft background music.

The whole setup was a far cry from the utilitarian therapy offices they'd been to after Eddie's accident all those years ago. When their father took off, Geraldine was nineteen years old, technically an adult and qualified as a legal guardian. But between his sudden disappearance and Eddie's medical issues, the police contacted the Department of Social Services to make sure the Connelly siblings had enough support. As a result, Tara, Eddie, and Geraldine endured many family therapy sessions and home visits. They would clean up, dress nice, sit together, and talk about how well it was all going. Basically whatever they had to do to keep busybody state workers out of their house and their business.

Tara didn't know anyone even remotely related to the mental health field, so she used the internet to find a therapist for Geraldine. Judy Horowitz checked several boxes: she'd worked with hoarders before, she accepted Geraldine's insurance, and she had room in her schedule relatively quickly, which was key. Geraldine promised to see someone, but each passing day upped the chances she'd back out. When they walked into the waiting room Tara had even silent-messaged Eddie to take the seat closest to the exit in case Geraldine decided to make a break for it.

They had sat Geraldine down at the kitchen table that awful night and confronted her about what they found. It was long and painful and exhausting. She tried everything. Indignation: *How DARE you invade my privacy*. Denial: *I told you, it's for my eBay business*. Playing the martyr: *After everything I do for this family, you're both turning on me* . . . Tara did most of the talking. She stayed calm and told Geraldine her behavior wasn't healthy, and they were worried about her. When sobbing and railing against the injustice didn't work, Geraldine sank to nasty comments: *You're the criminal who just got out of prison, Tara. You have no money, you're living off us, and* I'm *the one who needs help?* That's when Eddie told Geraldine the discussion was over, either she agreed to talk to someone or he was clearing those rooms out and throwing every last thing away. Which was a genius move. Geraldine stared at him for a long moment, her whole face shaking. Then she agreed to try one session as long as Tara and Eddie went with her.

Looking at her sister across the waiting room Tara felt a sharp pang of pity. Geraldine sat erect and stiff, her hands white-knuckling the straps of her purse. Her ginger hair was frazzled and in bad need of a cut and shaping. She was wearing stretchy slacks and a busy floral blouse, grandma clothes that didn't do her any favors. For some reason Geraldine had never been willing to put any money or time into taking care of herself, yet she'd probably spent thousands of dollars on all that junk. Her rooms had scared the shit out of Tara. She was no psychologist, but she knew an addiction when she saw one. And she'd watched a lot of women try to quit bad addictions, watched the suffering they endured.

"She's two minutes late," Geraldine said, checking her watch and standing up. "I really don't have time for this. We'll just have to postpone . . ."

Fortunately the inner door opened right then and a petite woman stepped out. She was maybe five feet—if that—with short gray hair cut in choppy layers. Her smile was wide. "Welcome, Connelly family. I'm Judy." Her bright eyes were accentuated by cat-eye glasses attached to a colorful beaded chain that wrapped around her neck. She wore black pants and a chunky black sweater. "I'm so sorry I kept you waiting," she said, clasping her small hands in front of her. "Got stuck on the phone dealing with an insurance provider who doesn't think mental health is important." She shook her head. "But you're not here to listen to my problems. Other way around, right?" Her laugh was genuine and unreserved, and it was impossible not to like her right away.

Tara had talked with Judy briefly on the phone when she scheduled the appointment. She stepped forward and introduced herself, then Eddie and Geraldine.

Judy shook everyone's hand but held on to Geraldine's for an extra moment. "Geraldine," she said. "Such a classic name." Then she opened her arms to include them all. "Such a nice-looking family. Please, come in."

They followed her into a large office with warm lighting and muted colors. There was a desk and a file cabinet at one end, but clearly the center of the room was where the therapy happened: plush chairs arranged in a circle around a coffee table with fresh flowers.

Once they all got settled Judy slid her glasses off, letting them fall against her chest, and folded her hands on her lap. "Let me begin by sharing with you my understanding of the purpose of today so we're clear. After speaking with your sister the other day, Geraldine, it sounds like you're considering therapy, and you wanted your siblings here to assist you in making that decision. Is that about right?"

Geraldine sat on the very edge of her seat, still gripping her purse in front of her. She offered an uncertain shrug.

"It's important that we all understand something," Judy said. "If Geraldine decides to work with me, I would be *her* therapist." She turned toward Geraldine. "I would be an advocate in helping you work toward *your* goals. Eddie and Tara would be welcome to take part in the process if you want, but you would be my client, not them."

Geraldine's shoulders seemed to relax the tiniest bit.

Judy gave her a reassuring smile. "Would you like to start by telling me why you're considering therapy?"

"Actually, *they* want me to go to therapy. They think I have a problem because I like to collect things."

"It goes far beyond collecting," Tara said. "It's taken over half the house, Geraldine. We checked the basement over the weekend." She didn't mention that she and Eddie set up traps down there after finding evidence of mice living among the mass of junk.

Geraldine drew a sharp breath. "Well, I don't know that everything down there is mine. I would have to check—"

"It's all yours, Ger," Eddie said. His low, deep voice was somehow gentle and firm at the same time.

She mashed her lips together for a moment. "Just because I save things doesn't mean I'm a *hoarder*." That last word was a harsh whisper and her cheeks flamed.

Tara understood why Geraldine was having such a hard time with that word. She was ashamed. Just like Tara was every time someone identified her as a criminal.

"May I offer an observation?" Judy asked. "I haven't seen your house, and people have different definitions for the word *hoarding*. But the bottom line seems to be that it is an issue, whatever we choose to call it." Her eyes swept around their small circle. "You all share a home, and this is creating conflict in the family. Maybe that's a good place to start?"

Tara and Eddie nodded.

Geraldine didn't look up.

"You know what else I see here?" Judy said. "I see a family who cares about each other, enough to be here today. Eddie and Tara, you've taken time from wherever you would normally be right now, to show your concern and support for your sister. And Geraldine, you were willing to come even though you're not sure about all this. I think that says a lot. Have you always been a close family?"

A *close* family? *Broken* seemed a better fit to Tara.

Geraldine responded first. "Yes, I think so."

Eddie nodded in agreement.

Tara didn't know how to respond. She felt close to Conor. She used to feel close to Eddie. And she wanted to support her sister, but . . .

"You don't think we're close?" Geraldine asked her.

"In some ways, I guess."

Eddie turned to Tara. "What does that mean?"

Tara waited to see if Judy was going to get the conversation back on track, but she appeared to be waiting for a response as well. Tara sat up a little straighter. "Well, if we're all so tight, why didn't I see you both more while I was at Taconic?"

"Good Lord, Tara!" Geraldine jerked her head toward Judy.

"She knows I was in prison. I told her on the phone."

Judy sat forward. "So, Tara, you were disappointed that Eddie and Geraldine didn't visit you more."

"This isn't really about me . . ." She hadn't planned to get into this; they were here for Geraldine. However, this line of questioning brought her anger to the surface. "But, yes. Eddie only came a few times, Geraldine even less. In truth? They kind of left me high and dry." Tremendous relief came with saying that out loud.

Neither of her siblings said anything.

"Eddie and Geraldine," Judy said, "would either of you like to respond?"

Geraldine pulled her head up. "Eddie couldn't visit you more because he got sick every time he went up there."

Eddie glared at her. "Geraldine . . ."

"It's true. He would come home a wreck, stay in bed for a day. After the last time he had a seizure."

Tara's eyes jumped to Eddie. He wouldn't look at her.

Geraldine went on. "Then he couldn't drive for a long time and he had to take pills. It was just too much for him, Tara. Seeing you in that place and leaving you there all over again."

That's what Eddie was trying to tell her that day in the truck. His answer had sounded so lame—*It was just too hard*. But it wasn't that the trip was a hassle, it had just taken too much of a toll. Before Tara was done asking herself why Eddie didn't tell her about that seizure, she answered her own question. It was for the same reason she never told him she got beat up once at Taconic. They didn't want the other to worry.

"What about you, Geraldine?" Judy asked in a soft voice. "Was there a reason you didn't go more?"

Geraldine waved a hand. "I don't like those places. And Tara didn't really care if I showed up."

"That's not true," Tara said.

"Yes, it is."

Eddie cleared his throat. "Geraldine didn't visit more because she likes to be needed. And Tara didn't need her."

"That's not true," Tara said again.

"It is true," Geraldine said. "Even when you were young, and I was supposed to be taking care of you, you never really needed me. You certainly never listened to me."

Tara couldn't argue with that. When she looked back on her relationship with her sister, it was one long battle. Geraldine trying to be Mom, and Tara blowing her off.

Judy offered a sympathetic smile. "Well, congratulations, Connellys. You are a normal, healthy, screwed-up family."

"Gracious." Geraldine brought a hand to her chest. "Why would you say we're screwed up?"

"Oh, I don't know, Ger," Eddie said. "Maybe because you're a hoarder, I'm a loser, and Tara's a felon."

It was so unexpected, and so spot-on, Tara coughed out an incredulous laugh.

Geraldine sucked in a very offended gasp.

Which made Tara laugh even harder. And once she started, she couldn't stop. Especially after Eddie got going too. Even Judy giggled with them—or at them—a little. Just as they would get it under control, one of them would set the other one off. Eventually they calmed down, and that would have been the end of it if Geraldine hadn't spoken.

"Geez Louise, I really don't see what was so funny."

That was all it took to get them going again, and it was such wild and breathless laughter that even Geraldine joined in here and there, despite herself.

For the rest of the session they were never quite able to get it fully under control, even after Judy took command again and gathered some family history, details about their living situation. But it put Geraldine at ease, enough to leave her purse on the floor by her feet and sit back against her chair. And at the end of the hour, when Judy asked if she'd be willing to come back and try meeting one-on-one, she said yes.

Tara experienced mild regret as they filed out of Judy's office. That desperate laughter had connected the three of them for a little while, bridged the gap of past hurts. But even though she was sorry it had to end, it was also the most hopeful she'd felt since the morning she'd walked out of Taconic.

~⋊~

When five o'clock rolled around a week later Tara took her time finishing up her work. Lance and Gordi were out running an errand, and they'd asked her to stick around until they returned, which was fine with her. She was enjoying her new job so much, it was a little disappointing when it was time to get going at the end of the day.

She'd been there for over two weeks now. Her work space was the table in the middle of the cramped room, and they pushed it against a far wall when the guys were streaming so she didn't appear on-screen. Gordi gave her his old laptop to work on until she could afford her own, so she hadn't asked them about other supplies. She was using sketch pads and pencils she'd brought from Taconic, which would only last so long. And she was pretty sure Gordi's mom was partially funding her employment. It was all tenuous, they were just making do until—fingers crossed— some money started rolling in. The fear hanging over her head each day was that subscriptions would drop off and this whole thing would fall apart. Which would be a real bummer because Conor and this job were the bright spots in her life at the moment.

A week after their therapy session with Judy the certain knowledge had settled in that there was no quick and easy solution to Geraldine's "collecting" problem; she still wasn't willing to get rid of anything when Tara offered to help over the weekend. Judy had encouraged Tara and Eddie not to challenge her much yet, so instead Tara went up to Conor's room, where he was playing *Fortnite*. She lay on his bed and asked for a joke.

"Why was the little strawberry crying?"

"I don't know."

"Because his mom and dad were in a jam."

Who knew where he was getting the jokes, but he was always ready with one when she asked.

She'd just finished packing up when the boys returned. They came over to the table and stood before her.

"This is for you," Gordi said. He glanced at Lance before laying an envelope on her desk.

As soon as her eyes landed on it she was sure it was a termination letter. The guys hadn't realized what it would be like to have someone in their space, they couldn't afford her, they didn't really need her.

She didn't reach for the envelope, just looked up at them.

Her expression must have said it all because Gordi held out a hand. "Oh, hey. It's just your first paycheck."

She took a breath. "Right."

"We actually put a little extra in there. It's only twenty-five bucks, but we thought you could put it toward a cell phone or something."

"Yeah," Lance said. "You're literally the only person I know who doesn't have a cell phone."

She picked the envelope up. "You guys really didn't have to do that."

"You already helped us save more than that each month by finding the better internet package," Gordi said. "And clicks were up like fifty percent last week because of your thumbnails."

That was good to hear. Gordi said it was her job to get clicks, and their job to convert views to subscribers. "Thanks," she said.

"No, thank *you*," Gordi said. "You know, whatever happened before"—he shrugged a vague reference to her confession about being in prison—"it brought you here. And we're really grateful it did." His smile was so earnest Tara couldn't stop herself from giving them both a hug before she left.

꙳

Grateful. That's exactly how she felt as she climbed in the truck, her first paycheck in a year and a half in her back pocket. She was bursting with gratitude in that moment, to be working with Lance and Gordi, listening to their banter all day and becoming part of it. To be learning and creating and driving on a sunny day. She was thankful to be out in the world and home with her family, looking forward to pizza for dinner because that's what they did on Wednesday nights. And it was true, all of these things were that much sweeter because of where she'd been just three weeks ago.

Gordi was right. Whatever came before had brought her to the here and now. And, like it or not, that included Taconic, because that's where she spent so much time studying, drawing, finding her style. She'd spent hours on end with her pads and pencils.

The pads and pencils . . .

She braked for a stop sign and stayed there a moment. There was someone else who deserved her thanks. Someone who helped her when she very much needed it and apparently expected nothing in return. Who does that?

She checked her rearview to see it was still clear and tapped her fingers against the steering wheel.

Well, shit.

Before she could change her mind Tara made a right toward town instead of heading straight home.

～

It was hard to stomach the idea of going back to that police station, and she wouldn't go inside. Some of the most horrible moments of her life had taken place in that building.

The night she was pulled over in her old Toyota and the cop found the pills, she had just crossed the Mill Street Bridge into Greenwich. After he officially arrested her, he placed her in the backseat of his cruiser while he dealt with her vehicle. Tara waited there, staring out the window, thinking about when her mom used to take them across that same bridge on day drives. They would wander past the jaw-dropping mansions of Belle Haven that overlooked Long Island Sound and discuss which one was fit to be Connelly Castle. Sitting in the back of that police car, hands cuffed behind her and all hope lost, Tara couldn't have felt further away from all of that. Further away from her mother.

Nolan and his partner had been waiting for her in that dreary interview room. The first thing Doyle did was flip a switch on a black box on the table and inform her their discussion would be recorded. She'd been scared shitless, her pulse and her mind racing. But they fetched her coffee, made small talk, cracked jokes about unlucky busted taillights. It didn't hurt that Nolan was nice to look at, with his thick dark hair, smiling eyes, and boyish grin. He and Doyle said they weren't interested in a low-level delivery girl, but they had to go through the motions. Even though she refused to give them anything, she went home that night feeling optimistic. Which, she later realized, was a setup.

When they showed up at the house that weekend and read her her rights it was the worst kind of shock. Eddie tried to intervene while Doyle was handcuffing her, and he would have been arrested too if Nolan hadn't put a hand on his shoulder and told him to think about Conor, who was in tears. That second interview was short and sweet.

They took her to the same room and flipped on the recording system, told her no more games, they knew she was working for Roland. They needed her to testify to that and tell them about his operation—*Talk to us and this all goes away*. Doyle took the lead that day, barking about her previous record and long prison sentences, insinuating she was a doormat for her drug-dealer boyfriend. She didn't set them straight on that last score. It was kind of perfect. They assumed she was protecting Roland, and she let them keep believing that.

When it was clear she wasn't going to give them what they wanted, a disgusted Doyle told her she had two days to decide between cooperating and going to prison. Then he stalked out of the room.

She remembered staring after him, wishing to hell she'd never met Roland Shea.

"Miss Connelly." Nolan was still sitting in his chair, elbows on the armrests, fingers laced in front of him. His gaze was direct but his voice gentle. "If you cover for him you will end up a convicted felon, and that will be on your record for the rest of your life. You'll never teach again."

That's when Tara dropped her eyes from his and blinked away tears that were trying to come.

"Any guy that cared about you would never let you go down for this."

She knew it was a ploy, but there was an urgency in his voice that caught her. And during the interview she'd noticed subtle glances and gestures that indicated maybe his heart wasn't in this as much as his partner's. That's why she decided to give it a shot.

"I don't know anything about his operation," she said. "You have no reason to believe me, but it's true."

His sigh was full of doubt, like he'd heard this story before.

"I *can't* give him to you. All you're going to do is take me from my family and put me in prison. Is that what you really want?"

He studied her for a long moment, long enough that she began to hope.

Tara clasped her hands together on the table. "Detective Nolan, is there anything you can do to help me?" She wasn't used to asking people for help, but she needed someone to give her a chance, slow this madness down. Maybe Nolan could convince the prosecutor this wasn't the smart way to go, or at least buy her some time. There had to be something he could do.

"You say you can't turn him in," Nolan said. "Tell me why. Give me *something*."

But when she opened her mouth nothing came out. If she told him she was protecting someone other than Roland, the next question would be: *Who?* And if she answered, if she told him the full story and saved herself, she'd be hurting other people. It was an impossible choice.

Nolan waited a long time for an answer, but when she said nothing he stood from his chair. "You have until Monday morning to decide what you want to do."

Then he'd walked her to the lobby and left her there without saying another word.

~⋉

She waited behind a clump of trees on the far side of the parking lot behind the police station. Maybe he was gone already, but the black Explorer was there, so she took her chances that he was too. When several people poured out of the building Tara ducked her head and pulled down the flat cap she was wearing. She wanted to catch Nolan alone. The group dispersed and he wasn't among them.

God, did she really mean to do this? She should walk away, forget the whole thing. DaCosta had been clear about this issue, and that woman was not messing around. Whenever Tara thought about their first meeting, how close she'd come to going back to prison, she felt sick. But there was only one way to know for sure whether he'd given her that money. And why.

To her relief, when he walked out the back door to the station a few minutes later he was alone. He carried no bag or briefcase, and he wasn't wearing a jacket, so his gun was visible in the holster on his hip. His hands were shoved in his pockets as he walked toward the parking lot.

Tara moved in his direction as he headed toward an old green Grand Cherokee parked in the end row. He was pulling his keys out of his pocket when he raised his eyes in her direction. She gave a subtle wave, and he checked back over his shoulder, toward the station, before moving closer to her.

"Hi," he said, a little wonder in his voice.

"I need to talk to you." She'd decided to just get to it, catch him off guard so she was more likely to get the truth.

"Okay," he said. But she heard the trace of wariness.

All of a sudden she felt foolish, and she had to remind herself that Jeannie had seen the credit card transactions. But she still winced when she asked him the question. "Did you send me money at Taconic?"

He didn't respond right away, but his sigh of resignation was all the answer she needed. "I thought your PO told you to leave this alone."

"She did."

"You're not too good at following the rules."

"Apparently, neither are you."

He raised his eyebrows in a *touché* kind of way. "Yes. I sent you money. But you were never supposed to know. Did DaCosta tell you?"

"No."

"How did you find out?"

"Why did you do it?"

He rested his hands on his hips. "I told you I felt bad about what happened. I know how much money means in there, and I just wanted to help. That's all."

She shook her head at him. "You know that's very hard to believe, right?"

"What is? That someone would do something nice for you?"

"That a cop who sent me to prison because I wouldn't cooperate would give me almost two thousand dollars while I was there out of the kindness of his heart."

His eyes rolled to the side. "When you put it like that, I guess it is hard to believe. But it's the truth. I'm just sorry if I caused you any stress."

Maybe he knew about her visit to Roland's. Obviously he and DaCosta had talked about her at some point.

"If it'll help," he said, "feel free to yell at me like your PO did. But can we get on with it? I've already had a long day."

She crossed her arms. "I didn't come here to yell at you. But I have no idea when I'll be able to pay you back—"

"Please don't."

"—so I'd like to tell you how I spent your money."

He held up his hands. "You really don't have to do that. Whatever you spent it on is fine—cigarettes, junk food, shivs." He shrugged. "It's none of my business."

Shivs. She felt the corner of her mouth pull up. "Come on, Nolan. I have this spiel in my head, and if you don't let me tell you it's just going to rattle around up there." She made circular motions with her finger.

It was his turn to smile a little. His sleeves were rolled up, and he folded his arms against his white button-down. She liked him better without the tie. "O-kay," he said.

She glanced around before she started. No one was within earshot. There was just the low hum of traffic in the background. "I spent most of it on paper and pencils. Specifically, sketch pads and drawing pencils."

His forehead pulled up in surprise.

"I admit to being a little extravagant with the pencils. They had to special order them. But you really need all different kinds, depending on what you're doing." Why would he know anything about pencils. She was babbling. "Anyway, I drew all the time. I made cards for my nephew and other women's kids, and worked on portraits. They took me to the nursery sometimes so I could sketch newborns for their moms. I also started working on some new stuff. It's sort of pop art style . . ." Jesus, she was babbling again.

But he was watching her closely, like he was hanging on every word. And it seemed as if those broad shoulders had relaxed while she talked.

"I got a lot better because I did it all the time. My last cellmate said it was like I was trying to draw my way out of there. Which I did, for hours, every day." She held his gaze now because she was getting to the main point of all this. "Those sketch pads and pencils helped me survive that place, and now I have a job as a graphic illustrator, which is pretty cool." She thought about how to finish, then flipped her hands up. "I just thought you should know that."

He swallowed before he spoke. "That was quite a spiel."

"Thanks."

A few more people spilled out of the door across the parking lot. The last thing she wanted was to see his partner again.

"I better go." Right before she turned to walk to the truck she added one more thing: "I hope your day gets better, Nolan."

She'd taken only a few steps when she heard his voice behind her. "It already did."

She paused, but didn't turn around, before she started walking again. When she arrived at the truck and saw in the reflection of the driver's-side window that he was still watching her, it sent a ripple of excitement through her core that she hadn't felt in a long time.

Chapter Thirteen

Geraldine didn't like having Tara in her room. Well, it was technically Tara's room, but it had become Geraldine's space, and it was full of her things. Although Tara had promised not to throw anything away, having someone else in there, even her sister—*especially* her sister—was like being naked and on display. But in Geraldine's last therapy session Judy had pointed out that a good faith measure, such as returning Tara's belongings, would go a long way toward keeping peace in the house. So Geraldine promised Tara they would finally do it Saturday morning.

When they entered the room Tara looked around with wide eyes, and Geraldine could see distaste in the way her mouth tugged down at the corners. She was judging, which she had no right to do. Everybody had their hobbies. At least Geraldine's wasn't *trafficking drugs*.

"Should I just start going through piles?" Tara asked.

"No." A sense of panic hit Geraldine at the thought of her sister touching her things. She had to fight the urge to push Tara out of the room and shut the door. "I'm pretty sure your stuff is in the closet," she said, pointing to the corner of the room, where the closet door was largely hidden behind boxes and bags. "We have to do this in an orderly manner."

"Okay." Tara glanced around, then pointed to a tall stack of newspapers. "What are all those?"

"It's the local paper. I have a copy from every week for the last six years."

"Why?"

"It's like a record of town history."

Tara's brow furrowed. "Right. And those?" She nodded toward a taller pile of *Good Housekeeping* magazines.

Geraldine picked up the top copy and flipped through. "This was Mom's favorite magazine—did you know it's been around since 1885? We order it at Bertucci's for the waiting room, and I take them home at the end of the month."

Tara took a deep breath and scratched her head. "We have to start somewhere, Ger."

"I know that." She put her fists to her hips. "Let's put clothes and linens to the left, everything else to the right."

They went to work, sorting through piles, creating a path to the closet. Geraldine caught Tara shaking her head now and then, turning away from stale odors wafting out of bags that had been sealed up for a long time. She just didn't get it. Geraldine had a reason for keeping every item in that room. Some of it was sentimental, like the Dolls of All Nations collection she'd had since she was a little girl; Eddie's old baseball uniforms, cleats, and trophies; Conor's baby clothes and toys. Memories were attached to all those irreplaceable things. And the various boxes of paperwork were important—copies of their taxes, medical bills and statements for the last seventeen years, all of Geraldine's pay stubs since she started at Bertucci's, every report card and standardized test result Eddie and Tara had brought home. The rest of it—used clothing, kitchenware, house decor—could come in handy at some point, or might even be worth some money. Though, Judy had asked her to consider the possibility that accumulating stuff like this might be filling an emotional hole. Geraldine didn't know about that, but she promised to think on it.

"Oh my God," Tara said, after opening a large cardboard box. "This is creepy. You have a stack of crucifixes in here." She held up a wooden cross with an iron Jesus nailed to it.

Geraldine grabbed the crucifix from Tara and put it back in the box, closed the flaps. "I'm going to donate them to the church bazaar."

"Then let's put this box in the hall, and we'll drive it over to the church."

"I'm not ready to do that."

"Why not?"

Geraldine didn't look up from the bag she was going through. "Because I don't know if anyone will want them."

Tara didn't say anything or move for a long moment, like she didn't know how to respond. Then she shoved the box of crosses to the right.

Once Tara was engrossed in the next box, Geraldine asked a question that had been bothering her all week, since Tara mentioned seeing that policeman. Brian Nolan. Apparently he put her in prison and then sent her money? That didn't make sense. And Eddie had flipped his lid when he found out she went to talk to him alone. "What's going on with that detective?"

"Nothing. Why?"

"It's just strange, him doing that for you." Geraldine didn't believe for one minute he did it to be nice. She didn't trust the police, had been living in fear of them as long as she could remember. For many years she was afraid they would catch her father. And after he left, when Eddie was in the hospital, they questioned Geraldine over and over again, like they believed she was covering up for him. They even threatened to take Eddie and Tara away from her if she didn't cooperate. "Are you going to see him again?" she asked.

"Doubt it." Tara sounded a little regretful.

But Geraldine breathed a sigh of relief.

"Look at this." Tara pulled a framed picture from a plastic bin and passed it over.

It was an old photo of Geraldine, from over twenty years ago. She was wearing a leotard and tights under a loose skirt, hair pulled up in a bun, the laces of her Mary Jane tap shoes tied in a bow. She stood in the middle of a long line of smiling girls dressed likewise, arms around each other's waists, their right knees lifted high in imitation of the Radio City Rockettes.

Tara scooted closer to look over Geraldine's shoulder. "I remember when you took dance."

"Yeah, I did it for a long time." Geraldine hardly recognized herself in the photo. It felt like it was from a different lifetime. She handed it to Tara. "Just put it back in that box."

But Tara held on to it. "You look so happy here. We used to go to your recitals, at that little studio in town . . . You were good. Why did you quit?"

"Why do you think? After Mom died I didn't have time for it anymore."

"And that's Jenny, right?" Tara pointed to the girl on Geraldine's left in the picture. She was the same height as Geraldine, but rail thin, her dark 1990s hair permed into a frizzy mass. "You guys were like best friends. Do you keep in touch with her at all?"

"She sends me birthday cards, calls once in a blue moon and invites me to lunch with some of the other girls from our high school class."

"Do you ever go?"

"No. Are you done with that box yet?"

Tara ignored her. "Why don't you go?"

Geraldine let out an exasperated sigh while she shoved a crate of old shoes to the right. She regretted mentioning Jenny's invites; this really wasn't any of Tara's business. "Jenny's just being nice, they don't really want me there. It would be uncomfortable for everyone."

"I'm sure they'd love to see you."

"For pity's sake, Tara. We have nothing in common. They're all married with kids, a couple of them work in the city. Now put it away or we'll never get done here."

Thank goodness Tara finally dropped the subject. They worked in silence for a while until Tara opened one of the few remaining boxes in front of the closet door.

"These are Mom's clothes." She held up a couple of dresses, one a floral pattern and one with polka dots. Then she pulled more items out, soft blouses and long skirts, held them up, laid them across her lap, and ran her hands over them. Tara had graceful hands, like their mother. She looked so much like her too, and she had her artsy tendencies. But her gritty edge was all Dad.

"Do you remember Dad complaining about how many clothes she had?" Geraldine asked. "He used to say she took up their whole closet."

"Did they argue about that a lot?"

Geraldine braced her hands against her knees. She wasn't used to talking about this history, but it was nice to have Tara's full attention. "They mostly fought about his side business. The cars. She would get on him about gambling, tell him he wouldn't need to steal if he stopped owing people money. He would say a laborer's wage couldn't pay for a family of five."

"Did she ever have a job?"

"No. She had a hard enough time trying to take care of us and the house. She was tired a lot. During the day she had to take a lot of naps."

"But didn't she, like, clean and do laundry and make dinner?"

"She did when I was younger, but then she pretty much stopped." Geraldine pulled a bag onto her lap and went to work on the twist tie, trying to signal an end to the conversation.

"When did she stop?"

"Gracious, Tara, I don't know." The stupid twist tie wouldn't open. She tried twisting the other way. "When you and Eddie were pretty young." She didn't know exactly when, but she remembered making the cake for Tara's sixth birthday and buying a gift with money she begged off Dad. She was thirteen at the time, and already good at managing things. Her mother often said so, while running her hand down Geraldine's hair or rubbing her arm—*There's my strong girl, Geraldine, taking care of us all.*

Tara didn't say anything but Geraldine could feel her sister's eyes on her, wanting more. And Judy had said being honest with her siblings would help them understand.

"Mom was actually sick for a long time," Geraldine said. "Long before she went to the doctor."

"Why wouldn't she go to the doctor?"

"It came from growing up the way she did, she didn't trust 'people in suits.' She wanted to try other things first. Like we went to Mass together every day after school for a while and said the rosary." Geraldine remembered kneeling next to her mother in the pew, eyes squeezed shut while she focused all her energy on sending those prayers straight to God. "I remember an uncle of hers in Ireland tried saying prayers over the phone that were supposed to help. And she went into the city to see a man from Dublin once. He was the seventh son of a seventh son and reported to have the power to heal through touch." She shook her head. "Mom had more faith in the idea of ordinary people with special powers than she did in modern medicine. Once she started coughing up blood Dad finally dragged her to the doctor."

"I didn't know all that," Tara said. "I thought she was only sick near the end."

That's because Geraldine went to lengths to hide it from Tara and

Eddie. Sending them out of the room when she sensed one of her mom's coughing fits coming on, cleaning up after her, making excuses when she spent so much time in bed. "Well, I figured there was no reason to have you and Eddie worrying about it. There was nothing you could do, you were both so young."

"So were you." Tara's voice was so soft it frightened Geraldine.

She started yanking on the end of the twist tie. "Dang it. This stupid thing won't open."

"Let me help," Tara said, her hands reaching out.

Geraldine jerked away. "I got it."

"Maybe we should take a break."

"After all your nagging, now you want to stop?" Geraldine turned to see that her sister's big blue eyes were moist and full of compassion. She started clawing at the bag with her fingers.

Tara put a hand on her arm. "Ger, stop."

Geraldine froze. She couldn't remember the last time someone reached out and touched her. Part of her wanted to yank her arm away, part of her wanted Tara to never let go.

"You took care of everything, didn't you," Tara said. "Even before Mom died."

"Not everything . . ." But most things. Geraldine believed if she took care of the house and the family, her mother could focus on getting stronger, getting better. So she cooked, cleaned, shopped, helped with homework, and signed report cards. She learned to pay bills, clip coupons from the Sunday papers to help get the food they needed.

And she worried. About everything, all the time. She worried about her little sister and brother, who ran wild around the neighborhood and wouldn't listen to anybody. Even before her father left she worried about money and keeping a roof over their heads. Then she worried about losing Eddie and Tara to foster care. While all her peers were focused on dances and dating and the future, Geraldine was taking care of two kids.

"I'm sorry," Tara said. "I can't imagine how hard it was for you. And I didn't make it any easier."

Geraldine closed her eyes tight. It was either that or cry. And right then she was feeling such gratitude for what Tara said, for the fact that she was sitting there beside her, that if she started crying she might never stop.

After a moment she opened her eyes to see her sister staring up at the poster of the County Down countryside that still hung on the wall. "I remember her telling us fairy tales right up until the end," she said, a wistful note in her voice.

Geraldine didn't understand why Tara still held on to those fairy tales. Probably because they were full of drama—warriors and goddesses and romance. But what good did they ever do anyone? None, as far as Geraldine could see. Certainly not their mother, who preferred to drive into Greenwich and daydream about mansions rather than confront her illness. Nor Tara, who had a long history of making impractical decisions that put her in a bad position. Like when she racked up credit card debt a couple years ago to buy a new laptop and help Eddie because he was out of work for a while after he broke his arm. Or when she got mixed up with a *drug dealer* and then refused to turn him in. Even now, she chose a profession that didn't pay a viable wage.

"You know," Tara said, "if I could remember more details about 'The Connellys of County Down,' like what our special powers were, I'd love to draw that story."

Geraldine recognized a hint when she heard one, but she didn't want to talk about special powers. She stood to pull a bin of magazines away from in front of the closet. "Okay. The moment of truth."

When she opened the door, there were two large boxes on the top shelf with TARA'S THINGS written on them. As soon as Tara opened them her face lit up. She plucked out handfuls of clothes, going on about favorite jeans, which Geraldine didn't get, because they were all ripped up. She recognized other items that had been staples of her sister's wardrobe: a military-style jacket with countless zippers, some T-shirts in loud colors, the chunky black boots Tara used to wear all the time. Her sister had always had her own style, one Geraldine never understood.

But, holy cow, was Tara excited about those boxes. So much so Geraldine regretted not digging them out sooner. Why hadn't she just gotten Tara her things weeks ago?

Standing there, watching her little sister rifle through old clothes and books like a kid on Christmas morning, more of Judy's words came back to Geraldine and hit her so hard she had to look away.

Judy said sometimes people who collected things the way Geraldine did felt more attached to the things than the people in their lives.

~

She woke Sunday morning with regrets. She didn't drink so she'd never been hungover, but she imagined this was how people felt after imbibing too much and making bad decisions.

Yesterday Geraldine agreed to let Eddie take the crosses to the church, and she and Tara took a box of children's clothing to Goodwill. But Geraldine had agreed to those things only because she wanted to prolong the day with Tara, who seemed so pleased with her. Now she felt like she'd been tricked, and she wondered about getting her things back. She just needed an excuse for Father Pat, and certainly the Goodwill hadn't already sold the children's clothes. Though, the woman who processed the donation said there was a great need for kids' clothing. Maybe she'd just let that stuff go. This way she could tell Judy she'd made real progress over the weekend. Besides, she had bigger fish to fry that day.

She made sure Eddie and Conor were getting ready, then laid out her own church clothes before heading for the shower. Mass started at ten and she wanted to be early so she could light a candle at the Virgin Mary statue and say a prayer. If she was going to fix her problems at work, she needed all the help she could get. The quarterlies were now three weeks late. Rita had taken last week off, which put even more on Geraldine's plate. It was all she could do to keep up with payrolls.

The good news was no one yet realized the taxes were late. The bad news was the estimated tax money, which they'd already received from their clients, was still sitting in the Bertucci business account. If it was there much longer Mr. Bertucci would begin to wonder why. She needed to hide that money until she processed the taxes. It's not like she'd be *stealing*, for pity's sake—just holding the money temporarily, until she sent it to the IRS. The only question weighing on her mind the last few days was where to put the money. It was too risky to put it in her own account, which was at the same bank as Mr. Bertucci's. Someone might make the connection. But now she had the answer.

It came to her like a gift from God while Tara was going through her boxes the day before. At the bottom of one was a statement for Tara's old checking account, the one Geraldine was supposed to have closed out for her when she went away. But Geraldine had forgotten all about it. She offered to take the statement to work and shred it, just to be safe. And Tara, who had opened a new account at a different bank, handed it over.

Now Geraldine had access to an open, unused bank account. Tomorrow she planned to move the estimated tax money over to Tara's old account. It wouldn't be exact, but it would be close enough, and she could make small adjustments later. It was pretty foolproof. The account was in a different bank, and Tara wasn't associated with Bertucci's Payroll Service. As soon as Geraldine paid the taxes she'd close out the account.

She finished getting dressed and headed downstairs, where Eddie and Conor were at the table eating cold cereal. They both wore khaki pants and polo shirts Geraldine found for them at Harriet's. The first thing Tara did with her paycheck was get Conor a haircut and buy him a new pair of glasses, to replace the perfectly good ones Geraldine had bought him. It was so like Tara to spend her money on such a thing rather than chip in more for household expenses.

"You both look so nice," Geraldine said, leaning against the counter.

Neither Eddie nor Conor responded. They just focused on their bowls with grim expressions. They were never excited about going to church, but it had been worse since Tara came home because she wouldn't even consider going.

So Geraldine was not thrilled to hear her coming down the back stairs at that moment.

She rounded the corner dressed in jeans with childish colorful patches, a boxy sweater, and a baseball cap. After pouring herself a coffee she came over to the table. She raised the cup to take a sip but lowered it when she saw what they were all wearing. "Wait a minute," she said, turning to Conor. "Don't you have a game this morning?"

He looked up at her with big eyes and nodded.

"He skips the game when it conflicts with Mass," Geraldine said.

Tara's face scrunched into disbelief. Her eyes swung Eddie's way.

He pulled his hand down his beard a couple times, like he was considering something.

Geraldine pushed off the counter. "It's the way we've been doing it."

"Conor," Tara said, "do you want to go to church, or play in your game?"

He just stared back at her.

"That's what I thought. Go change and get your stuff."

"Wait a minute . . ." Geraldine said. But Conor was already up the stairs.

"Eddie," Tara said, "you need to come watch your son play baseball."

He rose from the table and pressed his lips together. "Sorry, Ger. We'll go next week." Then he rushed after Conor.

Just like that, in a matter of seconds, Tara had upset everything again. Geraldine snatched their bowls off the table and started scrubbing them in the sink. She was going to have to come up with some excuse for Eddie and Conor missing church when she saw Father Pat—it might even set Conor back for making his Holy Communion. Now it would be more of a fight to get them to go next time. Tara still had no respect for how Geraldine did things, and Eddie just followed her lead. Didn't seem to matter to him that she chose a *drug dealer* over him and Conor a year and a half ago, while Geraldine had been here, day in and day out, taking care of them.

"Why don't you come to the game with us, Ger?" Tara asked. "Conor would love for you to be there."

Baloney. None of them cared if she was there.

"After the game the team gets pizza," Tara said. "It's fun. Just skip church today."

Geraldine turned off the water and dried her hands on a towel. "I can't just *skip church*. I'm committed to my faith."

"Okay. Then join us after."

"I have work to do after church."

"I can help after lunch," Tara said.

That took Geraldine by surprise. She focused on folding the towel into a neat rectangle.

"Seriously," Tara said. "I'm not a bookkeeper, but I know how to use a calculator and a spreadsheet. Kind of." She smiled.

For a second Geraldine thought about taking her up on that. She could accept her sister's help and it would be like yesterday again. Maybe she could even tell Tara about the pickle she was in, and they could figure it out together.

But then Tara would have even more reason to take over. Look what she'd done just that morning. Before Geraldine knew it, all her stuff would be cleared out of the house. Maybe even Geraldine herself.

"No thanks," she said. "It would take more time to teach you how to do everything than just doing it myself."

"Okay." Tara shrugged. "Let me know if you change your mind." She headed out to the front porch with her coffee.

Geraldine watched her go, which is when she noticed a picture had been added to the collection of family photos on the mantel. It was her dance class photo, the one Tara had found yesterday. Geraldine walked over for a closer look, studied it, tried to feel some kind of connection to the girl who used to love to tap-dance and talk about boys and laugh with her friends. Maybe that's why Tara had dusted the photo off and put it up there, to help Geraldine remember her younger self. *You look so happy here,* she'd said.

Geraldine thought about turning down Tara's offer to help with a little regret. She hadn't meant to sound harsh, but this was her job and she had a certain way of doing things. Tara would probably take one look at her systems and, like Rita, make all kinds of suggestions for improvements. Besides, Geraldine had a solution to her problem, but Tara couldn't know about it. She'd never agree to let Geraldine use her old account. And right now that was the only solution she had. So she didn't go after Tara. Instead she finished up the breakfast dishes before leaving for Mass.

But first she took the dance class photo off the mantel and hid it away in a kitchen drawer.

Chapter Fourteen

Brian had to get moving or he would be late for work. He'd slept like shit and woke with a sore head and cotton-dry mouth. That's how it usually went after a late night with Hank. The thought of strong coffee dragged him out of bed, and he hit the shower.

It had started with a call he and Hank responded to yesterday afternoon: a young woman who OD'd on heroin in a drug den on the south side of town near I-95. She survived thanks to a dose of Narcan, but they knew immediately it was Roland's product because of the Yankees logo on the little envelope. That was followed by a task force meeting last night after work. The team was staying positive, but the more everyone in the room hid their frustration, the more Hank and Brian felt the heat. They represented the police on this task force, and although Roland disappeared during someone else's watch, it might as well have been theirs. And since Hank was the veteran, he bore the brunt. Which is why Brian agreed to have a late dinner after the meeting, even though he knew it would make for a long night. His uncle didn't have anyone else to talk to at the end of the day. Besides, maybe it was Brian's chance to tell Hank he was going to Rosemary's wedding.

While they ate, Hank went on about the dumb bastards who let Roland get away. *Jesus, Bri. He pulled the oldest fuckin' trick in the book.* Brian nodded and agreed and let his uncle blow off steam because he knew the whole episode had been a reminder to Hank that he still hadn't fulfilled his promise to his old friend about taking Roland down. But when he ordered a third round of beers—always Heineken because Brian's dad had worked at their headquarters—and included shots of Bushmills, Brian decided the subject of Rosemary's wedding would wait for another time because he knew where they were headed. Hank only talked about Brian's parents after a good start on getting drunk.

On that tragic night eighteen years ago, Hank had lost his older sister and his best friend in one fell swoop. Michael and Julie Nolan and Hank and Rosemary Doyle were a tight foursome, spending weekends, holidays, and vacations together, lots of barbecues, card games, late nights. Hank and Rosemary were Brian's godparents, and it was assumed Brian's parents would serve the same role for their future kid. When that kid never came, it was Brian's mom who took Rosemary to the doctor in search of answers and sat with her in church praying for a miracle. And Brian's dad took Hank to Yankees games, planned family meals and trips. Even at a young age Brian sensed his parents were the glue keeping Hank and Rosemary together. Which only compounded his guilt after they died.

As the younger brother to the female victim, Hank had never been assigned to Brian's parents' case. But he'd read everything that had ever been documented about it, and he had lots of blame to throw around: the neighbors who heard gunshots that night but didn't see anything, the many detectives who worked the case over the years and couldn't solve it. The only person Hank didn't blame was Brian. He never theorized aloud that if Brian had been home, his parents never would have gone out that night, leaving the house an easy target for robbers. And in return Brian refused to burden Hank with his own grief. He got used to holding it in and sharing it with no one.

Feeling slightly better after a shower and shave, he took an Uber to Dunne's Pub, where he'd left his car the night before. They'd gone there for burgers and beers because that's where they always went. He grabbed a black to-go coffee from a diner before he climbed in the Grand Cherokee and headed to Port Chester.

He had hung in there until Hank ordered a fifth beer and a third shot. Brian passed on the shot but didn't feel like he could leave. So he stayed and listened to Hank tell old stories about Brian's mom, what a good big sister she was, how she kept Hank on the straight and narrow while they were growing up in Hell's Kitchen—*back before it was full of ritzy restaurants and luxury condos, Bri.* And Hank talked about Brian's dad, how he was book smart but still a regular guy, a class act and the best friend a man could have. But Brian was only half listening to Hank. His mind had drifted to the person it had been drawn to like a magnet for the last week. The same person it drifted to right then as he merged onto the expressway.

Tara Connelly.

Stunned. That's how he felt when she appeared at the station that day and made her speech about the sketch pads and pencils. When he put that money in her account he assumed she would spend it on the things most inmates did: extra clothes, food, maybe an iPod and music. To hear she used it on drawing supplies was completely unexpected, and to hear what she'd been drawing was . . . touching. Newborn babies, portraits of other prisoners, cards for kids. He wanted to ask questions, know more about all that, but he was afraid to interrupt. She seemed skittish, like the slightest disturbance would send her running. So he settled for soaking in her smile and the way her eyes would hold his for several seconds, jump to the side, and come back. How undeniably cute she looked in a flat cap, her hands flitting about while she talked, drawing attention to colored smudges on her fingertips. He could have listened to her all day.

He wasn't sure why she told him all that. Maybe it was gratitude, or pride. Either way she'd been willing to risk coming to the station because she wanted him to know how she spent that money. That had to mean something; he just didn't know what to do about it. He could imagine what his dad would say: *For one thing, you shouldn't have let her walk away, kiddo.* Brian's parents had met in college. His dad always said he knew Brian's mom was The One from the get-go, and he never gave her the chance to get away.

But this was far more complicated. Brian was one of the cops who put Tara in prison, and her name was still high on a list of known associates for Roland Shea. He didn't know why she wouldn't flip on Roland back then or what her relationship was with him now. Then there was DaCosta—*Stay away from Tara Connelly, for both your sakes.*

When Brian walked into the station, his uncle was waiting for him in the lobby.

"Hey, Sleeping Beauty," he said when Brian came through the door. He was leaning back against the desk sergeant's counter, jacket and tie on, hands shoved in his pockets.

"How long have you been here?"

"A while." Hank pushed off the counter. "Woke up early and decided to come in. You ready to go to work?"

"What do you mean?" Brian drained his coffee. He was going to need another one.

Hank threw a nod down the hall toward the interview rooms. "I picked up someone who might have a lead on Roland. Wanted to wait until you got here to start questioning."

"Okay." Brian tossed his cup in a corner trash can and followed Hank down the hall. Maybe this would turn something up. Brian didn't feel on his A game, but Hank could do most of the talking. He seemed fully recovered, chipper even.

When they reached Interview Three Hank didn't even give Brian a chance to ask who was in there. He just swung the door open.

Brian followed him inside. And froze.

For a split second he considered backing out of the room. Then she looked up and it was too late.

Hank moved to take the seat across from her. "Miss Connelly, you remember my partner, Detective Nolan."

"Yes, I do." She dropped her gaze from Brian's, but not before he saw the betrayal in it.

Hank pulled his chair in close to the table and glanced at Brian, who hadn't moved from where he stood by the door.

He pulled out the chair next to Hank and sat, his mind racing. Why the hell had Hank brought her in? He must have something. Maybe she'd been seen with Roland again or made contact with him . . .

Hank reached over to hit the power switch on the recording system. "Miss Connelly," he said, "we want to start by thanking you for volunteering to come in this morning."

"Volunteering?" She crossed her arms against the light denim jacket she was wearing. "You showed up at my work and told me, in front of my new bosses, that I was wanted for questioning and my parole officer would be informed if I didn't cooperate. Didn't feel very voluntary."

Brian's eyes jumped to Hank. Had he really done that? Veiled threats weren't against the rules when they had reason to apply pressure to someone. But harassing her at work without cause was over the line. He might have cost her the graphic illustrator job she'd just gotten.

Hank held his hands up. "You're free to leave. We just thought you might like to offer some assistance, and your PO would certainly look favorably on it."

Her face stiffened. "What do you want?"

"We're looking for a former associate of yours," Hank said. "Someone you were close to, maybe still are. We're having a hard time locating Roland Shea, and we thought you might be able to help."

"I have no idea where he is."

"See, you're answering awfully quickly," Hank said. "Maybe you should take a minute, really think about it." He paused, which was Brian's cue. There was an art to this process and part of it was passing the questions back and forth, keeping the person of interest off-balance. But Brian knew where Hank was going, and he couldn't do it.

When he said nothing, Hank picked back up. "You know Roland well, you two have history."

She dropped her head and sighed.

"Maybe you can guess where he went," Hank said. "Could be somewhere the two of you used to go, a place you spent time together. Or maybe you used to hear him talk about a safe house he had somewhere."

"I have nothing to do with Roland anymore," she said.

Hank rubbed his chin. "Then can you explain what you were doing at his house last month?"

Shit. Brian felt a sharp dropping sensation in his gut.

Tara's brows pinched together in confusion. Her eyes darted to Brian and back to Hank. "Did you guys see me there and report it to my PO?"

Hank lifted a shoulder. "Just doing our job. Can you tell us the nature of that meeting?"

When she let out a soft incredulous laugh, Brian got it. They shared a bad inside joke here, the knowledge that it was his fault she was at Roland's that day. But she never looked his way. "I went there because I thought Roland put money in my inmate account at Taconic. I wanted to tell him I would pay him back so I didn't owe him anything, but turned out it wasn't him."

Brian's mind flashed forward to the moment when she would tell Hank who did put the money in there. Of course she would, she had too much at stake.

"We chatted for another minute or two, and that was it." Tara leaned forward, forearms on the table, and held Hank's gaze. "I swear I haven't seen or heard from him since."

Hank studied her for a minute. "If we find out you're in contact with Roland, or helping him in any way, you'll get sent right back to Taconic." He wasn't letting up.

Her shoulders sank and she fell back against her chair.

This wasn't right. Hank had no reason for questioning her that morning other than desperation. The interview needed to end. "Miss Connelly," Brian said, "we just ask if you do hear from Roland, you let us know."

"Fine," she said, without looking up.

"And just so we're clear," Hank said, "that would include letting us know if you get any *personal* phone calls or texts from him."

That seemed to trigger something. When she raised her eyes they were defiant. "I don't have a cell phone."

Hank tilted his head, gave her a tolerant smile. "Well, then, if he sends flowers."

"I'm not really a flowers kind of girl."

Hank's smile disappeared. "This isn't a joke, Miss Connelly. Roland's dope almost killed another person yesterday."

Tara's whole body seemed to flinch. "I'm sorry about that, but I don't know—"

"Want me to add up how many he killed since you wouldn't turn him in eighteen months ago?" Hank asked.

She swallowed and looked down at her lap.

"We're done here," Brian said, standing up. "Miss Connelly, do you need a ride back to work?"

She stood from her chair and turned toward the door. "No, I don't."

"One more question," Hank said, standing up as well. "If it wasn't Roland who put that money in your inmate account, who was it?"

"My family." She answered before Brian even had a chance to consider speaking up. He couldn't help noting that her steady gaze and expression gave nothing away while she lied to Hank's face.

Hank grunted. "Kind of strange, isn't it? You assuming Roland put that money in there rather than your own family?"

One side of her mouth pulled into a wry smile. "You don't know my family."

Brian opened the door for her, tried to catch her eye as she marched past him. But she never looked up.

Hank started to head out the door as well, but Brian put up a hand to stop him. "You didn't tell me you turned her in to her PO. And you went to her job and threatened her?"

"We need to find this guy, Brian, before his dope kills more people. And I'm going to follow any leads we have, even if you have a little crush on her."

Brian felt his face heat up.

Hank leaned in and lowered his voice. "Don't you even think about it. You could lose your job." Then he pushed past Brian and left.

Brian watched him go, stumped by what had taken place in that room. First, his uncle's disregard for protocol, jeopardizing Tara's livelihood simply because he was frustrated.

Then there was the indisputable fact that Tara had covered for Brian. Even though she could have deflected attention by throwing Brian under the bus, she'd covered for him.

And she'd lied to the police to do it.

He didn't know exactly when he decided he was going to see Tara that night, though he was pretty sure it was before she left the interview room. It wasn't smart—talk about unprofessional behavior—and she would probably tell him to go to hell. If DaCosta or Hank found out, the shit would really hit the fan. But he couldn't let her believe he had a hand in that ambush.

Still, when he finally wrapped up his day around six and headed for her house, he felt like he was about to cross a critical line.

It was almost dusk when he pulled onto Gillette Street, the thin light of evening fading toward dark. He rounded the cul-de-sac and parked in front of her house. The red-and-white pickup was there, and an old white minivan. He locked his gun and badge in the glove box, left his jacket and tie on the passenger seat. He was not there as a cop. Which was his first step across that line.

He climbed out, locked the car, and started across the lawn, wondering what kind of reception he was in for. He hoped her brother didn't answer the door; he would not be happy to see Brian. She had a sister Brian never met. Whoever answered, he was going to have some explaining to do.

"*Nolan*." The rough whisper came from the side of the house, where Tara stood, most of her hidden behind the corner. He could see only her face and a shoulder.

He headed that way, and as he got closer she backed away from him until she was against a set of dilapidated stairs that led up the side of the house.

"What are you doing here?" she asked. Her arms were folded across her middle, and she searched behind him. Probably for Hank.

"I'm alone," he said. "I just want to talk. If you had a phone I would have called first. Though I'm guessing you would have told me not to come."

"Ya think?"

"I only need two minutes."

She glanced toward the house and sighed. "I don't want to worry my family. Just come upstairs." When she spun around to lead the way, he caught a whiff of her hair, that clean, light floral scent.

As he climbed the steps he assumed they were headed for some kind of bonus room. When they got to the top she held the door open for him.

"Thanks," he said. "I promise I'll be quick . . ." But he stopped because, after stepping inside, he realized where he was.

His first thought was that her room was feminine, but not frilly. It was a mix of warm colors and soft fabrics. He recognized a couple items: the flat cap hanging on a hook, the denim jacket on the back of a chair. The bed in front of him was unmade, clothing peeked out from half-open drawers, the shelves to the right were jammed with books, photos, and kid art projects. It felt lived-in and cozy.

But it was the splash of vivid colors to the left that fully captured his attention, enough that he just stared for a while. There were pictures of various sizes hanging above a desk, clothespinned across three rows of taut twine. Most of them were comic-strip style, action shots of young lively figures with speech balloons above their heads. Some depicted names of video games he'd vaguely heard of spelled out in graffiti-style letters and surrounded by, presumably, characters from those games. It was all bold colors and sharp lines and expressive faces.

"Wow. These are terrific," he said.

"Thanks."

He looked down at her desk to see an old laptop, next to a stack of sketch pads. He laid his hand on the sketch pads. There were maybe half a dozen, the covers worn with use. Some of them must have come with her from Taconic. When he turned to ask her that question he remembered why he was there.

He took time to consider his next words because once he said them he couldn't take them back, couldn't erase the fissure it would create between him and Hank. "I didn't report you to your PO. And I didn't know Hank was going to pull you in today, or I would have headed it off."

She pulled her black hoodie tighter around her. "I think your partner has it in for me."

"He has it in for Roland Shea. He thinks you're a way to get to him."

"I'm not."

"I believe you." Or, at the least, he badly wanted to.

Some of the tension seemed to seep from her shoulders.

"And I'm sorry I put you in a position where you felt like you had to lie about the money. I should have said something. I didn't technically break any rules by giving it to you . . ."

"But it raises awkward questions," she said.

"Yes." What a dick. She'd been threatened by Hank and dragged into the station that day, and Brian was worried about awkward questions. "I don't think it'll come up again, but if it does, just tell the truth."

Her mouth took on a rueful slant. "Don't worry about it, Nolan. I'm not a rat, remember?"

He nodded, not sure how he felt about being in the same club as Roland Shea: guys she would keep secrets for. "I remember."

They both looked away, joint acknowledgment of the things they couldn't talk about.

She slid her hands into the pockets of her hoodie. "Anything else?"

Yeah. He wanted to pull up a chair, flip through those sketch pads, ask about her family and her work. He wanted to know about her time at Taconic, if she'd ever been in danger or mistreated. He wanted to close the gap between them, take her hand, brush those loose strands back from her face.

But then what . . . *Don't you even think about it,* Hank had said. *You could lose your job.*

"I guess not," he said. "I'll get out of your way." He looked up at the wall again, tried to take mental snapshots of her work so he could recall it later, then headed for the door. He was almost there when he stopped, about-faced, and walked back to stand in front of her. Close enough that his eyes could trail the light freckles from one side of her face to the other. "Do you think you could ever get past the fact that I arrested you and sent you to prison?"

Her head tilted. "I don't know. Could you get past the fact that I transported those pills and did a year and a half for it?" He saw a challenge in those piercing eyes. Maybe a little hope too.

"I got past that a long time ago," he said.

A corner of her mouth curved up, but she crossed her arms. "I think seeing you could violate my parole."

"I think seeing you could end my career."

"I don't really know where that leaves us."

He didn't either, but he knew he didn't want to go yet. "Thank you for covering for me today."

"You're welcome."

Before he could think it through he leaned forward and gently brushed his lips against her cheek, lingering for just a second.

When he pulled back her face flushed, and she started to smile but stopped when someone knocked on her door.

"Tara?" A kid's voice. The nephew.

"Yeah?"

"I thought we were going to work on the spaceship."

Brian grinned at the confirmation that she had indeed listened to his suggestion the day he drove her home.

She rolled her eyes at him. "I'll be right there, Con-man. Give me two minutes."

"Okay," he said, his voice fading as he thumped back down the stairs.

"Sounds like you have a date with your nephew and some LEGOs," he said.

"Yeah, I do."

He was already thinking about how and when he could see her again. "Do you really not have a cell phone?" he asked.

She shook her head.

"That's all right," he said, backing away. "I'm a detective. I'll figure it out." He opened the door and stepped outside, closing it gently behind him.

She was still the former girlfriend of a drug dealer, and Brian had lots of questions about that. The threat of DaCosta hung over both their heads. Hank would keep Tara in his sights until they found Roland, and Brian had gone way over the line with that kiss.

But as he quietly descended those rickety steps so as not to alert her family, he just didn't care.

Chapter Fifteen

Normally Andrea provided some notice when she was coming to visit. Not a lot, Conor's mom wasn't much of a planner. But typically she called Eddie a day or two ahead to get the all clear. So he and Conor were surprised when she was waiting at the house Thursday afternoon. Eddie kept the truck that day so he could attend Conor's baseball practice. They'd been working on his swing, and Conor wanted Eddie to come watch him. Tryouts for the traveling team were coming up that weekend, and Conor's heart was set on making it.

When they saw Andrea smoking a cigarette and leaning against her old, bright yellow PT Cruiser, they exchanged a look. Eddie could see the mix of excitement and dread on his son's face. Conor was always happy to see Andrea, but the visits were inevitably a letdown. It was natural for him to keep hoping his mom would change, but it was tough to watch fresh disappointment sink in every time.

"Wait here a sec, Con," Eddie said, before climbing out of the truck. He wanted to get a good look at Andrea before Conor got too close. Though she knew better than to show up high, particularly now that Tara was back.

Andrea had always been a beauty, kind of exotic with a touch of glamour. She had dark glossy hair and full lips, a tiny waist and long legs. As usual she was showing them off in a miniskirt and ankle boots with a high heel. She used one of them to stomp out her cigarette as Eddie approached, then stuffed her hands in the pockets of her leather jacket. It was when she pulled her big sunglasses off that Eddie could see the shine was wearing off, even though she wasn't quite thirty yet. That was bound to happen after almost a decade of living the club life. Her green eyes were lined too heavily, her lipstick too red. She looked tired, probably strung out, but sober at the moment. Which was about as good as it got with Andrea.

"Hiya, Eddie." She gave him a nervous smile and wiggled her long red nails over his shoulder at Conor. "I was just hoping to say hello to him. I'm sorry I didn't call first. I didn't know I was gonna be up this way until it happened."

Eddie knew better than to ask what brought her up this way. She often coordinated parties for wealthy people who lived in Westchester or on Long Island, hooking them up with all the product they needed for their fun. "All right," he said, waving Conor over. "But he has practice soon."

She glanced at the house and lowered her voice. "Tara isn't here, is she?"

He shook his head.

"Hi, Mom," Conor said, walking up next to Eddie. His arms swung back and forth against his hips.

"Hey, baby!" She crouched down a bit and held her arms open, several bracelets swinging from each wrist.

Conor gave her a hug.

"You want to come inside while we grab him a snack?" Eddie asked.

"Sure." She kept her arm around Conor while they made their way across the yard and up the porch steps, squeezing his shoulders and ruffling his hair. When Andrea did visit she kept her eyes and hands glued to Conor the whole time, like she was trying to soak him in and make up for all that lost contact.

She and Conor sat at the table while Eddie scrounged up a couple granola bars and a glass of milk. Andrea fired questions at Conor about school and baseball and friends, same questions she asked every time she saw him, though she never seemed to remember the answers.

"So what else is new, baby?" She put her chin in her hands and watched him eat.

"I'm helping Tara with her job," Conor said around a mouthful of granola bar.

"Is that right?"

"Yeah. I helped her stop smoking too. Right, Dad?"

Eddie nodded. It had to be tough for Andrea, listening to Conor talk up Tara.

"How'd you do that?" Andrea asked.

"I tell her a joke when she gets a craving. I could do that for you too, if you want," he said, twirling his glass on the table. "You could just call me when you need a joke."

She laid both her hands on his forearm. "I would *love* that."

Conor half smiled and nodded at her.

Eddie couldn't watch it anymore. "I'll go grab your bag, Con." He headed upstairs, listening to Andrea tell stories about celebrities she'd seen in the club, like her ten-year-old son gave a shit about that. She just didn't have anything else to offer him.

He found the bag and dropped down on Conor's bed, wanting to give them a couple minutes. Once again Eddie thanked God or the universe or whoever that Tara was back home. There was nothing like a dose of Andrea to make him appreciate his sister and what she did for his son. Though it had cost Tara. He would never forget that day eight years ago when he came home from work to find two cops at the house. They were standing in the living room, Andrea crying on the couch with a bruised and bloodied mouth, and Tara sitting at the table, bouncing Conor on her lap.

Tara had come home a little earlier to find Conor wearing just a diaper, wandering around the front lawn on a chilly October afternoon. She'd scooped him up and taken him in the house, where Andrea and some girlfriend of hers were stoned out of their minds on the couch watching TV, passing a bong between them. Tara dressed Conor and set him in the playpen upstairs, went down to the living room, and called Andrea's name. When Andrea lumbered up to a standing position and asked what was going on, Tara pulled her fist back and hit her square in the face.

After getting rid of the bong, Andrea's furious friend called 911 and stayed to make an official report. So even though Andrea would not have pressed charges—she avoided cops like the plague—the police had no choice but to arrest Tara for assault. They took her in that afternoon, and she was released on her own recognizance a couple hours later. The charges were dropped once the details came to light, but they'd booked her, which was enough of a record to rule out minimum security when she was sentenced for the drug charge.

Eddie headed back downstairs to the kitchen.

"Look, Dad," Conor said. "Mom gave them to me." He held up a pair of Beats headphones, similar to ones he already had. The plastic Best Buy bag was sitting on the table. She'd probably just bought them on her way over.

Andrea was chewing a fingernail. "I can get something else if you don't like them."

"They're great," Eddie said.

"Yeah," Conor said. "I really like them."

She breathed a sigh of relief.

Eddie held up Conor's bag. "We should get going, bud."

"You know, Mom," Conor said, "you could come to my practice if you want."

Andrea froze, surely picturing the same thing Eddie was: her standing at the side of the field in her clubbing clothes, alongside Little League moms who would give her dirty looks and a wide berth. Conor knew it too, and still he invited her. That just about broke Eddie's heart. He was only eleven when he lost his own mom, but he had good memories to cling to. Like listening to her fairy tales, giving her the play-by-play of his baseball games, the way she would often reach out and put a hand to his cheek—*Thank you for always making me smile, Eddie.*

Andrea tilted her head. "I'm so sorry, baby. I wish I could go, but I have to work tonight."

Conor nodded and rose from the table. "That's okay." He took his bag from Eddie and headed outside.

"You're doing a great job with him, Eddie," Andrea said.

"It's been good for him to have Tara home again."

Andrea nodded with a rueful smile. "She always was so great with him."

He appreciated her saying that, but really he just wanted her to leave. He would be forever grateful to her for giving him Conor, but being around Andrea reminded Eddie of some of the worst times of his life.

She stood and turned to go, and he followed her outside, hanging back a bit so she could give Conor a hug and a bunch of empty promises before she left.

It wasn't all her fault. He'd been partying pretty hard himself for a few years before he met her, trying to self-medicate away the effects of his brain injury, which only made them worse. He met her during a haze of binge drinking and bar fights. But less than a year later, when he found out she was pregnant, he stopped all that. He owed that to her too.

But if Eddie'd had the balls to kick Andrea out sooner, Tara would not have had that assault charge on her record. For that matter, she wouldn't have gone to prison at all because she never would have come in contact with Roland Shea. He was Andrea's dealer; she brought him into their world.

After Andrea hugged Conor goodbye, Eddie walked her to her car. She wasn't much of a mother, but every time he saw her he thought it could be the last. All it would take was one pill or one snort too many at the club one night.

"Can you get me a schedule of his baseball games?" she asked when they arrived at her car. "I'd like to try to make one of them."

"Sure," Eddie said, knowing full well she never would.

She slipped on those oversize sunglasses to hide the red-rimmed eyes. "Thanks, Eddie. I promise I'll call next time." She drew a shaky breath and looked down. "Just keep taking care of him, okay? And tell Tara . . . Tell her thank you for me." She flashed him the saddest of smiles and got into her car.

He waved through the window and watched her fight tears while she started the engine and pulled slowly forward. It was at the last second, when she was just about past him, that he noticed them. Several small semitransparent envelopes in the center cupholder, the Yankees logo stamped on them. Roland's product.

God damn it. He knew in an instant what had brought Andrea up this way. She was working for Roland, setting up deals, or maybe even selling for him down in the city.

"Come on, Dad," Conor called from the truck.

Eddie felt such an intense surge of anger toward her for bringing that shit anywhere near their son that his head started to hammer and he saw white for a moment. When it mostly cleared he walked over and climbed in the truck next to Conor, but he didn't start it right away. He needed to take a few breaths, settle his mind and his hands before he drove. They sat in the truck, both of them watching the bright yellow PT Cruiser drive down Gillette Street.

"Are you okay?" Eddie asked Conor.

He took his glasses off and rubbed the bridge of his nose. "Yeah. Are you okay?"

"Yeah. But I could use one of those jokes about now."

Conor thought for a second. "What did one toilet say to the other toilet?"

"I have no idea."

"You look flushed."

When Eddie laughed out loud Conor beamed. Then Eddie did something he couldn't remember doing for a long time. He reached out and put a hand on Conor's head, felt his son's soft hair beneath his calloused palm and fingers. "Thanks for that."

He was ready to drive. Better than any pill or relaxation technique, reaching out and touching his son soothed it all quite a bit.

◇

The next evening Eddie and Conor rode the elevator up to Lorraine's fifth-floor apartment. She and Katie lived in a plain stucco building with wide balconies. It was centrally located, just north of town. They could walk to restaurants and shops, the train, and Lyon Park. The units were older and small but had been refurbished a few years ago and were in fairly high demand, so Lorraine had to be doing okay for herself.

He tried like hell not to scratch his neck as they stepped off the elevator and headed down the hall to her apartment. Tara gave him some kind of lotion to put on after she dragged him to a barber who trimmed his beard and shaved his neckline that afternoon, and she told him not to scratch—*It'll get bright red and itch even more.* He asked why she made him do it in the first place if she knew that was going to happen, but she just shook her head. *Had to be done, Eddie.* She'd been in that kind of mood the last couple days, almost bubbly. She even woke him up that morning—before work—to go running. When he said fuck no, she called for Conor's help, which was dirty pool. Eddie had risen, and with Conor cheering them on from his bike, he went for a run with her. Well, he'd mostly walked, and it was less than two miles. But it was a start.

The itchy neck and shin splints were well worth it when Lorraine opened the door and her eyes widened in pleasant surprise. She looked good in her out-of-work clothes, a short-sleeve navy-blue dress that went to her knees and flattered her slender shape. And her hair had a little wave to it.

"You look nice," he said.

"Thanks. You too." She gestured to his face. "I like it."

He ran a hand down his beard, which was a much quicker trip now. "My sister said it was time." Tara also told him not to wear a hat, but she lost that battle.

Lorraine stepped back and waved them in.

Eddie gave Conor a gentle push across the threshold. He wasn't thrilled about coming along, but Lorraine had invited him, and Eddie felt a little more comfortable having him there. It had been a while since he'd spent one-on-one time with a woman other than his sisters. Last week Eddie had submitted his application for the project leader position, and tonight Lorraine was going to show him the forms he'd need to be familiar with for the interview. *If* he decided to move ahead with the interview. That was a big if, and it depended on whether he could get comfortable with the paperwork.

Lorraine brought Conor a Sprite just as Katie came walking into the kitchen.

"Oh, hi, Conor," she said, crossing her arms and cocking her hip. She looked as thrilled to have Conor there as he was to be there.

"Hi." He focused on cracking open his soda.

"So I hear you're good at LEGOs," Katie said. She was a full head taller than Conor and skinny as a rail.

Conor shrugged.

Katie huffed out an exasperated sigh. "Well, I'm working on a princess castle my grandma gave me. It's like a million pieces, and you can help me if you want to."

Conor shrugged again. "Fine."

"Come on," Katie said, rolling her eyes. "It's this way." She led Conor down a hallway and he followed, head and shoulders drooping. Like he was being led to the gallows.

"She's a little bossy," Lorraine said once the kids were gone.

"We live with my sisters. He's used to bossy women."

She led him over to her kitchen table, where a stack of papers sat in a neat pile. He was tempted to accept a beer when she offered, but he wanted to stay as clearheaded as possible so he just asked for some water.

They each took a seat, and he waited for Lorraine to start digging into the pile of forms, but instead she clasped her hands on the table.

"Eddie, before we get to the forms, can you tell me what about them is so hard for you?" It was probably without conscious thought, but she winced. Like she felt sorry for him or was afraid of offending him.

"It's not like I can't read them or understand them. I used to fill out some of them all the time, like general work orders and the foreman's site report." He shifted in his seat. "But as the company grew the forms got complicated, there was a lot more math. Like the estimate sheets and all the schedules, and we started using the computer for everything. I know they're supposed to be easier but I could never get the hang of the . . ." He mimed touching a screen because he couldn't think of the damn word.

"The tablets?"

He nodded, feeling like an idiot. It was Lorraine who helped Dunbar Construction modernize the last few years by going largely electronic.

"Then maybe we start by getting you comfortable with the tablet," Lorraine said, hopping up to grab one from her kitchen counter. "They really are simple once you get used to them . . ." She started tapping buttons, waking the thing up.

They really are simple. She didn't get it. None of this was ever simple for Eddie. There were reasons he'd stepped down to general laborer, and one of them was so he didn't have to put up with people looking at him with pity in their eyes or pretending to be busy while he took forever to figure shit out. This was a mistake.

He stood and stepped back from the table. "I really appreciate it, Lorraine. But I don't think this is going to work."

Her brows twitched together. "Where are you going?"

"Look, I just can't do this." He waved toward the tablet in her hands, the papers on the table.

"Yes you can."

"I barely graduated high school, Lorraine. It took me five years, and the only reason I did was because Tara did half my homework and teachers felt sorry for me, spending so much time in the hospital. And when

I *was* in school I copied everything off my friends." He took a breath and slowed down. "I'm pretty good with my hands, but not with this." He tapped a finger against his temple.

She turned the tablet off and put it aside. "Can you sit back down, Eddie?"

He was tempted to just call for Conor and hit the road. He'd been kidding himself, thinking he could figure this stuff out.

"Please?" she asked. "Let's start over."

There was no way he was changing his mind about going for the project leader job, but Lorraine was kind, she laughed at his jokes. And he got the feeling she'd put some effort in tonight.

He took his seat again.

"How long were you in and out of the hospital?" she asked.

"Years."

"You missed a lot of school?"

"Weeks at a time."

"What was that like?"

He was about to say "It sucked," but he already knew she'd follow up with more questions—she was good with the questions. And she deserved to know the whole truth. Not just because she was trying to help him get this job, but if she were, by chance, thinking about something else between them, she needed to know. So he told her. It was a little halting, and out of order, but he told her. A lot.

How the doctors were slightly amazed when he woke up after the accident because, with such a skull fracture, they thought he was a goner. How worried they were about the swelling in his brain and then possible clots and infections. He told her how bad the pain was, and about the memory loss and vertigo, the endless hours of physical and occupational therapy. He also told her about the sheer frustration of being given a clean bill of health and released from the hospital, only to find himself back there a few months later.

It might have been the longest Eddie ever spoke in one go. He checked on Lorraine while he spoke, to make sure he wasn't saying too much or upsetting her. But she never shied away, just listened, her expression full of compassion.

"You went through all that without your parents?" she asked.

"Yeah, but I had my sisters. They were there all the time, coming in after work and school, on the weekends. But it was hard on them. Geraldine was still a kid herself, and she had to deal with doctors and social services, all the paperwork. And Tara was so young and scared . . ." He paused to swallow a lump that came with the memory of waking up more than once to find Tara crying by his bedside. "She used to spend nights in my hospital room, even though she wasn't allowed to. Which drove Geraldine nuts."

Lorraine laughed. She had a nice laugh, soft and sincere.

"All of that," Eddie said, taking off his cap and running a hand through his hair, "was my way of telling you that I deal with this TBI all the time, and there are some dark days. I don't always have the best judgment, my memory is spotty, and I have a hard time organizing my thoughts. If I get tired or anxious it makes it worse. And I still take meds for seizures, sometimes for migraines. But I've cut down on the sleeping pills lately."

When she placed her hand on Eddie's, his heart rate jumped up. "Thanks for helping me understand, Eddie."

He turned his hand over so he could take hold of hers.

"Look," she said, "I've watched you deal with all this for a long time now, and I know it gets really hard sometimes. But you always keep going, no matter what. Usually with a smile and a kind word for everyone. That's why I think you'd make a great project leader. But if you don't want to go for this job, that's fine with me." She smiled and squeezed his hand.

He hated to let go, but the kids came wandering in.

"How's it going?" Lorraine asked them.

Katie led Conor to the fridge. "Pretty good. We got the first floor done so I told Conor he could have a Popsicle."

Conor gave Eddie a pointed look. "Are you guys done yet?"

Eddie glanced at Lorraine.

Her brows and shoulders shrugged—*Up to you*. No pressure, but she was still willing to help him, if that's what he wanted.

He hadn't let himself want much in a long time, but the truth was he wanted the project leader job. It would be good for him and his family. And Lorraine really seemed to believe he could do it.

"Sorry, Con," he said, picking up the tablet. "We need some more time. Lorraine's going to show me how to use one of these damn things."

Chapter Sixteen

_____

On Monday morning Tara had to make the trip to New Rochelle to meet with Doreen DaCosta for an official six-week check-in. Eddie had offered to drive her for moral support—*or in case you lose the power of speech again*—but she didn't want him to miss more work, especially when he was going after a promotion. Besides, she'd have to get used to going alone; she'd be doing it for the next two years. But considering what happened last time she met with her PO, she hadn't slept much the night before, and she was on edge all morning. Enough to ask Conor for a joke at the breakfast table.

"Did you hear about the kidnapping at school?"

"No."

"Don't worry. He woke up."

Now she sat across from DaCosta, waiting while she read through the repetitive paperwork Tara had to complete for each visit. They'd already run through a long checklist of questions about the status of Tara's family and living situation, employment status, her current physical and mental health.

"I see you did the drug and alcohol education class," DaCosta said. She wore the same gold hoop earrings, but the press-on nails were different this time, a rainbow of iridescent colors.

"Yep." A whole Saturday spent in the basement of the Port Chester Community Center, watching melodramatic videos and taking quizzes about the evils of substance abuse.

"And all your UAs are clean."

"I told you, I don't use."

DaCosta looked up at her testy tone, which Tara regretted. But it was humiliating, making weekly visits to the local drug testing center—not to mention the morning she was called in for a random test and had to leave work. Gordi and Lance were cool about it, but still.

"I don't know about this job," DaCosta said, shaking her head. "You're working for a couple kids who play video games on YouTube? Sounds like a bad setup for someone on parole for a drug charge."

Tara had expected this line of questioning. "They run a clean show. Their audience is younger kids, so there's no violence, no talk about drugs or sex, not even bad language. I brought some examples of the stuff I'm working on." She reached into her bag, pulled out copies of thumbnails she'd created, and handed them to DaCosta.

She studied them for a moment, and one side of her mouth pulled up. It was the closest thing to a smile Tara had seen from her.

"They're just starting out," Tara said. "But they have good momentum going."

"You like the work?"

"I love it."

"That counts for a lot." DaCosta handed back the drawings. "I'll go with it for now."

Tara felt like she should thank her, but for what—letting her keep her job?

"What about your social life?" DaCosta asked. "It's okay to be getting out, seeing friends. You just can't be around anyone who's using or has a criminal record."

"Between the job and my family I don't have much time for that. I went out with my brother and his work friends one night, that's about it."

"How was that?"

"Fine. A little awkward. Some of them knew I was in prison . . . It was hard to know what to talk about."

"That's normal. But you gotta decide how to handle those situations 'cause that's how it's gonna be now. Some parolees put it right out there, tell new friends they did time and see how they react. Some get good at changing the subject. It helps to have a small group that knows what you've been through so they can support you."

Tara nodded.

"You seeing anybody?" DaCosta asked.

Jesus. It felt like no aspect of her life was sacred anymore, there was zero privacy.

"A boyfriend or girlfriend can have a big impact on your progress," DaCosta said. "I'm not asking for juicy details, just if you got someone in your life."

An image materialized in Tara's mind: Brian standing in her bedroom, his hand on her sketch pads while he looked up at her work on the wall. "No, I'm not seeing anyone." She wasn't. But it kind of felt like a lie.

"It's smart not to rush into anything." DaCosta went back to her checklist. "Have you had any interaction with law enforcement since I saw you last?"

Tara's heart skipped a beat. This was the discussion she'd been dreading. If she admitted she'd seen Brian—more than once—DaCosta would know Tara had broken her promise and further investigated the commissary money, which could potentially get Jeannie in trouble too. Not to mention what might happen to Brian. She chose her words carefully. "The cops asked me a few questions last week about Roland Shea, I guess he's missing. I told them I didn't know anything."

"They pull you into the station?"

"Yeah, just for a few minutes." Tara shrugged a shoulder, hoping that would end the conversation.

"Who pulled you in?" DaCosta asked.

"One of the detectives who originally arrested me. Doyle."

DaCosta's eyebrows shot up. She laid down her pen and wrapped one hand around the other. "Did Detective Doyle question you alone?"

Damn. "His partner was there too."

"Nolan? What *exactly* did they want?" DaCosta's eyes never left Tara's face while she brought a hand to her chin, started rubbing it with an index finger topped off with a shiny lime-green nail, looking very much like the human lie detector she probably was.

"They thought I might have some idea where Roland went. I told them I couldn't help, that I have nothing to do with him anymore. And that was it." Tara held the other woman's gaze, made sure not to fidget.

She studied Tara a little longer. "You know, they got the right to ask you questions, but not to harass you."

Something clicked for Tara then. DaCosta might be a hard-ass, but it was largely because she was looking out for Tara. She fleetingly thought about coming clean—*I know Nolan gave me the money. We talked about it and it's okay.* But she just didn't trust DaCosta would let it go at that.

"If you hear from either of them again," DaCosta said, "for any reason, I want you to call me right away. Got it?"

"Got it."

DaCosta picked up her pen again and made some more notes. She wrapped it up shortly after that. They scheduled another in-person meeting for next month, and DaCosta mentioned decreasing the frequency of the drug tests if they kept coming up clean. Her last words before ending the meeting were "Good job, Miss Connelly."

Relief washed over Tara when she left that office, and she counted her blessings as she drove back to Port Chester. Her job was safe for now, Eddie was going for a promotion, Conor was doing well, Geraldine was getting the help she needed. Tara didn't know what to make of this thing with Brian, but it was kind of exciting. Six weeks after leaving Taconic she felt like she was beginning to take back some control over her own life.

When she pulled into town and passed the shitty strip mall where Value Maids was located, she mentally flipped off Rudy Russo and his last words to her—*You can't escape your past.* She hoped never to see him again, but she would have liked him to know how wrong he was about her.

~

She'd been working with Gordi and Lance for almost five weeks, and subscriptions were up 10 percent to over sixty thousand and still climbing. The first real benchmark, the one that would make them feel somewhat legit, would be a hundred thousand. That's when they could start making decent money on ads and reach out to potential sponsors. They were moving in the right direction, but one thing Tara realized quickly was Gordi and Lance weren't very good at the business side of their business. Their financial records were a mess, which, at the moment, wasn't a big deal, since there was little money to manage. But there was also no tracking going on as to which thumbnails and videos were drawing the most clicks and subscriptions. The guys played games and posted videos, watched the overall subscriber number, but that was about it. Tara suggested a weekly meeting when they could sit together and start getting the administrative side of things in order. So early Friday morning the three of them huddled around the tiny kitchen island with coffees Gordi brought from Dunkin'. He had a crush on one of the baristas there, which is why Tara sent him for the coffees.

"How'd it go?" Tara asked him. "Did you talk to her?"

"A little."

"She means other than ordering the coffees, dude," Lance said.

"Oh." Gordi adjusted his glasses. "Well, no, not really. But she smiled at me."

"That's her job," Lance said.

"No, it's a start," Tara said. "But your challenge tomorrow is to ask her how her day is going. Can you do that?"

"Yeah." But he gulped like it was already stressing him out.

They kicked off the meeting by conducting an analysis of current numbers. After taking a look at the stats, there were a couple of highlights: thumbnail caricatures Tara posted of Gordi and Lance were a big draw, as well as one video during which the boys placed an impromptu bet as to who would achieve the highest score that afternoon. And the next day even more kids tuned in to watch Gordi throw a chocolate cream pie in Lance's face.

They were in the middle of brainstorming other gambits that would gratify middle school humor when someone knocked on the front door. Gordi jumped up and jogged across the room to answer it.

"Can I help you?" he asked whoever was on the other side of the door.

"Hi, I'm looking for Tara Connelly? I think she works here . . ."

Tara's eyes jumped in the direction of the door. She couldn't see him, but she knew the voice right away.

Gordi crossed his arms. "Who's asking?"

Lance stood and moved to the door beside Gordi.

"I'm Brian."

"You a cop?" Lance asked.

Tara decided to let the boys run with it. They'd been shaken up when that Doyle prick appeared last week. She came back from the police station that afternoon afraid they might be freaked-out enough to let her go. Instead they apologized for not intervening. *Sorry we just stood there like idiots, Tara,* Gordi had said, looking downright shamefaced. *He took us by surprise. But we'll be ready if it happens again.*

"Yes, I'm a cop," Brian said. "But I'm also a friend."

Is that what he was? Tara didn't know what to think since his visit to her room.

"We don't have to let you in here," Gordi said.

"Or talk to you," Lance said.

"No, you don't have to talk to me or let me in. Maybe you could just tell her I'm here."

"We never said she was here," Gordi said.

"Yeah," Lance said.

When she heard Brian exhale in exasperation, she figured it was time to step in. She walked over behind the boys. "Hey, guys, it's okay. I know him."

Gordi didn't take his eyes off Brian. "You sure, Tara?"

"Yeah. I got this."

They backed away. "We'll be right here if you need us," Gordi said. "Remember, my mom's a lawyer."

"Yeah," Lance said.

"Thanks." She stepped out onto the porch and closed the door behind her.

"Wow," Brian said.

"They were here when your asshole partner came for me the other day."

"Protective. I like it." He was dressed for work—she'd never seen him in anything other than a button-down—and his loose navy-and-white-striped tie lifted a bit in the breeze.

"You really shouldn't be here," she said, looking up and down the street.

"Don't worry. I made sure I wasn't tailed."

She couldn't help but smile at the teasing edge to his tone.

"I'm sorry to bother you at work," he said. "But you're a tough woman to get hold of."

"I kind of like it that way."

When he gave her a crooked grin, his eyes crinkled at the corners. "Would you have dinner with me tonight?"

Tara slid her hands in her back pockets. "You mean, like, a date?"

"Yeah, a date. You know, you have a couple drinks and a meal, you talk . . . You've been on dates before?"

"Yes. Just not with cops who have arrested me in the past."

If her remark gave him pause he didn't show it. "What if I promise to leave the cuffs at home? And the badge and the gun. My ID even. I'll just take one credit card so I can pay."

She couldn't help thinking that *she* should pay. Didn't she owe him almost two thousand dollars? "What about your job?" she asked.

He waved that off. "Let me worry about that." His face became serious, his eyes searching hers. "What do you say?"

This was not a good idea, going out with someone who always seemed to have the upper hand. And, given their beginning, where could this whole thing possibly go . . . But then she thought about the other night. Having him in her room, and that kiss. How it felt to be that close to him, his lips against her cheek. Just thinking about it made her heart pound till she was sure he could hear it. "Okay."

He grinned again. "Where should I pick you up?"

"Here." She still wanted to keep her family out of it.

"See you about six." He turned and jogged down the stairs.

"Your partner tell you where I worked?" she called after him.

He gave her a breezy shrug. "I told you. I'm a detective."

Yes, he was a detective. Which was kind of the problem.

But she waved goodbye, already wondering how the hell she was going to focus on work for the rest of the day.

꩜

A little before six she ducked into the bathroom to freshen up. The downstairs powder room had become hers, Gordi and Lance always used the upstairs bathroom. They were thoughtful that way. Both of them would make good boyfriends someday, if they ever got out of the house and interacted with actual people.

Eddie had the truck that day, which meant she couldn't stop home and change before dinner. The jeans and boho floral blouse would have to do. But that was okay. The soft green tones complemented her hair, which was always piled on top of her head by the end of the day. She refreshed her mascara, the only makeup she bothered with, because it defined her pale eyes a bit.

When she came out of the bathroom Brian was there. Gordi was giving him a tour, answering questions about their equipment and videos, showing off some of Tara's artwork on the walls. Although Brian seemed to have won Gordi over, Lance stood back with his arms crossed, the usual stoic expression on his face. Tara joined him, and he leaned toward her. "You sure about this guy?"

She gave him a sheepish smile. "Not really."

They left shortly after that, and conversation was pretty seamless on the drive to the restaurant. Brian asked a lot of questions about the You-Tube channel and how it all worked. She was grateful for the distraction. It kept her from focusing too much on the smell of his car. She didn't know if the hint of spice and citrus was cologne or just him, but it caused a fluttering in her stomach.

He took her to Brennan's, an Irish pub in West Manor. It was busy, but not yet packed with a full Friday night crowd. They were seated in a green leather booth and the hostess said someone would be with them in a few. But as soon as Tara looked at the menu, she knew she wouldn't be able to eat. Her nerves were shot. Part of it was being on a date for the first time in over two years. Part of it was that the date was with him. One minute she told herself this was a huge mistake, the next minute she wanted to slide over next to him.

"I hope this place is okay," he said. "It won Best Local Pub in Westchester for three years in a row."

"This is great." She glanced around at the various maps of Ireland on the walls, the pictures of the Irish countryside. "My mom was from County Down."

"Have you ever been there?" he asked.

"No. I'd love to go sometime. I have family over there I've never met. My parents used to talk about taking us there, but they've both been out of the picture for a long time, so we never got the chance to go." She focused on her menu, thinking she'd spare him the details of all that sad family history for now.

But then she realized something.

"You already knew that, didn't you," she said.

He looked up from his menu.

"I mean, you've read some kind of file on me, right? So you already know my mom died when I was nine, and my dad took off when I was twelve. You know about my assault charge. You probably know my brother, Eddie, has a traumatic brain injury."

He shifted in his seat and dropped his eyes. He couldn't deny it.

She yanked her shoulders up. "You might already know my sister's a closet hoarder, even though I just found out."

He cocked his head. "I didn't know that last one."

"This is not how it's supposed to work," she said, shutting her menu. "Usually when you go out with someone you share the good first. When you're ready, you share the bad and the ugly. But you already know all of it."

A waitress approached the table, but before she could speak Brian asked her to give them a few minutes. Then he put his menu aside. "Okay. Let's even this out." He sat forward in his seat, forearms on the table. "The first thing you should probably know is that my partner, Hank Doyle, is also my uncle."

"Seriously?"

"Yes. And you're right," he said. "He's an asshole sometimes. The next thing is I was married. I rushed into it when I was twenty-six, and it lasted four years. She lives in the city now, sells high-end real estate to the rich and famous. She had some romantic notion about being married to a cop." His brow furrowed. "I think I was worried about ending up alone, like my uncle. We were completely wrong for each other, and she couldn't even wait until we split to find the next guy."

Whatever Brian Nolan's faults, Tara decided then and there his ex was a fool.

He kept going. "I dropped out of college and wasted a few years before I joined the force. When I was nineteen I caused a minor accident because I was driving drunk, but I got out of it because of Hank. He helped me out of a few scrapes with the law back then, which, I know, isn't fair really. But he cut me slack because I was dealing with some heavy stuff. That leads me to this last one . . ." He scraped a hand through his hair. "I lost both my parents when I was fifteen. They were shot and killed."

Tara drew a sharp breath and held it while she absorbed his words. There was the shock of hearing how his parents died and the realization that, like her, he'd lost them both when he was far too young.

"It happened in our kitchen," he said. "It looked like they came home and surprised an intruder, or intruders. We don't know because the case has never been solved, and it never will be. Whoever did it got away with it." His eyes never left hers, and she recognized the pain he carried in them, a bottomless pain that came with such loss. "But to be honest, I'll always believe it was my fault. If they hadn't left the house that night, chances are no one would have broken in. But I blew off my curfew, and I know damn well they went out looking for me." He paused, blinked a couple times, flopped back against the booth like he was suddenly drained. "Now *you've* read *my* file."

Tara didn't know what to say, what words would be worthy of such raw honesty. She offered the only ones that came to mind. "That was quite a spiel."

"Thanks."

She wanted to say more, but a surge of abrasive laughter drew their attention to the bar area, where a group of people had taken over several tables. It was irrational but Tara resented them—along with the other noisy patrons and bustling waitstaff—for intruding.

"I'm not hungry," Brian said. "Are you hungry?"

She shook her head.

"Wanna get out of here?"

She nodded.

～

When he reached out his hand to lead her from the restaurant she gripped it with both of hers, and she didn't let go until he opened her car door and she had to climb in. There was no real discussion about where they were going. He simply said, "My place isn't far from here," and she nodded. What was there to talk about? It's not like her place was an option.

They barely spoke on the drive. She could sense a nervous anticipation building between them, and it was like they were both afraid of diminishing it with filler conversation. Considering he'd just bared his soul to her, words seemed insufficient. But while he drove she was hyperaware of him, the intensity in his eyes when they slid her way, the nearness of his arm, the way his hands gripped the wheel.

He exited the Taconic Parkway just north of downtown White Plains. The busy neighborhood was a mix of houses and apartment buildings, close to the Pace University law campus. He lived in a fairly nondescript six-story brick structure with large windows. The lobby was lined with mailboxes, and a small elevator took them to the third floor, where she followed him down a carpeted hallway.

"Don't expect too much," he said, stopping in front of a door halfway down the hall. A small plaque to the side read *#312*.

"You've seen my place, remember? The tiny room, in the attic, in the house I share with my siblings."

"I like yours better." He pulled keys from his pocket and unlocked the door, holding it open so she could enter first.

She walked into a living area that was separated from a galley kitchen by a small counter with two barstools tucked under it. The apartment was contemporary style, with wood floors, sleek appliances, modern cabinetry. It was tidy and functional but screamed Single Man. The countertop was bare, a large TV was the center of focus, and there were no personal touches, other than a shelf of paperbacks. She would have bet money that, after his divorce, he saw this staged apartment and rented it as is, furniture and all.

He dropped his keys on the counter. "Pretty cliché bachelor pad," he said.

She stepped over to the window, which faced the back of the building. There was a ground-level pool down there, adjoining a large grassy area. Everything about his place indicated a comfortable existence. But maybe a lonely one too.

"Can I get you something?" he asked. "I have beer or white wine."

It seemed unlikely Brian Nolan was a white wine drinker. He probably

kept it on hand for just such an occasion. Or maybe he bought it specifically, hoping she'd come here. "Beer's fine," she said.

While he went to the fridge for drinks she wandered over to the
bookshelf and ran her fingers along the spines. "Detective novels. Now,
that's cliché."

He brought her a bottle of Heineken. "It would be a lot more cliché
if I'd read any of them."

They both laughed, and when their eyes met it brought her back to
the things he had told her at the restaurant. Now that they were standing
face-to-face in the quiet, no distractions, she said what she'd been thinking. "I'm so sorry about your parents."

"Thanks." He glanced down at his bottle. "I kind of laid a lot on you
back there. I hope I didn't overshoot."

She shook her head.

For a moment the surrealness of the situation struck her. She was
standing in the apartment of a cop who helped send her to prison, but
felt badly enough about it to give her money without hope of gain or rec-
ognition. Even before that, going back to that third interview, he seemed
to have her best interest at heart. And the way he was looking at her now
caused a thrilling shiver throughout her whole body, like all her senses
were on high alert. But there was some anxiety wrapped up in it.

"Brian, there's something I should tell you."

"Okay." His brows ticked up and she saw a wariness in his eyes, like
he was afraid she might say she wasn't interested, or she had a boyfriend,
or maybe some disease.

She reached down to place her bottle of beer on the coffee table. "It's
just . . ." This was embarrassing. "I haven't done this in a long time."

There was unmistakable relief in the way his shoulders settled. "We
don't have to do *this* tonight." He angled his bottle toward the couch.
"We can sit and talk. Or order a pizza and watch TV. I don't care."

She could tell he meant it by the earnest expression on his face. He
would be fine just spending time talking with her. But she didn't want
to talk.

She took the bottle from his hand and put it down next to hers. Then
she stepped to him, close enough that she had to tilt her head up to his. "I
didn't say I didn't want to. It's just been a while."

His eyes roamed around her face, which was warming up, as if she could feel his gaze touch down on her hair, her cheeks, her lips. She laid her hands on his chest so she could feel the rise and fall of it through his shirt. That seemed to give him some kind of permission because he took her face in his hands.

When he first brought his lips to hers it was light, tentative, like he was testing the waters. But it didn't take long to become more serious, slow, deep kisses that went on until they had to come up for air. At some point she offered up a silent thanks that he was good at it. When her arms went around his neck, he slid his hands down her back, pressing her against him.

She didn't know if he was being thoughtful or trying to drive her crazy by waiting for her to take the lead, but that's what happened. She went to work on his shirt, slipping open each button so she could run her palms over his skin. Only then did he lift her blouse over her head and trail his fingertips across her shoulders. Desire hit her hard and fast. It had been a long time, but it wasn't just that. It was him. His light stubble against her cheek, his solid arms around her, his warm hands on her body. The way he was gentle and urgent at the same time.

When she paused the action he drew back a bit and searched her face, like he was looking for a sign that she was changing her mind. But she just asked a question: "I assume this cliché bachelor pad has a bedroom?"

He took her hand and led her across the living room, into a bedroom she didn't take notice of because he pulled her to him as soon as they made it in there, and they were tangled up in each other again.

After that, most conscious thought was gone for a while. Instinct took over. He was still a cop and she was still a criminal, but Tara figured everything that came before had led them to that moment.

Chapter Seventeen

———————

At work the following Monday morning Brian could not keep his mind from straying to that night no matter how hard he tried to focus on the tedious task at hand: watching hours of CCTV footage from the Costco parking lot. He and Hank had been at it most of the morning.

Hank ejected the latest disc from the machine. "I'll go grab the next couple DVDs and fresh coffees," he said, rising from the table and whistling as he headed out to his desk. He was in a better mood the last couple days.

The good news was Roland Shea was back in town. As mysteriously as he disappeared from the Costco parking lot ten days ago, he turned back up at his house Friday night. The bad news was it meant Brian and Hank had worked Saturday and Sunday because there was no way they were letting him go again. Brian was looking forward to the light at the end of this long Roland tunnel. Sending him away would be a nice payoff after two years of work, and it felt like it would close the chapter on any involvement Tara ever had with the guy.

But Brian's frustration level was peaking. He hadn't been able to see Tara since he dropped her home Friday night. She didn't stay over at his place because she didn't want her family to worry, and he wasn't sure she was ready to have him come by the house. But he couldn't talk to her because she didn't have a damn phone, he never thought of getting an email address, and the whole thing was beginning to feel like a dream.

He hadn't planned to blurt out the darkest moments of his life sitting across from her in a busy pub, but he could tell she was close to calling the whole thing off when she talked about him reading her file: *This is not how it's supposed to work.* She was right. Before he even met her he knew details about her family history, her personal life, her occupation. He had access to her bank and cell phone records, forced his way into her home to arrest her. Even his good intentions, giving her that money, put her at a disadvantage. How could she *not* feel like he had all the power. So he decided to level the playing field as much as he could. And once he started talking he kept going, admitting things he had never told anyone before. After that he couldn't imagine staying in that busy restaurant and backsliding into small talk over a meal.

Hank returned and unwrapped the next DVD Costco had sent over. The whole point was to see when Roland returned to his car and how he got there, look for any indication of where he'd gone or who he'd been with. Hank slipped the next disc into the player and once again the north-west section of the Costco parking lot appeared on the TV. Roland's SUV sat in the lower left corner, where it had been since he vanished. Hank hit the fast-forward button, but at a lower speed so they didn't miss anything.

On Friday night, when Tara said there was something she should tell him, Roland crossed Brian's mind, the idea that they were still involved in some way. Then he feared she was going to say their date was a mistake, and she just wanted to go home. When she told him, with trepidation in her eyes, that it had been a long time since she was with anybody, he was humbled by her honesty. He found he was nervous, didn't want to disappoint. So he went slow and took cues from her, in case she changed her mind or felt like she was rusty. But she seemed to know what she wanted, and she didn't move like she was rusty.

Afterward they ended up ordering that pizza and drinking some of those Heinekens. But they hardly put a dent in any of it before he couldn't take it anymore: her on his couch, bare legs tucked under her and hair loose around her face, wearing only his partially buttoned shirt. They'd gone for Round Two right there in the living room.

"... see that, Bri?"

Brian jerked his coffee, spilling a bit on the table. "What?"

Hank was pushing buttons on the DVD player. The video on the screen stopped, rewound. "I asked if you saw that." He started the video again and after a few seconds a car pulled into the Costco parking lot and stopped directly behind Roland's SUV. It sat there a few moments, then

Roland climbed out of the passenger seat, waved at the driver, and headed to his vehicle. The other car took off, as did Roland shortly after.

The driver of the other vehicle wasn't visible on camera, but they had the make and model of the car, along with a partial license plate, so it wouldn't be too hard to track the person down. It was an added bonus that the car was a little unusual, not only in color, but also Chrysler stopped making that model almost ten years ago.

Which meant there were only so many bright yellow PT Cruisers in the Greater New York area.

~

The next day he decided to reach out to Tara the only way he could think of, but it was a gamble, and he didn't want to screw it up. Which is why he decided to call in Rosemary for backup.

When they met in town during her work break that morning she was wearing the same general secretary clothes she'd been wearing as long as he could remember: modest skirt and blouse with low heels, brown curls framing her face. She gave Brian a tight Rosemary hug and kissed him on the cheek, told him he looked good though he could stand to gain some weight, the same thing she always told him.

"Now," she said, glancing at the flower shop they were standing in front of, "what are we doing here?"

"I want to send someone flowers, but I have no idea what to send—I've never even been in one of these places. And you know about this stuff, with all your gardening . . ."

Rosemary's eyes grew and she smiled wide. "Who are you sending them to?"

"A woman."

"Yes, Brian. I figured they were for a woman. Who is she?"

He'd forgotten his aunt would want details. "Her name is Tara."

She clasped her hands together in front of her. "Oh, that's a lovely name. And how did you meet?"

He didn't want to lie to Rosemary, so he considered saying it—*I arrested her*—figuring they might have a laugh. Until she found out Tara went to prison for drug trafficking. "We met through work," he said.

She waited for more and then sighed. "I guess that's all I'm getting for now. So, let's do this."

They entered the shop and Brian was immediately grateful he'd called her. It was overwhelming, the multitude of colors, scents, sizes, and shapes of flowers on display, filling the space and lining the shelves of a huge cooler. His cheeks burned when Rosemary walked right up to the counter and explained that Brian wanted to have a bouquet delivered to "a new lady friend." When the florist smiled and asked what he was looking for, he offered a helpless shrug.

Rosemary put a hand on his arm. "The important thing with flowers is sending the right ones, for her and for the situation. Think about what you're trying to say. Is this a special occasion? Are you two serious, or just getting to know each other? Maybe you're going for a little romance . . ." She lifted her shoulders in question.

None of that was right. There was no special occasion, and though this thing with Tara was new, they were way past just getting to know each other. He rested his hands on his hips and glanced around the store, considered what he was trying to say to her, why he'd even thought of doing this in the first place. Then he looked back at Rosemary. "She thinks she's not a flowers kind of girl. I want to change her mind."

Rosemary grinned. "Something tells me I'm going to like this Tara. You should bring her to the wedding."

The wedding. The one Brian still hadn't told Hank he planned to attend. And it was only a few weeks away. "We'll see," he said.

Rosemary turned to the woman behind the counter. "Well, you heard the man."

They took it from there, and Brian didn't even blink when the florist charged $140 to his credit card.

～⤙

By Thursday afternoon he decided, one way or another, he was going to see Tara before the day ended. So he told Hank he needed a night off.

"Oh yeah?" Hank said, looking up from across the desks. "Is it that marketing girl?"

"Just some stuff I have to take care of."

Hank chuckled. "Sure. Tell her I said hello."

Brian let it go. He wasn't breathing a word about Tara to his uncle until this Roland Shea business was definitely over. "Thanks."

"And listen," Hank said, "I booked us on that fishing boat off Montauk next month. On the seventeenth. Already requested the day off for both of us."

Brian's gut twisted. The seventeenth. Rosemary's wedding date.

His uncle lowered his voice. "Figured we'd get out of here for the day, you know?"

Jesus. Brian had waited too long. "Look, there's something I was going to mention to you . . ."

But Hank's desk phone rang. He held up a hand to Brian while he answered it. Then he covered the mouthpiece. "Gotta take this. A new report."

Brian nodded. As soon as Hank got off the phone, he would set the record straight and offer to go fishing another time.

While he waited he checked his email inbox to find a DMV report pertaining to the yellow PT Cruiser from the Costco camera footage. The vehicle was registered to an Andrea Leary. He stared at the name for a moment. It was vaguely familiar. She was twenty-nine, lived in lower Manhattan, had a couple minor drug charges on her record. He read through the report a few times, but if Brian had come across her before, he couldn't remember when.

Across the desks, Hank ended his call and hung up. "That was a possible theft or fraud I have to follow up on tomorrow afternoon. Local guy, owns a payroll company. He says there's cash gone from his business account, tax money that didn't end up where it was supposed to go."

"Is that right?" Brian couldn't care less about a new payroll company case. He was trying to decide how to give his uncle the bad news.

"Yeah," Hank said. "But he sounded pretty old, a little out of it. We'll see what I get tomorrow."

"Hank, that fishing trip sounds great," Brian said. "But maybe we could—"

"It's partly a thank-you, Bri. I've been a pain in the ass lately, and I'm sorry." He offered a sad smile. "I know you put up with a lot."

Brian was momentarily stunned into silence by that very un-Hank-like apology. And the remorse in his uncle's eyes when he offered it. "It's okay," Brian said.

Hank sighed. "Sorry. I interrupted." He waved toward Brian to continue.

But he couldn't tell him. Not after what Hank had just said, and not sitting at their desks. At the least Brian could take him to Dunne's and talk to him about it over dinner. But not tonight.

He pointed to his computer screen. "I was going to tell you the PT Cruiser is registered to an Andrea Leary. Lives down in the Village. Ring any bells?"

"No. Does she have a record?" Hank asked.

"Just some petty drug stuff going way back. I feel like I've heard the name before, but I'll have to think about it."

"Well," Hank said, giving him a cocked brow, "since you're gonna be busy with the marketing girl tonight, you can dig into it tomorrow."

Chapter Eighteen

Geraldine had to drag herself out of bed Thursday morning. She'd slept terribly the night before, and her mind felt groggy, her limbs heavy and slow. Really what she wanted to do was soothe her soul by making a cup of tea and sitting among her things. First in her room, then across the hall in Tara's old room. After that she'd spend a couple hours in the basement, saving the shed out back for last. But she'd make darn sure no one else was home before she went to the shed—it was the only place she had left. Eddie and Tara never thought to look out there.

She would have called in sick for only the third time since she started working for Mr. Bertucci, but he'd phoned her the night before to say he would be by that afternoon to check in. Besides, she had a session with Judy first thing that morning. If she canceled, Eddie and Tara might use it as an excuse to start throwing her stuff away.

As soon as Geraldine walked through the door Judy mentioned how tired she looked, and she started asking questions in her lulling voice, reminding Geraldine their time together was just for her, she was in a safe place. So Geraldine sank into the comfy client chair and admitted she hadn't been sleeping well. And when Judy asked why not she said she was overwhelmed lately, falling behind—"just a little"—at work, frustrated with how things were going at home.

And it felt so good to unload, to have someone really listen and try to understand, that Geraldine kept talking. When Judy asked what was causing the stress Geraldine said it was Tara because that seemed the best way to sum it up. She talked about how her sister had disrupted everything since she came home, how she didn't respect any of Geraldine's rules. Dinnertime was never consistent now, Eddie and Conor wouldn't go to church anymore. Tara's "job" drawing video game characters didn't contribute enough to the household budget.

"I hear your frustration," Judy said. "But it might help to keep in mind that Tara's been through a lot lately. Transitioning back home can't be easy. She essentially has to rebuild her life."

"Well, she did it to herself," Geraldine said. "Frankly, Tara just needs to grow up already. I mean, she still clings to our mom's old fairy tales, for pity's sake, and she tells them to Conor. Fills his head with heroes, romance, and supernatural beings."

"The fairy tales sound kind of beautiful," Judy said. "And they can be useful too. They teach us life lessons, give us comfort and hope."

"That's what church is for, but Tara turned her back on that a long time ago."

"You could argue that fairy tales and religion are alike in some ways. They were both created to help people cope with life's hardships. And they only work when someone has faith in them, believes them to be true."

Geraldine gave her a doubtful look. "Fairy tales aren't real. Especially the one Mom made up about us."

Judy smiled. "Your mom made up a fairy tale about the three of you?"

"Yes. She called it 'The Connellys of County Down.'"

"That's wonderful. Tell me about it."

"I think I forgot some of it." Geraldine couldn't remember the last time she let herself think about that story.

"Just the gist then."

Geraldine reached for the water glass Judy always had sitting there for her and took a sip. "If I recall, Eddie, Tara, and I spent our days trekking through the County Down countryside, looking for Connelly Castle, our rightful home." She rolled her eyes at the silliness of it. "One day Tara got it in her head that the castle might be on the other side of the Fairy Forest. So, *of course*, she ran off to see if that was true, and she dragged Eddie with her. And, *of course*, they ended up getting trapped in the forest so I had to go after them."

"Did you find them?"

"Yeah, I found them and pulled them out of the bog." The more Geraldine talked about this, the more unsettled she felt. She rushed through the rest. "After that we had to use our special powers—Mom gave each of us a special power—to get through the forest together and find the castle."

"What was your special power?" Judy asked.

Geraldine took another sip of water, tried to wash down the sudden constriction in her throat. "In the story, I was . . . strong. I took care of Eddie and Tara."

Judy's whole face softened, as did her voice. "That's how your mom saw you, Geraldine."

Without warning the constriction spread to Geraldine's chest. She looked away from Judy and drew in a deep breath, cleared her throat. "Anyway, Tara won't let it go. She's always asking me for details."

"When Tara asks about the fairy tales or shares them with Conor, it might be her way of remembering and mourning things she lost in her childhood." Judy was quiet for a moment. "Do you ever think about the things you lost? It must have been extremely difficult for you, taking on all that responsibility at such a young age."

"It was a lot of work and worry, that's for sure."

"I can only imagine. You were a teenager who had to support a household and raise two kids. Not everyone could or would do that, Geraldine," Judy said, tilting her head the way she did when she seemed to think she was making an important observation. "You kept Eddie and Tara safe and sound, got them through their school years, through Eddie's hospitalizations. It's really quite remarkable, and you should be very proud of that."

Geraldine felt her face heat up. She hadn't really thought of it that way before. During those years, while all that was going on, she mostly just felt . . . inadequate. There was never enough time to do everything—work, take care of the house and bills, watch over Eddie and Tara. And there was never enough money. That's when she had started holding on to things, afraid to throw something away in case they needed it later or it became valuable in the future. She shrugged a shoulder. "I was the oldest, so I had to figure it out."

"Yes, and you had to sacrifice a lot to take care of Eddie and Tara, didn't you? Your own childhood, friends, passions . . ."

That photo came to Geraldine's mind, the one Tara had found and put up on the mantel: her younger self dressed in her tap dancing costume, standing next to Jenny in a line with the rest of their class. Geraldine hadn't looked at it again since shoving it in the kitchen drawer. "It was my job to keep our family together."

"And that's exactly what you did."

When Geraldine raised her glass to gulp more water her hand was shaky.

"Maybe before we meet next you could try a little assignment," Judy said. "Find a few quiet minutes for yourself and write down the things you lost when you were younger."

"Oh, I don't know," Geraldine said, leaning over to put her water glass on the side table. "I'm very busy with work."

"Okay. Maybe just start the list, and you can work on it as you have time. There are no wrong answers or silly answers."

Geraldine flipped her hands up in question. "What good will that do me?"

Judy briefly pressed her lips together. "I think it could help you find some compassion for yourself. And you deserve that. You really do."

If Judy hadn't ended their appointment right after that, Geraldine would have.

~

Six whole hours later, her mind still drifted to that session. It felt good to vent to Judy, but these talks were getting more and more uncomfortable. And Geraldine hadn't even told Judy the biggest reason she'd been awake all night. It was because there was no more denying it, *something* was going on between Tara and that Brian Nolan. And the last thing Geraldine needed right now was for a policeman to be hanging around.

When she arrived home from work the day before yesterday, a huge bouquet of flowers had been sitting on the front porch. This was no Stop & Shop selection, someone paid a professional florist a lot of money to put it together. It was an explosion of delicate flowers: small pink roses and peonies, amber mums and orchids, scarlet carnations and lilies. Airy greenery was mixed in, and it was all gathered in a burlap wrap, tied with a red ribbon. It was one of the most beautiful things Geraldine had ever seen in real life. Which is why her first thought was they'd been delivered to the wrong house. But the envelope attached to the ribbon said *Tara* in an elegant script.

Geraldine scooped up the fragrant flowers and brought them in to the kitchen table, where she stared at them for several minutes, tempted to throw them away. Nothing good could come from this. Tara had enough to be thinking about, like getting a real job. She didn't need to be distracted by some man. And what kind of guy would even want an *ex-convict*? Tara would end up getting hurt. As the big sister Geraldine should at least see who sent them.

She used a knife to slip the envelope flap open, which was barely sealed so maybe it wasn't meant to be a secret anyway. Then, with growing dread that settled in her stomach like a brick, she read the card. Over and over again, until she heard the truck pull up the driveway. She slipped the card back in the envelope and waited. It was too late to throw the flowers away.

When Eddie, Tara, and Conor piled in, they noticed the bouquet immediately.

"What are those?" Eddie asked.

Geraldine jerked her shoulders up and down. "They were on the front porch when I got here."

"Wow," Tara said. "They're gorgeous."

"They're for you," Eddie said with a sly grin, pointing to the little envelope.

When she reached for it and slid out the card, Eddie leaned over, trying to read it across the table. Geraldine could have told him what it said: *Sure you're not a flowers kind of girl? —Brian*

If Geraldine had been holding out hope there was nothing going on between her sister and that policeman, the slow smile that spread across Tara's face killed it dead.

"What was *that*?" Eddie asked.

Tara's eyes darted to him as she pulled the card to her chest. "What?"

"That smile." He pointed to her face and looked at Conor. "Did you see that?"

Conor raised his brows and nodded.

"Who are they from?" Eddie asked.

Tara slid the card in her back pocket. "No one."

"Bullshit."

"Potty mouth, Eddie!" Geraldine said.

Tara picked up the bouquet and headed for the stairs to her room.

"Hey," Eddie called after her. "I want to meet him, Tare." He took his hat off and laughed a little. Then his eyes landed on Geraldine, dropped briefly to her throat, where her fingers played with her cross. "What's wrong with you?"

"Nothing," she said. "I just think she has more important worries than dating right now."

"Jesus, Geraldine. Can't you just be happy for her?" Eddie had shaken his head and climbed up the stairs then, without giving her a chance to respond.

~≺~

It was just about four fifteen, which was when Mr. Bertucci said to expect him, so once again Geraldine would not be getting to the quarterly taxes that day. Lucking into Tara's old bank account had been an answer to her prayers. She'd moved the tax money into the account without raising any flags, and once the IRS processed the payments, she would close it for good. No one would ever be the wiser. Now all she had to do was get the quarterlies done. The problem was she kept putting it off, because the Q folder sitting in her bottom drawer grew by the day and even looking at it now made her break out in a sweat.

As Mr. Bertucci parked in front and made his way inside, he looked even older and frailer than the last time Geraldine had seen him just a month ago. He declined coffee and dropped into a chair, like the walk from his car had exhausted him.

"It is with a heavy heart I come today, Geraldine."

She folded her hands on her desk and waited. Perhaps Mrs. Bertucci had taken a turn for the worse.

"I think there may be money missing from the account," he said.

The room spun in a violent way for a moment as Geraldine absorbed those words.

He held his hands up. "I don't know for sure, but it appears there may be some kind of fraudulent activity going on."

She swallowed so her voice would sound steady. "What makes you say that?"

"Dunbar Construction got a call from the regional IRS office asking about their quarterly tax payment." He shrugged. "I knew you sent those in weeks ago so I figured it was a misunderstanding."

"I'm sure it is—I can follow up right away, Mr. Bertucci."

"I already did. I figured why bother you with this, you did what you were supposed to do, eh? So I checked the account." He sat forward in his chair, elbows on the armrests. "The money is not there, Geraldine. There is at least ten thousand dollars that's unaccounted for, maybe more."

She stopped breathing. This was it. The whole house of cards was about to come tumbling down. Mr. Bertucci knew she took the money, and she was going to be *fired* and sent to *prison*. What would happen to all her things?

He reached over and patted her arm. "I know how upsetting this is, my good friend. The most important thing is this: you can't blame yourself. This kind of thing happens these days." He waved his hand about. "These hackers, they get into accounts all the time now."

Maybe this wasn't it after all. Geraldine leaned forward on her desk and used her most pragmatic voice. "Mr. Bertucci, there's probably a good reason for this. For instance, there's usually a delay between when the money leaves our account and the IRS processes it. If you just let me follow up, I bet I can figure out what's going on."

"That would be wonderful, Geraldine. If I'm missing something, surely you will catch it. But, in the meantime, I called the police."

Geraldine began to feel sick. "You did?"

"I spoke to them today, a Detective Hank Doyle, and I explained everything. He's coming tomorrow to talk in person."

"Oh my."

"Yes, he seemed very good." Mr. Bertucci gathered his palms together and pushed his hands toward Geraldine. "You will be here, eh? You can provide details. And Detective Doyle said if it appears the money was stolen, they will try to trace it."

Could they do that? Trace the money? If they could, they would find it in an account under the name of Tara Connelly. Who'd just gotten out of *prison* and had a *drug felony* on her record. Geraldine searched Mr.

Bertucci's kind eyes and thought about just blurting out the truth—*I fell behind and I didn't want to worry you* . . . It wasn't good, but nothing was beyond repair yet, was it?

Though, he still might press charges, and he would have to fire her because he could never trust her again. She would lose her income, the job she loved, and the one person in her life who truly appreciated her. She would have nothing.

Maybe she could still find a way out of this.

She came around the desk and knelt down next to him. "Mr. Bertucci, you know I'll do anything I can to help."

Chapter Nineteen

Before Tara left work Thursday afternoon she received some unexpected news. At the end of the day Gordi and Lance wheeled their desk chairs over to her table.

"You're getting a small raise next paycheck," Gordi said, big smile on his face.

"Yeah," Lance said.

"I appreciate it, guys," Tara said, packing up her bag. "But you can't afford to give me a raise."

Gordi turned his hands over. "We had dinner with our financial backer last night, and she says we're not paying you enough." They all knew the financial backer was Gordi's mom. "Oh, she loved the button-down shirts by the way."

Tara grinned. "Told you."

"And she cried happy tears when I told her Gordi asked out the barista," Lance said.

Gordi's face went bright red. "I think what really did it was when I said we were registering for those coding classes this summer. She knew it was your idea before we even told her."

Tara had suggested the coding classes earlier that week, sold the boys on the idea of working toward financial independence and having more options in the future.

"Yeah," Lance said. "Gordi's mom thinks you're a hero."

Tara was still riding high from their discussion later in the evening when she headed down to the kitchen to add fresh water to Brian's flowers and just stare at them for a bit. They were stunning. She couldn't remember receiving such a perfect gift before. It had been good timing too. Granted, she didn't have a phone. But after not hearing from him for three days she had begun to wonder if she'd made more of their night together than he did. She didn't want to get carried away; however, despite their turbulent history, or maybe because of it, she felt so drawn to him that night. So much so it scared her. It was like they were doing this whole relationship thing backward. Usually dating came before the sex, and they hadn't even had a meal together yet.

After setting the flowers front and center on the table she took inventory of the fridge and cabinets, searching for dinner possibilities. It was actually Geraldine's turn to cook, but she was working in her room again. She was doing a lot of that lately, staying upstairs, only coming down briefly to eat, so they hadn't seen much of her. But she was going to all her therapy sessions. Judy called Eddie just that afternoon, with Geraldine's permission, to schedule another family session. And Geraldine hadn't bought anything from Harriet's in a couple of weeks. That was progress.

Tara had just decided to throw leftovers together in a veggie noodle soup when there was a light rapping on the front door window.

Brian was standing there, waving at her through the glass. Even as she checked the stairs to see if anyone was coming down, pure excitement pulsed through her.

She stepped out onto the porch and pulled the door shut behind her.

"You really need to get a phone," he said.

"I know. I'm going to—"

He leaned forward and stopped her with a soft kiss. "Hi," he said.

"I love the flowers."

"That's good. I was afraid that might go the other way."

She laughed, but she was thinking about what to do next. Invite him inside, where her family would join them at any moment? She'd be happy to just go with him right then. Out to dinner. Or back to his apartment.

But then the door opened, and Eddie stuck his head out. "What's going on . . ." When he saw Brian standing there, his curious expression clenched into anger. He stepped out next to Tara and raised an arm to tuck her behind him. "What the hell are you doing here, Nolan? Come to collect on a debt?"

Tara touched Eddie's shoulder. "No, Eddie. It's okay."

"Get inside, Tara," he said, keeping his eyes on Brian. "You got a lotta balls showing up here."

Brian held his hands up. "Wait a sec—"

"Turn the hell around"—Eddie jabbed a finger over Brian's shoulder—"and get back in your car."

"I'm not here on the job."

"What the hell does that mean?" Leading with his chest, Eddie stepped closer to him.

Tara tugged on his arm. "Eddie, stop. It's all right."

He turned to her.

"It's okay," she said, nodding to confirm.

His face twisted up in confusion, and he stared at her for a while before his eyes jumped to Brian and back to her. Slowly his expression cleared and he faced her full-on, his back to Brian. "You gotta be fuckin' kidding me, Tare," he said. He looked more desperate than angry.

"It's okay," she said again. "Really."

His gaze, filled with dread, slid around to Brian. "Are you the one who sent the flowers?"

Brian nodded.

Eddie puffed out a long incredulous breath, leaned over to brace his hands against his knees, and shook his head. Then he stood, lifted his hat off, and put it back on. "Well then, maybe you should come in for a beer," he said, his voice laced with resignation.

"Oh, no," Tara said. "He doesn't have to—"

"I'd love to," Brian said.

Eddie headed inside. Tara watched Brian follow him and enter their front door for the second time. But this time, he'd been invited.

～✦～

While she chopped vegetables to throw in a simmering broth and threw together a mixed green salad, Tara paid close attention to what was happening in the next room. Another surreal moment: her brother bringing Brian a bottle of Bud and making awkward conversation in their living room while she cooked dinner.

She prepped the food and listened while they exchanged surface histories. Brian answered Eddie's questions: he was originally from White Plains and had always lived there, no family other than his aunt and uncle, he'd been on the force for ten years. And Eddie did the same: the Connellys had always lived in Port Chester, Eddie had a ten-year-old son upstairs, he'd been with Dunbar Construction since graduating from high school. Tara couldn't help thinking that Brian already knew all that about Eddie, and then some.

When she noticed Conor standing halfway down the stairs she wondered how long he'd been there, gripping the railing and gaping at the man who had barged in one morning and taken his aunt away in handcuffs.

"Hey, Con-man," she said.

Eddie and Brian took notice and stood as Conor came down, his eyes locked on Brian.

"Con," Eddie said. "This is Brian."

"It's nice to meet you, Conor. I've heard good things." Brian held out his hand.

But Conor only offered an apprehensive frown. "I remember you."

Brian dropped his hand. "I'm sorry about the last time I was here. I've felt badly about it for a long time." His eyes flicked to Tara's and then Eddie's. "Maybe at some point you can give me another shot."

Conor's expression softened a bit and his mouth puckered to the side, but he stayed quiet.

"You know what, Conor," Tara said. "I think we could all use a joke about now."

He thought for a moment before turning to Brian. "What happened when all the toilets were stolen from the police station?"

"What?"

"The cops had nothing to go on."

Brian laughed. "Can I use that one at work?"

"Yeah." Conor looked Tara's way then, and she gave him a wink and a grateful smile.

While Eddie and Brian took seats at the table, Conor ran to get Geraldine for dinner. Tara dished up soup and salad.

"Sorry," she said to Brian. "You came on leftover night. Not my best effort."

"Are you kidding? I live on vending machines and takeout."

Eddie took a swig from his beer. "Tara's a good cook, but did you know she's a vegetarian?"

"Nope," Brian said, glancing up at her. "That wasn't in the file."

Conor came back down, followed by Geraldine. She stopped at the bottom of the stairs.

"Hey, Ger," Tara said, transporting bowls and plates to the table. "This is Brian Nolan."

He stood to say hi and offer his hand. She reached for it slowly, like she wasn't sure she wanted to.

"Nice to meet you," she said.

"So you're the big sister."

"And you're the policeman." It sounded like an accusation.

Brian gave her a hangdog smile and nodded.

She openly stared at him. It wasn't with hostility really, more anxiety. But Geraldine had always been so nervous around the police.

Eddie cleared his throat. "Why don't you sit, Ger."

She looked down. "I think I'm going to eat in my room this evening."

"Why?" Tara asked.

"If this isn't a good night," Brian said, "I can leave . . ."

"No, it's not you, Detective Nolan," Geraldine said. "I just have a lot of work to do in my room."

"Please, it's just Brian."

She offered a smile, but it was shaky. After that she grabbed a bowl of soup and headed up the stairs.

"What was that?" Tara asked Eddie after she heard Geraldine's door close.

He rolled his eyes and shrugged. "Who knows. Let's eat."

～

Baseball was a main topic of conversation during dinner because all the boys at the table had played, or were currently playing, and they all rooted for the Yankees. Conor was the star of the show, since he'd just learned he made the traveling team. He also answered lots of questions about

Fortnite, and helped Eddie and Brian better understand what Tara did for a living.

It was hard to put into words how grateful she was to Eddie. He could have—understandably—sent Brian away, told him not to come back. At the least, he could have made the whole thing more uncomfortable. But he brought Brian another beer during dinner, bragged to him about Tara's drawings, sent Conor to fetch some of her comic strips from his room. Even his gentle teasing—*You took your life in your hands offering Tara that ride home from Taconic. Bet that was a fun trip*—went a long way toward making Brian feel welcome.

Cleanup after dinner was a group effort. Then Eddie and Conor decided to head upstairs.

"It was good to meet you again, Brian," Eddie said. "I like you better this time."

"Me too," Conor said.

They started up the stairs, but Eddie turned back. He bumped his cap up and crossed his arms. "I was just thinking, it was one hell of a coincidence you were at Taconic the morning Tara needed that ride home." His tone was almost doubtful, and Tara wondered what he was getting at.

But when she looked at Brian there was no missing the way his neck flushed. "Yeah, it was," he said.

Eddie's face broke into a knowing smile before he followed Conor up the steps.

Brian went back to drying a pot at the sink.

Tara watched him work, questioning whether it could be true, if he really planned to be there that morning. If, even after giving her that money, he wanted to see her, tell her he was sorry. The idea that she'd been on his mind to some degree for a year and a half was a little overwhelming. It was also exhilarating.

But he seemed embarrassed. "I should go," he said, setting the pot down on the counter. "I didn't mean to barge into your family dinner."

"You were invited."

He tossed the towel on the counter and turned to her. "Look, I did go up there that morning to talk to you, make sure you were okay. It wasn't an accident. I didn't tell you because it always seems like I'm"—he scratched his head—"I don't know, calling the shots between us, or setting you up in some way. Showing up unannounced." He braced a hand against the counter and looked down. "That's not what I want."

Tara stepped close and laid her hand on his. "I'm just glad you didn't pull over and kick me out of your car that morning. Because I was a real bitch."

He smiled, then let his forehead fall down gently against hers. "When can I see you again?"

He was seeing her now, but she knew that's not what he meant.

"If you give me five minutes and meet me up at the side door to my room, you can see me then."

"Deal."

~

Tara wanted the five minutes so she could talk to her sister. When she knocked on her bedroom door Geraldine opened it just enough to stick her head out.

"What is it?" she asked.

"I wanted to check on you. I'm sorry I surprised you by having Brian come to dinner. It wasn't planned."

Geraldine sighed. "Most of what you do isn't planned, Tara."

Tara tried to remember her sister was coming from a place of caring, that she was worried. "He's a good guy, Geraldine."

"Is this serious? You and him?"

"Well, it's new. But yeah, I think it might be."

Everything about Geraldine seemed to sag in that moment, her shoulders, her chest, her whole face.

"I promise you," Tara said, "I'll be careful. I know what I'm doing."

Geraldine shook her head and spoke so softly Tara almost didn't catch it. "No, you don't." Then she closed her door.

Tara thought about knocking again, demanding an explanation for such dramatic behavior. But it was probably just one of Geraldine's moods. She got like this when she couldn't control everything, make the rest of them do what she wanted.

So Tara gave up on it for the night and went to her room, where she received a much warmer welcome.

∼

Never was she more grateful to Geraldine for moving her to the attic, on the opposite side of the house from the rest of the family. She and Brian went slow, took their time with each other. Afterward they lay in her bed, wearing nothing but the top sheet, talking in low voices. The only light came through the window from a pale moon.

He told her how much he liked Eddie and Conor, apologized for upsetting Geraldine. She told him not to worry about Geraldine, she wasn't good with new people. Or most people, really.

"I can't remember the last time I was part of an actual family dinner." He was on his back, one arm folded under his head. "When I lived with my uncle it was fast food in front of the TV, but my parents and I used to eat together every night. No matter how late I had practice, my mom wouldn't put dinner on the table until I got home."

Tara was on her side, facing him. After their mom died the Connelly kids often ate alone, left to scrounge up whatever they could find for dinner. "What did your parents do?" she asked.

"My dad worked for Heineken, he was in sales. When they moved their headquarters to White Plains in the 1990s he became a senior manager. My mom stayed home for a long time, then later she was a receptionist in an insurance office." He paused. "You want to see a picture?"

She nodded.

He grabbed his pants from the floor next to the bed and pulled out his cell phone, tapped and swiped a few times before he handed it to her. "That was taken not long before they died."

The screen was filled with a photo of a lanky teenaged Brian standing between a man and a woman, one of his arms flung around each of them, big grins on all their faces. They were dressed up, like maybe they'd just come from church or dinner out. Brian had his dad's solid build and slanted smile, but his mom's twinkling eyes. Tara sensed from their expressions and body language, the way they leaned into one another, that they'd been a close family, probably easy with affection and laughs.

"What were their names?" she asked.

"Michael and Julie."

She studied them again, put names to the happy people who had died shortly after this picture was taken. For a moment she was so overcome with sorrow for the little family the tears almost started to flow. So she let her eyes roam around the rest of the photo.

"Is this the house you grew up in?" she asked.

"Yeah. It's not too far from my apartment."

It was a two-story blue house, Cape Cod style, and it sat on a large corner lot. His upbringing had been so different from hers—two loving parents, a stable home, security. Tara had none of those things, certainly not an uncle-cop who got her out of trouble with the law. She had Eddie and Geraldine though. She grew up in survival mode, always waiting for the next blow, but Brian's entire foundation was yanked away in one fell swoop. How sad it was that every time he looked at this photo he was reminded his parents were gone, that all his fond memories were likely tinged with a deep sense of loss. She knew what that was like.

She zoomed in on the picture a bit. There was a car parked in the driveway of the Cape Cod: a dark green Grand Cherokee. "Is that your car?" she asked.

"Yep. That was right after my dad bought it brand-new. It was my mom's dream car, so it was a big day in the Nolan house." His smile was wistful. "My uncle kept it for me until I got my license."

She handed his phone back and watched him take one more long look at the photo before turning it off. Almost like he was saying goodbye for now.

"What about you?" he asked. "Do you know where your father is? Have you talked to him since he left?"

For a second the old reflex wanted to kick in: just say no and change the subject. A certain shame came with talking about a criminal dad who'd abandoned his kids. But Brian had shared so much with her.

She shook her head. "He sent money for a long time. He even wrote to me at Taconic and asked if he could visit. But I didn't respond. He was a shitty father who made money stealing cars." Before the words had left her mouth she realized how hypocritical they must sound to him. In his mind, wasn't she a shitty person who once made money selling drugs? For a moment it was so tempting to tell him the truth about that night, why she was crossing that bridge with the pills under the passenger seat. But that secret didn't belong to her alone. "Anyway, after what he did to Eddie, and the way he left, I just don't want to know him." She winced. "Does that sound terrible to you?"

"No." He wrapped his arm around her and she sank down against his shoulder. "If I promise to be gone early, is it okay if I stay?" he asked.

"Yes." To confirm it she slipped her arm around his middle.

It didn't take long for her to start drifting toward sleep. Lying there alongside him, tucked into his arms, was quite possibly the safest she'd ever felt in her life.

Chapter Twenty

The next afternoon, while Hank went to interview the owner of the payroll company about his fraud complaint, Brian stayed at his desk to research Andrea Leary, the woman who had dropped Roland at his car at Costco the week before. She might be helpful in buttoning up the case against Roland. And, more than anything, Brian needed to be done with Roland Shea. The guy was like a dark shadow hanging over him and Tara, and Brian wanted to finally shake him loose.

After last night—having dinner with her family, talking in bed the way they did, spending the night with her—there was no denying the plain truth staring him in the face: Brian was falling hard. A rocky beginning was putting it mildly when it came to him and Tara, but that's probably why he felt so close to her. They never went through that whole get-to-know-a-certain-version-of-each-other-first thing; they'd cut right through that bullshit. Maybe what made them improbable also made them right for each other. Brian had spent over half his life feeling a step apart from everybody around him. After his parents died the way they did, there was no way to fit in again. It was easier to keep some distance because no one understood. But it felt like Tara did. Probably because she'd lost so much during her own childhood and had always been on the outs too.

Without a doubt there were things to work through. He needed to understand why she ever became involved with Roland Shea. There was a time when the explanation seemed simple to Brian, even obvious: either she needed the money or she fell for the wrong guy. But it was getting harder to square either of those motivations with what he was learning about her. Or maybe he just didn't want to believe either one was true.

He gave his head a shake—time to get back to work—and checked the notes he had on Andrea Leary. Here's what he knew: she was twenty-nine, lived in lower Manhattan, and worked as a hostess in a nightclub-heavy section of Greenwich Village. Perfect cover for distributing drugs for Roland or, at the least, brokering deals. He plugged her name into the database and her record popped up on his screen. There were the two possession charges, both so minor she was let off with fines. One was from four years ago in Manhattan. But the older charge, from nine years ago, had taken place in Port Chester. Maybe that's when she first connected with Roland.

He pulled up her address at the time: 418 Gillette Street.

Shit. He knew exactly where he'd seen the name Andrea Leary before. She'd been listed in Tara's arrest report from eight years ago. As the victim. This was the woman Tara punched in the face. Eddie's ex, Conor's mother.

Brian leaned back in his chair, laced his fingers behind his head. What the hell did this mean . . . Probably nothing. Eddie mentioned Conor's mother wasn't in the picture much. Even if Andrea was distributing for Roland, it didn't have anything to do with Tara. But it didn't look good, another link between her and Roland. At least that's how Hank would see it. Brian could already hear his uncle: *Roland, Tara, this Leary woman—they go way back, Bri. Probably been working together the whole time.* And he'd definitely want to talk to Andrea. Who knew what she'd say to protect herself—she might be very willing to throw Tara under the bus, especially if there were still hard feelings about that old assault. And maybe there was jealousy too. It was obvious how close Tara was to her nephew. There was no way around it—if they brought Andrea in for questioning it could hurt Tara.

Brian could ask her about Andrea, ask if she knew anything about the woman's involvement with Roland, but that would be akin to asking Tara about her own involvement with Roland. They'd be right back to cop and suspect. He wasn't sure what the answer was, but he did know that, for now, he would have to keep this info from Hank. Which meant Brian was crossing another line.

He leaned his elbows on the desk and put his head in his hands. Who the hell was he kidding. There were no more lines, he'd crossed them

188 | Tracey Lange

all long ago. And he didn't mean the night he kissed her cheek, or the morning he gave her the ride home from Taconic, or even the day he decided to put that money in her account. The first time was the day of Tara's third interview. That's when Brian had really passed the point of no return with her.

They'd asked her to come in for a final meeting. No grand show with handcuffs, just come to the station at an appointed day and time. Brian had wondered if she'd make a run for it, but she showed up as requested. When Brian, Hank, and Tara took their usual seats at the table in Interview Three, Hank flicked on the recorder and asked one question: "Miss Connelly, are you willing at this time to talk about who you were working for when you transported illegal opioids across state lines earlier this month?"

One of her hands played with a homemade bracelet on the other wrist, a pipe cleaner with chunky beads on it. She didn't raise her eyes. "No," was all she said.

Hank shook his head. "You understand this is the last time we're asking? After this, you sign your statement and we officially charge you with trafficking, which will get you at least two years, probably more."

"Yes." She focused on the bracelet. Gone was any defiance or fight.

Hank patted the table and stood. "Okay. We'll be back."

Brian rose and followed him out the door, but with reluctance. This was her last chance.

He and Hank stopped in the next room, on the other side of the one-way mirror. She slumped in her chair, touching and staring at the bracelet like it was the only thing in the world that mattered at the moment. Brian thought back to the kid, the nephew who cried while they arrested her. She was probably the only mother he had.

"Guess that's that," Hank said, shaking his head. "Foolish girl. I'll go make the call and get her statement for signature."

"Wait," Brian said. "This doesn't feel right. I thought we were trying to nail Roland, not a struggling art teacher who takes care of her family. Putting her away was never our intention." They had lost sight of that somewhere along the way. Maybe because she made them look bad when she wouldn't cooperate. She wasn't innocent, but it felt to Brian like this was less about justice and more about punishing her for not giving them what they wanted. They'd assumed the worst about her, never considered there might be something else going on. *I don't know anything about his operation . . . You have no reason to believe me, but it's true.* That's what she'd told Brian after the previous interview. Right before she asked for his help, and he turned her down.

"She knows what she's doing, Bri, and the wheels are in motion. The prosecutor needs something after all the resources that have gone into this, and we need to send a message to Roland. If she's not willing to give up her boyfriend, she's got to go down." He left to get the paperwork.

A sense of panic began to build in Brian, the feeling they were making an irrevocable mistake. He had maybe five minutes to change her mind. He poured a coffee and took it into the interview room.

"I brought you this," he said, placing the coffee in front of her. "Sorry, all out of tequila."

She didn't reach for the coffee.

He needed to get her talking. "Your name. Tara. It's Irish, right? My mom used to say all Irish names mean something. Does yours?" When Brian was growing up, his mother loved to tell him his name meant "noble." He didn't feel very noble at the moment.

"It means 'Celtic goddess of great beauty.'"

"Really?"

"No. It's Gaelic for 'rocky hill.'"

Neither of them laughed at her joke.

"My mom liked to say the goddess thing," she said, gazing into her coffee with a dull stare. "She was good at telling stories. She used to tell my sister, brother, and me a fairy tale about three siblings who had special powers and used them to save each other."

Brian had seen this before, when suspects knew they were done. Sometimes a sort of detached calm took over. She was resigned.

He asked a question, not because he thought it would yield useful info, but because he thought he might still reach her. "What was your special power?"

When she raised her eyes they were watery. "I don't know," she said, her voice shaky. "My mom died when I was young, and I don't remember." She swallowed the emotion down.

But he recognized it instantly, that feeling of utter loss. When parents die so early they take too much with them—their children's security, their strongest guiding light and biggest cheering section. It was like being left to free-fall through life with no safe place to land.

In that moment Brian hadn't given a shit about Roland Shea, or making the prosecutor happy, or slowing the flow of drugs. He just wanted to throw her a lifeline. He reached over and flicked off the switch on the recording system.

Her eyes jumped to his.

"They're not going to back down," he said, effectively separating himself from Hank, the department, the whole task force.

"I know."

He leaned forward, closer to her. "Just turn him in."

"I told you, I can't."

Brian heard Hank's footsteps in the hall. He reached out and gripped her wrist. "Don't sign anything until a lawyer looks it over and *not* a court-appointed lawyer. It won't make this go away, but it'll help." Then he let go and flipped the recording system back on just as Hank walked through the door.

She stared at Brian for a moment but recovered as Hank took his seat and slid a document across the table to her, along with a pen.

"That's a transcription of your statement," he said. "Read it over, make sure it's correct, and sign on the dotted line."

Tara looked down at the document, her eyes moving around the page, though it didn't appear to Brian she was reading it. Hopefully she was thinking about what he had said. She picked up the pen and, for a second, he thought she was going to sign, that she was ready for all this to be over.

But she laid the pen back down. "I'll sign it as soon as a lawyer looks at it."

Hank turned to Brian with a questioning brow, as if to ask what the hell happened in the last few minutes to change her mind.

Brian kept his face neutral and shrugged a shoulder.

"Let me get this straight," Hank said. "Now you're asking for a lawyer?"

"Yes."

He let out a loud sigh. "All right. Do you want us to call a public defender?"

She hesitated, probably because lawyers were expensive. But then she shook her head. "No. I'll call my own."

Hank nodded. "Then I guess we need to get you a phone."

When he stood to grab the phone from the far end of the table, Tara's eyes moved to Brian's. She gave him the slightest nod, an acknowledgment, maybe a thank-you. He nodded in kind, which she probably took as "You're welcome." But what he was really thinking was that he should have done so much more.

Hank set the phone down in front of her. Then Brian stood and followed him out of the room so she could make her call. He didn't see Tara again until the morning she was released from Taconic. But it helped a little when he heard her lawyer negotiated her sentence down to eighteen months.

"You taking a nap?" Hank asked, tossing his jacket on the back of his chair and taking his seat.

Brian lifted his head. "Just reading over some notes."

"Get anything on the Leary woman?"

"Maybe." Brian closed her file on his screen. "She lived in Port Chester a decade ago, so that's probably how she knows Roland. And she's a hostess at a club in the Meatpacking District."

Hank grunted. "Thriving drug scene down there. You find anything else on her? She got any family here?"

Brian held his uncle's eye. "Not that I could find yet, but I'll keep digging. How'd it go with the payroll company?"

"Okay. Nice guy. Ernesto Bertucci, from the old country. Looks like he might be right about some money missing, but he had a tough time with the details. His office manager was supposed to be there for the interview, but she called in sick today." Hank waved his notepad around. "He swears she's solid, been working for him for fifteen years. But there might be something there."

"What's the office manager's name?" Brian asked, pointing to his keyboard. "I can run a quick check."

Hank seemed to study Brian for a moment, then he looked down at his notes and rubbed his chin, like he was considering something. "It's just some local woman. But don't worry about it. You stay on the Leary lead, and I'll follow this up myself." He closed the notepad. "By the way, we both got the seventeenth off. For the Montauk trip."

Brian hung his head. He was keeping a few secrets from Hank at the moment, but it was time to clean this one up.

"We'll do some fishing," Hank said. "Get a steak dinner at that place we like, my treat. It'll be great." He lowered his voice, leaned toward Brian. "Thanks again for coming. Tell you the truth, I still can't believe she's marrying someone else." He lifted a hand and shook his head with the sad wonder of a man who would forever love the woman he'd driven away.

That's when Brian knew he wasn't going to Rosemary's wedding.

"I'm grabbing some real coffee from the corner place," Hank said, rising from his chair. "Want one?"

Brian shook his head and watched his uncle walk toward the lobby. There was some relief in having made the decision, which had really been inevitable from the get-go. He wondered why he didn't just say no when Rosemary first asked him, but then her words came back to him—*It would mean the world if you would stand up with me during the ceremony.*

She would be disappointed but not surprised. She'd understand; she always did. When Brian had canceled or cut short all those dinners and visits over the years because he didn't want to leave Hank alone, she had never once complained. Rosemary was used to settling for scraps from Brian.

That was the thought that drove him out of his chair. He didn't know if he was angrier at Hank or himself. He only knew he didn't want to be there when his uncle returned.

❧

He didn't bother to grab his jacket, just headed out to his car. A hard spring rain was coming down, but he kept going. By the time he climbed behind the wheel, he was fairly soaked, and he had to turn the wipers on high. He made his way across town, frustrated by the slow traffic that became inevitable whenever water hit the road.

He pulled up to the house, parked out front, and walked through the rain to the front door. After knocking he braced his arms against the sides of the doorframe and waited.

When the door opened Lance was standing there. "Hey, dude."

It wasn't until Lance's brow furrowed that Brian realized how he must look—rain dripping from his hair, shirt stuck to his skin.

Lance half turned and called over his shoulder. "Tara?"

A moment later she appeared. "Hey," she said, a smile starting and then fading fast. She stared at him with those light eyes, which were a stark contrast to the loose black sweater she wore. It fell off one shoulder, revealing a lacy strap.

When Lance slipped back into the house, she stepped across the threshold. "Are you okay?"

The alarm on her face made him realize he hadn't really thought this through, showing up at her job in such a state. "Yeah, I'm fine. I just . . ." He sighed. "I just wanted to see you."

He expected questions, but she just said, "Okay," and reached up to wrap her arms around his neck, pulling him to her, wet clothes and all.

His hands dropped from the doorframe and slid around her. Relief washed through him as he lowered his head to her shoulder.

After a long moment he pulled back but didn't let go. "Sorry I interrupted your day," he said.

She smoothed wet hair back from his forehead with her hand. Then she smiled. "Wanna get out of here?"

～

They went to a coffee shop and talked for so long it turned into dinner at Brennan's—they stayed to eat this time—and then spending the night at his place. He told her all about Hank and Rosemary, that she was getting married again and Hank couldn't handle it and Brian was stuck in the middle. He explained their history, their failed attempts to have a child. How they'd taken him in after his parents died, and how that loss took such a toll on their marriage even Brian wasn't enough to keep them together. He also told her that every time he visited the cemetery he asked his parents' forgiveness for not coming home that night, because his single act of juvenile defiance had set so many terrible things in motion. Tara listened and commiserated, her eyes full of compassion. But she also asked questions about his mom and dad, like she wanted to get to know them. And it gave him a chance to remember the good, dig up old memories and funny stories.

And Tara told her own stories. How she remembered her mother as fragile, but also beautiful, inside and out. How she and Eddie had been thick as thieves and generally blown off Geraldine's attempt to play parent. How scared and lonely she was when Eddie was in and out of the hospital in high school. The three of them had a tight bond that came with facing common enemies in their youth: a checked-out father, Eddie's debilitating injury, a fear of well-intentioned social workers. Brian could sense the complicated nature of their relationships though. Geraldine drove Tara crazy, and Tara felt guilty about that. Eddie's lack of faith in himself made her tremendously sad. But when she talked about Conor, it was all smiles and light. She called Eddie Friday night to say she wouldn't be home and spent ten minutes catching up with Conor, asking questions about his day. She was crazy about the kid, and he was crazy about her. Listening to her talk and joke with Conor on the phone, Brian was struck by two realizations: Tara must have been a great teacher. How sad it was she'd never be able to do it again.

When he rose from bed Saturday to scrounge up breakfast and pulled on jeans and a T-shirt, she threw her arms high and cheered—*Thank God. I thought all you owned were suits.* They spent the afternoon walking the trails at Saxon Woods Park, and when they got back to his apartment he proposed a deal: if she stayed another night, he would wash her clothes, since they were the only ones she had. She said she'd never had a man do her laundry before and took him up on it. And she laughed when he put them on an extra-long cycle so she had to wear his boxers and T-shirt that much longer. It meant ordering dinner in, but that was fine with Brian.

When the doorbell rang shortly after, he figured it was the food and didn't even hesitate before opening the door. But it wasn't a delivery guy standing there. It was Rosemary, wearing a long coat and one of her fancy little hats.

Her eyebrows shot up when she took in his T-shirt, jeans, and bare feet.

Brian plowed his fingers into his hair. "Damn. I forgot about church."

She laughed and shook her head at him. "No big deal. I can wait while you get ready." She walked right past him into the apartment, dropped her purse on the kitchen counter, and took off her coat. "We'll just stop at the cemetery after Mass rather than before . . ." She stopped because she'd finally turned around and noticed Tara standing by the couch. Wearing Brian's clothes. From across the room Brian could see the blush creeping up Tara's cheeks while she shifted her weight from foot to foot.

Rosemary brought a hand to her chest. "Oh, I'm so sorry." But a smile pulled at her lips. "I guess I understand why you forgot about church."

Jesus. Talk about awkward. But they were in it now. "Tara," he said, "this is my Aunt Rosemary."

"Hi," Tara said. "It's nice to meet you . . ."

Rosemary had already crossed the room to take Tara's hand in both of hers. "You too, dear. But I apologize for barging in."

"That's fine." Tara looked to Brian. "If you have somewhere to be I can take off—"

"No-no-no," Rosemary said, waving her off. "Brian lets me drag him to Saturday evening Mass once in a while, but I'm perfectly fine on my own." She glanced at him but then gave her full attention back to Tara. "Tell me, did you like the flowers?"

Tara smiled. "They were beautiful."

"Good. And Brian tells me you two met through work?"

"I guess that's true . . ." Tara said.

"What's your position at the department?"

Brian had done it again. Put Tara in a position where she had to lie. "Tara doesn't work at the department," he said. "She's a graphic illustrator."

"How interesting," Rosemary said, bringing a hand to her chin. "But, wait. Then how did you meet through work? Oh, I hope it wasn't because he was investigating a crime and you were the victim."

Tara shook her head. "No."

Rosemary looked from Tara to Brian, awaiting further information.

"It's a long story," Brian said.

His aunt's eyes widened as she got the hint. "Oh. Well. Another time then. I better get going anyway, but it was so lovely to meet you, Tara."

"You too."

After Rosemary bustled back into her coat and purse, Brian followed her to the door and held it open for her. She waved at Tara over his shoulder, stepped out into the hall, and leaned toward Brian: "You should definitely bring her to the wedding." Then she gave him a quick hug before she left.

The wedding. Brian closed the door, sagged back against it.

"She seems great," Tara said, dropping down onto the couch. "You haven't told her you're not going to the wedding?"

"Not yet." He pushed off the door. "Listen, about that whole 'we met through work' thing. She asked me about you the day I bought the flowers, and I didn't really know what to say . . ."

"It's all right, Brian. I get it." When her gaze drifted downward he worried the Rosemary episode had thrown cold water on their whole weekend. But then she looked up at him again with a teasing glint in her eye. "Do you really spend your Saturday evenings at church with your aunt?"

He shrugged. "Like once a month or so."

She pressed her lips together like she was trying to suppress a smile.

"Oh, you think that's funny?" he asked.

Her smile burst through.

"I can't believe you're laughing at me right now."

"No, I'm not. Seriously." She sat up straighter. "Actually, I think it's kind of hot."

"Really?"

She nodded.

"So, just how hot do you think it is"—he dove onto the couch beside her—"like on a scale of one to ten? Because I also mow her lawn sometimes and clean out her gutters twice a year."

When she dissolved into laughter and let him ease her back on the cushions, he figured their weekend was back on track.

～

On Sunday morning, while still lying in bed, they stumbled onto the topic of Taconic. Tara mentioned she was applying for special permission from the Department of Corrections to visit her old cellmate, Jeannie.

Parolees had to go through extra hoops to get approval before visiting current inmates.

"Were you guys close?" he asked.

"Yeah. She got me through my last six months. Though she would say I got her through her first six months. She was petrified when she got there."

He took a breath and asked the question. "Were you scared when you first got there?"

"Yes."

He couldn't see her expression because they were spooned up, her back to his front. So he waited to see if she would say more.

"The most afraid I've ever been in my life was when I thought Eddie was going to die. But that was a close second."

"Tara, did anyone ever hurt you in there?" He squeezed his eyes shut, afraid he'd asked too much, more afraid of her answer.

"Once. Early on. I went a little too far with the tough girl act." Her head shook against the pillow. "I sat at the wrong table in the rec room, the one closest to the TV. A couple of women told me to move, but I ignored them. They walked away, and I thought that was it. But later that day in the cafeteria, when I took my tray up to the line, a group of them pulled me into the kitchen . . ." She paused, and Brian could feel the tension in her body, against his chest and under his arm. "They took turns hitting me for a few minutes, to put me in my place. They didn't cause any real damage, but I was black-and-blue for a while."

"I'm sorry," he said, feeling like he'd personally put her in that position.

"It's okay. I borrowed a shiv and got some of them back a couple of days later."

He propped himself on his elbow and looked down at her.

"I'm kidding," she said, giving him a side-smile. "I never sat at that table again."

He lay back down, slid his arm tighter around her.

After a few moments she turned to face him, her eyes wide and shiny. "Have you really thought about us, Brian? I mean, outside of this . . ." She waved her hand around the bedroom, the apartment, the little bubble they were in. "You're a cop, and I have a permanent record."

He knew what she was getting at, especially after Rosemary's visit the day before. Tara's conviction would follow her throughout her life. Wherever she went, whatever she did, it would always be there. When she applied for a job or a residential lease or a bank loan, there'd be a background check. When she met people or made new friends she would either have to hide her past or be judged for it. And so would the people in her life.

Brian had considered all that. The truth was he didn't care what most people thought. It would be tough for Hank, but hopefully he'd come to accept it. Rosemary would be shocked, but she'd get over it. So he tried to impart all the sincerity he felt when he said, "That doesn't bother me."

What did bother him was not understanding why. Why she became involved with a guy like Roland Shea, to the point where she delivered drugs and went to prison for him—gave up her teaching career for him. But Brian didn't want to have to ask her to explain that. He wanted her to *want* to explain it to him.

She seemed to sense that afterthought. Although she smiled briefly at his answer, there was doubt in it. And then she studied him, teeth grazing her bottom lip, like she was debating saying more.

When she sat up to reach for a glass of water on the nightstand, he sat up alongside her and waited, hoping to hell she was ready to talk to him about it. Because he realized now the dark shadow hanging over them wasn't Roland Shea. It was Tara's unwillingness to trust Brian with the truth.

She took a sip of water. "So," she said without looking at him, "do you think they'll approve my application to visit Jeannie?"

He ran a hand down his face to hide the disappointment.

"They should, right?" she said. "I've stayed out of trouble since I was released."

Kind of, he almost said. She'd kind of stayed out of trouble. Except when she went to Roland's house. And used some illicit prison connection to find out Brian had given her that money. "Yeah," he said. "But I think they're pretty particular about granting that permission to parolees." If he had left it there, the discussion would have been over. But he felt his pulse picking up as disappointment gave way to frustration, which is why he said what he did next. "On paper you might look a little . . . stuck to them."

She turned to him. "Stuck how?"

"Well, you still live with your siblings, who are both kind of a mess, and you work for a couple of gamers barely out of high school. You don't have your own transportation . . ." He almost stopped when her brows lifted high in surprise, but he wasn't done making his point. "You don't even have a cell phone, for Christ's sake." He chuckled to soften his words, but there was no humor in it.

She tipped her head. "Is that any more stuck than being your uncle's bitch at thirty-three years old?"

They locked eyes and Brian could see his own shock mirrored in hers. They'd just spent the weekend sharing intimate information, and now they were using it against each other.

"Wow." He sighed and dragged a hand through his hair. "I'm sorry. I shouldn't have said those things."

She looked down and shook her head. "I'm sorry too. That was harsh."

He wasn't sure how to come back from that. Changing the subject seemed the best way to move them onto safe ground. "Will you still let me take you to breakfast?" he asked.

"If you still want to."

They rose, dressed, and walked to the restaurant without saying much. The tension thawed a bit during brunch, and they spent an hour wandering around the farmers' market downtown before he dropped her home. But he sensed the strain between them the rest of the day, and he didn't know how to fix it. They'd had their first argument, which was bound to happen at some point, and it wasn't even much of an argument. It had lasted a few seconds, there'd been no yelling or crying, they'd both apologized.

But he knew what lingered was the sting of the truth in what they'd said to each other. The most honest words didn't have to be loud or dramatic to cut deep.

Chapter Twenty-One

———————

Eddie was running late for their family therapy session Monday morning. When he arrived to pick Tara up from work and take her to Judy's office, she was waiting on the front porch, arms folded across her overalls, one of those clunky black boots tapping the floor.

He hit the brakes and leaned over to push open the door for her. "Sorry. I got held up." While she climbed in he loosened the tie she had knotted for him earlier that morning. He hadn't worn one since Conor's christening. Tara was the one to knot Eddie's tie that morning as well.

Once she was in her seat he gave her the bad news first. "I got a call from DaCosta this morning. I think she's getting tired of having to go through me to reach you."

Tara rolled her eyes. "I know, I know. I need to get a cell phone. What did she want?"

"She said you have to report for a drug test at noon today, and she's going to meet you after that so she can see where you work."

"She's coming to my *job*? Today?"

"Guess so." Eddie watched her slump in her seat. "It's no big deal," he said. "Just drop me back at work after this appointment and take the truck. And Gordi and Lance won't mind her visit, they'll be happy to put in a good word for you." He pulled away from the curb and started toward Judy's office, slipping the tie from around his neck and wrangling open the top two buttons on his stiff shirt. "Listen, I have some good news too. I'm late because the interview went long. Mr. Dunbar and I talked for close to an hour."

She perked up. "Seriously? Tell me."

"I guess he was disappointed when I stepped down last year. I was honest about my concerns with the paperwork and my off days, but he thinks they can accommodate that, start me out with smaller projects. He said I'm reliable, all the guys like me, and I'm an important member of his crew. I think he really wants to give me a chance, Tare."

"That's awesome, Eddie!" She gripped his arm with both her hands and gave it a shake. "Did you tell Lorraine yet? You owe her a huge thank-you."

"I already thanked her." His face got hot as he made a left onto Main Street. "I kissed her, right there at her desk."

She barked out a stunned laugh. "You did not."

"I did." Immediately after the interview with Mr. Dunbar, Eddie walked straight to Lorraine's small office down the hall. She asked how it went and he didn't answer, just tugged her up by the hand, wrapped his arms around her, and spun her around. When he put her down he planted a kiss, fast but firm, right on her mouth. Her shy smile was one of the prettiest things he'd seen in a long time, but then he had to run out of there for this session. Not very romantic. "You think I jumped the gun?" he asked.

"Did she call for help? Or slap you?"

"No."

"Then, no. I don't think you jumped the gun. But I do think you should leave Conor and Katie with me one night this week and take her to dinner."

"You sure about that? I kind of figured you'd be busy with Detective Nolan." He twitched his eyebrows up and down at her.

"Shut up."

"I didn't know if you were gonna come home again or just move in there."

She went red and looked out her window.

Eddie rolled to a stop at a red light. "You got it bad for him, don't you."

She offered no response.

"Don't worry," he said. "He feels the same way."

"How do you know?"

"Because of the way he looked at you at dinner that night. Even a dummy like me could see it."

She paused for a moment. "We had an argument over the weekend."

"It happens. You'll get over it."

Her eyes dropped to her lap. Knowing Tara, she didn't trust it yet. She'd always been primed for a letdown when it came to relationships in the first place, and here she was, falling for a cop who put her in prison. But maybe this was the good to come from all that.

"He seems like a good guy who'll treat you right, Tara. I'm happy for you."

One corner of her mouth pulled up. "Thanks, Eddie."

He nodded. "But I definitely want to be there someday when your kids ask how you guys met."

She rolled her eyes at him. But the little smile stayed put.

~

When Judy answered her door they rushed in, apologizing for keeping her and Geraldine waiting. But Judy was alone.

"Geraldine's not here yet," she said. "This is unlike her, she's always early."

Eddie pulled his phone from his pocket. "Maybe she got the time mixed up . . ." While Judy and Tara took seats, he called Geraldine's cell, which went straight to voice mail. He tried her office number next, and Rita answered over at Bertucci's. He asked to speak with Geraldine.

"She's not here today, Eddie."

He'd watched Geraldine load up in her van to go to work that morning. "What do you mean?"

"She called in sick again."

"'Again'?"

"Yeah. She was out last Friday too, said she has some kind of stomach bug. You didn't know?"

"No." He looked over at Tara. "Geraldine say anything to you about being sick? Missing work?"

She shook her head.

Rita lowered her voice on the other end of the phone. "Eddie, you probably know Geraldine and I don't get along well. But, honestly, you might want to see what's going on with her. She's been acting weirder than usual lately."

Eddie had met Rita twice, and she'd struck him as a pretty straight shooter. Geraldine didn't like her, but that didn't count for much because his sister saw most people as some kind of threat. "Like how?"

"She's been giving me useless work to do while she seems to be slammed. I figured it was because she thinks I never do anything right." She let out an irritated *psh*. "But after coming in this morning and digging into things a little . . . I think she's behind and trying to hide it? I've found a lot of mistakes in recent payroll reports, and I don't know where the quarterly tax forms are. It's kind of a mess."

Eddie's head started to pulse. He thanked Rita and hung up, then joined Judy and Tara, and filled them in. While Tara's expression grew confused, Judy's settled into something like resignation.

She slid her glasses off and let them fall against her chest. "I can't say I'm surprised to hear she's having a hard time. It's one of the reasons I asked you both to be here today. My goal was to talk about some things that have come up recently in my sessions with Geraldine. At the moment I'm concerned about her."

Eddie exchanged a puzzled look with Tara.

"But she seems to be doing okay," Tara said. "She hasn't been to Harriet's in weeks."

"Are you sure about that?"

Tara considered the question. Like Eddie, she was probably realizing the only proof they had of that was Geraldine's word and the absence of green plastic bags in plain sight. "No, I guess not. But she's been so busy with her job lately, even working at night in her room. And over the weekend."

"Rita said she's behind on things," Eddie said.

"Then what the hell has she been doing?"

He shrugged.

Judy folded her hands in her lap. "There's a good chance she's simply sitting among her things, maybe sorting through and trying to organize. If she's experiencing high levels of stress lately, that would be a way for her to find comfort. Remember, Geraldine feels very attached to her things. Hoarding is a form of self-medication, like any other addiction."

This just didn't make sense. Eddie raised a hand to pull his cap off and relieve a little pressure, then remembered he wasn't wearing one today because of the interview. "But that job means everything to Geraldine. Why would she jeopardize it?"

"That's a good question," Judy said. "Something seems to be triggering her lately. She's so anxious she can't focus on work, and now she's avoiding it. She admitted to me last week that she hasn't been sleeping, and her thoughts seemed somewhat disjointed. I think she's really struggling, and part of her is asking for help. She approved this family session and granted me permission to speak with you both, yet she didn't show up."

Tara sighed. "It's me, isn't it? My coming back home. I interfered with how she was running things."

"This isn't your fault," Eddie said. His head was starting to hurt in earnest. Jesus, ten minutes ago he'd been looking forward to a promotion and taking Lorraine on a date. Now Geraldine was off the rails. He'd been stupid to believe he was on the cusp of some happiness, to think he actually deserved that after what Tara had done for him, after what he had *let* her do. And Geraldine's problems probably had something to do with having to care for a younger brother with a brain injury, deal with his depressions and hospitalizations, help him raise his kid. How is it anyone—Tara, Lorraine, Mr. Dunbar—had any faith in him . . . Shit. Here came the flashing lights and blind spots that were a pregame show to a main migraine event. He focused on trying to relax his muscles, starting with his neck and shoulders, determined to keep the pain at bay.

"Are you okay?" Tara asked. "You want me to get your pills from the truck?" Concern was written all over her face.

"No, thanks." He was so tired of people looking at him that way, tired of being a sympathy case. His sisters needed his help now, and his brain wanted to check out as usual. The pills would ease the pain, but they made him tired and numb. He pictured the flow of blood through his head slowing down, from a raging river to a spilling stream. A biofeedback technique half a dozen doctors and therapists had suggested along the way.

"Your coming home has been challenging for her, Tara," Judy said. "We all know she struggles with changes to the routine, giving up control over these things. And, at the same time, she's afraid of disappointing you. But I don't think it's as simple as that. I sense there's been much more pressure at work lately too."

Tara shook her head and scooted forward in her chair, like she was getting ready to leave. "She won't be able to handle it if she loses her job. I have to find her and figure this out before it goes too far."

"Just hold up," Eddie said, his voice rising a bit, along with his frustration level. This is how it started with Tara. Her deciding she needed to fix things for the rest of them.

She ignored him. "I'll talk to Mr. Bertucci, explain everything."

Judy turned to her. "Do you think maybe Geraldine should sort out her own difficulties at work? I know you want to support her, but why do you feel the need to do it for her?"

Eddie answered the question before Tara could. "Because that's what Tara does." He didn't know if he'd planned the accusatory note, but he was okay with it. "She decides to figure it out herself because she doesn't think the rest of us are capable of doing it."

Both their faces swiveled his way.

Tara's eyes narrowed slightly, like she wasn't sure what he was getting at. "I'm trying to help."

Eddie knew that was true. He also knew firsthand that her help could cause harm, cause long-term guilt and shame for the person she was helping. "Maybe you should let Geraldine deal with her own goddamn mess."

Judy leaned back in her chair a bit, as if subtly removing herself from a conversation that was going where it needed to go without her assistance.

"What's your problem?" Tara asked him.

"You make decisions alone when it affects other people."

Her face pulled back, like she'd been scolded.

They both knew what this was really about. It was about what happened a year and a half ago.

When she spoke, her words were slow and deliberate. "You have something you want to say to me, Eddie?" This is the closest they'd come to talking about it since before she went to prison.

"Yeah. I don't think you do the rest of us any favors when you don't let us carry our own burdens."

Tara stayed quiet but didn't drop her eyes, which gradually filled. One blink and the tears would fall. Her expression was stiff, unreadable. Like she had too many emotions going on to pin one down.

Eddie felt a sharp ache in his chest, looking across at her. His little sister, who had sacrificed so much for him. He softened his voice. "I love you for doing it, Tare, but it needs to stop. For all our sakes."

She bowed her head, and he could tell she was working to get it under control.

He shot Judy a glance, and she nodded slightly in encouragement. He felt his shoulders relax, and the pain in his skull had dulled. The relaxation strategies had helped. Or it could have been unloading things he'd needed to say for a long time.

After a while Tara raised her head and cleared her throat.

Eddie was ready to talk about it in front of Judy, all of it, if Tara was.

But she changed the subject. "What do you suggest we do for Geraldine right now?" she asked Judy.

Eddie half listened while Judy encouraged them to be gentle and supportive when broaching all this with Geraldine, help her problem solve what was happening at work and come up with a plan. But he was also watching Tara closely, searching for a reaction to what he'd said.

Judy wrapped it up by asking them to keep her updated and offering her services over the next couple of days if they needed it.

After that Eddie and Tara left her office in a sad silence, and he didn't know how to break it. He wondered how things would change between them now. Although he didn't regret what he said, he knew he'd flipped the tables on her.

Tara had never once held it over his head that she'd gone to prison for him. Instead, today, he'd held it over hers.

～

They were quiet on the drive. Tara stared straight through the windshield, her hands gripping the wheel tight, like she was gnawing on some mental bone. Maybe thinking about what to do for her sister. Maybe thinking about how betrayed she felt by her brother.

"Listen," Eddie said, "what I said back there . . . You know I'll always be grateful for what you did."

"I know." But she didn't look at him or say anything else.

When she pulled to a stop in front of the Dunbar offices a few minutes later, Eddie was reluctant to get out. Their earlier ride to Judy's office had been full of hope. He wanted to get some of that back. He wished Conor was there so they could ask for a joke.

"It's going to be okay," Eddie said. "We'll sort out whatever's happening with Geraldine."

She nodded, but it was halfhearted.

"Tara, please don't let this drag you down. Not when so much good is finally going on for you." He needed her to believe that because he could say the exact same thing to himself.

"Okay." But she still wouldn't look at him.

"Don't forget about DaCosta, and the drug test at noon."

"I won't."

"I'll see you here after work?"

"Yep."

He couldn't think of anything else to say so he reached over to put a hand on her shoulder for a moment. He could feel the hum of stiff tension under his fingers, like she was simmering on the inside. But she offered no response so he climbed out of the truck and headed toward the office. Right before he reached the front door he took a last look over his shoulder to see the truck make a left to head north on Main Street, away from town. Which meant she wasn't heading back to work.

Never was Eddie more frustrated with the fact that she didn't have a cell phone. What the hell was she doing? Probably looking for Geraldine on her own, or heading to the Bertucci office to save Geraldine's job. He should have known she wouldn't let it go. He just wished she had enough confidence in him to let him help.

He headed into the office, hoping Lorraine would be able to give him a ride home before long. He was done sitting back, letting other people figure it out while he hoped for the best. Tara was getting his help whether she wanted it or not.

And he wasn't kidding himself that this was selfless. After what she did for him, he just didn't believe he had the right to be some kind of happy unless she was too.

Chapter Twenty-Two

Tara headed straight for home, where she hoped to find her sister.

I don't think you do the rest of us any favors when you don't let us carry our own burdens.

Well, you're welcome very much, Eddie.

He couldn't be serious. Was she really supposed to put him in danger back then, let him go to prison—leave Conor—for years? Not to mention the detrimental effects that kind of stress would have had on Eddie. He would have been too vulnerable in prison, probably come out with permanent physical or psychological damage, if he made it out at all. No. If he felt guilty, so be it. She had done the right thing.

As for Geraldine handling her own problems . . . She was maybe on the cusp of being fired, and without that job she'd have nothing. She would slip further into this hoarding nightmare. Tara couldn't just "let Geraldine deal with her own goddamn mess."

Eddie was right about one thing though: there was a lot of good going on for Tara now, and she couldn't let her sister derail it. For one thing, she loved her job, and she wasn't going to take time off to babysit Geraldine. Then there was Brian. Being with him was so effortless, so comfortable. It was that illusive idea she'd always heard about but never experienced, the feeling that they just made sense together, got each other in a way no one else could. But Tara was already bringing enough baggage to the relationship without an older sister who was spiraling.

It was her fault they'd said hurtful things to each other yesterday. After coming so close to telling him the truth about Roland, she stopped herself. Keeping that secret had become a reflex. She'd done the time, protected her brother, kept everybody in the dark . . . If the truth came out now, why the hell had she done it? It was like her sacrifice would amount to zilch. Brian was still police. If she told him the truth, he might feel compelled to turn Eddie in. At the least she'd have to ask him to carry their secret too. Worst of all, he would judge Eddie. He'd wonder what kind of brother—what kind of *man*—could do what he did . . .

Though, the truth was if her past or her family was going to scare Brian off, it probably would have happened by now. On their first date she told him he already knew all the bad and the ugly. That wasn't true, he didn't know all of it. But he knew most of it, and for a long time, as far back as that last interview, when he flipped the switch on the recorder and risked his job to help her, he'd been able to see past the mess: the troubling family history, her criminal charges, even the idea of a drug dealer boyfriend. Despite all that, he'd opened himself up to her.

But that trust needed to go both ways. What kind of future would they have if she was less than honest with him? She'd grown up in a house full of dishonesty. No one talked about their mom being sick for so long. They knew their father stole cars but kept it secret from everyone, before and after he left. Tara, Eddie, and Geraldine spent years telling doctors, teachers, and social workers what they wanted to hear so they'd be left alone. Even now, she and Eddie had lied to everyone, and Geraldine was a closet hoarder. God. In some ways they were still those three kids, scrambling to hide their shame from the world.

That's not what she wanted with Brian. She wanted what they had to be true and clean. She wanted to be rid of all secrets.

Sure enough, the minivan was at the house. Tara pulled into the driveway and went inside, calling for Geraldine. There was no response, even after Tara climbed the stairs and knocked on her bedroom door. She opened it and peered inside. No Geraldine.

Across the hall, she checked her old room. No Geraldine.

Down two flights of stairs to the basement. She flipped on the lights. No Geraldine.

Tara climbed the steps to the kitchen, considering where else her sister could be hiding. Maybe she was just walking the neighborhood, killing time. But that didn't feel right. Judy said Geraldine was likely finding comfort among her things. If she wasn't in her rooms or the basement, the next best option was probably Harriet's, which was within walking distance. Tara picked up her pace, deciding that's where she'd look next.

She headed back out to the truck, but just before she climbed in, she caught movement out of the corner of her eye and turned toward the shed across the yard, which had a small window next to the door. She hadn't been in the shed for years, forgot it was there most of the time. Every year the whole decaying structure leaned more to the left. It was a hiding place when they were kids, but since then it had only been used to house a bunch of junk—rusty bikes, sleds, old tools.

When she looked closely, she could see a path of lightly flattened grass from the porch stairs to the shed. Someone had gone back and forth recently. She made her way to the corner of the yard, relieved to see no padlock on the door. After taking a deep breath she gripped the metal handle and slowly pushed the creaky door open.

The shed was maybe ten feet by ten feet. The old tools and equipment had been shoved to one side to make room for half a dozen cardboard boxes and several clear plastic bins containing VHS tapes and used board games. There was a mountain of clothes on the wooden workbench.

"Tara?"

She spun to see Geraldine standing in the shadow behind the door. Her eyes were wide, and one hand fiddled with the cross at her throat.

Judy had encouraged a soft approach. "Hi, Ger," Tara said, keeping her voice neutral. "What're you doing out here?" She glanced past Geraldine to see a wicker chair in the corner under the window, beside an upturned crate. There was a large mug on the crate, with a tea bag hanging over the side.

"I'm not feeling well," Geraldine said. "It's probably nothing, but it's best practice to stay home, just in case. I wouldn't want to pass a bug on to anyone else, especially poor Mr. Bertucci."

"Why didn't you tell us?"

"I didn't want to worry anyone."

Tara nodded, wondering where to go next. There was a wariness in her sister's expression, and Tara could see the lack of sleep now, in Geraldine's pallid skin and slack features. It looked like she was barely keeping it together.

"What're you doing here?" Geraldine asked. "Why aren't you at work?"

"I came to find you. I was worried when you missed our session with Judy. And Eddie talked to Rita, found out you called in sick."

"Well, I'm fine." She shrugged and moved to the workbench, started sorting through clothes. "While I'm home, I figured I would go through this stuff, think about what to donate to Goodwill."

Tara checked her watch. She still had an hour before she had to report for that drug test. Maybe she could convince her sister to go back to work. "Ger, what's going on at Bertucci's?"

She kept folding clothes, assigning them to various piles.

"You've missed two days," Tara said. "And Rita's finding lots of mistakes. Tell me what's happening."

"Gracious, Tara. You disappear all weekend, and *you're* demanding answers from *me*?"

"What does that have to do with anything?"

Geraldine whipped toward her so fast Tara backstepped. "Why did you have to get involved with him?" Her finger jabbed the air inches from Tara's face. "Why couldn't you just focus on being back home with us and getting a real job? Instead of *hooking up*"—a rough whisper— "with a man. And I know he stayed here last week, I saw him leave. I can't believe you did that with Conor in the house."

"You're upset that I have someone in my life?"

"He put you in *prison*, for pity's sake. What's he even doing with you—have you asked yourself that? Why a policeman would be interested in a woman who *trafficked drugs*? You need to get him out of our lives. He could ruin everything." She turned back to the bench and tore apart a pile of clothes she'd already folded.

The vehemence of her reaction momentarily stunned Tara. This wasn't about her corrupting Conor or hooking up with a guy. *He could ruin everything.* It was Brian in particular.

"Why are you afraid of him?" Tara asked. "Is it because he's a cop?" Nothing scared Geraldine like the idea of getting into trouble with the police. But she was way too nervous to ever do anything illegal . . . Unless she thought she might lose her job. In that case her desperation might outweigh her fear.

Tara kept her voice steady. "Did you do something at work? Something you shouldn't have done?"

Her sister didn't respond, but her hands slowed and lowered to the workbench.

"I can help if you tell me, Ger. We can figure it out together."

Geraldine balled up her fists and dropped her head. "I'm sorry," she said. It was almost a whisper.

"For what?"

"It was such a good plan. Your old account was just sitting there . . ."

Her old account? Tara had no idea what Geraldine was talking about, but a low ringing started in her ears.

"If I just had another week or two," Geraldine said, still speaking to the floor, "it would have been fine. No one would have realized."

"Realized what?" Even if that account was still open, what could Geraldine have possibly done with it? There'd been no money in it to steal. Just the same, the ringing was getting louder.

Geraldine turned to her. "I never meant to involve you. I don't want you to go back to that place."

That place. Those words slammed into Tara and caused such a sharp moment of vertigo she thought she might puke. She gripped the edge of the workbench and waited for it to pass, fleetingly thinking of Eddie, how often he must feel like this, as if the world beneath him might fall away. Geraldine could only be talking about one place. "What did you do, Geraldine?" she asked in a coarse voice she didn't recognize as her own.

Geraldine gave her head a quick shake. "Nothing. Never mind, I'll figure it out." She focused on folding clothes with every bit of her attention, hands flying about, trying to move fast enough to outrun this conversation. "You go back to work and let me get on with this."

Tara wished she could do just that. Walk away from these questions and answers that felt like they would change everything, and not in a good way. But that wasn't an option. And she was done with the gentle approach. She grabbed her sister's upper arm and pulled her around, held tight when she tried to squirm away. "You tell me what you did right now, or I start throwing your shit away."

Geraldine just shook her head again.

"Fine." Tara let her go, reached for the nearest box. Then she kicked open the shed door and tossed the box outside. It flew several feet and landed on its side, spilling shabby throw pillows onto the lawn.

"No, Tara!"

But Tara grabbed the next box, which was heavy—books maybe—and did the same. And it felt fucking great. She'd been tiptoeing around Geraldine since she got home, trying to make it work. And all Geraldine did was judge her, ooze disapproval at every turn. Peck away at anything good that happened for Tara.

"Please, stop," Geraldine said, her voice a shrill cry.

Tara chucked a third one, and several mirrors broke and spilled out when it landed. What had her sister "involved" her in? She went back in the shed for the next box, but Geraldine was standing in front of her stuff, trying to protect it.

"No more, Tara." She looked half-crazed, arms splayed, face blotchy and trembling.

Tara felt like she was barely hanging on to control herself. "Tell me the truth or I throw the next box."

"I can't tell you . . ."

Tara pushed past her, grabbed the next box.

Geraldine followed her as she headed out to the yard with it. "I promise I'll fix it—wait . . ." She tried to catch the box when Tara tossed it, but it bounced off her arms to the ground.

Back to the shed. Two more boxes, then Tara would move on to the plastic bins.

"I didn't get the quarterly taxes done on time, okay?" Geraldine said. "And I needed a place to hide the money for a little while."

Tara turned to see her sister on the ground, among shards of mirror, reaching about to gather the sad contents strewn about the grass. She walked over and crouched down in front of Geraldine. "What money?"

"The tax money." Geraldine stuffed things back into busted boxes, moving so frantically she didn't even seem to feel her knees crunching against the glass on the ground.

Regret hit Tara hard, as it always did when she lost her temper with Geraldine. And she was seized by a wave of pity for her sister, who was so scared of the world right now she was retreating from it as much as possible. Tara took a deep breath and held her hands up. "Please stop, before you cut up your knees more."

Geraldine looked down at the spots of blood that had seeped through her jeans. She scooted back, away from the glass, away from Tara.

Without getting any closer, Tara sat down cross-legged on the grass. "I promise I won't throw any more boxes," she said. "But, Ger, you need to tell me what you did."

Geraldine stared down at her hands, which were squeezed together so tight her forearm muscles were visibly strained under the skin. "I took the quarterly tax money from the Bertucci account and put it in your old one. It was only going to be there for a couple weeks, until I got the taxes done."

Jesus Christ. Geraldine had stolen money and put it in Tara's bank account. "How much money?"

"Almost twenty-five thousand."

It was a good thing Tara was sitting because it felt like everything in her collapsed. There was nothing like spending time in prison to educate someone about the law. That kind of money qualified for grand larceny in the third degree. Two to seven years. Probably more if someone had a previous record.

She brought her hands to her head. "My God, Geraldine. Why the hell didn't you just tell Mr. Bertucci you needed help? He would have understood—everybody makes mistakes."

When Geraldine yanked her head up her eyes were like daggers. "That's easy for you to say. When *you* made mistakes we had a meeting with the principal. You got detention or went to summer school. If *I* made mistakes"—she poked herself in the chest—"we could lose the house or have no money for food. Eddie could get sicker, or CPS would put you two in foster care. *I* couldn't make any mistakes."

Tara's shoulders settled with the weight of that, the truth of it. She'd always recognized her sister's dogged adherence to rules and routine, her need to control everything. Tara had believed it was because Geraldine was judgmental and thought she knew best. But that wasn't the root of it. She wasn't trying to impose her will on them really. She was trying to protect them. Geraldine was afraid of making mistakes because the cost would be too high. She'd been afraid of that her whole life.

"I didn't think anyone would notice the money was gone," Geraldine said. "But the IRS called, and Mr. Bertucci realized it was missing. He called the *police*." That last word was barely a squeak, and her eyes filled. "They came to the office, that's why I stayed home."

Tara felt any hope of fixing all this trail away like the wispy end of a dream that can't be recalled. The police were already involved.

The police. Brian. How long would it take for him to hear about it? He believed Tara had been working for a drug dealer not that long ago, now this. Stealing money from her sister's boss. She imagined telling him the truth—*None of it is how it looks*. She knew it to be true, and it still sounded far-fetched. Even if he wanted to believe her, certainly he'd always wonder. And she couldn't expect him to jeopardize his job to help her with this. He'd want to steer clear of her and her family. She couldn't blame him.

Perhaps Rudy Russo had been right after all. *You can't escape your past.*

Alongside the despair, panic started to edge in as Tara realized that Geraldine first skipped work last Friday. Which meant the police had been investigating this for several days. How long would it take to trace that money? As soon as they did they would assume Tara stole it and come looking for her.

Geraldine was crying hard now, her body shaking, tears streaming down her face. "I don't know what to do. I can't go to *prison*, Tara." She hiccupped through a sob. "I . . . I wouldn't survive there."

No, she wouldn't. Not intact anyway. Geraldine's sloppy, childish weeping reminded Tara of certain women in Taconic. Women who were easy victims because they were afraid of their own shadow and would never fight back. Not against stronger women looking to take advantage of them, and not against the desperation that threatened to suck their spirit dry forever. Geraldine's life was already small and sad, fraught with anxiety and loneliness. It had been that way since she was a kid, left alone to raise two other kids. She'd been through enough. Tara would not let Geraldine go to prison.

But that meant letting the police believe Tara had taken the money, that she was a thief. Déjà vu from eighteen months ago. Except this time, although Tara wasn't willing to let her sister go to prison, she wasn't willing to go back there herself either. That left only one option, and time was running out. She didn't know where she was going, or for how long, only that she had to go now. She'd figure out the rest later.

She bolted up to a standing position so fast it brought on a head rush. Then she ran over and knelt close to Geraldine. "Look at me, Ger."

She raised her face, which was streaked with tears.

"You're not going to prison."

Cautious hope edged into Geraldine's eyes. "What do you mean?"

"It's going to be okay," Tara said, placing her hands on her sister's shoulders. "But I need you to do exactly as I say right now. You have to pick this stuff up as quickly as you can and get it back in the shed. And then you need to stay in there for a while. Can you do that?"

"Where are you going?"

"The only way this works is if I leave."

"For how long?"

"I don't know."

"But—"

"Now you don't come out of that shed for anyone but Eddie. Understand?" She stood, pulling Geraldine up with her. "I mean it. You *only* come out for Eddie, and make sure he's alone first."

"Okay, but we should talk to him—"

"Listen to this part carefully. When Mr. Bertucci and the police ask you about that money, you tell them you don't know anything about it. You've been home sick the last few days. Keep it that simple." It would work. The police would have no problem thinking the sister with the criminal record was the one who stole the money.

"But if I do that," Geraldine said, "they'll think it was you."

"I'll be fine." Tara started backing toward the house.

"Tara, wait . . ."

"Just do what I said, Ger. Okay?" She wasn't entirely successful at keeping the note of hysteria out of her voice. She had to go now.

Geraldine stared at her across the yard for a moment, maybe letting the implications sink in, maybe debating whether she could live with them.

So Tara offered what she hoped was a reassuring smile. Then she spoke the words she knew her sister needed to hear: "Everything will be fine. I promise."

With watery eyes Ger pressed her lips together in a return smile.

"Okay." Then she dropped to the ground and started shoveling items in boxes.

Tara ran into the house and up to her room, grabbed an old backpack from under the bed. She tried to think about what she'd need, but her mind was racing, already listening for the sound of a car pulling into the driveway, possibly even distant sirens. So she ended up just throwing handfuls of random clothes in the bag. She grabbed a few things from her desk, including the precious little cash she had—$18—and ran her eyes over the drawings hanging on the wall. If she wasn't so panicked she would have sat down and cried at the thought of bailing on Gordi and Lance this way.

When she went back outside Geraldine was still rushing to get the boxes back in the shed.

Tara waved and called to her: "I'll be in touch soon."

Geraldine waved uncertainly, but the relief on her face was visible even at this distance. At least Tara had done that for her. She hopped in the truck, started the engine, and pulled out, firming up a plan in her mind. It was pretty simple: keep driving until she was far, far away. But there were a couple of stops she had to make first.

She flew down Gillette Street but then forced herself to slow down so she didn't get pulled over for speeding. While she drove she kept her eyes peeled for Eddie, police cars, Brian's Grand Cherokee. He had to know by now . . .

With that thought a fierce ache gripped her chest. She knew this feeling. It was loss. She was grieving Brian, and what they might have had.

Chapter Twenty-Three

Brian left Port Chester mid-Monday morning to head into the city. He'd been a little worried about how to disappear from the station without raising Hank's suspicion, but Hank was nowhere to be found that morning. He was probably working that payroll company case, which was just as well. Brian was still trying to reconcile himself with the point Tara had made yesterday, in her very Tara way: *Is that any more stuck than being your uncle's bitch at thirty-three years old?* She had sideswiped him with that one, and he couldn't get it out of his head.

It took thirty minutes to hit the West Side Highway in Manhattan, which took him south along the Hudson River. Traffic was relatively light and soon he was passing the Midtown piers, where ferries carried people across the river to and from New Jersey. A few minutes later he got off at Fourteenth Street and headed into the clogged streets of the West Village.

He was betting late morning would be the best time to catch Andrea Leary at home. She worked nights, probably slept in. He'd decided against contacting her first, in case she got spooked. He didn't know any more about this woman than he did last week, had no idea what he'd be dealing with. It might be a waste of time, but there was a chance she could offer useful info about Roland. Maybe she could even shed light on Tara's relationship with the guy, which would be well worth the trip.

He found Andrea Leary's building on Thirteenth Street, a crumbling five-floor walk-up. He thought he might have to deal with a locked exterior door, maybe an intercom system, which would make it easy for her to ignore him or send him away. But the front door was unlocked. The dim lighting and the vestibule littered with refuse said security wasn't a high priority in this building. The nightclub hostess gig must not pay much.

Three sets of narrow stairs later he found Apartment 4B. He had to knock several times before he heard movement inside, but he kept it light, undemanding.

She answered by opening the door slightly, the chain still fastened. A pair of tired green eyes peeked out. "Yes?"

Brian didn't move any closer, just offered a disarming smile that had worked in opening doors in the past. "Hi. I'm sorry to bother you, but are you Andrea Leary?"

Anxiety rippled across her face. "Why?"

"My name's Brian Nolan." He pulled out his badge and ID, held it up so she could get a close look. "I was hoping to talk to you for a few minutes." He gave her a helpless shrug. "I'm sorry I couldn't call first. I didn't have a phone number."

Her wary gaze flicked from the badge up to his face.

"Miss Leary, you're not in any trouble. I just have a couple questions about Roland Shea."

She sucked in a sharp breath and pulled back from the door, and he could see it. She was scrambling for the quickest way to get him gone.

He lowered his voice to a just-between-us level. "You see, I'm a little worried about his possible involvement with some friends of mine. The Connellys."

She froze.

"I thought you might be able to help," he said.

"You know the Connellys?"

He nodded. "I just had dinner with them last week, at their house. I met your son, Conor."

She pulled the door open as far as the chain would allow. "You did?"

"Yeah. He's a great kid." Brian laughed a little. "Smart. He told me a really funny joke."

Her whole demeanor softened, and the only word he could think of to describe what he saw in her expression was longing. "He's doing good?" she asked.

"Sure seemed like it. He was talking about school and *Fortnite*, his buddies . . ."

While he spoke, Andrea closed the door enough to unfasten the chain. Then she pulled it open wider, her eyes glued to Brian like she didn't want to miss a word. She wore a short, black robe, her dark hair pulled back in a messy heap. She was attractive, but there was a worn, fragile quality about her. Like it wouldn't take much to knock her down, physically or mentally.

". . . and baseball, of course," Brian said. "He talked a lot about that."

She folded one arm across her middle, and her other hand gathered the robe together at her throat. "Yeah, I've been wanting to get up to one of his games. It's just really hard with work and everything."

"I bet," Brian said, because he sensed that was what she needed to tell herself.

"You can come in, I guess, for a minute."

"Thanks."

She held the door open and he stepped into a narrow living area. It was old-school tenement: sloping wood floors, dingy shower stall in the kitchen, a cast-iron radiator with paint flaking off. Her one window looked out onto the brick wall of the next building and offered almost no daylight. He noted a tiny table with two chairs, a love seat with a flowery slipcover. But what his eye was really drawn to was a shelf crowded with dozens of photos. Every one of them was Conor at various ages.

"Eddie and Tara send me pictures," she said, picking up a pack of cigarettes from the table and tapping one out. "They're good about that." She held up the cigarette and a lighter. "You mind?"

Brian waved at her to go ahead. So it would seem Andrea and Tara had gotten past that old assault charge, at least to some degree.

She lit and inhaled. "How do you know the Connellys?"

He hesitated, wondering how honest to be with her. But maybe it would help, her knowing he was personally involved. "I've gotten close to Tara lately."

Her eyebrows arched. Then a corner of her mouth curled up. "Be careful not to piss her off," she said. "Tara's got a helluva right hook."

"I don't doubt it."

She took a drag off her cigarette. "You really had dinner with them all?"

"Well, with Eddie, Tara, and Conor. I met Geraldine, but just for a minute." He tilted his head. "I don't think she likes me."

"Don't take it personally. Geraldine's a strange one." She rolled her eyes. "But you said something about helping them . . ."

"Andrea, I'm sure you know about Tara being in prison, why she was there. Her past relationship with Roland Shea."

She shrugged a shoulder. "I wasn't around for all that."

"I have coworkers who think she might still be working with him in some way. They're watching her closely, looking for any connection between her and Roland. And you were recently spotted with him." He held up a hand. "Just dropping him at his car ten days ago. But as you can imagine, with your ties to the Connelly family . . . It makes them wonder."

She took a tense pull off her cigarette, side-blew the smoke away from him. "What do you want, Detective?"

"I want Roland Shea out of the lives of Tara and her family."

"She has nothing to do with Roland anymore."

"I believe that. But not everybody does." He kept his voice soft. "You have to understand. A lot of people want to put Roland away, and they'll do whatever it takes. He's ruined too many lives."

Her eyes drifted toward the floor.

"People I work with have seen the damage he's caused firsthand. They've found the OD victims, taken kids out of homes because the parents are hooked on his heroin."

Andrea pulled her arms across her middle, the cigarette still clasped between two fingers. She seemed to be shrinking as she stood there, her thin frame closing in on itself. It made sense, he was describing her to some degree. Brian didn't know exactly what Andrea did for Roland, but clearly she was another victim. There was a vacancy behind her eyes, even to her apartment, like only a shadow of her former self resided there. But she loved her son.

"Roland is going down, Andrea. Soon. The only question is who he's going to take with him. Personally, I don't want it to be Tara. And I think you know that would hurt the whole family."

She bit into her bottom lip. He didn't need to spell it out. One of the people that would hurt the most was Conor.

"And after meeting you today," he said, "I'd rather it not be you either. But I'll be honest, I'm not the only cop who's going to come talk to you about this. And the next conversation will probably go a different way."

She continued to chew that lip, and he could see her mind working behind those jumpy eyes. "What do you want from me?" she finally asked, shaking her head and tamping out her cigarette in a nearby ashtray.

"I don't know," he said, which was the truth. "I only know the sooner he goes away, the sooner we're all free of him."

She looked up at the word *free*.

Brian glanced over at the shelf of pictures. "Conor's only ten, Andrea. There's still time to be his mother. You're the only one he's got."

Her arms fell to her sides, and her whole body seemed to droop. She stepped over to the little dining table and dropped into a chair. "I don't know how much I can help. I'm just an errand girl. He doesn't talk to me about much."

Brian believed that. Roland was too smart to entrust one of his own customers with the details of his business. "I'll take whatever you got," he said.

She propped an elbow on the table, put her chin in her hand, and gazed out her desolate window.

He waited.

After a long moment, she looked up at him. "What if I could tell you when and where he'll be meeting with his Mexico connection next?"

⤳

He was so eager to get back to Port Chester after leaving Andrea's apartment he wished he was in the Explorer so he could throw on the flashing lights and blow past everyone. He'd spent another hour with her, going over details at least three times, stopping occasionally to reassure her when she needed it. He knew he wasn't speaking out of turn when he told her she would be protected from prosecution. The task force would be happy to grant her immunity, considering what she was giving them. He had, however, promised not to use her name until a deal was worked out. In the meantime, she would remain his confidential informant.

But they'd likely have Roland in custody the following week. At Roland's request, Andrea had arranged a private VIP room in her club where he could conduct business with his supplier. Apparently he trusted her enough to do that.

As he merged back onto the highway heading north, he took a moment to savor the win. Because even though they weren't there yet—something could still go wrong—they were that much closer. Andrea wanted to work with him. The more they talked, the more certain he'd been. Maybe it was the idea of being free from Roland, maybe it was the link Brian provided to Conor. But even in the short time he was with her, he could see a tentative sense of purpose move into Andrea's eyes and posture. This could be healthy for her, a first step to getting clean and rebuilding a relationship with her son.

He called Hank's cell, hoping to update him, but got his voice mail so he tried the station.

"He was here for a little while," the desk sergeant said. "But he took off again."

"Any idea where he went?"

"It had something to do with that payroll case he's working. The bank was able to trace the stolen money. He's probably following up."

Alone? Hank and Brian often did preliminary research on reports separately. But once there was some meat to a case, like chasing down persons of interest, they generally worked together . . .

He decided to call Tara at work—the one place he could reach her by phone—to tell her he wanted to see her that night. They needed to talk about all of this. He would tell her about Andrea, explain what led him to her. He wanted Tara to hear it from him.

But it was also time to ask her for the truth about Roland. Meeting Andrea had crystallized it for him. Andrea was scared and alone and battling addiction, but she was willing to help put Roland away, something Tara had refused to do. She wouldn't even talk to Brian about him, which could only mean she still had some kind of feelings or loyalty for the guy. Enough to want to protect him. And Brian simply couldn't live with that.

Gordi answered the phone when Brian called and said Tara wasn't at work. "She left here this morning for some family thing. She was only supposed to be gone for like an hour, but she's not back yet."

Brian knew the "family thing" was a therapy session for Geraldine. But that had been at ten. He checked the time: twelve fifteen.

"What's really weird," Gordi said, "is she hasn't called. That's not like her. And we can't call her."

Something must have come up after the therapy session. Maybe Eddie was having one of those rough days she'd talked about. Or Conor was sick . . . She really needed a goddamn cell phone.

"Listen, Gordi," Brian said. "I'll track her down and ask her to check in with you."

"I hope everything's all right," Gordi said. "Hey, let her know we hit the next benchmark this morning. Seventy-five thousand subscribers. We were hoping to celebrate with her. It's because of her, you know?" He paused. "Just let us know she's okay."

Brian said he would and hung up. Flashing lights or no, he edged his speed up.

His heart sank a bit when the pickup wasn't in the Connelly driveway, but he decided to park and check anyway. He climbed the porch steps to see Eddie inside, sitting at the kitchen table, his head in his hands.

Brian knocked on the window to get his attention.

When Eddie looked up, his expression stiffened. He got up, came to the door, and yanked it open. "What are you guys, tag-teaming us now?"

"What are you talking about?"

"Your partner was just here." Eddie threw an arm toward the street. "I'm surprised you didn't pass him on the road." He turned and stalked back to the kitchen.

Brian closed the door and followed him inside, trying to tamp down a rising dread. "What was Hank doing here?"

"Looking for Tara."

"Where is she?"

"Hell if I know." Eddie rubbed his forehead with his fingers.

"What did Hank want with her?"

"Something about money stolen from the Bertuccis. He said it ended up in an account in Tara's name." He pointed a finger at Brian. "I'm going to tell you the same thing I told him. She didn't steal any fucking money."

"Of course not. Bertucci . . . he owns a payroll company, right?"

"Yeah. Geraldine works for him. She's been there fifteen years."

"Is she the office manager?"

Eddie nodded.

The other day, when Brian asked for the name of the office manager, Hank said not to worry about it, but he'd been looking at his notes, had her name right there in front of him. Hank had known it was Tara's sister, and he'd kept it from Brian. But Brian had been busy keeping his own secrets from Hank too.

"Geraldine probably knows something about this." Eddie spread his arms wide. "Her van's outside, but she's nowhere to be found either." He narrowed his eyes. "Why is your partner so fixed on Tara?"

"He thinks she might still be working with Roland in some way."

Eddie dropped his head.

"I know it's not true," Brian said. "But he's stuck on it. She wouldn't give him up back then, and you guys went to see him after she got out . . ."

"Let me ask you something, Brian. Why do you think Tara wouldn't turn on Roland?"

There it was. The million-dollar question. The one that had nagged at Brian for eighteen months, and still did. Maybe because the only answer he'd ever come up with was so disappointing.

He shrugged. "They have history. I think your sister's a loyal person, sometimes to a fault."

"History?" Eddie shook his head at Brian. "Do you really think Tara was ever dumb enough to get involved with Roland Shea?" he asked. "You are right about one thing though. She is loyal to a fault, especially to certain people."

It hit Brian like a sucker punch. The only reason why Tara would give up a year and a half of her life by refusing to turn in a drug dealer. Jesus. The most disappointing part of the whole thing was that Brian hadn't realized it sooner.

"She did it to protect *you*," he said.

Eddie pulled out a chair and took a seat. Then he leaned forward with a heavy sigh, thick forearms on the table, like he needed the support. "I was the one working for Roland. I did it for almost six months."

Brian dropped into the chair across from him, still feeling dazed.

"A couple years ago I broke my arm and couldn't work for a while. Tara and Geraldine were supporting me and Conor, we were getting buried in bills, especially my medical bills . . . Conor's mom got me the job." He flipped his hands over. "Roland paid me to make the weekly delivery to Greenwich. It was fast, easy money, and I kept doing it even after I went back to work because it helped so much. Tara didn't even know about it. She would have kicked my ass."

Brian had a million questions, but he waited for Eddie to continue. Something told him Eddie had been waiting to tell this story to someone for a long time.

"The night Tara got busted, I was supposed to make a delivery to some new guys from Stamford. Roland was nervous about it because these dudes were scary. All I had to do was make the drop, but one of the worst migraines I ever had came on a couple hours before. Probably the stress." He shoved his hands through his hair. "I was a mess. Lost most of my vision, I was puking and shaking. Tara wanted to take me to the ER. She wouldn't let up, so I told her what I had to do that night." He closed his eyes. "In all my life, I never saw her so angry. When she was done yelling at me, she told me I should take one of my pills and get some sleep, that she would wake me up in time."

"But she tried to make the delivery for you," Brian said.

Eddie nodded. "First she went to Roland and told him tough shit, I wouldn't be making the run that night. But he said that wasn't an option that late in the game, not with these guys. So they made a deal: she'd make the drop, but I was officially quitting." He scraped a palm down his haggard face, and in that moment Brian could see the toll this had taken, the weight of the shame that still pulled at Eddie. "When she got home and told me what happened, I wanted to drive straight back to the station, tell you guys the truth. But she said that was stupid, she'd already been busted, and I couldn't just step in and take her place. I told her I'd give up Roland and go to prison myself to clear her, but when we met with Roland the next day, he said if I turned him in, his people would retaliate. He also told her that I'd been running pills and heroin across state lines for months, and more people had seen my face than his. So if she turned him in, I would go down too. For a long time."

He thrust his face toward Brian, his eyes begging for understanding. "I fought Tara *so hard* on it. Told her she'd never teach again, that this would always be on her record. But she said our whole family could be in danger if I came forward. And she talked about Conor, how he already had one absent parent, and I would be out of his life for years, miss his whole childhood. Hell, I told her Conor would be a lot better off with her, but she said he'd grow up with everyone judging him, knowing his dad was a loser. We knew what it was like to grow up like that . . ."

Brian remembered now, wondering how she could have chosen to leave her nephew when it was obvious he needed her. But Tara had been too afraid of losing Eddie. She said it herself just yesterday: *The most afraid I've ever been in my life was when I thought Eddie was going to die.* So not only did she go to prison for her brother, but she had also convinced him it was best for everyone.

Maybe Brian should have been angrier at Eddie, for running drugs in the first place, getting a migraine that night, letting her take the fall. Technically Brian had an obligation to report this to the task force. But he saw no point to all that. It was clear Eddie had been haunted by this since the night it happened, and to some degree he would be forever.

He slumped back against his chair. "Some days I don't know if I can live with that for the rest of my life."

"You have to. Otherwise she did it for nothing." Then Brian offered Eddie what he could. "If it helps at all, she was right. If you had come forward, it wouldn't have let Tara off the hook. You might have made a deal where she avoided prison, but you would have had to give up Roland. And you would have gone away for a lot longer than eighteen months."

Eddie nodded, but it was perfunctory. Like he'd already played that scenario out a thousand times and still couldn't square himself with what happened. He probably never would.

"Where could Tara be now, Eddie?" Brian asked.

He shrugged. "I don't know what she told you about our sister, but she's got issues. My guess is Tara's out there somewhere"—he flung a hand toward the front door—"trying to help Geraldine. I'm just afraid she could end up back in prison for doing it."

"That's not going to happen. I'll find out what's going on." Brian stood from his chair. "I'll call as soon as I know anything. And you let me know if she comes back here, or if you hear from her."

Eddie stood as well. "Will do."

Brian was in a rush to get going, but before he left he thanked Eddie for telling him the truth. Such relief came with knowing she'd been protecting her brother rather than Roland, and it just made so much more sense. She would have told him herself at some point in the future. And Brian wanted that with her, a future.

But first he had to figure out what the hell was going on with Hank and this payroll case, which would be difficult because Hank was deliberately keeping him in the dark. Maybe he'd sensed something was going on between Brian and Tara, but for the first time in his life, Brian and his uncle were not on the same side. The cold truth was they didn't trust each other right now. And Brian had no idea how they would come back from that.

All he knew right then was he had to find Tara before Hank did.

Chapter Twenty-Four

Once Geraldine got all her stuff back in the shed she took time to organize some of it, which was soothing after such an upsetting day. While she worked she replayed Tara's words in her mind—*Everything will be fine. I promise.*

She had resettled most of her things when Eddie was dropped off at the house by Lorraine. Geraldine almost followed him inside, but Tara said to make sure he was alone so she waited a few minutes. Good thing she did because Eddie was having a busy day. First a dark SUV drove up and a big man got out and went into the house for a bit. He looked very official in his jacket and tie and sunglasses, and Geraldine had a bad feeling about him. Then, not five minutes after he left, Brian Nolan pulled up. She had ducked back under the window to hide, careful not to make a peep.

Brian was probably searching for Tara, but Geraldine had no idea where she went. *The only way this works is if I leave.* How sad Tara looked when she said that. She usually had such good posture, but, in that moment, her shoulders curved over her chest, like something had emptied out of her.

Geraldine had just checked her watch—almost two o'clock—when she finally heard Brian's car start up and drive away. After giving it a few more minutes she left the shed and made her way to the house. The fresh air felt good after being cooped up for so long, and she lifted her arms to let the light spring breeze cool her clammy skin. When she climbed the porch steps she saw Eddie sitting at the kitchen table, staring at his phone.

He pulled his head up when she opened the door. The strain around his eyes and mouth said he was fighting a bad headache. "Where the hell have you been?" he asked. He sounded mad, but it was still a relief to see him. Eddie was always patient with her.

"Out in the shed," she said, taking the seat across from him.

"Have you been in there all day?"

"Yes. I keep some things out there."

He let out a confused huff and shook his head, like his afternoon couldn't get more puzzling. She expected questions about why she was skipping work and hiding in the shed, but he gave her a pointed look and asked something else. "What's going on with this missing money at Bertucci's, Ger?"

"What do you mean?"

"You probably saw the police were here. They said someone stole money from Mr. Bertucci, and it ended up in Tara's account."

"That doesn't sound right," she said, pulling on her cross until she felt the chain dig into the back of her neck.

Eddie's facial muscles stiffened. "If you know something, you have to tell me. Right now."

But if Geraldine told him Tara was running away, he'd jump up and go after her. He might even catch up to her. Then the truth would come out about what Geraldine had done.

"She could go back to prison," Eddie said. He sounded scared. Probably because he took it so hard when Tara was there the last time.

Geraldine didn't want Tara to go back to that place either. Even though things were kind of nice when she was gone. Geraldine loved her sister, but she was like a whirlwind that had blown in and disrupted everything.

When Eddie spoke next, his voice had an edge to it. "I'm not letting her go back there, Geraldine."

Letting her? "Sometimes I think you forget she earned that prison sentence, Eddie."

He closed his eyes. "You don't know what you're talking about."

"I'm just saying, she was trafficking drugs." It occurred to her she hadn't whispered those last words. She must be getting used to them.

"Tara wasn't trafficking drugs," Eddie said. "I was. She was just trying to help me out of a jam that night." He turned over his hands, like he was appealing to her. "She went to prison for me."

"Oh, for pity's sake, why would she do that?"

"So I would be safe, and I wouldn't have to leave Conor."

She opened her mouth to question him further but then realized it made sense. Tara had always worried so much about Eddie. The only time Geraldine could remember seeing her kneel and pray was next to his hospital bed. And she did love Conor to pieces.

"Is that what really happened?" she asked.

"Yes."

All of this had gone on behind Geraldine's back. Eddie and Tara had hidden it from her. "No one ever told me that," she said.

"We figured it would put you in a bad position if you knew. You'd have to lie to people, including Conor. We didn't want you to have to do that."

But she knew it was also because they didn't think they could trust her with that secret. She'd always been so concerned with following the rules.

"Did you tell the police the truth?" she asked Eddie.

"I told Brian."

"What's going to happen to you?"

"I don't know." But he didn't look worried really. He looked relieved.

She felt a swell of emotion. Even with his thick build and gruff beard and potty mouth, she would always see her little brother in the soft eyes and kind smile. Like Tara, Geraldine had spent a lot of her life worrying about Eddie, and she understood why Tara had gone to prison for him. Maybe sometimes breaking the rules was the right thing to do. "Tara did that to protect you," she said.

Eddie nodded. "And I think she's out there right now trying to help you out of some mess."

Yes, she was. Geraldine's eyes started to sting. Tara had saved Eddie, and now she was trying to save Geraldine. She was giving up everything to take care of her family.

That's when Judy's words rang loud and clear in Geraldine's mind: *You had to sacrifice a lot to take care of Eddie and Tara . . . things that were important to you . . .*

Geraldine stood and moved to the kitchen drawers, opened one up, and pulled out her dance class photo. She never made that list Judy asked for, but in a sense this picture said it all, symbolized what she had lost when she was younger. It was a before picture. Not long after it was taken Geraldine lost her mom, then her dad and any semblance of security. Throughout high school she gradually quit everything extracurricular—choir, dance, her friends—because she had to watch Tara and Eddie after school and work on the weekends. She would do it all over again, of course she would. Because she loved her brother and sister.

But then why was she thinking about letting Tara take the blame and return to prison? Just so they could go back to dinners at six thirty and church on Sundays? At some point she had become so rigid with everyone, including herself. Especially herself. Because she was afraid of making mistakes and losing the people she cared about. But she'd been so busy trying to control everything, she was at risk of exactly that—ending up alone. Judy had wanted Geraldine to make that list so she could have some compassion for herself. But she also needed to have compassion for Tara.

Eddie stood and moved beside her, looked down at the picture. "Damn. Look at you." He smiled. "Did you know Tara used to make me walk into town with her sometimes just so she could watch you practice at that little studio?"

"She did?"

He nodded. Then his smile faded. "Do you know where she is, Ger?" He seemed to hold his breath while he waited for her answer. Because he was hoping to save Tara, just like in Mom's fairy tale. But in the fairy tale they all saved one another.

Geraldine shook her head. It was the truth. She didn't know where Tara was, not even which direction she was heading in. "I'm sorry," she said. "I don't know where she went."

He sighed in disappointment and sank back down into his seat.

She tried to swallow a painful ache in her throat, but it wouldn't budge. There was something she could do to help Tara now. She could follow Eddie's lead and tell the truth. But she was so scared. She could get arrested and go to Taconic or somewhere like it. And she would be so ashamed if people knew.

But she'd felt the same way about her collecting. For years she'd lived in fear of people learning her secret and judging her for it. But when the truth came out it wasn't as bad as she assumed. Eddie and Tara hadn't disowned her or forced her to throw everything away. Judy hadn't locked her up in a loony bin. Besides, she could only imagine the shame that would come with letting everyone believe her little sister stole that money. This was Geraldine's chance to save Tara, and she might not get another one.

Eddie sat staring out the window with his hand to his chin, as if trying to figure out what to do next. But Geraldine knew what to do, and she was pretty sure she could do it with his help.

She walked over, set the photo back on the mantel, and turned to her brother. "Eddie? Will you come with me to talk to Mr. Bertucci?"

Chapter Twenty-Five

———————

Right about the time Tara was supposed to be reporting for her drug test, she pulled into Edison Elementary. The school secretary recognized her right away, knew she was listed as an authorized caregiver in Conor's file, so she agreed to pull him out of class for a few minutes.

Initially he looked worried, his brow furrowed above his glasses when he met her by the front desk. "Is everything okay?" he asked.

It was not until that very moment that she realized she hadn't really thought about this. She didn't want to upset him, just see him before she left. Because she didn't know when she would see him again.

She put a hand on his shoulder and forced a smile. "Yeah, everything's okay." As she guided him away from the reception area, she thought about what to say. She couldn't exactly tell him she was on the run from the police and leaving indefinitely. Maybe just that she was heading out of town for a few days . . .

But when she turned to face him she couldn't lie. So she came as close to the truth as she could get. "I'm having a tough day, Con-man. And I could really use a joke."

"Okay." His face scrunched up for a moment. "Why wouldn't the shrimp share his treasure?"

"I don't know."

"Because he was a little shellfish."

She laughed, because she couldn't cry.

"Better?" he asked.

"Yep."

"See?" He smiled and shrugged a shoulder. "All you have to do is ask for help."

She smiled back and nodded. Then she hugged him, told him she loved him, and managed to make it out of the building before the tears came.

Her next stop was about getting some money. She didn't have enough on her to fill the tank, let alone buy food and keep traveling for a while. There was only one person she could think of to go to for help. Someone who not only owed her, but would also understand the position she was in. After all, he'd run away from home himself seventeen years ago.

She pulled into a convenience store near I-95, where she asked for directions to the return address on her father's letter. The young clerk smirked and, before jotting them down for her, told her she really needed to get a phone. Although she knew the Bronx wasn't far from Port Chester, she still experienced an internal jolt when she realized he was only thirty minutes away. She had no idea how long he'd been this close.

As she headed south on the highway, moving that much closer to him, her resolve faltered. The idea of seeing him sent waves of apprehension through her. She had rejected his attempt to communicate in the past, and now she was showing up out of the blue asking for money. But when Tara really considered why she was so nervous about seeing him, she realized it had as much to do with her reaction as his. Before she was old enough to understand her dad wasted precious money on gambling, covered debts by stealing cars, avoided a sick wife and kids who needed him—before she realized all that, Bobby Connelly had just been her dad. Her fast-driving, cigarette-smoking, wisecracking dad.

Her mother had been pretty and soft-spoken, with a touch of elegance. But there had been something inaccessible there, as if she kept part of herself tucked away where no one could quite reach it. Some of it was probably because she was sick for a long time. But Tara suspected it also had to do with disappointment. She had left Ireland looking for the American dream. Instead she found a good-looking charmer who talked a good game but couldn't deliver.

Where her mother seemed delicate and sad at times, her father had been lively and warm. Tara still remembered he was the only person who could get her mom to laugh out loud. He didn't lecture his kids or get too angry or worry about bedtimes and homework, never seemed to take much seriously. And even after her mom died and Tara knew he should be more present, she was quick to forgive because when he was around it was so nice. She used to get upset with Geraldine because she would nag him when he was home—about money, the house, needing help with "the kids"—and Tara was his biggest defender when anyone dared to say he was derelict in his parental duties.

Which is why she took it so damn hard when he left the way he did. It was bad enough he almost killed Eddie, the person she relied on most in the world. But then he disappeared. She waited weeks for him to come back, holding vigil beside Eddie's hospital bed, assuring Geraldine and all the adults around them he would return. As time went on and she saw what Eddie went through in the following years, she had shoved her father into a small room in the back of her mind and locked it tight.

His address was four blocks off the highway. Kingsbridge Road was a steep hill in a busy working-class neighborhood with lots of older, utilitarian brown and yellow brick buildings. They had security doors and metal fire escapes; air-conditioning units hung out windows. Tara found a parking space across the street from his building and hopped out before she could start doubting this plan again. He mentioned in his letter that he was bartending night shifts, so there was a decent chance he was home during the day. Otherwise, she'd have to wait.

With equal parts relief and dread she saw the name R. CONNELLY next to the buzzer for Apartment 3H. She didn't press it right away, considered how to respond if he answered—most likely with, "Who's there?" She could blurt out her name and hope he let her in, or she could say she had a delivery and get up to his door before she announced herself. She decided on the latter and hit the intercom, but the security door just clicked and buzzed. He'd let her in without checking.

Both sides of the small foyer were lined with rows of vertical mailboxes. The hallway went off to the right and left after that, as far as she could see in the dim light, but she headed up the staircase straight ahead of her to the third story. The linoleum floors were old, the walls were painted a bland blue, and the apartment doors were metal with at least two locks on each of them. Whatever life her father was living now hadn't upped his financial status, and chances were slim he'd have a lot of cash to spare. But anything would help. She made her way down the quiet corridor and knocked on 3H. She shored herself up with a deep breath at the sound of unhurried footsteps and a lock being turned.

When he first opened the door she thought she had the wrong apartment. The man standing before her was not the Bobby Connelly she remembered. This man was old, with gray hair on his head and gray whiskers on his wrinkled cheeks, and he wasn't as broad as her father. But he was so stunned to see her standing there she had time to take a second look. She realized that although the color had faded from his hair, it was still thick. And his shoulders and arms, visible because he was wearing only an undershirt with his jeans, were still muscular, just covered in looser skin. But it was his eyes that confirmed it beyond a shadow of a doubt. He had dark, round, expressive eyes, just like Eddie's.

She could see some of the same internal dialogue going on for him behind that shocked gaze, his mind denying it was her while recognizing her with certainty at the same time.

"Tara." When he said her name in his deep, scratchy voice, there was no question in it, only wonder.

"Hi."

His brows ticked up. "It was you I buzzed in?"

She nodded.

His mouth trembled in a nervous half smile. "I thought you were the UPS guy. He buzzes around this time till someone lets him in." He swallowed and looked down, brought an embarrassed hand to his undershirt. "Sorry, wasn't expecting company."

Tara stayed quiet. She wasn't ready to explain why she was there.

He stepped back and pulled the door open wider. "Will you come in? I just made coffee."

"Okay." She stepped inside and followed him down a narrow hallway, past a living room with a braided rug, a recliner, and a TV. Across from it was a kitchenette with a little round table under a window in the corner. The whole place was wallpapered, but it was so faded she had to squint to make out the design. A fleur-de-lis pattern.

He removed a short-sleeve shirt from the back of a chair, threw it on, and started buttoning it, nodding toward the other chair. "Would you like to sit down?"

This wasn't a family reunion. She was here on business. But she figured they both needed to be a little comfortable with each other if they were going to have this conversation, so she took a seat. The New York *Daily News* was open on the table, and a pair of glasses sat on top.

He moved to the counter to pour two coffees. After he set them on the table he gathered spoons, sugar, and cream.

Tara had experienced a few surreal moments lately, but here was another one: the burly father she hadn't seen since she was twelve serving her coffee and pouring half-and-half into a ceramic dispenser instead of just putting the carton on the table.

He set everything down and sat across from her.

She added sugar to her coffee and took a sip, trying to decide where to begin. But it was hard to think while he was staring at her.

"You look so much like your mom," he said.

She immediately felt a pinch in her throat—the very reaction she'd been afraid of—and took another sip to loosen it up.

He folded his arms on the table. "How are you? It looks like you made it through Taconic okay."

"How did you know I was there?"

"I still got a couple buddies in the old neighborhood. Once in a while they come across a piece of news and pass it on." He glanced down at his coffee. "When I heard it was a drug charge, I worried maybe that was an issue for you now."

"No. I was just making a delivery." She was fleetingly tempted to add that she'd been filling in for Eddie. Probably because this man was still her father, albeit a negligent one. But then she felt ashamed. Ashamed that she cared what he thought enough to almost throw her brother under the bus.

"Can I ask about Geraldine and Eddie? And I hear Eddie has a son."

She didn't want to talk to him about Conor. It was a protective thing, like keeping him a stranger to his grandfather might lift some of the burden of their family's history off Conor's shoulders. "Eddie's good. He's been in construction since high school. He still struggles with the brain injury, but he's a hard worker and a good dad." She was pretty sure she'd partially meant all that as a by-contrast dig.

But he just pressed his lips together. "You and Eddie always had a special thing."

"That 'special thing' came out of surviving our childhood together."

He nodded. An acknowledgment, or admission, of sorts. At least he wasn't going to try to pretty up the past or defend himself in some way.

"Geraldine's a bookkeeper. She's been with the same company for fifteen years now. She was a big help to Eddie while I was gone."

"Sounds about right for Geraldine. She's been handling money and taking care of things since she was far too young." He sipped his coffee. "And what about you? You're settled in back home?"

It was now or never, no time to dance around it. "I'm in some trouble actually. I need money so I can get out of town. That's why I'm here."

He brought a hand to his chin and studied her for a long moment. Then he stood from the table and moved to a drawer next to the fridge. She wondered if that's where he kept some cash, if it was going to be that easy, but he just removed a pack of Marlboros, a lighter, and an ashtray. "I hope you don't mind," he said, sitting back down, "but I think I'm going to need one of these." He pulled one out and stuck it between his lips. Then he held the pack toward her and cocked an eyebrow.

She hesitated, but not for long, before mentally apologizing to Conor, pulling one out for herself, and accepting the lighter from him.

He inhaled deeply. "What kind of trouble are you in?"

"The kind that could send me back to prison."

"Another drug charge?" She didn't sense judgment from him. More like he was assessing how bad her situation was.

"No. They think I stole money from Geraldine's boss."

"But you didn't?"

She took a tense draw off her cigarette. "Look, it's a long story."

"What do your brother and sister have to say about this?"

That was a little too close to playing Dad for Tara's comfort. "It doesn't matter. Can you help me out or not?"

He flinched, like he'd been scolded for overstepping. They both knew he had no standing here. "I'm just asking if you've really thought this through."

"Yes. And I don't have any choice."

He shifted in his seat, considered his next words. "That's how I felt, after the accident with Eddie. I thought it would all come crashing down.

The cops would find out about the cars, I'd be arrested. Not only would I go to prison, but the guy I worked for . . . He ran a chop shop out of Harlem, and he was scary. I knew he'd hold you kids over my head. I didn't want to go to prison, but I also believed leaving was the best way to protect you. Disappearing seemed the only option." His forearms were resting on the table, and he leaned forward over them. "But take a good look around, Tara. This is what running will get you."

She did look around then. At the dish drainer by the sink that held one plate, one glass, and a fork. The lone jacket hanging on the coatrack in the corner. The single recliner in the living room that faced the TV. She searched for signs of another person spending time in this space, being part of his world—clothing, pictures, personal items—but there were none. The apartment, much like his life, she suspected, felt small and lonely.

He took a drag off his cigarette. "I have some cash, and I'll give you everything I got on hand if that's what you want . . ."

She could hear the unspoken *but* in his tone. Through the light haze that hung between them she saw restraint in the set of his jaw, like he knew he couldn't tell her what to do, but he was trying to serve as a cautionary tale.

Tara didn't want to run, but if she went back home she didn't know how to keep her sister and herself out of jail. Not that she'd given it a whole lot of thought. When Geraldine told her about the money, Tara had simply panicked. She hadn't talked to anyone about it, not Eddie or Brian, not even Geraldine really, who had set all this in motion. What had Eddie told her just that morning? *You make decisions alone when it affects other people.* That's exactly what she'd done here.

Maybe her father sensed her hesitation because he held up a finger. "You want to see something?" he asked, pulling an old-school, black leather wallet from his back pocket. He slipped a small photo from the billfold. "I took this before your mom died, and I've been carrying it around ever since."

She picked up the picture, which had tattered edges and had been handled so much even the creases were worn smooth. It was a photo of her, Geraldine, and Eddie, one she'd never seen before. They were standing in front of the maple tree in the yard, Geraldine and Eddie next to each other, with Tara—shorter than both by a few inches—in front of them.

Her father pointed to the photo. "Whenever I look at it, I think of that fairy tale Mom used to tell you guys, about the Connellys of County Down. Do you remember it?"

"Sort of." She ran her eyes over the picture again, trying to glean elements of the story her mother used to tell. Though they were all smiling wide at the same time there was nothing else remarkable about the photo. They wore jeans and sweatshirts, Geraldine carried a backpack, Eddie had a hat on. Maybe a first-day-of-school snapshot. "Do you remember it?" she asked.

"You hear something enough times, you never forget it."

"Do you remember what our special powers were?"

His eyebrows went up, probably at the note of urgency in her voice. "Sure I do." He pulled a hand down his stubble a couple times, a pure Eddie gesture. "Now, Geraldine was the protector. She was angry as hell when you took Eddie and ran off for that forest, but she went after you right away. She found you guys trapped in the bog and used a rope to pull you out. She always had that backpack full of warm clothes, food, tools—everything you needed. She kept you all safe."

Tara had sort of expected that.

"And Eddie," her father said, his voice softening a bit. "He was the heart of your little team. When things got hard, and you and Geraldine were arguing—like you always did—or you wanted to quit, Eddie kept you going. He had his cap, and he would turn it backward rally style, like in baseball." He mimed grabbing the brim of an invisible hat and spinning it around. "Then he would tell a story, make you laugh, carry you a little ways. Whatever you needed to make it through that forest."

She smiled. That sounded about right. But at the same time there was a fluttery feeling in her stomach because she didn't know what was coming next. In the picture, Geraldine had her backpack and Eddie wore his cap, but Tara wasn't carrying anything. She was just standing there, in front of them.

"And you," her father said. "You went off to find that castle in the first place. That's why your mom gave you an internal compass that was never wrong, because you always wanted to explore." There was pride in his smile. "And no matter where you were, or what was happening, if it was pitch-black outside or the fairies were trying to trick you guys . . ." He shrugged. "You always knew the right way to go."

She drew in a breath, somewhat stunned by a sudden memory of her mother's words: *You were the True North, Tara.* And she felt closer to her mother than she had in so long. Almost as if, for the briefest second, she was in arm's reach.

"You know," he said, "what I liked most about that fairy tale is that you all saved each other. You knew the way to go, but you needed Geraldine and Eddie to get there."

She couldn't help but offer up a rueful smile. He'd done a good job of making his point: she didn't have to be in it alone.

Somewhere along the line she had stopped trusting that. After losing her mother and almost losing her brother, after being infinitely let down by the man sitting across from her, she had become tired of disappointment catching her off guard. She decided relying on herself was the only way to avoid getting hurt again. But look at the fallout, not just for her but also for the people she loved. She wanted Eddie to have more confidence in himself, yet she showed little faith in him. She rode roughshod over Geraldine, which only made her feel more out of control. Even though Brian was willing to accept the idea that she'd been involved with a drug dealer and his business—that's how much he cared about her— still she didn't trust him with the truth. She thought of Conor and his words earlier that day: *All you have to do is ask for help.* What would she be teaching him by running away?

Her father had run, but he'd still been in a prison of sorts. A prison of regret and loneliness. Maybe that's why he wanted to visit her at Taconic, because he understood what she was going through better than most.

He tamped out his cigarette, and she did the same.

"Well?" he said. "Should I get the cash?"

Time to decide what she was doing. She had violated her parole today—three times. She failed to show for the drug test, skipped out on the meeting with DaCosta, and left the county without permission. Maybe the police had traced the money and were already looking for her. Returning to Port Chester could mean going back to prison for a while.

But looking across the table at her father, a glimpse of her potential future, she couldn't believe she'd actually considered running away, leaving Brian and her family, Gordi and Lance and the job she loved. Whatever consequence she had to face, the life she'd been building was worth fighting for. She felt her shoulders relax. "No."

His sigh was full of relief.

It struck her then. Her father was the *only* person who'd wanted to visit her at Taconic. And he saved her from making a terrible decision today.

"Thank you," she said.

His brows lifted in surprise, and for the first time since she walked in, his eyes went glassy. He nodded once in response.

"Before I go," she said, "can I borrow your cell phone to make a call?"

"Would a landline do?" he asked, pointing behind her, toward an old yellow wall phone with a long cord. "I never got around to getting a cell phone."

Despite it all she had to smile. "A landline will work."

He left the room to give her some privacy, and she made the call. But in the end she had to leave a message. It was the best she could do at the moment.

After that her father rose from his recliner and followed her down the hall to the front door.

She stepped across the threshold and turned back to face him, not sure what to say.

"I know I don't have the right to ask," he said. "But when things settle down for you, I'd really like to see you again. And Eddie and Geraldine, if they're open to it. Maybe meet my grandson someday."

Tara paused before responding. There was still a lot to come to terms with, considering what he'd done, but today was a beginning. "I'll keep that in mind. And I'll talk to Eddie and Ger about it."

The gratitude showed in his eyes before he said it. "Thank you, Tara."

She offered him a small smile. Then she turned and left.

～

A swirl of emotions was going on as she walked outside and jumped in the truck, but she focused on her next steps. She needed to talk to

Geraldine—who still might be sitting out in the shed at this point—about coming clean with Mr. Bertucci, doing some damage control. And Tara wanted Eddie to be part of that discussion. It would be tough for Geraldine, but together they would help her through this. And she would come out stronger for it on the other side.

But the first order of business was finding Brian. For the first time since leaving Taconic she wished she had a cell phone. With each passing second her sense of urgency grew: as soon as he heard about the stolen money in her account he would try to get in touch with her. And if he learned she had left town . . . It couldn't look much worse.

The idea of losing him brought on a profound sadness. There was so much she already loved about him. The warmth in his eyes and his smile, how well his sense of humor matched hers. How safe he made her feel. That was Brian's special power. It was like he provided an invisible shield between her and the rest of the world. If she was drawing him, what would symbolize his shield . . . What would be his magic backpack or rally cap? Probably the suit. The one she teased him about.

She was only a block from the highway when she noticed the flashing lights behind her and realized she was being pulled over. Her hands immediately started to sweat against the wheel. But even if they were already looking for her, what were the odds they would have tracked her down here? Maybe she'd been speeding or cursed with another busted taillight. After pulling off into the parking lot of a strip mall, she turned the truck off, sat very still, and waited, talking herself down. Hopefully, at worst, she was in for a traffic ticket of some kind.

When she looked in the rearview mirror to see a black SUV, her heart sank at the idea that it was Brian. She wanted to be the one to find him rather than him coming after her. But when the driver stepped out and started toward her, she realized it wasn't him. It was Hank Doyle, Brian's uncle. He walked to the truck and tapped his knuckles against the window.

She rolled it down. "Detective Doyle?"

"Miss Connelly. I'm going to have to ask you to step out of the truck, please."

Traffic was loud in the street, and she hoped she'd misheard him. "I'm sorry?"

He leaned a little closer. "You're going to need to step outside, please."

"Can I ask why?"

"I can explain, but I think it would be better if we spoke out here." He took a step back to make room for her to open the door.

She didn't have to get out of the truck, certainly not without a reason. But this was Brian's uncle, his only family, and she'd gotten off to a bad start with him a long time ago. She opened the door and stepped down out of the pickup. "Is everything okay?" she asked.

He pulled off his sunglasses. "Miss Connelly, did you have permission from your parole officer to leave the county?"

"I was on my way back right now."

"I'm going to have to ask you to come with me. You're wanted for questioning in regards to some missing money."

She held her hands up in front of her, like that would slow all this down before it got out of hand. "I know about that. I was on my way back to Port Chester."

His "mm-hmm" was full of doubt.

"It has to do with my sister—"

"We can talk about all that at the station."

"I'm not going to the station."

He sighed. "Miss Connelly, I'd rather not force this, but I will if I have to. I've obtained a warrant for your arrest, but we can do it without the cuffs."

Her legs went weak. "If I can just call my sister. I don't have a cell phone, but you could try her."

His hand shot up. "We're not going to have this discussion on the side of the road." There was no compromise in his voice or expression.

She only had one hope left, though it was fading fast. If Hank knew about the money, Brian must know too. But he wasn't there. "Where's Detective Nolan?" she asked.

He slid his sunglasses back on. "Miss Connelly, Detective Nolan isn't going to help you with this."

She felt her shoulders slump. Maybe Brian had removed himself from the whole situation. Given her disappearing act, he probably assumed she was guilty.

"What's it gonna be?" Doyle asked.

She had no choice here, he was going to take her in one way or the other. "Fine. Should I follow you up to the Port Chester station?"

"I figured we'd just head to the Fiftieth Precinct, right up the road here. Use one of their interview rooms. It shouldn't take long."

That sounded hopeful. As soon as she got to a phone she could call Geraldine. Besides, this way she didn't run the risk of bumping into Brian. She wanted to catch him alone—certainly no Hank—while she explained everything.

"Your car will be safe parked here," he said, gesturing to the mini-mall.

She glanced at Eddie's pickup, then at the Explorer.

"Okay." She locked the truck, dropped the keys in her pocket, and followed Hank to the dark SUV she'd vowed never to ride in again.

Chapter Twenty-Six

———

Eddie hadn't known it was possible for someone to cry for so damn long. Didn't tear ducts dry up at a certain point? But Geraldine had been at it for a while. She started at the kitchen table, when she explained why she wanted him to go with her to talk to Mr. Bertucci. The more Eddie heard, the angrier he got—*Jesus Christ, Geraldine. You fucking set her up.* But as soon as the words left his mouth he realized with a horrible shock how hypocritical they were. Because Eddie had done the same thing to Tara. Not intentionally, but he'd put her in the same position: taking the fall for his crime. At least Geraldine was owning it sooner rather than later.

After she came clean with him they called Mr. Bertucci and asked him to meet them at the office. She cried during the drive and while they waited for him. For the most part it was just a slow, quiet stream of tears and blowing her nose. Though tougher moments would trigger a few sobs—when the old man came through the door, when she admitted moving the money. Eddie stayed calm, encouraged her the best he could. He tried to be reassuring for both of them, especially Mr. Bertucci. Because if he believed they could work through this together, he'd be more willing to withdraw his complaint.

But Mr. Bertucci was having a hard time absorbing what Geraldine was telling him. He sagged in his chair, hands dangling between his skinny knees. "But, Geraldine, I don't understand. After all these years . . . Why could you not tell me?" He lifted a hand, brought his fingertips together, shook it while he spoke. "I even came to you, asked if you needed help, eh?"

Geraldine dropped her head.

"That's just it, Mr. Bertucci," Eddie said. "Ger thinks the world of you, and she loves this job. She didn't want to let you down."

He nodded but still wore a puzzled expression. Apparently, where Mr. Bertucci came from, if people cared about each other they didn't lie to their faces and threaten their livelihood.

Geraldine cleared her throat and sat up a little straighter. "It's true, Mr. Bertucci. I didn't want to worry you or disappoint you. And I thought I could fix it all so nobody got hurt. I *still* can fix it." She paused. "Or Rita can do it. I can give her everything she needs."

Eddie knew how hard it was for his sister to make that offer, to give up trying to control what happened here.

"And you say the money is in an account in your sister's name?" Mr. Bertucci asked.

"Yes, but she knew nothing about it." Geraldine shuffled through the papers in her lap, found what she wanted, and handed it to him. "I printed out the bank statement. You can see it's all there, every dime."

He pulled glasses from his shirt pocket and put them on so he could read through the statement.

When Geraldine glanced at Eddie with worried, puffy eyes, he gave her an encouraging nod. Despite it all, he was proud of her. She was scared shitless of what might happen, assumed it would be the worst—*Everyone will know what I did, Eddie. I could go to jail*—but she was still doing the right thing. And Eddie believed she would feel much better when this was all over. He'd felt like the worst kind of loser while confessing to Brian, and he wouldn't have blamed Brian if he hit him—part of him *wanted* Brian to hit him. But even though Eddie would always carry that guilt, there was relief in taking some kind of responsibility.

Mr. Bertucci lowered the statement to his lap. "Detective Doyle said he traced the money." He turned to Eddie. "This looks bad for Tara, yes?"

"It does. But we're going to the police station after this, so Geraldine can explain."

Geraldine offered a firm nod in confirmation and held up an accordion folder. "Mr. Bertucci, this is all the paperwork for the outstanding tax payments."

He took the folder and flipped through.

Eddie checked his phone. Nothing new from Brian. He hadn't found his partner or Tara in the last couple hours, which made Eddie a little frantic. Maybe that Doyle asshole had found her. Maybe she'd done something reckless to help Geraldine, just like she did a year and a half ago for him.

He took a slow, deep breath. The headache that had started earlier in Judy's office was still there, lying in wait at the perimeter of his brain, applying pressure until it found an opening—like a rush of anxious thoughts—where it could sidle in and start playing havoc.

Mr. Bertucci closed the folder and patted it with his fingers. "Geraldine, it hurts deeply that you lied to me. But I don't believe you intended to steal from me, or harm the business."

"No, Mr. Bertucci. I would never do that."

He nodded. "But I'm sure you understand I cannot have you in the office manager position any longer." His expression was so sad. Eddie was pretty sure it was as difficult for the old guy to say it as it was for Geraldine to hear it.

Her voice was almost a whisper. "I understand."

"I want you and Rita both here tomorrow," he said. "We will all go through this folder and get the quarterlies done. Move the money back into our account and do this properly. Then, you will take us through any outstanding payrolls and errors. *All* of it"—he chopped the air with a hand—"so we can clean everything up."

Geraldine nodded. "Whatever you need me to do."

Mr. Bertucci shifted his attention to Eddie. "Then I suppose I should accompany you to the police station. They will want to know we have this sorted out, eh? Hopefully, that will be enough to stop them from pressing charges."

～

Mr. Bertucci wanted to stop home and check on his wife before they talked to the police, and Eddie needed to pick Conor up from practice, so they arranged to meet at the station in an hour. While Eddie drove the van to Conor's school, Geraldine sat in the passenger seat, staring out the window. She seemed to be done with the crying.

Lorraine had been a lifesaver. She left work to give him a ride home earlier that afternoon, and when Eddie asked if Conor could hang out at her place for a bit after practice, she said no problem. She even offered to pick him up, but Eddie didn't want to spring it on Conor that way. His whole evening routine was going to be upended, he'd have lots of questions, and Eddie wanted to keep his worrying to a minimum. Lorraine hadn't pried at all, even though Eddie offered only a vague explanation—*I got some stuff going on with my sisters.* It's not that he didn't want to tell her more, but one thing would lead to a long story, including what he'd done for a living for a little while. Not something he could breeze over in a five-minute drive.

Geraldine let out a long, shaky sigh.

"You did good, Ger," Eddie said.

"What am I going to do for a job? I need a job, Eddie." She turned to him with wide eyes. "Unless they arrest me today."

"They're not going to arrest you." Eddie felt fairly confident about that, especially with Mr. Bertucci on their side. He pulled into the school parking lot, next to the practice fields, and spotted Conor among the crowd of kids gathering their equipment. "We're going to meet with Brian," he said. "I already called him about it." Brian had been on his way into some meeting, where he was hoping to finally catch his partner, so Eddie only had time to tell him they could clear up the Bertucci business. "He knows us," Eddie said. "We'll explain everything, it'll be okay." But the doubts were still nagging him.

Conor grabbed his bag and headed toward the van, picking up speed when he saw Eddie behind the wheel. The surprised smile on his son's face momentarily lifted Eddie above the mess of this day. He got out to slide open the back door.

"What're you doing here, Dad?" Conor slung his backpack into the van and jumped in.

Eddie got back in the driver's seat and explained he was helping Aunt Geraldine with some work stuff. Then he broke the news that Conor would be spending a little time with Lorraine and Katie. He tried to sound upbeat, mentioned Lorraine was planning to order pizza for dinner.

"But, *Daaaad*, Katie's so bossy, and all she's gonna wanna do is build her stupid princess castle." He flopped back against his seat.

"Sorry, Con. But Aunt Geraldine and I need to take care of a few more things."

Conor glanced at Geraldine, then took a longer look at her. "Is everything okay, Aunt Geraldine?"

She didn't turn her head, only said, "Yes, Conor."

His brows pushed together. "Where's Tara? Why can't I stay with her?"

"She's not home yet," Eddie said, starting up the van.

"She came to school this afternoon. She stopped by for a joke."

Eddie exchanged a look with Geraldine. That didn't sound right, Tara interrupting Conor's school day to ask for a joke.

"Did she say anything else?" Eddie asked him.

"Just that she was having a tough day."

Damn. Tara had disappeared but stopped to see Conor on the way to wherever she was going. Like maybe she was saying goodbye.

"But she'll be home from work soon," Conor said. "Can't I stay alone for a little bit—"

"You know what, Conor?" Geraldine turned in her seat. "I could really use a joke right now."

Eddie watched Conor stare at her, slightly stunned at the request, coming from his no-nonsense aunt.

After a moment, he asked, "How do you make a tissue dance?"

"I don't know."

"Put a little boogey in it."

It took Geraldine a few seconds, but then she got it, and she laughed long and hard, harder than Eddie could remember her laughing. Part of it might have been how appropriate that particular joke was today, but Eddie figured it was also an emotional release. Whatever it was, it was good to see. Hopefully it would provide some strength for the last step in all this.

Conor watched her laugh with a big grin on his face. Eddie caught his eye in the rearview mirror and winked.

He also threw Ger a grateful smile when she looked his way. She had asked for a joke to distract Conor, and it worked.

Sure enough, when they arrived at Lorraine's, Katie was waiting to lead Conor back to her room to work on the castle.

"Come on, Conor. I really want to get this thing done already so I can get on with my life."

Conor followed, head down, so Eddie was sure to know he wasn't happy about it.

Geraldine was waiting in the van, so Eddie and Lorraine were left alone.

"Thanks again for this, Lorraine. For everything." He bumped his cap up. "Sorry the day got so hectic for me."

"That's okay. But listen, Mr. Dunbar spoke with me this afternoon." She looked up at him with bright eyes and a big smile. "He's going to offer you the job, Eddie."

He wanted to pick her up and swing her around again, and she looked ready for it. But something held him back. "Well, it's thanks to you," he said.

"No." She waved him off. "It was all you."

"Seriously, Lorraine. I was hoping to take you to dinner to celebrate, not ask you to babysit."

A light blush crept up her cheeks. "That's okay. I don't know what's going on, but I think it's nice you're close to your sisters, that they can lean on you like this." She was looking at him like he was some kind of hero.

That's when Eddie realized what his hesitation was about. Lorraine wouldn't be looking at him like that if she knew what he'd done. She might not want anything to do with him ever again.

She leaned toward him and whispered: "We can do dinner another night. And maybe try that kiss again."

Eddie wanted that. He really did. Life was looking up—a promotion, managing his headaches better, stepping up for his family—and he knew Lorraine had a hand in that. But he was done being dishonest. He pulled his cap off and held it in his hands. "Lorraine, we have to talk when I finish this business with my sisters. I need to be honest with you."

She brought an uncertain hand to her mouth, like she was afraid she'd misread things.

"There's something I need to tell you. Something stupid I did a while back, and it hurt people."

"What was it?"

He checked his phone for the time and shook his head. "I'm so sorry, I have to go right now—I have to do this thing for Tara. But then I will come back here and tell you everything. After that, if you still want me to kiss you, there's nothing I'd rather do."

Lorraine studied him for a long time, her expression tough to read. There was hope in it, though he also saw the apprehension. She'd been hurt before by an unreliable man. But she said, "Okay," and gave him a close hug before he left.

Eddie headed out to the van, where his sister was waiting, her nerves probably starting to unravel again. He had to help Geraldine through this last frightening step, make sure Tara was clear of this hurdle. Then he'd return to Lorraine and tell her the whole truth.

And he would do whatever he had to do, wait as long as he had to wait, to prove her right for believing in him in the first place.

Chapter Twenty-Seven

Brian was worried. It had been hours since anyone heard from Tara, and he'd had no luck tracking down his uncle that afternoon. His last hope was that Hank would show for the five o'clock task force meeting at the station. He better. Because Eddie was coming in after that with Ernesto Bertucci to apparently straighten out this whole mess. Brian planted himself by the front desk in the lobby so he wouldn't miss Hank when he walked through the door. But five minutes before the meeting was scheduled to start there was still no sign of him. Brian turned to the desk sergeant. "You sure you haven't heard anything from him?"

"Christ, Nolan. How many times you gonna ask me the same thing?" He shook his head. "Why don't you check the message that's on your voice mail? That might have something to do with it."

"What message?"

The desk sergeant pointed to the switchboard with his pen. "Your light's blinking. Maybe Hank left you a message . . ."

But Brian was already rushing back to his desk, where the red light on his phone was flashing. Damn it. He'd kept his cell close by all afternoon, but he'd never thought to check his desk phone. He grabbed the handset and pressed the voice mail button. After a beep the message started:

"Hey, Brian, it's me."

At the sound of Tara's voice, his legs went loose. He dropped into his chair and covered his other ear with his free hand to shut out the background noise.

"Sorry about leaving a message on your work phone, but I don't know your cell number." A weary chuckle, then a sigh. "I was really hoping to catch you. I have so much I need to tell you . . . I'm sorry I waited this long—I know that's what you wanted over the weekend, I was just scared. I've never been good at trusting people . . ."

He could hear shaky emotion in her voice.

"But I trust you, Brian. All the way. And I'd like to tell you everything, if you'll still let me. I'm heading back to Port Chester now, and I'll go straight to the station to find you. But listen, I don't know what's waiting for me there . . . I have no idea what you've heard at this point, but I really fucked up today. I panicked and made some decisions that could land me back in Taconic." She paused, sniffled, and when she spoke again he had no doubt it was through tears. "But I want to come home, and I know I can face whatever's coming if I have you."

Brian's heart soared at those words, and he had to remind himself he was sitting in the bullpen when he realized he was close to shedding tears himself.

"I'm in the Bronx right now—part of the long story I have to tell you. But I should be there by three. And Brian . . . I can't wait to see you."

He heard the relief in her voice as she ended the call with those words, but then he checked his watch: 5:25. She'd left the message three hours ago. Something had gone very wrong.

Before hanging up he forwarded the message to his cell phone. Then he headed back to the lobby, where the desk sergeant pointed down the hall toward the conference room. Brian caught up to Hank as he was about to walk into the task force meeting.

"Hank, we need to talk about Tara Connelly," he said. "She didn't take that money."

"Jesus, Bri. A former drug dealer with an assault on her record. Is it that hard to believe she stole this money?"

"She was never a dealer, and she didn't steal anything."

His uncle's sigh was loaded with disappointment. "Never thought I'd see the day when your judgment was this compromised. You've lost all perspective when it comes to this woman, she's playing you."

"No, she's not—"

"No? Then why have you been lying to me about her connection to Andrea Leary? I ran her record myself." Hank stepped closer and lowered his voice. "You think I haven't noticed something going on between you two? Like the day I brought her in for questioning and you barely said a word. You've been thinking with the wrong head, Brian."

"She didn't do what you think she did."

Hank raised his brows and tilted his head, as if to say Brian had just proved his point. "How long's it been going on?" He held up a hand. "Let me guess. Since that day I brought her in? I know you went to her house that night."

"Were you *following* me—"

"Or was it before that, like the day you drove her home from Taconic?"

Brian felt himself recoil in disbelief. Not just because Hank had figured it out, but also because of the lengths he must have gone to—tailing him, calling the prison to ask questions. "Talk about losing perspective— you've been *investigating* me? Like a suspect?"

Hank put a hand on Brian's shoulder. "I'm just looking out for you. You're risking everything—your job, your future, your pension—for a woman with some serious charges on her record. That whole family's a fuckin' mess you don't need to get sucked into. I don't want you to get hurt." He turned and walked into the conference room, where the meeting was getting underway.

Twenty minutes later, without using Andrea's name, Brian had explained to the task force what his new confidential informant was going to deliver. He should have been enjoying the moment: surrounded by colleagues, the object of their kudos because two years of work on the Roland Shea case might finally come to fruition. And it sounded like Andrea would get the deal he promised her. Right then though, he only wanted the meeting to end.

When the prosecutor looked to Hank and asked what he thought of the "chip off the old block," flicking a thumb toward Brian, Hank offered a weak smile. He clearly wasn't in the mood to offer praise, which was fine, because Brian wasn't in the mood to hear it from him.

Hank headed for the door when they wrapped up a few minutes later, but Brian stopped him.

"We have another meeting right now," he said.

"With who?"

"Ernesto Bertucci. Find an open room and I'll go get him." Brian didn't give him a chance to question it, just turned and headed to the lobby.

Hoping to God Eddie was right about putting this Bertucci matter to rest.

～

Brian knew Tara's older sister had issues, but what a shit show.

Geraldine made it through her story, apparently for the third time that day. Eddie gently redirected her once in a while, when she got stuck on repeating that she never intended to break the law, but for the most part he just let her talk. He seemed cautious about putting words in her mouth, probably because Hank's skepticism was written all over his face the whole time she spoke.

When she finished, Mr. Bertucci stepped in. "Detectives, Geraldine is a good girl, eh? She made a terrible mistake, but all of the money is accounted for." He waved his hand over the bank statement sitting in front of him. "She is taking action to correct the situation as quickly as possible, and I want to please withdraw my complaint, Detective Doyle."

Hank didn't respond, only rubbed his chin with a thumb and index finger.

Just to make sure it was crystal clear, Brian asked a question: "Geraldine, did Tara help you with this in any way?"

"No."

"Are you saying Tara knew nothing about all this?"

"She thought I closed that account for her a long time ago." She pulled up in her chair a bit and spoke with a firm voice. "Tara had no idea what I was doing."

When Brian gave Hank a pointed look, he dropped his gaze.

"Will it be a problem?" Eddie asked. "Withdrawing the complaint?"

"It shouldn't be," Brian said. "No charges have been filed yet. We can contact the prosecutor's office in the morning, explain what happened." He looked to his uncle for confirmation.

But Hank was staring at the table, his mouth a stiff line.

"Thank God," Eddie said, nudging his cap up and rubbing his forehead. "If we could just find Tara and let her know."

"She left me a voice mail," Brian said. "She said she was on her way here to find me. But that was almost four hours ago now."

"It's getting late," Eddie said. "I'm worried."

"I know where she is," Hank said, standing from his chair and clearing his throat. "I had an arrest warrant—"

Brian shot up from his chair.

His uncle held up a hand. "The judge signed off when I got proof of the bank transaction."

"You arrested her?" Eddie asked, standing as well, but staying on his side of the table. "Is she here?"

"No," Hank said. "I issued a BOLO and she was spotted heading south, so I followed her. I thought she might be going to do some business for Roland."

Eddie yanked his cap off. "Jesus. She has *nothing* to do with Roland Shea."

Brian put a hand out toward Eddie. They didn't need to get into another confession now. "Hank, where is she?" Brian asked.

"I picked her up in the Bronx."

"What the hell was she doing there?" Eddie asked him. "She doesn't know anyone in the Bronx."

Hank shrugged. "She was visiting someone. When she came out, I pulled her over and brought her into the Fiftieth to question her. She's still there. They're holding her on suspicion of grand larceny."

Before he knew what he was doing, Brian grabbed his uncle by the lapels and backed him up against the wall. "You left her in a cell in the *Bronx*?" In the background he heard Geraldine gasp.

Hank tipped his chin up in defiance. "How the hell was I supposed to know her own sister set her up? It was by the book, Brian. She's on a twenty-four-hour hold. It looked bad, and I was afraid she was pulling you into all of it."

"How do we get her out of there?" Eddie asked.

Without releasing Hank, Brian twisted his wrist so he could read his watch. Then he let go and brought his hands to his head.

"We can post bail, right?" Eddie said.

"You can't get her out tonight," Hank said, tugging on his jacket to straighten it out.

"She has to spend the night in there?" Eddie turned to Brian. "There's nothing you can do?"

Brian shook his head. "The prosecutor's office is involved now, they have to sign off. We can call them first thing tomorrow morning."

Everyone was quiet while that settled in.

Geraldine was the first to break the silence. "I'm so sorry," she said to no one in particular, maybe everyone in the room. Or maybe it was only meant for Tara.

~

Brian could watch the pastel predawn light creeping up from the horizon in the east because he was still awake, sitting on his couch, where he'd been all night. He had drifted off a few times, his head lolling forward or backward, but then he would snap awake and remember Tara was sitting in a holding cell, likely not getting any sleep either. When the edge of the sun finally showed itself, he decided it was time to get started on his busy morning. He left his apartment, hopped in the Grand Cherokee, and headed north.

He had called the Fiftieth Precinct last night to check on Tara and warn whoever was on the other end of the line that she'd better be safe. But the Fiftieth wasn't his home base, so his demands were only worth so much. And that part of the Bronx was a mixed bag. There was no telling who she'd been locked in a cell with for the night. He made the call after things calmed down, after they all had to admit there was nothing more they could do for Tara till morning, and the small, dejected crew—Eddie, Geraldine, and Mr. Bertucci—went home.

Brian parked in the lot and started down the cement path that wound through the headstones. He'd thought about coming straight here after leaving the station the night before, but it was too dark. He'd decided to wait until there was a little light, so he could see their stone, the two overlapping hearts, one engraved with his mother's name and dates, the other with his father's. He and Hank had picked out that stone, along with the quiet plot under the shade of an oak tree. Despite the dewy grass he sat on the ground—he was too tired to care—and leaned back against the tree, resting his forearms on his knees.

He'd come to catch his parents up, and he started by telling them he was going to Rosemary's wedding, that he realized now he wasn't helping his uncle by keeping secrets from him and letting him feel sorry for himself. It wasn't healthy for either of them. They'd both been stuck for a long time, and they needed to move on.

Brian could almost hear his father's response: *We knew that a while ago, kiddo. Glad you're finally getting it.*

He also wanted to tell them about Tara. He started with a basic bio, pictured his parents shaking their heads at her tough childhood. Both of them would appreciate that she was an artist. They'd be concerned to hear she'd been in prison, but less so when he explained why. And he imagined they'd approve of his efforts to help her while she was there. When he told them she felt responsible for far too much, his mother would likely invite him to look in the mirror. He was certain his parents would have liked her. His dad would have been won over by her independence and grit. And his mom would have particularly appreciated how devoted she was to her family, and the way she was with Conor.

More than anything Brian wanted to lay eyes on her, make sure she was okay. He'd listened to her message several times during the night. *I trust you, Brian. All the way . . . I know I can face whatever's coming if I have you.* She had panicked and run yesterday. But, despite knowing she might be in for more prison time, she'd been on her way back to him. And that, he told his parents, was what mattered.

When the sun was high enough to warm him through, and traffic in the streets started to pick up, he figured it was time to get moving. He stood and brushed off the wet seat of yesterday's rumpled pants, stepped close to his parents' stone, and laid his hand on top, like he always did when he said goodbye. But he didn't ask them for forgiveness this time, and he suspected they were relieved about that. He knew now there was no nobility in wallowing in his own guilt, and the only person who had yet to forgive him for not being home that night was him. He thought he could do that now.

His next stop was Parole Services, where he wasn't at all surprised to find Doreen DaCosta at her desk before the normal workday started. She looked up when he knocked lightly on her open door.

"Good morning, Ms. DaCosta," he said, stepping into her office. He had a large carton of coffee in each hand and placed one on her desk.

"Detective Nolan?" Her eyebrows arched. "You look like you haven't slept all night."

"That's because I haven't slept all night." He dropped into one of her guest chairs.

She leaned back in her seat and laced her fingers in front of her. The long nails were bright white now, with little stars all over them. "Lemme guess. This has got something to do with Tara Connelly."

He nodded. "It has everything to do with Tara Connelly."

"You know she broke parole again yesterday? Several times?"

"I do."

She gestured to her phone. "And this morning I got a message about some warrant for grand larceny."

"I know about that too."

"Mm-hmm." Her eyes darted to the coffee he'd put on her desk. "I hope you didn't think you could come down here and bribe me with that. Because the truth is it looks bad for her."

"It does. But I'd like to fill you in on a few things." He paused to emphasize the next word. "Please."

Her sigh was long and loud and exasperated. "You know, I met her 'bosses'"—air quotes—"yesterday. She was AWOL for our meeting, but they insisted on showing me around their 'office'"—more air quotes— "and telling me how important she is to them. Her brother left me a forever voice mail last night, trying to explain everything. And here you are at the crack of dawn, no doubt to convince me to give her another chance. Now I don't know how a train wreck like Tara Connelly got so many cheerleaders, but can you tell me why I should believe she's finally gonna get her shit together?"

Brian pulled his cell phone from his jacket pocket and held it up. "Maybe we start by letting her speak for herself. I have a message you really need to hear."

～

Twenty minutes later he hopped back in his car and headed toward Hank's. They were due for a tough talk. Brian would start by telling him he was going to Rosemary's wedding, then they needed to talk about the job. He had thought about it while sitting on his couch in the dark all night, and he planned to tell his uncle they shouldn't work together anymore. Brian's anger had subsided, he believed Hank was looking out for him. But their relationship had just gotten too muddled. He didn't think Hank would disagree.

Brian had even considered requesting a transfer, working out of another location. But once that thought occurred to him, another, unexpected possibility presented itself. Maybe he could do something else altogether, something other than being a cop. It didn't take a genius to deduce that on some level he joined the force because of what happened to his parents, to try to find justice and redemption in solving crimes. He also did it to follow in his uncle's footsteps.

Maybe this was an opportunity to figure out what he really wanted to do. He liked helping people who needed it, but there were different ways to do that, some of which didn't involve dwelling on the dark side of human nature. He'd rather be more of an advocate, assist them with understanding and navigating the criminal justice system so it couldn't be used against them. He'd learned a lot about people the last ten years, and he wouldn't mind using that knowledge to help lift them up rather than lock them up.

As he drove toward Hank's, the sun brightening a cloudless blue morning, Brian imagined Tara's reaction to all that: *That was quite a spiel.* And he smiled.

Chapter Twenty-Eight

_____

Technically, Tara hadn't broken her vow to never wake up in a prison cell again. But only because she never slept. Even if she wanted to, the rigid seat and constant noise weren't conducive. There were no bunks in this holding cell, only cement benches against cement walls, and one vile communal toilet in the corner, barely hidden behind a half wall. Fortunately, there were only four other women in the cell. The guard who put her in there called it a Monday night lull.

Hank's interrogation the day before hadn't taken long. He read her her rights, and she agreed to talk to him. But just like twenty months ago she played dumb, insisted she knew nothing about the missing money, even when he said she might be looking at grand larceny. Tara wanted to talk to Brian, Eddie, and Geraldine before telling Hank Doyle anything. His agenda seemed almost personal, and she suspected he was fishing to some degree because he didn't charge her, though he decided to hold her overnight.

She sat forward and stretched, twisted side to side, working out the kinks that had set in after sitting in the same position all night. But she tried not to make a sound. The younger woman in stilettos and heavy makeup slumped over a few feet away was finally asleep. She'd come in during the night, drunk or stoned or both, crying and ranting. Which went on until she vomited and passed out.

There was no way of knowing what time it was because there were no clocks in the cell, not even a window to guess by. Complaints about the holding cell notwithstanding, Tara preferred it to the relative privacy and comfort of a regular cell because that would have meant she was moving further into the system. They could hold her for only twenty-four hours without officially charging her, so in a holding cell there was still the hope of being released or bonded out.

The problem was she had little chance of either if no one knew she was here. She'd asked for her phone call, but when they told her she couldn't call her family because they might be connected to the crime she was arrested for, she didn't know who else to call. She didn't know Brian's cell number. Besides, she didn't like the idea of trying to explain everything to him while standing at a bank of dirty pay phones with a line of women waiting their turn. She wanted to wait until she could face him, tell him the whole truth.

When the cell door opened, Tara was hoping for some coffee. But a guard stuck his head in and called her name. "Your lawyer's here."

She hesitated before following him out of the cell and down the hall. She hadn't asked for a lawyer, but perhaps they'd assigned her a public defender. Which couldn't be a good sign. Wouldn't that mean they were officially charging her?

The bare-bones interview room was a striking contrast to the woman who waited there, sitting tall and straight, with her hands folded on the metal table in front of her. She wore a quality navy suit over a white blouse, brown curls cut in a short bob. The streaks of gray made her look more chic than old. She seemed too polished for a public defender.

She stood to shake hands when Tara entered. "Hello, Tara. I'm Linda Cohen. Eddie hired me to represent you."

Tara took the seat across from her. "Eddie knows I'm here?"

Linda nodded. "He found out last night. Unfortunately, it was too late to get you out. I'm sorry about that." She gave Tara a sympathetic press of the lips.

Tara imagined what the other woman must be seeing. She hadn't looked in a mirror for more than a day, which was also the last time she'd showered, changed clothes, brushed her hair and teeth. God, maybe she even carried the waft of Crying Girl's vomit.

"The night go okay?" Linda asked.

"Yeah."

"Well, the good news is you'll be out of here within the hour." She spoke with the utmost confidence, and Tara wondered where Eddie had found this woman. And how he was going to afford her. "I spoke with the prosecutor's office and they are declining to pursue any charges. They're getting final signatures, then they'll send it over here, and you'll be released."

Tara felt her shoulders relax. "Great. But why are they dropping the charges?"

"Your sister"—Linda flipped open the file in front of her—"Geraldine. She came forward last night. Apparently she was temporarily hiding money while she cleaned up some mess at work. Not sure of the nitty-gritty, but she explained it to her boss and to the police. Her boss withdrew the complaint and the prosecutor's office agreed not to pursue charges." She closed the file and folded her hands on top again.

"Geraldine came clean to the police?"

"Yes. She went to the station with your brother and told them the whole story." Linda cocked her head and lowered her voice. "If she were my sister, I'd want to throttle her. But let's make sure we don't see you back in here for assault."

She was right. Tara should be furious with her sister. But if Geraldine were present at that moment, Tara was pretty sure she'd just hug her. Linda wouldn't understand that. She didn't know that Geraldine confronted one of her greatest fears last night, and she did it for Tara.

"Now, there's still the fact that you violated your parole yesterday," Linda said. "New York is trying to move away from incarcerating parolees for technical violations, but it's really up to your PO. If it goes to a hearing, I'll represent you."

So Tara's fate would be decided by DaCosta, who generally had a zero tolerance policy when it came to parole violations.

Linda checked her watch, maybe tracking billable minutes.

"Sorry you had to come here," Tara said.

"No problem. Just hang in there a little longer." She held up a hand. "I promise I'll be calling the prosecutor's office every half hour until I know you're out of here."

"Thank you," Tara said as they both stood from the table. "Can I ask, where did Eddie find you?"

Linda tilted her head, as if confused. Then she chuckled to herself. "I'm sorry, I forgot to mention . . . I'm Gordi's mom. Eddie called the boys last night to let them know you were okay, and Gordi put him in touch with me."

Tears sprang to Tara's eyes. It was part gratitude, part humiliation. She could only guess what this woman, who had once thought highly of Tara, must be thinking of her right then. And Linda had to know the Connellys couldn't afford to pay her much.

"Oh, hey." Linda's face morphed into concern, and she reached across the table to put a hand on Tara's arm. "It's okay, I'm happy to help. Gordi and Lance believe in you, and that's good enough for me." She smiled Gordi's warm, earnest smile. "Just do me a favor. Keep working on their wardrobes and those coding classes, okay?"

~⋉~

Crying Girl was still asleep, but she had stretched out to take up the whole bench. The other seats were occupied, so Tara nudged her until she moaned and curled back up to make room. Then Tara sat in the same corner spot she'd been in all night, pulled her knees up to her chest, and tried to think through all the implications of what Linda had told her.

Relief had flooded her from fingertips to toes when she heard about her imminent release. She'd tried to stay optimistic all night, but just being in a cell again made her feel hopeless and isolated. Those old instincts to withdraw kicked in—mouth shut, eyes open, guard up—like she was once again preparing for the worst.

But her family had been busy while she'd been sitting in this cell all night, busy stepping up in ways she couldn't have imagined. Her sister had confessed. And it appeared Eddie had taken charge, helping Geraldine, dealing with Mr. Bertucci and the police. Tracking Tara down and finding her a lawyer. *Gordi and Lance believe in you,* Linda had said. It appeared Tara still had a job, that despite the drama the guys wanted her to stay on board.

The only relationship in her life that was Status Unknown was Brian. By now he would have heard about Geraldine coming clean; he might have even been present for it. But Tara had run away, violated parole, and was facing an uncertain future. She'd left him that message, but maybe it had been too little too late. She couldn't blame him if he was ready to give up on her.

When the cell door opened next, a guard stuck his head in and said the four magic words: "Connelly, you're being released."

She stood and followed him out the door, back down the hall to the discharge desk, shaking her head in wonder when they passed a wall clock. It was ten fifteen. An impossible amount of shit had taken place in the past twenty-four hours.

The guard moved behind the desk and pulled a large envelope off a shelf behind him. He opened it and shook out the contents: her watch, ID, keys, a few loose dollars. Then he double-checked the empty envelope. "No cell phone?" he asked.

She sighed. "No." When he pushed the contents toward her, she stuffed them in her pockets. "Can I call my brother for a ride home?" she asked.

"I'm pretty sure he's out there waiting for you," he said, nodding toward the lobby. "Just sign here for your items."

She signed and moved to the exit door, thankful Eddie was already there. If she'd ever been this tired before, she couldn't remember when it was.

Someone buzzed the door and she pushed through to the lobby, which had several windows and was so bright she blinked against the flood of light. As her eyes adjusted she searched for Eddie among the few people seated in the dingy vestibule.

When she first spotted him standing against the far wall, part of her wanted to run back inside, bang on the door until they buzzed her in. She'd been prepared to see Eddie, let him give her a bear hug, drive her home while he explained what all happened the previous night. But it wasn't Eddie standing there, slumped back against the wall. It was Brian.

All the emotion she bottled up over the last day started to rise in her chest. She was so happy to see him she wanted to cry, but she had no idea what he was thinking at this point.

When he pushed off the wall and walked toward her, she could see the toll the night had taken. He looked like how she felt, disheveled and exhausted. And it appeared he'd slept all night in yesterday's clothes. Or, like her, *not* slept all night in yesterday's clothes.

He stood before her for a second and seemed to breathe a big sigh of relief before he pulled her toward him.

And she felt it immediately, the safety that came with being in his arms.

After a moment he pulled back. "Are you okay?" he asked.

"Yeah. Did you get my message?"

He nodded.

"I meant all of it," she said. "I want to tell you everything, about Roland, and why I wouldn't turn him in . . ." She glanced around, wishing she didn't have to do this in the lobby of a police station. But she didn't want to wait a minute longer to tell him the truth.

"It's all right," Brian said. "Eddie told me everything."

A rush of questions came to mind, but she asked the most important one. "Is he okay?"

"To be honest, I think it was really good for him."

She could see that. It was clear to her how much guilt Eddie was carrying around. But he'd confessed to Brian, to the police. "Is he in some kind of trouble now?"

"No," he said, his voice firm. "He's not going to be in any trouble."

Gratitude swept through her, but this meant Brian was going to keep their secret. He would lie to his uncle and the people he worked with because of her.

"I don't know how to feel about what you did for him," he said. "But I understand why you did it."

Maybe he understood it, but Tara didn't know if that meant he could live with it.

"I talked to DaCosta this morning," he said.

She froze and held her breath, afraid to ask anything.

But he smiled. "You're just going to wear an ankle monitor for a while."

Even after replaying those words in her head—*just going to wear an ankle monitor*—she couldn't believe it. "How did you do that?"

"I played your message for her."

The relief was dizzying, but that meant Brian had told DaCosta about them. He'd saved her, but he'd risked his job to do it.

"I'm sorry you had to break the rules for me," she said.

He cocked an eyebrow. "Tara, I've been breaking the rules since I met you." His wide smile reached his eyes, and there was no regret in them.

It wasn't until right then that she realized it **was** okay that he had saved her. Because maybe she had saved him too.

"Thank you for coming down here," she said.

"I was actually here on another matter," he said. "But I thought I'd offer you a ride home. They could call you a taxi, but that'll cost you."

In an instant she was transported back to that morning at Taconic. The other time he'd picked her up from jail.

"I'm headed to Port Chester anyway, so it's no problem . . ."

That did it. Her vision blurred, and she threw her arms around his neck. People were looking, but she didn't care. And they stayed that way awhile before she stepped back and swiped at her cheeks.

"I got you something." He slid his hand in his pocket, pulled it out, and proffered a cell phone. "You must keep this on your person at all times," he said. "Day and night, now and always."

She laughed through the last of the tears and took the phone. "Okay."

"Now, wanna get out of here?"

"Yes."

"That's good, because there are some people who want to see you." He led her to a window that faced the street.

Tara looked out to see Geraldine and Eddie standing next to each other on the sidewalk, with Conor in front of them. They were waiting for her.

Brian braced an arm against the wall by the window and shook his head at them. "They're quite a crew."

"Yeah, they are."

"But you really need to tell your family to stop confessing to me."

"I'll do that."

He took her hand and nodded toward the exit. "Ready?"

She slipped the cell phone into her back pocket and smiled. "Ready."

Acknowledgments

———

Thank you . . .

Stephanie Cabot, for helping me find the heart of this story and having faith I would get there. My own fairy tale came true when we met in Kauai three years ago.

Deb Futter, for once again putting your finger on what was missing and helping me make this book the best version of itself.

Rachel Chou, Christine Mykityshyn, Jennifer Jackson, Jaime Noven, Anne Twomey, Randi Kramer, Heather Orlando-Jerabek, Rebecca Ritchey, and everyone at Celadon and Macmillan. I cannot imagine what more someone could possibly want from a publishing team.

Noa Rosen, Helena Sandlyng-Jacobsen, and the whole crew at Susanna Lea Associates, for all your support and help with the important details.

Gillian Green, Cormac Kinsella, and the team at Pan Macmillan, for taking my first book to the UK and Ireland, and being such a pleasure to work with.

Jessie Weaver, for always answering my texts, reading anytime I ask, and being able to tell me what's not working when I can't figure it out. I'm so grateful we decided to swap first manuscripts way back when.

Carol Merchasin and Steve High, for your encouragement, your honesty, your humor, and your keen eyes. You were part of this story from the very beginning. I treasure our weekly meetings and hope they never end.

Beth Mondry, for reading an early draft and asking great questions. Bob Murney and Kim Young, for inviting me to be part of the writers' group that started it all and continues to be so important to my process.

Vernita Ediger and Darlene Nastansky, for drilling down and offering such valuable nuanced feedback.

All the readers who gave my first novel a chance, spread the word, and encouraged me to write another one. It is truly a gift to hear from you, to know I've touched you in some small way. It's why I do this.

Kathy Murphy, for being so supportive and reminding me to take credit for some things.

Kevin O'Hare, for reading the first draft and offering great advice.

Louis O'Hare, for our daily chats, which always made me smile, and for being my go-to resource when it came to both New York and County Down. You are missed every single day.

Will Lange, for your endless encouragement; your sharp, analytical mind; and your willingness to offer feedback on things big and small, even while you're serving our country overseas during this tumultuous time. I don't have the words to express how proud I am to be your mom.

Ben Lange, for inspiring Gordi and Lance and for your great patience in educating me about the world of gaming and YouTubers. I appreciate your willingness to let me trap you in my office and ask infinite questions. I don't have the words to express how proud I am to be your mom.

Fred Lange, for being my rock, for knowing me better than I know myself sometimes, and for putting up with my special brand of crazy. I couldn't do any of this without you.

About the Author

Tracey Lange was born and raised in New York City. She graduated from the University of New Mexico with a degree in psychology before owning and operating a behavioral health-care company with her husband for fifteen years. While writing her debut novel, *We Are the Brennans*, she completed the Stanford University online novel-writing program. She lives in Bend, Oregon, with her husband, two sons, and beloved German shepherd.

CELADON
BOOKS

Founded in 2017, Celadon Books, a division of
Macmillan Publishers, publishes a highly curated list
of twenty to twenty-five new titles a year. The list of
both fiction and nonfiction is eclectic and focuses on
publishing commercial and literary books and
discovering and nurturing talent.

CELADON
BOOKS

Founded in 2017, Celadon Books, a division of
Macmillan Publishers, publishes a highly curated list
of twenty to twenty-five new titles a year. The list of
both fiction and nonfiction is eclectic and focuses on
publishing commercial and literary books and
discovering and nurturing talent.